BETRAYER

C.C. URIE

For Conrad and Charlotta

TRIGGER WARNINGS
WARNING: SPOILERS

- Larken is in multiple aircraft accidents and has severe PTSD because of it
- Larken is emotionally abused by her mother and older brother, and her father is an alcoholic
- A war takes place throughout this Trilogy and there is blood, shootings, stabbings, and other injuries
- One character is a narcissistic abuser who becomes obsessed with his victim and has lustful thoughts about her, makes several innuendos, and tries to stalk her which may be upsetting to some readers
- This Trilogy deals with adult themes like abandonment, self-worth, relationships, and other complicated emotions

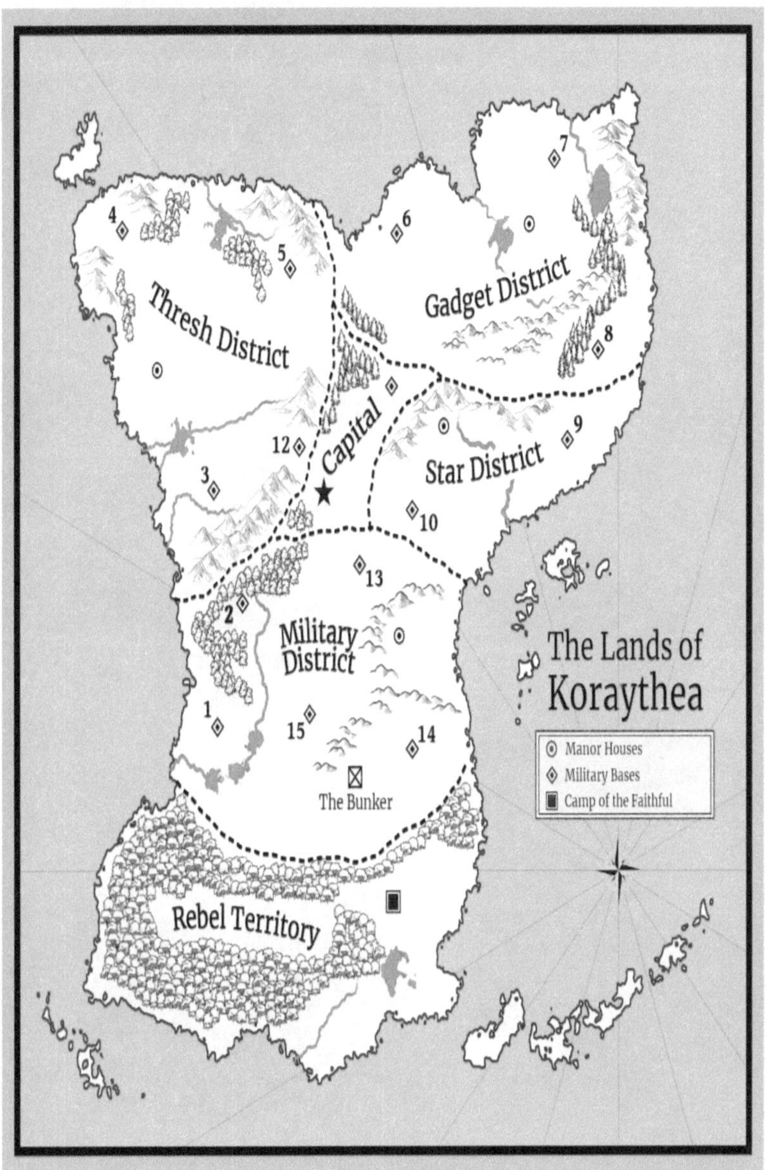

Thresh District
Gadget District
Star District
Capital
Military District
The Bunker
Rebel Territory
The Lands of
Koraythea
Manor Houses
Military Bases
Camp of the Faithful

CHAPTER 1

"And you're sure this is what you want?" Cornella Hale asked. Her sharp eyes, the same color as crystalized caramel, were narrowed in his direction.

She looked down her nose at Dominic as if she were the Magnate herself, instead of just a Luminary's wife. Wearing black dress pants, white stilettos, and an elbow-length light grey cashmere sweater that hung off both shoulders, Cornella flaunted the thin frame that she hadn't passed on to her daughter. Her light brown hair had been pulled back into its usual twist, not a single strand out of place. The shade of lipstick that stained her calculated frown reminded Dominic of blood, which he found fitting since she looked ready to pounce on him like a wild animal.

"Yes," he answered. "I've never been more sure of anything in my whole life."

Cornella crossed her arms and began to circle him once again, looking for any chinks in his armor that she could exploit. She took in his perfectly tailored uniform, and Dominic felt more and more aware of his weaknesses as she eyed him. The clicking of her heels sounded in the tiled council room, echoing as if they were well-timed gunshots. Cornella thrived on making sure that everyone knew she was the one with power, and she didn't care what tactics she needed to use to prove it. Dominic knew this, and even though he had been the one to present her with the answer to all of her problems, he still felt like a fly caught in her web. He didn't move, let alone speak, deciding that all of his focus would be better used to ensure that his face didn't give away how much he needed her to agree to his request.

"Liam won't like it, you know," she mused, once more appearing in front of him. Cornella paused, her fingers tapping at her left bicep one at a time. "*But* I don't think Larken will like it very much either."

"I am determined to change her mind." Dominic fought not to let his anger color his voice; jumping to Larken's defense would earn him no favors where Cornella was concerned. "I will do whatever—"

Cornella huffed a feminine laugh that didn't quite sound like it should belong to her. The act changed her features from a woman who looked like she would never be satisfied to the beauty that had caught Trogar's eye all those years ago. The laughter still colored her voice as she asked, "You—*what?* Will do *whatever it takes* to make her happy? My darling Captain, not gallivanting with everything that has a pair of breasts would make her happy."

Dominic stood his ground, still fighting to keep his face straight. He didn't say what she expected him to, not wanting to give her the satisfaction of claiming that he had changed. The only person that needed convincing was currently running laps in one of the training fields. Which one, he didn't know; she wouldn't tell him, no doubt wanting to workout in peace.

"Oh dear," Cornella uncrossed her arms, her eyes twinkling with mirthful glee. "I've hurt your feelings."

Dominic bowed his head slightly, looking to the floor. "I assure you, Lumina, worse things have been said about me."

"Oh, *I know.*"

Dominic lifted his gaze to see her walking up to the white and gold marbled seat embellished with little carvings of the sun. It was reserved for the Luminary, not their spouse. Trogar hadn't been in the thing for years, Cornella having claimed control of the Military District after his first public incident. The man had shown up a drunken mess to a council meeting with the other Luminaries and the Magnate and had passed out before they had even started discussing the battle plans. Since then, Trogar had been tolerated as the Luminary, but it had been the Lumina who was really in control.

Lounging atop the stone, Cornella sighed, resting her chin on her left fist. She looked him up and down again. Her lips pursed, like thinking about him put a bad taste in her mouth, but Dominic didn't back down. He would see this through until the end, only accepting the answer he wanted. Still, her scrutiny had his shirt sticking to his back, despite the coolness of the room.

"Tell me, Captain," she finally said, breaking the bone-crushing silence. "Why would you agree to help me?"

Dominic took in the opulence of the room around him. The tables that had been pushed to the side, the bronze and cream tiles that stretched across the floor, and the crystal lights that had the council room looking more like a throne room. This had been all that Larken had ever known, the only way she had been able to ask anything of her vile mother. It only hardened his resolve as he stared into Cornella's skeptical eyes. "What makes you think I'm doing this to help you?"

Her red lips twisted. "Yes, I forgot. You're doing this out of the goodness of your heart to save Larken from a loveless home." Cornella's eyes glinted. "I think we both know the real reason you're doing this, so let's not pretend anymore, shall we?"

Dominic bit his tongue before he could say something he would regret. Instead, he forced his face to look easy, like she had figured him out. "Yes, well, what can I say? I hate the word *no*."

Cornella relaxed even more into her seat, crossing her legs and steepling her fingers. "Your offer, though well thought out, seems a little *one-sided*. So, what else is it that you are wanting?"

"I have made my request, Lumina. No tricks, no hidden agendas. All that's left is for you to give me an answer."

"Forgive me, Captain, but it is a bit hard to believe that someone such as yourself would be content with so little."

"I have to disagree. I think it's you who is on the lesser end of the arrangement."

"Is that so?" Cornella's eyes flashed as she grinned, and Dominic regretted opening his mouth. "Then you wouldn't mind if I made a few requests of my own?"

"Not at all, Lumina."

Cornella looked somewhere over Dominic's shoulder and motioned for someone to come forward. Heavy boot falls sounded as she said, "I am in search of a *Captain* of sorts, an honorary General if you will." A man appeared in the corner of Dominic's eye, the fierce scowl on his face prominent as he bowed to Cornella. She continued, "I have been putting together a little group to help regulate the District and keep the Faithfuls where they belong. The last thing we need is them burning down any more homes. I need someone to help look over things, now that Mr. Tanner will be moved elsewhere."

Dominic chanced a glance at the man next to him, who stood taller by about two inches. His jaw was stubbly and looked to be cut from stone. Black hair hung in his face, and a dark impatience seemed to surround him. Dominic didn't recognize the man, but still asked, "His new position?"

"Your close and personal friend as you get used to your new responsibilities, as well as my daughter's new bodyguard."

Dominic hated the man immediately. It was bad enough that he had to deal with Deckard, but now this guy? He glared at Cornella, and her teeth glinted as she grinned at him. She had trapped him in her web, and there would be no untangling himself. If Dominic wanted to keep a close eye on Larken and keep this guy away from her, he would have to do *exactly* what she wanted and hope that she would uphold her end of the deal.

Dominic was still trying to find the right words, when she mused, "Come now, Captain, you can't expect me to let my pride and joy out into the world without a protector after your last outing, can you?"

"General Maxwell and I had it under control," he growled.

"Yes, and the media are still discussing how *in control* you were three days later." Dominic seethed quietly as she added, "As well as the new responsibilities that you would agree to, I would need you to find a new Chief Administrator for Base 14. Someone *trustworthy*."

"As I assume my new *friend* is trustworthy?"

Cornella laughed as the man next to him grumbled in a thick accent, "I don't have a problem keeping what's in my pants in my pants, mate."

Take Larken away.

Keep her out of the District.

New title with responsibilities.

Find a Chief Administrator.

The list kept getting longer and longer. Dominic knew that he would do whatever it took to get what he wanted though, and apparently, so did Cornella. There was only one option before him, and he had played right into her hands.

"How do I know you'll keep your word?" he asked, knowing that she would dangle her daughter in front of him for as long as she could use him.

Cornella smiled like she thought his distrust was adorable. "My dear Captain, if I hadn't intended to accept your offer, I never would have insisted Larken come home." Her eyes flashed. "Just like you asked me to."

CHAPTER 2

"*The Military Sweetheart is at it again, showing the world exactly why she shouldn't be messed with.*" The reporter, a woman in her late twenties, had a nasally voice that grated against Soren's nerves. She also wore too much makeup that clashed horribly with her orange locks.

Soren ground his teeth as the image on the television switched to a video of Larken with Braves and General Maxwell.

"*What was supposed to be a fun night out quickly turned to a warning for all men who are hoping to win Miss Hale's heart,*" the reporter continued, as the grainy figure of Larken backed into Braves, shaking her head at some sleazy-looking guy who could barely stand up.

They looked to be at a bar of some sort, one that she had no business going to. She had on a white blouse and a pair of jeans that hugged her hips. Soren's hands burned as they tried to remind him of how those hips felt, how warm they had been, but he dug his nails into his palms, suppressing the memories. Larken turned, and General Maxwell put his arm around her, trying to shield her from the creep. The guy lurched forward, grabbing a handful of her backside. Larken stiffened, turned, and then punched the guy in the face.

The video cut back to the reporter, who looked to be hiding a smirk, but her eyes danced in approval. *"The ex-cadet is no stranger to violence, having attacked her own stylist, Cameron Brady, not even a year ago. Not to mention all the other would-be suitors who tried to get close to her since her return."* Pictures of Larken shouting at men and hitting them filled the screen. *"With her twenty-first birthday approaching, we have to wonder who will be making the guest list, and who won't make the cut. But after the way the last few weeks have gone for her, I think it's safe to assume that there won't be many single men in attendance."*

"Is Larken in trouble?" Jing asked Loxly, burrowing into his side. "Papa says it's bad to fight."

"No, Darlin', she isn't in trouble. She was just standin' up for herself."

"Well, then," Jing looked up at Loxly, "do you think she'll invite me to the party?"

Loxly brushed her chin with his knuckle. "I don't think we'll get invited. Her mom doesn't like us talkin' to her."

"Her mom is *mean!*" Jing huffed, crossing her arms and pouting.

Soren ignored Loxly's agreement as the reporter said, *"As for the mystery man that the Military Heiress had been caught with, no one seems to know where he came from, or where he went."* A picture of Soren smiling down at Larken as she covered her mouth to hide her giggles had been pulled up. He could remember the exact moment that that picture had been taken, and his gut clenched. *"We can only wonder if he is the cause of Miss Hale's recent outbursts, or if he will make a showing at the party. The—"*

Not able to take it anymore, Soren grabbed the remote from the coffee table and turned the television off. No one said anything and they actively didn't look at him. Well, everyone except Hinlee, who glowered at him. Brecker leaned into her and murmured, "Leave it alone, Hin."

As if she couldn't help herself, Hinlee said, "Oh, what a shame Larken wasn't asked to stay in a safe place with people who care about her and are able to help keep those creeps away. Not to mention, give her a party that she would actually enjoy."

Not in the mood to have this conversation again, Soren stood and walked out of the dorm, deciding that it would be better to run until his feet were stumps than think about what he didn't do. What he didn't say.

It had been three weeks, and Hinlee reminded him every chance she got that it was his fault Larken that was gone. The worst part, though, was that he knew the mechanic was right. He had seen the broken hope in Larken's eyes, the hope that maybe there was someone who needed her just as much as she needed them, and he did nothing. He just let her leave, and Soren could no longer pretend that he had done the right thing. He might not have been ready to offer her what she had really wanted, but now he would never get the chance. Because instead of being honest with her, he had let her walk away.

Tell me that none of this matters and that you don't care about any of it. Ask me to stay, Soren.

Soren walked into his personal gym, hating himself more than he had the day he let her go. He didn't even stop to stretch before he broke out in a run. Nothing felt like it should. Their pew in the tabernacle felt too big, the dorm too quiet, and the gym too empty. The practice droids were too tall, and they had no tricks hidden up their sleeves while he sparred with them. Worst of all was the heaviness of his lungs, the words left unsaid weighing his chest down, constantly making him feel short of breath. The laps started blending together as her goodbye chased him, no matter how fast his legs moved.

Ask me to stay, and I will.

Soren thundered to a halt. The running didn't help, it only made him feel like a coward. He wished that he didn't keep thinking about her, that he could forget everything about her. Forget the way she literally crash-landed into his life and always had him at his wit's end. He was going insane—hearing her laugh everywhere, seeing wheat-colored hair out of the corner of his eye, smelling nonexistent grapefruit when he walked down the hall to his room. Her memory followed him, refusing to leave him alone, taunting him with those final words. But her goodbye hadn't bothered him as much as what she had said after the crash.

These men aren't Faithfuls. I should have told you sooner, but I—that doesn't matter now. But, I know for a fact that these aren't—

The memory of the gunshots that cut her off had him flinching. Walking over to the wall, Soren leaned against it and sank to the ground. He rested his elbows on his knees, letting his hands hang limply in front of him. What had she meant? What had happened that made her wonder if there were other groups aside from the Faithfuls in the first place? Those people were the same that had gone after her again and again, so what changed? What made this other group different?

Soren thought back to the first day that he met Larken, the day of the first crash. Both times, the aircraft had been shot out of the sky by people hiding on the ground. He couldn't really compare that to the ambush, because they weren't flying, but all three times their electronics had cut out. The only major difference that he could think of was that when they were ambushed, the Faithfuls had seemed to shoot at them as more of a warning than to kill them. The men he had watched chasing Larken and General Maxwell seemed to have no problems hitting them however they could, just like the men at the crash site had no problem shooting him.

Soren's side throbbed once at the memory, and he forced his hand to stay where it was. He didn't talk about that night with anyone, not even Levi, and his squad hadn't pushed it. They had all done what they could to accept that Larken was gone. Hinlee and Loxly talked about her like she was just visiting the Manor and would eventually be back, that they would somehow see her again. At least, Loxly tried to pretend anyway. Soren could see every extra hour added to the sharpshooter's flying log.

Brecker didn't complain about the cafeteria food like he used to, even though everyone could tell that he wanted to. He had been the one to suggest they all take their meals in the dorm in the first place, but with her gone, it just wasn't the same. Levi had stopped cooking altogether, spending as much time as he could at the rehabilitation center instead. Rather than spend time with any of them, he helped the soldiers who had been hurt relearn to use their limbs. The Second was as closed off and broody as he had been when he first came to base, seeming to take her absence the hardest. And Soren… well, he ignored everything and everyone.

Resting his head back against the wall, Soren let out a deep breath, closing his eyes. She was there again, just like always, looking up and smiling at him, calling him an idiot. His throat went tight, remembering all the things he had wanted to tell her in the aircraft, remembering how close he had come to kissing her. Anger spiked through him again, and Soren shot to his feet, blaming her for forcing him into something he hadn't been ready for, then getting upset when he couldn't give her what she wanted. It was all her fault that everyone felt miserable, that they were now blaming *him*, that he was…

Soren needed to get out of there; he shouldn't be alone. Bad things happened when he was alone, and he didn't want to think about any of it anymore. Not about her, or why she left, or what she said, any of it. Larken was gone, and there was nothing that could bring her back—no petitions, no request forms, and not him.

Leaving the little gym, Soren decided instead to go to the Captains' gym, thinking working out around people would leave him less likely to think of anything aside from how annoying they were. And, if he was lucky, Braves would be there, and Soren could ask him for a spar and finally have an excuse to pulverize him. It wasn't likely though. The man had been in every single picture that was taken of Larken since her return home. At parties, shows, or any of the events Larken was expected to attend as a Luminary's daughter. Of course, Soren couldn't help but imagine Braves's annoyance every time he saw the picture of Soren and Larken in the garden that got pulled up every time her love life was discussed in the media. But the reporters didn't know that the people smiling in that photo didn't exist anymore.

Reaching the Captain's gym, Soren pushed in and immediately had about twenty sets of eyes on him. All conversation stopped, and he glowered at everyone. Some were smart enough to look away, while others kept staring, wanting to get a good look at the Captain who had lost the greatest asset to his squad. Larken's presence on base hadn't completely faded out; the number of sponsors that wanted to be associated with the base the Daughter of the Military had been a part of skyrocketed. Stars and wealthy Gadgets that followed Larken had started claiming soldiers from Base 14, wanting to help the squads that Larken had fought beside, clearly not knowing Larken's peers were the reason for her hard times.

Someone cleared their throat beside Soren, and he scowled, looking at whoever was stupid enough to come and talk to him. Kelly Pratchett stood to his right, looking up at him with her big brown eyes. One of the six female Captains, and one that most soldiers wanted to have a tumble with, Kelly went for what she wanted and didn't hold back until she got it. And with the way her eyes kept dropping to his chest and arms, Soren had a pretty good guess what her current goal was.

"Captain Pratchett," he grunted.

"Captain Deckard." She smiled like she enjoyed the taste of his name. "How are you? It's been a while since we've been able to catch up."

"Same as last time," Soren said, walking over to the communal weapons rack and grabbing a brass spear.

Kelly followed him, laughing. "You're the same as you were six months ago?"

"Yup."

"Well, I guess that means you're still short-fused and brooding," she teased.

"Guess so."

"Just as funny too," she added, eyes crinkling as she smiled coyly at him.

Soren only grunted and walked over to where the lifeless practice droids sat.

Kelly followed, ignoring his blatant rudeness, and asked, "Wouldn't you rather have a living partner?"

Soren looked at her, raising an eyebrow. She stood half a foot taller than Larken and was capable enough…just not Larken. Kelly rose an eyebrow of her own in a challenge, daring him to take her up on her offer. Soren looked away first.

"No, I'm fine."

Kelly hummed softly like she approved of his answer. "Next time then."

He noticed her swaying hips caught more than one eye as she walked away, and Soren forced himself not to look. Forcing himself not to think of Larken's hips, Soren turned on one of the androids. He thought a moment about the difficulty level he wanted, and then turned on a second android. Setting them both at hard, he led them to a less crowded corner of the gym and went on the offensive.

The glass tip of the spear clinked against chrome as Soren attacked. He couldn't tell anymore who he was more upset with—himself, or her. He felt pulled between two impossible choices: to blame himself for not being ready for that much honesty, or to blame her for leaving when her mother called her back.

Her mother…

Soren's gut twisted at the thought of her. What was she doing to Larken this very second? He just couldn't shake the feeling that Larken's mother was up to something, and that was the real reason she had told her daughter to come back home. It just seemed odd to him that no one in Larken's family had cared enough to see if she had even survived the first crash, and suddenly they were worried that she wasn't safe enough. Then there were the men that had shot them out of the sky in the first place.

Just like that, Soren was lost in his thoughts again. It was too much; he couldn't keep thinking about what had been left unsaid. He needed to figure out how Larken knew that the men weren't all Faithfuls and *exactly* how she was tied into this whole mess. There were also the recent fires to consider. The homes of several high-ranking military families had been burned down, and the media blamed the Faithfuls. But the families had never been shy about their beliefs in Maxim, so why would they destroy possible allies?

Not to mention, attempted murder sounded more like the other group Larken had tried to tell him about. What he needed to do was to look into the retaliations of the Faithfuls. He needed to see if they had always been more peaceful, or if they had ever done more than just protect themselves.

With more of a direction of where to begin his search, Soren ended his spar in four moves. Leaving the defeated androids where they were, he put the spear away and made his way back to the dorm. He needed to be alone, to think about these new realizations.

When had he become so indecisive? Whenever he was alone, he needed the distraction of others. But when he was around people, Soren could only focus on getting away. He blamed Larken, like he did for everything now. And instead of the hurt that caused, Soren would focus on his new leads. First, he would look into the Faithfuls. What exactly did they stand for, and how could stealing the Daughter of the Military away from base help them? Maybe the answer would tell him why Cornella Hale suddenly felt so protective of her daughter, and why she had taken Larken from him.

CHAPTER 3

The sun beat down on Larken's head, threatening to burn off her hair. Sweat stung her eyes and ran freely down her back. Even though she was glad to be back in shorts, they did nothing to cool her down as she ran lap after lap. She shot another glare at Vallen, blaming him for her discomfort. He only stood there and glared back, bald head shining in the sun. Face set in his signature frown, he acted like the heat was no more than a mild annoyance. It only aggravated her even more.

Larken was about to shout at him, bully him into running with her, when Carl called, "Can't you hurry those laps up? It's hotter than Shadric Barlow's latest hit out here."

She looked over at the stylist who wore nothing apart from his purple swim trunks as he sprawled out on a lawn chair, sunbathing. Larken seriously considered shooting one of the little legs off the thing, just to watch him fall, but a warning from Vallen had her looking straight ahead. She sucked in a hot breath, her lungs on fire, and pushed her legs to keep moving. The air sat still, no breeze willing to blow away the impossible heat. The genetically enhanced yellow roses that bloomed on the bushes around her were wilting slightly, and Larken wished that the sprinklers would turn on just so she could run through the mist.

They never did, and she was forced to run her ten remaining laps in misery.

When she had finally stopped, Larken felt like dropping to the ground. The packed dirt had been baked from its normally dark brown color to a sun-bleached tan. Even the soil protested the heat, and Larken laughed bitterly. Forcing her feet to move, she trudged to the table that sat by Carl's chair and reached for one of the waters a staff member brought out three laps ago.

Vallen appeared at her side, saying, "They spoiled you by letting you work out in the air-conditioning."

"You sure you're not just a sadist?"

Carl barked a laugh that covered Vallen's growl. Larken smirked and took a gulp of her water. She had been surprised at how easily she fell back into her old life; the only memories of her time at base were Carl and the pearl that still rested against her chest. Larken thought about ripping it from her neck and throwing it away so many times that it wasn't even funny. But she couldn't ever bring herself to do it. Carl, on the other hand, had taken her offer of employment willingly, not even giving himself time to think about it. It had been a thirty-second conversation of Larken making the offer and him asking when he started. He had moved into the Manor, taking a vacant room in the same wing as her and Vallen. Larken had even offered up a room for Candy, who had jumped at the chance to live rent-free and pester her boyfriend about engagement rings every chance she got.

Vallen, still grumbling about the sadist comment, asked, "And when did taking it easy ever save anyone's life?"

"Saves my life every day," Carl offered, face still tilted towards the unforgiving sun. His sunglasses were impossibly dark, and Larken couldn't tell if he was even looking at them.

"That's because you're lazy," Larken said, lifting her glass for another drink.

"*Lazy?*" He turned his face to her.

"I didn't see you running out there with me."

"That's because I'd rather not smell like unwashed man."

Larken paused, considering her options, and then poured the icy contents of her glass onto Carl's naked chest. He yelped, jumping up from the chair so fast that it toppled over, and Candy's warm laughter rang out across the training field, covering a distant howl from one of the wolf hybrids. Dressed in a red two-piece the same shade as her hair, Candy made her way out of the Manor, a folded chair in one hand, a fancy drink with an umbrella in the other.

"Serves you right," Candy chastised, her warm alto voice reminding Larken of brown sugar. "You should never tell a woman that she smells."

"If I was telling Larken she smelled," Carl growled, flicking off an ice chip that clung to his skin, "I would have said, *Larken, you smell.*"

"I'm going to go shower," Larken grumbled, not at all looking forward to the evening that Carl had planned for her.

"Be ready in an hour!" he called after her as Vallen righted Carl's chair and sat in it.

Candy stopped Larken on her way back into the Manor, offering her the drink. "You want this? It's strawberry."

Larken smiled, unable to help herself. Candy was incredibly kind, and it was a wonder that this sweetheart had ever bullied Carl into anything. Larken took the drink and downed a half-frozen sip. The cold felt amazing against her too-hot throat, and she nodded a thank you to Candy. Sucking down more of the frozen, non-alcoholic slush, Larken reveled in the sugary flavor as she walked into the Manor. The cool air hit her exposed skin, causing her to shiver, and she ducked into the nonexistent shadows out of habit, hoping that she caught at least *some* of the cameras' blind spots.

She heard footsteps behind her, and then an accented voice as smooth as honey asked, "He's not pushing you too hard, is he?"

Turning, she found Medic Ezra Lattic walking her way. His caramel-colored skin glowed in the sunlight, and his wavy hair looked as messy as usual. "I don't think Vallen knows what *pushing too hard* means," she replied.

"I think I have to agree with you."

"He's still out in the training field if you need him."

"I'm here for you, actually. Needed to make sure you were handling your change in schedule okay."

Larken rolled her shoulder. "I can't say that I don't miss getting the chance to relax, but I'm fine."

"You sure?" he asked, looking like he didn't quite believe her.

"Positive."

"Well, let me know if anything changes."

"I will."

Larken waved and made her way down the hall to her room. She regretted not asking Ezra to walk with her; the bright tile offered nowhere safe to hide, and she felt too exposed. Aware of every camera that zoned in on her, she hurried along like they didn't bother her. Her shirt still clung to her back, wisps of her ponytail stuck to her neck, and she couldn't wait to hop into the shower. She finished the drink by the time she reached her room and left it on a nightstand. Kicking off her shoes, Larken wasted no time crossing over to her bathroom, ignoring the new olive green carpet under her feet.

When Larken had gotten home, she ripped apart her whole room. Pulling up the sand-colored carpet, throwing the pale blue sheets into the hall, taking a sledgehammer to the tiles in the shower. Before her time in Squad 19, Larken would have done anything to be near the sea, even decorating her room to look like the one place she would never see. Now, she couldn't look at it without thinking of that strip of blue just past Field E, of the way he had looked at her as she looked out that window, of the pearl that hung around her neck. Larken's hand flew up and grasped the stone again, ready to finally yank it free instead of giving in to her hurt, but when she tugged just enough for the chain to dig into her neck, his hands were there again, brushing against her skin and fastening it.

Larken's eyes burned as she dropped the necklace. The pearl bounced gently against her chest before settling, and Larken pulled off her shirt. She peered over at her door to make sure it was locked, but relaxed when she remembered that Cam was no longer her stylist. Carl would never break that trust with her; he always knocked and waited until she was ready for him. When she had brought it up to thank him, he had been horrified to learn that Cam had behaved that way. He had then insisted that he would never do that because he would hate it if Candy were to be treated the same.

Stripping off the rest of her clothes, Larken stepped into the now peach tiled shower. The warm water rinsed away the sweat, and Larken lathered up a washcloth with a body wash that smelled wrong to her. It had been the same one she had always used before, the same one that she had always loved, but now she hated it. She missed the honey and peach body wash she had used at the dorm, the grapefruit and orange blossom shampoo and conditioner that he had complained about so often.

Larken reached for the knob and turned the water all the way to cold. Freezing water pelted her, making her yelp and forget the turn her thoughts had taken. True to form, it didn't take her long to find her way back, though. Her eyes burned again, trying not to think about the people she had left behind, the things that he hadn't said. She couldn't blame him; she saw in his eyes that he wasn't ready to be that vulnerable with her yet, but she hadn't asked him for a proposal. Larken only wanted to know that he wanted her to stay, and now she never would. She would never see him, or any of them, ever again, and it would be best for her to forget her time in Squad 19 altogether.

Scratching at the door told Larken that Estelle had found her way from Vallen's room back to hers. Larken stood under the spray, wishing she could disappear and not have to deal with any of this anymore. It wasn't lost on her that standing in the shower and wishing for more time was how all her problems had started. If she had known then what would happen, Larken would have stayed locked in the bathroom. If she had, she would never know what it was like to have friends, what it was like to go to tabernacle, or what it was like to be held by him.

Turning the knob harder than she needed to, Larken got out of the shower and toweled off. She threw on her robe and rubbed at her hair with the damp towel. Estelle shoved her way into the bathroom as soon as Larken cracked the door and ran to the shower. Standing over the drain, the small dog sniffed at the suds that hadn't quite gone down yet. Dropping the towel, Larken made her way to her bed. Falling back on it, she stared blankly up at her ceiling, not caring that her wet hair soaked her sheets. Somehow, she felt both raw and numb, torn between wanting to forget everything and not wanting to forget a single second.

There was a knock at the door, but she didn't respond. That didn't stop whoever it was from coming in.

"Well, don't you look extra pathetic?"

Larken didn't move as she heard Carl walk into her room. She could picture him looking at her like he always did, arms crossed and a look of baffled exasperation on his face. He sighed, and she felt him drop onto the bed next to her.

They stared up at the ceiling together silently, before he asked, "You doin' okay, kid?"

Larken let out a long breath through her nose in answer.

"Wanna talk about it?"

"No."

"*Good,*" he sighed, relieved.

Larken snorted. "What if I had said yes?"

"I would have listened like the caring, selfless individual I am." Larken looked over at him to find him smirking at her. "Then I would have told you that you're not the only one with problems and to suck it up."

"*Caring and selfless?*" Larken mocked.

"You know it, babe." Carl groaned as he sat up, now dressed in khaki shorts and a pink polo that made his navy hair look darker than it really was. "Now, get up. We have a lot we still have to do before next week."

Larken groaned and threw her arms over her face. Even the detergent that had been used to wash her robe smelled wrong.

"Get over it, Princess. You're going to pretend to be a normal girl for one evening and come dress shopping with me."

She let her arms fall back and lifted her head to look at the stylist. He watched her expectantly, and she said, "I don't know what part of what you just said to make fun of."

"Might I suggest the part about you being a normal girl?" he offered.

"*Funny.* I was leaning more towards the part when you asked me to go dress shopping with you."

"Whatever gets you off of that bed. We can't be late for the tram. They won't wait, even if you are *Larken Hale.*"

Larken ignored the guilt that twisted her stomach and pushed up from the bed. Even though she wanted to complain about the shopping trip and drag her feet, she didn't. Carl had been more than understanding about her incurable fear of flying, making sure that they took the tram whenever they left the Manor. The first time she used it, she fell in love with the simplicity of the tram, as well as the cute little Tudor-styled homes with window boxes overflowing with flowers that they passed. Dominic would rent high-class hovercrafts for her, hating the crowded trams that made multiple stops before their destination. The one thing that did surprise Larken though, was that she learned she didn't mind Vallen's hoverbike. He was the only one she trusted enough to get on one with, but there was something about speeding through the streets and open roads with him. Those rides made her forget her problems, and they were the closest she would ever come to finding her wings again.

Larken let Carl drag her into her closet and didn't put up a fight as he pulled clothes out for her. He often teased her about her lack of fashion sense, having grown close with her over the past three weeks. When she wasn't sweating with Vallen or out with Dominic at some military function, Larken spent her time with Carl discussing color palates and outfit choices. His first day on the job, he brought what had seemed like every single type of fabric to her room and had her touch all of them, asking what she liked. He went from there, creating outfits and often asking for her honest opinion.

Carl made sure her closet had been filled with the things that she liked and felt comfortable in, instead of the daring outfits that Cam thought showed off her *assets* the best.

When Larken crinkled her nose at the stiff-looking goldenrod shorts, Carl shook his head with a small smile. "Just put them on. I promise they're comfy."

"Why Carl, have you been trying on my clothes while I'm not here?"

"I have, and my butt looks better in them than yours ever will," he shot back. "Let me know when you're decent."

Carl left, pulling the door shut behind him. Larken, still smiling, quickly got dressed. He had been telling the truth; the shorts were incredibly comfortable and soft despite how they looked. The cream top with thin black stripes she pulled on fit loosely, made of a breathable fabric that she couldn't stop touching. Larken scratched at her scalp, mussing her already tangled hair even more, before pulling on brown leather sandals.

Opening the door, she asked, "Where did you find this shirt?"

"I take it you like the material?" Carl mused as he watched her run her fingers over it again.

"I do, actually."

"Good, I thought you might so I ordered a few more tops made of the same stuff."

Carl sat her down at the vanity and got to work on her hair. If it had been up to her, she would have put it back in a ponytail or a bun, not wanting to get too hot. Carl had a different idea, though, and gave her loose waves. He then put on the barest amount of makeup, finishing the look by painting her lips a pale apricot.

Carl started putting his things away when Larken asked, "Does Candy want to come with us?"

He smiled but didn't stop working. "I'm sure she would. Why don't you go ask her while I finish up he—"

Larken's communicator started buzzing, the chime that sounded after each vibration making Carl go silent. Dread settled in the pit of her stomach, and she thought about smashing the device so she could pretend that it never started going off. Larken didn't even have to look at the screen to see who was summoning her to the council room.

Groaning, Larken said, "You better order a hover. I don't think we're going to make the tram on time."

"Right, I'll go tell Vallen where you're going. You better not keep her waiting."

Larken put on the invisible mask that she wore whenever her mother wanted to talk to her. Her stomach cramped, telling her not to go, but she forced herself to stand anyway. Carl gave her shoulder a comforting squeeze, and she left her room. Each step she took made her that much more apprehensive. Her mother had been nothing but cold towards her since her return, and Larken couldn't understand why she had been brought home. As far as she knew, the only person who had really missed her had been Wardell, and even he hadn't talked to her much since she'd been back. Her father hadn't even realized that she had been gone, thinking that she had been out at the theater or something when he was sober enough to notice her absence. Liam hadn't said a single word to her, only sneering at her whenever they passed each other in the hallway, and both Vallen and Carl had to keep her from repaying him for all of his interviews.

Other than Vallen and Ezra, only one other person had truly been happy to see her home. The day after her discharge had been announced, Larken had received a message from an unknown number, telling her that they were glad she was safe and that they would like a second chance at a first impression. She didn't ask who it was, she didn't even message back. Larken didn't know if she was ready for what Fisher Fillmar was offering her, and she didn't want to think about what had happened when they first met. Larken wanted to forget about that night in the garden, not wanting to compare herself to the man who also hadn't been ready for some-thing that life-changing. But how was it a fair comparison when she asked for one request, and Fisher wanted to step in as her real father?

Larken stood outside the council room doors, not realizing that she was already there. Pulling her thumbnail from between her teeth, she tried not to think about how mad Carl would be about her biting her nails and gingerly opened the door. Peering inside, Larken sought out her mother. Cornella sat lazily on her father's chair, and two men stood before her. One Larken recognized; she would know that uniform and blond hair anywhere. The other one though…Larken thought she would remember seeing someone that big and intimidating. Even from all the way at the back of the room, Larken could tell he frowned at her mother and that he was done with whatever conversation they were having.

Cornella caught Larken's eye, and a devious smile danced across her lips. "Ah, there she is." Dominic's spine stiffened as her mother said, "So kind of you to finally join us, Larken. We have been waiting for quite some time now."

"My apologies, Mother." Larken hated that her voice sounded so meek. She wanted to sound confident, like what her mother said didn't matter to her, but it did and she knew it always would. "I left as soon as I got your message."

"Well, the important thing is that you're here now." Cornella's eyes moved back to Dominic, like she was about to watch a show, and he was the star. "There is someone that I would like you to meet."

Larken said nothing as she walked forward. Stopping between the stranger and Dominic, Larken clasped her hands behind her back and looked at her feet.

"Captain Braves and I have been discussing you, and given recent circumstances, we both thought that you need more than just General Maxwell watching over you."

Larken kept staring at her feet, but she didn't miss the way Dominic balled his hand into a fist.

"We thought a bodyguard would be the best option."

Larken chanced a glance at her mother, who was still grinning as she watched Dominic.

"Larken, I would like you to meet Delvon Tanner, a member of my personal team that will be keeping an eye on you from now on."

Moving as slowly as she could, Larken turned to the mystery man on her right. His boots were the same ones that all the other security guards that patrolled the Manor wore. Slowly, her eyes moved up his bulky form, until they landed on a set of grey eyes that she recognized.

Larken's heart fell to her feet as the man smiled and purred, "Hello, love."

CHAPTER 4

Larken couldn't breathe as she looked at the man who had held her at gunpoint the night of the opera. Without her permission, her hand flew up to her neck and scratched at the spot he had run his nose across. He smiled at her, following her fingers with his eyes. Everything around her blurred as her stomach threatened to turn inside out. Then, her mother's words hit her.

"He's a member of your personal security team?" she asked, turning to her mother so fast that she almost fell.

"Of course, only the best for my daughter." Her smile was cold and calculating, and Larken shivered as she looked back at Delvon.

Narrowing his eyes, he warned her silently to keep her mouth shut, and Larken swallowed thickly. His being there meant that whoever those other people were had infiltrated the Manor. That, or her own mother had given the order to have her killed…twice.

Larken shivered again, his grey eyes freezing her blood. Taking a small step back, she felt as Dominic's warm hands grabbed her arms.

"That was all, Larken. You may leave while I finish my discussion with the Captain."

Dominic squeezed her arms reassuringly, and she looked up

over her shoulder at him. He gave her a smile and a wink. "I'll message you tonight, okay?"

Larken nodded dumbly, her eyes once again meeting Delvon's. She stared until her mother cleared her throat, and Delvon led her out of the council room by her elbow.

Each step she took away from her mother had her thinking more and more clearly. By the time the doors had shut behind her, Larken was furious and ready to fight. Delvon pulled her down hall after hall, getting away from the council room and away from the other security guards. She let him lead her around, knowing that the moment he stopped, she would make her move.

Passing open doors and servants muttering about the recent fires, Larken stared at the man yanking her down the halls. She wondered if he knew about them, if he was involved at all. Maybe he was the one responsible for the families whose lives were now ruined…or maybe she was just speculating since he could have easily killed her.

Not that she could say much about the fires. Vallen tried to keep them from her. She didn't mind though; Larken didn't like the thought of her friends having to deal with them. The idea of them rushing into a burning mansion or war camp gave her a stom-achache.

When they reached a darkened corridor that he had deemed suitable enough, he stopped with his back to the only camera. Glaring down at her, he said, "Finally."

Delvon pushed Larken up against the wall, his right hand going to her hip, his left tangling itself in her hair. The smell of pine and salt surrounded her as he pulled her head to the side and angled his right above hers.

He looked deep into her eyes and whispered, "Before you say anything, I need to know if you are the kind of person that believes everything your mother says."

Larken opened her mouth, but her words stuck. Delvon, the man that had almost killed her a month ago, was giving her the opportu-nity to talk to him about it. To the security team, they looked like nothing more than a couple trying to keep their passion a secret, and because of that, they would be forced to turn off the audio to give the daughter of their Luminary privacy.

Give them two sentences instead of one before deciding if they are an enemy or an ally.

Larken smirked. "Are you?"

Delvon returned her smirk with one of his own. "Well then, I do believe I owe you an explanation, love."

"I think so," Larken agreed, putting her hands up on his shoulders.

"I can't tell you everything, not yet. I still have my orders. All you need to know is that I work closely with your mother and report to General Maxwell."

"What about the crash?" Larken asked, pushing her fingers into his hair. "I know the men who attacked me both times weren't Faithfuls."

"Clever girl."

"So, if you're not a Faithful, and you work with my mother, then what were you doing at the crash site?"

"I was checking on you, of course."

"I'm surprised you're still alive."

"Why is that?"

"If you report to Vallen, then I can only assume it was him you were talking to that night." Larken let go of his hair, grabbing a fistful of his shirt instead. "And Vallen doesn't let anyone talk to me that way."

"Aye, he put me through the fight of my life but understood I had a part to play. Couldn't very well let your boyfriend catch on to who I was."

Larken let go of him as fast as if he had burned her and tried to push him away.

She scowled as he towered over her and murmured, "Not so fast, love. You don't look like you should."

"And what is that supposed to mean?"

Instead of answering her, Delvon pressed his lips to her neck just under her ear. Larken stiffened. He pulled away almost as soon as he kissed her, and her face felt hot. "There, now you look like you've been kissed."

"I was kissed, you moron."

"Don't get used to it," he said with a wink. "You're not my type."

Delvon backed up, and Larken felt as furious as she did embarrassed, but one look at the camera had her glad for her blush. At least now she looked like a frazzled girl, instead of someone who had wanted a private conversation. Together, they walked silently back to her room, Larken shooting glances Delvon's way. At first, she had thought it was because she actually knew him, but the longer she walked next to him, she felt like the crash wasn't the first time they had met.

"See something you like, love?"

Larken rolled her eyes. "No, I just can't decide if you look more like a dog or a bear."

He gave her a feral grin. "I'll take that as a compliment."

"Take it however you want," she muttered, not looking at him again.

They reached her room, and Delvon walked in and dropped into the chair in front of her vanity. Larken sighed, looking over her room. Vallen leaned against her wall, and Candy and Carl sat on her bed. She would need to start looking into furnishing her sitting room. In the past, she and Vallen would just hang out in his sitting room, but the list of people in her life seemed to keep growing.

"I see you found another stray," Vallen grunted.

"A good-looking one too," Candy agreed, now dressed in a pale pink sundress that complimented her thin figure. Her hair had been done up in fat curls that were pinned to the top of her head, her bangs pushed over her left eye.

"*Umm*, I'm sitting right here!"

Candy leaned over and kissed Carl on the cheek. "I know, sweetie."

Carl harrumphed, making Candy giggle. Candy stood and asked, "Well, is everyone ready then?"

Vallen pushed off the wall, smacking Delvon in the back of the head on his way over to Larken. Delvon grumbled as he stood, and Larken grinned.

"I'm assuming he deserved that," Vallen said.

"Of course he did." Larken took her communicator from Vallen, checking for a message she knew wasn't there.

Candy moved to her side, peeking at the screen. "Still nothing?"

Larken shook her head and sighed, releasing her disappointment. "It doesn't matter. Tonight is about finally having some fun."

"Weren't you just complaining about going shopping a little bit ago?" Carl asked.

"I can complain again if you want."

"Always so accommodating; no wonder you're known as the *Military Sweetheart*."

Candy smacked Carl in the gut with the back of her hand, causing him to grunt. Larken only smiled, following Vallen out of her room. She listened to Candy whisper-shout at Carl for being insensitive and tried not to laugh. They made their way like that through the Manor, Larken still checking her communicator every few seconds even though she told herself she didn't care.

When it eventually did go off, Larken almost dropped it in her haste to see who it was. A request for a video call appeared on her screen, and when she saw Loxly's name, she seriously considered ignoring it. Her heart squeezed as her thumb hovered over the decline button, and then she decided to answer. Instead of the messy brown hair and crooked smile that she had expected, a familiar pudgy face filled up her screen, and Larken's eyes burned.

"Larken, are you in trouble?" Jing asked, her dark eyes crinkled in concern.

"No, sweetie, I'm not in trouble. Why do you ask?"

"Because I saw—"

"Jing, what are you doin'?" Loxly's voice interrupted.

Larken's throat went tight as the girl answered, "I wanted to make sure Larken wasn't in trouble."

"That doesn't answer my—hold on, is that my communicator?"

Jing continued to ignore Larken, looking at Loxly who was somewhere behind her. "You said I could play on it."

"Yeah, *play*, not make video calls."

"If she was busy, she wouldn't have answered."

Jing shrieked, and the communicator fell from her hands. The pounding of Loxly's boots could be heard, and Larken readied herself.

When his face filled her screen, Larken couldn't help the sniff that escaped her. He sighed, that crooked smile parting his lips as he breathed, *"Little Bird."*

A hot tear rolled down her cheek before she could stop it, and she brushed it away roughly. Her voice sounded tight as she spoke. "Hey, Loxly. How have you been?"

"We all miss you like crazy." He looked a little guilty. "Didn't want to call in case—"

"My communicator is only monitored by Vallen," she assured.

His crooked smile split into a full-on grin. "Probably shouldn't have told me that."

Larken laughed, and it shook free some of the cobwebs in her heart. "Loxly, you could call me at 2:00 in the morning, and I would still want to talk to you."

"You say that now, Little Bird, but I don't think 2:00 am you would agree."

She grinned. "Probably not."

"Larken!" Jing called from somewhere. "Can I come to your party?"

"Jing," Loxly warned.

Larken's heart broke. "I'm sorry, sweetie, I don't get to pick the guest list. It's more of a social networking event for my parents than a birthday party."

Jing was silent for a moment, and then said, "That sounds awful."

Larken laughed. "I agree. I wouldn't even go if it wasn't my birthday."

"Will you at least have cake?"

"I think the caterers decided on gelato and chocolate-covered fruit."

"What's *gelato*?"

"Hoity-toity frozen mush," Loxly answered.

The group reached the doors and spilled out into the drive. The heat covered Larken like a suffocating blanket, and the back of her neck started to sweat as they waited for the hover.

Loxly looked back to Larken, his eyes worried. He asked softly, "Are you okay?"

"I'm…managing."

Loxly nodded.

"The others?"

"Levi's takin' it pretty hard, but he's survivin'. Hinlee misses you, and Brecker's hatin' that he has to eat at the cafeteria again."

Larken nodded, not daring to ask about the one person she wondered about the most.

Loxly, not needing her to say it out loud, said, "He isn't talkin' and shuts himself away a lot."

Without thinking, Larken reached up and grabbed the pearl. The hover pulled up, and the glossy black paint nearly blinded her as it reflected the sun. Heart breaking all over again, she looked back at her communicator and said, "Loxly, I'm really sorry, but I have to go."

"Big plans?"

"Dress shopping for the party."

Loxly's face went stern as he barked, "You tell that Carl if you show up to your party in another dress that looked like that red one, we'll fly over there and kill 'em."

Larken laughed over Carl's protests of, "*I didn't pick it out!*"

"Tell everyone I miss them."

Loxly rose a dark eyebrow. "Everyone?"

Realizing she still gripped the pearl, Larken forced herself to let go of it. "We'll talk again soon."

"See ya, Little Bird."

Larken ended the call just as Jing called, "Bye-bye Larken!"

Letting out a long breath, she stuffed her communicator into her back pocket. Candy put her arm around Larken's waist. She smelled like cherries, and Larken let that comfort her.

"At least he's just as miserable."

"I don't care how he's feeling," she lied.

Carl pulled Candy to him, leading her to the hover. Larken could hear him mutter, "I thought I told you not to bring that up."

"She's in *pain*, Carl. I just want her to know she has someone to talk to."

"She knows, Candy. She just doesn't like talking about *him*."

Candy's retort was cut off as Carl ushered her into the hover. He climbed in after her, and then Vallen crowded in, leaving Delvon to hold the door open for her.

Larken took his offered hand, and as she started climbing in, he asked, "Your boyfriend mad at you or something?"

Larken pulled her hand free and used it to shove him. Delvon fell against the hover, chuckling as he righted himself and followed her in. Larken climbed over Vallen and sat herself down between him and the window. She hadn't even been around Delvon for two hours, and he was already on her nerves. He still smirked as he sat in the open seat at Candy's right.

Candy talked to Carl the whole way to the boutique where he had set up the fitting. She asked about what he was planning on wearing to the party and what would complement his outfit best. Then she started asking about what he had planned for Larken, and he told her that he wouldn't know until she picked a dress. Larken knew her indecision probably caused him a great deal of stress, but she couldn't bring herself to care just now.

He's just as miserable as me...

Larken shook her head, trying to clear it, and realized that her fingers had wandered back up to the necklace. Growling low in her throat, Larken dropped her hand and crossed her arms, forcing herself not to touch it. She really should get rid of the stupid thing; all it ever did was remind her of things she wanted to forget. Larken looked out the window, ignoring the way her eyes burned.

Vallen nudged her gently, and she whispered, "I don't want to talk about it."

He didn't bring it up again, grabbing her hand so she wouldn't dig her fingers into her flesh anymore. She appreciated the gesture, loving Vallen even more for his worry. But he only held one hand, and the other eventually found its way back to the pearl.

CHAPTER 5

Loxly walked into his room without knocking, and Soren already wanted to shout at him. The sharpshooter crossed his arms and leaned against the closed door. "I was lookin' for ya yesterday, but you disappeared, like usual." When Soren didn't say anything, Loxly asked, "Wanna know who I talked to last night?"

He still ignored Loxly, the sit-ups unable to distract Soren like they had before being interrupted.

"Of course I do, Loxly. I would love to know who you talked to that you thought would be worth interruptin' my self-imposed house arrest," he said, mocking Soren and making him even more annoyed.

"Well, Cap," he continued as if it really had been Soren who spoke, "Jing hijacked my communicator and video called Larken."

Soren stopped for only a second, chest an inch from his knees, before dropping back against the floor.

"She was really upset and didn't ask about you."

Soren locked his jaw, not wanting to say something that Loxly would be able to use against him later. His fury rose with every passing second, and he began to worry about what would happen if Loxly continued to stand there and rub salt into his wounds.

"I told her about you anyway, about how you've been shuttin' yourself away and been ignorin' everyone."

Soren paused against his knees again, forcing himself to stay seated and not break Loxly in half.

"It really seemed to bother her."

"And what do I care what bothers her and what doesn't?" he asked, finally snapping.

"Because, even though she acts like it doesn't hurt her, she still has that necklace on. Just like you say you don't care but don't leave your room if you don't have to." Loxly pushed off of the door and opened it. He paused, about to leave, and looked back at Soren. "I just thought you'd wanna know."

Soren dropped to the floor as the door clicked shut, and he lay there for a while. The anger and hurt threatened to swallow him. It made Soren want to punch something. So what if she still had the necklace? That didn't mean anything. She probably only had it on because it matched the outfit that new stylist had picked out for her, not because she actually missed him. He needed to forget her, just like she had no doubt forgotten him. If she had really missed them, *him*, she would have reached out before now.

Before he knew what he was doing, Soren had his communicator out. He did a web search for Larken Hale, and he told himself that it was just to prove his point. His screen was soon flooded with images of the blonde, a hundred different links for him to choose from. Soren started scrolling through photos, looking only for the ones of her and Braves. Selecting one from the first public event after the opera, Soren zoomed in on her chest. Resting against the yellow lace of her dress was the pearl. Rage threatened to blind him as he looked for another.

Each photo he found of her, whether dressed for a black-tie event or a casual outing, she had it on. Guilt twisted his rage into nausea. From the photos, it looked like she never took it off. Soren tossed his communicator away, not caring where it landed. Things weren't supposed to be this way. She was supposed to be angry with him for not telling her to stay, just like everybody else was. She wasn't supposed to still be hurting, still clinging to the one thing he had given her. Larken had gone back to her old life, leaving him behind.

She wasn't supposed to be remembering him, because that made it so much more difficult for him to stay mad.

Soren pushed himself up, deciding that he would go workout somewhere that Loxly couldn't bother him, when his communicator went off. He looked around for it, finally finding it under his bed, the bed that he only had because of Larken. Everything around him had been saturated with her. His bed, the new weapons he had ordered, the furniture, the appliances—it had all been possible because of her. Because he had shouted at her and bullied her when she had first arrived. Soren couldn't say if he would have acted any differently towards her if he had known how things would have turned out; he could only wish that the ache in his chest would go away. He hated seeing her every time he closed his eyes, hated that he expected to find her sitting in her spot on the couch, covered in that ridiculous jacket, every time he heard Loxly laughing in the common room.

Soren heard his communicator *pop*, and he forced himself to relax his grip on the device. He looked at the screen and saw that he had a message, a summons to a meeting for all the Captains that started in fifteen minutes in the courtyard. Jumping at the chance to distract himself, Soren rushed out of his room, not even bothering to acknowledge Loxly's goodbye.

Through the halls and past the cafeteria, Soren started to notice that he wasn't the only one now making his way to the courtyard. Several Captains fell into step with him, saying nothing as they walked. Some had their weapons at their hips, and some had wet hair plastered to their faces and necks. Only then did Soren actually wonder what was so important that they needed all of the Captains in one place at the same time. Soren's stomach flipped, momentarily wary that it might be a trick, that the Faithfuls could be using this as an opportunity to hit their base. But the only time he had encountered the Faithfuls outside the battlefield, they hadn't seemed malicious. At the time, they had only wanted Larken; it was the other group that had wanted them all dead. Could they be connected to this summons somehow? After the Faithfuls were able to get onto base the day Larken was shot, he didn't know how much he could trust the Base's security. Especially when there was another group out there who had access to the same sort of spyware.

The heat hit Soren in the face as he filed outside with the others. The dry sun had his shirt sticking to his back in seconds, and his hair clung to his forehead. Brushing it out of his eyes, Soren made his way to his spot in line. Second row, second on the right, he stood there, waiting for the other Captains to finish arriving. The courtyard spread across the center of the base, housing a few flowerbeds and a single fountain that had spouts so small that the running water barely made a sound. Some of the squads used the area as a public hangout, but Soren never understood the draw of it. He would much rather play cards with his friends in comfort than sit in the dirt and have to talk over other conversations. Some of the soldiers even used the space to work out, opting for the fresh air instead of a smelly gym. Soren would have to agree with them on that point if he hadn't been awarded his own personal workout space. One that no one apart from the people he allowed inside could use.

Once it looked like everyone was there, except for Braves, a man that Soren didn't recognize stepped up onto the edge of the fountain. He stood ramrod straight, his posture telling of his years in the military. The dark suit he wore looked to be a size too small, and his tie appeared to be choking him. His oily-looking blond hair shone in the sun, his clean-shaven jaw clenched. He stood there for a moment, looking over every person in the first few rows. When his eyes landed on Soren, he smirked.

"I am Major Avery Sutton, and I am the new Chief Administrator of Base 14."

Soren kept his hands at his sides, already able to tell that this man was bad news. He held himself like he thought he was better than everyone else, and with Braves's absence, Soren's suspicions grew. If this man actually liked throwing his power around like Soren assumed, then he would be making a public example of Braves. Since the Captain of Squad 22 was missing, Soren could only surmise that the two had an understanding. And with the way Sutton was currently boring holes into his head, he could also safely assume that the man had been warned about Squad 19.

"I wished to call you all here," Sutton continued, his voice oily as his hair, "to introduce myself and tell you what I expect from the squads on this base. First, there has been an increase in the amount of media attention Base 14 receives. Therefore, we will be changing a few things so we appear presentable to the rest of the country and those who may wish to join our ranks." The man's eyes fell back on Soren. "Because of this spike in public interest, every squad will be expected to fill each open slot."

A grumbling rose up around Soren as he glared back at Sutton.

The Chief Administrator raised a hand, silencing all complaints. "Each of you has received a list of applicants, and it will be first-come, first-serve. You have until the end of the month to fill any empty rooms you may have, or someone will be chosen for you."

Soren stuffed his fists in his pockets, not wanting Sutton to see that his words affected him. No one had gone into Larken's room since she had left, and Soren planned to keep it that way. He wouldn't let some stranger come in and change everything again. Squad 19 had functioned with five members since Soren took over, and they would do it again. He had no problem petitioning General Maxwell for a squad cap if he needed to. Her room wouldn't be touched, and that was that.

"Secondly, with the Faithful threat rising as well as the number of fires, all recreational time will be suspended until further notice."

More complaints sounded, louder this time.

Sutton spoke over the crowd, saying, "You will use your dorm shifts as time to recuperate and relax, and until we are certain that this base is impregnable, this is how things shall stay."

The Captains to Soren's right and left both glared at him. He had to give Braves credit; if his plan was to get everyone to blame Squad 19 for all their problems, he'd succeeded.

"And lastly, we will be doubling the force of our attacks, so we will be implementing a two-week rotation where we will be sending five squads to the frontlines every other week, instead of the two squads every month. The Captains of the chosen squads should have already been notified and will be shipped out tomorrow. You will also receive a schedule for the next three months." Sutton grinned, finding pleasure in the growing anxiety around him. "Whether your squads return fully intact will determine when you will once again join the rotation. That is all."

No one moved until Sutton hopped off of the fountain lip and started walking back in the direction of his office. Some of the Captains Soren had once considered friends turned to openly glare at him, while others gathered in panicked groups and started whispering about the war or the most recent fire. Soren felt torn between staying back to fight every single person who glared at him and wanting to call General Maxwell and see if he was aware of these new developments. He would also have to tell the rest of his squad what was going on eventually, but his racing thoughts stilled as a soft hand brushed against his elbow.

Soren looked to find Kelly staring up at him. He scowled at her, but she only smiled and asked, "Pretty crazy, huh?"

He only grunted, not wanting to talk to her.

"You aren't shipping out tomorrow, are you?"

Soren shook his head, deciding he would collect his thoughts back at the dorm, away from all the hushed voices and blatant hostility directed at him.

Kelly followed. "Good, I'm glad. I would hate for you to leave when we just started talking again." When Soren didn't return her relief, she continued, "I do have three open spots in my squad though. I'll have to start going through the applicants. I'll find some younger girls. Make sure they have a place where they feel comfortable."

Soren ignored her as she talked about her plans, wanting only some quiet to think. He needed to find out who exactly Avery Sutton was and who his connections were. Soren couldn't go on assuming that Sutton had ties with Braves simply because he couldn't stand either of them. He needed facts, and he knew who could help. Only, reaching out to General Maxwell made his stomach twist. As Larken's unofficial adoptive father, he no doubt knew what had happened between the two of them, even if she hadn't shared it with him. What would he do if Soren reached out to him? Would General Maxwell listen to him because that was his job, or would he blow Soren off because of what he had done to Larken?

"Are you even listening to me?" Kelly asked, pulling him from his thoughts.

"What?"

She stopped in front of him, crossed her arms, and looked up at him with a teasing smile. "I asked if you had plans tonight. I usually go for a run at sunset around base during the warmer months, and I was wondering if you would like to join me."

The hope in her eyes had his stomach sinking as he remembered how a pair of teal ones had looked at him like that not too long ago. Feeling uncomfortable, Soren said, "Sorry, no. I have plans."

Her face fell, and she smiled sadly. "Worth a shot, right?"

Soren grunted, not knowing what she was talking about. She wished him a good rest of his evening and disappeared into the crowd. Soren made his way back to the dorm, feeling more confused than ever.

CHAPTER 6

S oren gave himself three days before reaching out to General Maxwell, leaving him with roughly three weeks to pick a new squad member. The others hadn't taken the news well, and Levi had already been written up twice for breaking the noses of two other field medics for trash-talking Larken and the rest of Squad 19.

Soren had taken to overriding their schedules, making sure that they worked out in his private gym, went to the shooting range during meal times so it would be mostly empty, and used squad funds to order in so they didn't have to eat in the cafeteria. Brecker, Hinlee, and Loxly all ate together at the table, working around their new schedules. Levi and Soren ate in their rooms, not wanting to talk to anyone as usual. Soren waited for the day that Levi would finally snap and come after him, putting the blame where it was due, but he never did. Soren didn't know if it was because the Second knew that he was itching for a fight and wanted to punish him even more, or if it was because Levi wasn't sure if he could keep from killing him yet.

Music sounded from the common room, and Soren had to force himself not to go out and smash the stereo to bits. It wasn't Shadric Barlow, but it was a song that Larken had often listened to while she cooked. The melody had seared itself into Soren's memory, and he knew the words that would come next. The man sang of second chances and sleepless nights as the melody swelled and died down. The part that he waited for quickly approached, and then the bridge hit. Instead of the harmonies of a female voice singing alongside the guy, it was only him carrying out the depressing words.

Something snapped in Soren; he never knew that this song wasn't a duet. She had sung it so often that he *knew* this song, but he hadn't really known anything. One day, Larken had been here, happy and singing, and then she left.

"That's good. She only does that when she's really happy. If she's dancing, then I have nothing to be worried about."

She had been happy here, so why did she leave him? Why couldn't he just say that one, *stupid* word? Why couldn't he have asked her to stay? Even if she couldn't stay, at least they'd be on better terms. But now, he only had androids to spar with, lonely meals in his room, and enough rage to blind a bear.

Soren's communicator started buzzing, and he looked at the screen. General Maxwell was returning his call, and he forced himself to take a deep breath and answer. "Captain Deckard."

"What happened?" Soren didn't expect to hear the worry in General Maxwell's voice. Maybe he assumed that Soren would only reach out to him if something really bad had happened. Unfortunately for the General, that was exactly what was going on.

"Base 14 is in trouble."

There was a long sigh, and then General Maxwell said, "Tell me everything."

Soren did, starting with Sutton's introduction and ending with the harassment Squad 19 currently faced.

General Maxwell didn't say anything for a moment, most likely processing everything Soren had said. Then he growled, the noise making Soren's communicator vibrate slightly. "So, what you're telling me is, you have no solid proof that Sutton is working with Braves, but he has been targeting Larken's old squad, and that Squad 22 has been let off easy despite their Captain sniffing around where he doesn't belong?"

Sniffing around where he doesn't belong. Soren could only assume that General Maxwell meant Larken.

"Yes."

General Maxwell fell silent again, and then he said, "I'll take care of it."

"Thank you, sir."

"Deckard."

"Yes?" Here it was; General Maxwell was finally going to rip into him for hurting Larken the way he had.

"I need you to do something for me."

"Yes, sir."

"I no longer have eyes at Base 14. I need you to tell me if something unusual happens there. I don't care how insignificant, I want you to call and report to me. Can you do that?"

Soren's tongue stuck, not expecting that order.

"Deckard?"

"Yes, I can do that."

"Good, recruit the rest of Squad 19 as well. I'll be in touch."

With that, he hung up. Soren held his communicator to his ear for a second longer before letting it drop to his bed. Leaning back, he stared up at the ceiling, feeling worse than he would have if he had been shouted at. His communicator chimed, and Soren held it up over his face.

Send me the list of applicants.

Soren forwarded General Maxwell the list, noticing that a few applicants' pictures already had the word PENDING written across them in red letters.

Dropping the device back onto the bed, Soren pushed himself up. Now was as good a time as any to tell his squad what he had just volunteered them for. On the way out of his room, Soren clipped his hip on his desk and sucked in a sharp breath. Something fell and clattered to the floor. Not able to let whatever fell just sit there, he bent down and started groping for whatever it was. His hand touched something cool and smooth, and he wrapped his fingers around it. Pulling it out, he saw it was the green bottle of lotion that he had meant to return to Larken, but never had.

Memories of that night flooded his mind. The night she had told him about her shoulder, how he had been lost in a eucalyptus-scented cloud, and the first time he had almost kissed her. Unable to help himself, he popped the top and smelled the contents. He closed his eyes, and she stood before him, looking up at him and smiling. His heart hurt, but he didn't open his eyes, not yet. He needed to see her a little longer, to be near her even if it was only in his mind.

The image slipped away, like it knew he wanted it to stay, and he opened his eyes. Soren set the lotion back on his desk and left his room. He pounded on Levi's door on his way to the common room, letting him know that they needed to talk. All conversation stopped as he stood there, waiting for his Second. Levi's door opened, and he appeared at Soren's side. His glare told Soren all he needed to know, and he knew that one of these days, Levi was going to give him what he deserved. Soren glared back, accepting the challenge.

"What's up, Decks?" Hinlee asked. "You sending one of us off next?"

"*Hin!*" Brecker hissed.

She only glared, refusing to apologize.

"I just finished talking with General Maxwell," Soren announced.

They all perked up suddenly, even Levi. Hinlee's mouth fell open, and she asked, "*What?* Does that mean Larken is coming back?"

"No," he answered, watching them deflate again. He lowered his voice and added, "But I think she might still be in trouble."

Silently, they all found their seats on the couches. Soren leaned in and quickly explained everything. He told them his personal thoughts about what had been happening on base and how General Maxwell's suspicions only made him more certain that there was more going on than Soren originally thought.

They were all quiet until Levi asked, "Is this safe to be talking about here?"

"Larken was here; there's no way General Maxwell would let her stay somewhere that was being watched for any reason other than security," Soren said. "And someone has been in the dorm every second since she left. When would they have had time to bug this place?"

"True," Brecker agreed. "This is probably the safest place to have a conversation like this."

"So, what does that mean for us?" Hinlee asked. "What sort of things should we be looking for?"

"Honestly, I'm not sure," Soren admitted. "He just said anything unusual."

"Would he consider Loxly's increased intake of coffee unusual?" she teased.

"I would suggest Hinlee's hair," Loxly shot back, "but General Maxwell doesn't have any, so he might not think it's that weird."

Hinlee threw a pillow at him, and he caught it, making a face at her.

"Should we tell you first or just report to him?" Brecker asked.

"It doesn't matter to me, but I would still like to know."

"And he agrees with you that Braves is the reason behind all of this?" Levi questioned.

"I don't even know if that's what I think, but I find it hard to believe that the number of base-wide write-ups has doubled in just three days, and his squad members are the only ones who seem to be getting off easy."

"It is weird," Levi agreed. He had that look on his face that said he was thinking hard. "But is he honestly smart enough to pull something like this off? I mean, he's pretty inept."

"Which is why I can only say I think he's connected to it somehow."

"You don't think it's Cornella, do you?" Hinlee asked, her voice small and eyes worried.

Soren's gut twisted. "That would explain why General Maxwell asked us to help, and why he had no idea what was happening here."

Hinlee covered her mouth. "What about Larken? Is she safe?"

"My guess is that she's a lot safer with General Maxwell than she was here," Levi said.

"Yeah, I guess..." Hinlee's voice trailed off. Soren understood her unspoken words; he didn't like the idea that Larken might be safe somewhere else either.

Soren glanced at Loxly, who was being uncharacteristically quiet. Everyone turned to him as well, and Soren raised an eyebrow. Loxly frowned, looking like Rich, and asked, "Who were his eyes on the inside in the first place?"

"Why do you ask?"

"Just..." he leaned forward and stared at his clasped hands. "Bear with me here, it's just a thought. But what if General Maxwell had a connection to the Faithfuls?"

"How could you say that?!" Hinlee accused.

"Let him talk," Levi grumbled, his brow furrowed. Either Loxly had talked about this with the field medic before, or he had come to the same conclusion.

"We don't know how they got past all the barriers and onto Field E. No one could answer any of my questions, and it only made sense that someone helped them from the inside."

"What are you saying?" Soren asked, not liking where this was going.

"What if," Loxly met his gaze, "he had someone spyin' for him in the Faithfuls, and when they told him about the plan to ambush Larken, he had to put them into hiding?"

I blame myself.

General Maxwell's words echoed in Soren's mind. It made sense, that he had been warned but didn't make it to base in time. He would blame himself, thinking that Larken's injury had been his fault for not moving fast enough. Soren blamed himself for the same thing. But that still didn't answer his questions about the other group that kept trying to kill her. Sure, the Faithfuls had broken into base and had tried to kidnap Larken, but how did that other group play in? Did General Maxwell even know about them? He had to;

he couldn't protect Larken and not figure it out, but the idea still didn't sit well with Soren.

"You okay over there, Decks?" Hinlee asked. "You don't look well."

"I think Loxly might be onto something." He stood, making his way for the door.

"Where are you going?" Brecker called, peering around Hinlee so he could watch him.

"I'm going for a run."

CHAPTER 7

Larken huffed, trying to catch her breath. It had been a while since Vallen had insisted on sparring with her, and she had forgotten how fast he could be. It didn't help that she had been distracted, still caught up in the nightmare she had the night before. Larken had been plummeting towards the earth, once again trapped in that aircraft with Soren. She had begged and pleaded with him, asking for him to do something, *anything,* to try and save them. But he only stared at her quietly, telling her with his eyes that he wasn't ready.

Larken hissed as Vallen's sword grazed her bicep, opening her skin. Blood trickled down her arm, and he yelled at her for not paying attention. She was about to shout back at him, but Carl called, "Watch it! Don't bruise the produce!"

Larken stopped her counterattack to gape at Carl. Even Vallen had stopped to stare at him.

"What?"

"Did you just compare me to an apple?"

"Peaches bruise easier. Plus, it would make a cute nickname," Carl tossed back with a wink.

"If you start calling me Peach, I'm gonna sneak into your room at night and shave your head."

Carl put his hands up in supplication. "Understood."

"Good." Larken tossed her sword to the ground, examining her wound. The air stung it, and she frowned. Turning to Vallen, she asked, "You gonna patch up this mess?"

Vallen, who was messing with his communicator, grumbled, "It was your own fault for not paying attention. Go fix it yourself." Then he left, tapping at the device as he did.

Larken scoffed and turned to Carl. The stylist let his eyes drop to her bicep once before looking away, his face green. She rolled her eyes as Delvon chuckled from somewhere behind her.

"Need help, Princess?"

"Not from you, I don't."

Still chuckling, Delvon left his spot in the shadows and followed her back to her room. Looking over her bed, she didn't see Estelle, and Larken knew that the android was sleeping on Vallen's couch. The small dog liked his sitting room a lot more than Larken's bedroom, not that she blamed her. Larken wasn't a big fan of her room either. She ignored Delvon as she began fishing through her drawers, searching for her dermis gun.

"Looking for this?" Delvon asked, leaning against her dresser, the clear blue dermis gun in his hand.

"Give me that."

"Only if you give me something first," he teased, flicking his eyes to the camera behind her.

Larken forced a smile and sat on the chair in front of her vanity. She crooked her finger at him, and he smirked as he prowled toward her. He dropped to one knee and cupped her cheek. He pulled her close, pressing his forehead against hers. She could smell the scent of salt and pine that she was quickly becoming accustomed to. "Don't scare me like that."

Larken didn't protest as he moved his cheek to hers. His thick stubble felt like prickly velcro. "I'm sorry," she murmured. "I'll try to be more careful."

His lips brushed her ear. "Is there still a blue light in the corner of the camera?"

Larken looked and whispered, "Green."

Delvon pulled back. "Keep your eye on it, but make it look natural. When it's blue again, that means they unmuted the camera."

Larken nodded, and Delvon gently grabbed her arm, looking every bit the concerned lover. Slowly, he ran the gun over her flesh; she looked down long enough to watch her skin stitch back together.

"I have a job for you."

"Sorry, I don't have much free time. Better find somebody else."

"It will fit into your schedule just fine, Peach."

Larken forced a smile. "I *will* hurt you."

"We need eyes on Braves," he continued like she hadn't just threatened him. "We have reason to believe that he's working with the new Chief Administrator for Base 14."

"What makes you think that?"

"The fact that I heard your mother ask him to find someone."

"Then what do you need me for?"

"We need you to figure out what he's doing before he does it. We were blindsided by a few changes he made, one of which ensured that Squad 19 could be taken care of."

"What do you mean *taken care of?*"

"Exactly what it sounds like, love."

Larken's stomach fell. "And you think Dominic is trying to—" She clamped her mouth shut, not willing to say the words aloud.

"That's what we need you to find out." He tossed the gun onto her vanity, the plastic clattering against the white wood. "Think you can handle it?"

"There isn't anyone else you could use?"

Delvon smirked at her. "He isn't interested in anyone other than you at the moment."

Larken took a deep breath, nodding. She looked up in time to see the camera switch from green to blue. Smiling, Larken leaned forward. "Dominic insisted we go out tonight, but maybe we can sneak away when I get back."

"I'll hold you to it," he said with a wink. Delvon stood and then asked, "Do I get to help you change?"

"Don't push your luck," Larken muttered, grabbing her communicator and messaging Dominic to let him know they could meet up later.

Delvon laughed, the sound deep and warm, sounding nothing at all like she thought it would. She couldn't help a small smile of her own. Carl peeked his head through her doorway, eyes wary. "All patched up? Or do you need me to go get Medic Lattic?"

"Nope, good as new," she announced as Delvon handed her a tissue. She used it to wipe away the blood and then tossed it in the bin. Larken smiled at Carl and said, "Change of plans. I will need your help with my outfit for tonight after all."

"I thought you weren't going out."

"Well, I am now."

Carl crossed his arms and leaned against the doorframe. "Should I be worried?"

"No."

"Why don't I believe you?"

Larken sighed. "Come on, Carl. I need your help."

"And how exactly am I going to be helping you?" he asked, raising an eyebrow. Carl wore a faded grey button-up and apricot-colored shorts, and it annoyed Larken how easily style came to him.

"I need to look good tonight," she grumbled, refusing to look at her sweaty self in the mirror to her right.

"How good we talkin'?"

"Irresistible."

Carl didn't say anything as he stared at her, but Larken knew that he wanted to laugh. Delvon chuckled silently beside her as well, but she didn't think it was for the same reason. He would find more humor in her pending discomfort, whereas Carl found his joy in her swallowing her pride and asking him to help dress her for once.

"The occasion?"

"Dominic, Delvon, and I are going to a club tonight."

Carl's smile faltered the slightest bit at the sound of Dominic's name. It told her he misunderstood the situation as a night of fun instead of work. He nodded once, a wicked gleam slowly appearing in his eye. "I know just the dress."

<hr>

"Many people are under the impression that yellow is a color of friendship." Cornella ran her fingers over the back of Dominic's chair as she walked by. Dressed in the form-fitting deep blue dress she had worn to a press conference earlier that day, Cornella gave off the impression of elegance and poise. No one would know that the woman who dropped back into her chair at the head of the table was really a spider parading around as a Lumina. She sighed and continued, "But they would be wrong."

Dominic tried not to let his impatience show. He had to meet Larken in an hour, and Base 7 was forty-five minutes away. Showing up late wasn't something that he liked doing; he would rather be early and get a good feel for his surroundings. He liked knowing where his escape routes were and seeing who might be willing to come home with him. But even though he had Larken now and didn't need to look for one-night stands, he couldn't break the habit of wanting to be early.

Forcing himself to appear interested, he asked, "Why would they be wrong, Lumina?"

She smiled softly, her red lips twisting as she tasted the secret she was about to let him in on. "Because yellow is the color of *jealously*, Captain."

The yellow rose pin that clung to his navy uniform felt suddenly heavy.

"It is the force that drives men, and no one is immune."

"What makes you say that?"

"Jealousy will make anyone do anything. It is what makes men take up arms for land that they think belongs to them, it is what makes women style themselves to catch the eye of a man they can't have, and," her eyes glinted maliciously, "it is the reason that you agreed to our little arrangement in the first place."

"I thought that I might be able to help you, Lumina. That's all."

"Are you not chasing after my daughter as you do so? Are you not having Chief Administrator Sutton *punish* Squad 19 for interfering with your relationship with her?"

Dominic couldn't say anything; it didn't make him proud to admit that she was right. The plan they had worked out was going perfectly, and in it, he had found the perfect opportunity to get back at the one person who had tried to come between him and Larken over and over again.

Cornella raised a thin eyebrow, expecting an answer. He gave her a rakish smile and said, "I worked out a plan, just like you asked me to. Squad 19 being affected by it is just a happy accident."

"Indeed," she agreed. "Just as I'm sure Squad 22 benefiting from your arrangement with Sutton is a *happy accident*."

Dominic shrugged; he couldn't care less what was happening to his squad. If things went according to plan, in just over a month, he would be far away from here, Larken at his side. He could only hope that she would understand. He was doing this, *all of this*, for her.

"Tell me, how have the transitions at Base 7 been going?"

"No one suspects a thing, Lumina. As far as the soldiers are concerned, the new recruits are eager cadets trying to prove themselves."

"Good." She leaned back in her chair, the dim light playing off her pale skin. "And how have you been managing your subordinates? Are they giving you any trouble without Mr. Tanner at your side?"

Dominic balled his fists under the table. Just the sound of his name had him seeing red. Larken had been pulled from the arms of one man and tossed right into the arms of another. Even now, as he sat there, trapped with Cornella, Tanner was there with her. Forcing his voice to sound calm, he said, "Things have been going smoothly. I've encountered no trouble."

"Good, good." She smiled. "I'm so glad to hear it."

Dominic looked at the clock behind her head. If he left right this second, he would only be five minutes late, plus whatever time it took to change in the aircraft.

"Perhaps you wouldn't mind showing me what you've been working on here? I've been curious about what new strategies you've been implementing."

Telling himself to smile, he said, "Of course, Lumina." Dominic stood, not daring to pull out his communicator. He would just have to do this quickly and hope that Larken was still there when he managed to finish.

CHAPTER 8

Music filled the club, and bodies writhed together to the sway of the melody. A booming bassline to the song reverberated through the floor and up the stool that Larken sat on. Clouds of smoke hovered over the dance floor, reflecting and blocking the lights that pitifully tried to illuminate the room. Larken felt a little guilty trying to deceive Dominic like this, but if the lives of her friends were at risk, then she needed to know. She felt uncomfortable, but she couldn't argue with Carl's results. Larken received many appreciative glances as she sat alone at the bar. A few men had even been brave enough to ask if she wanted a drink, and a few braver than that had asked her to dance. Larken turned them all down, not interested in what they were really offering, and with each man she turned away, she felt more and more confident that Dominic would like what he saw. If he ever showed up that was.

Larken stirred her drink, the ice clinking against the glass. The carbonated pomegranate juice was almost the same shade as her lips, and the bartender, who had the signature dark hair and eyes of the Military District, had ignored her after dropping it off. Since she wasn't drinking, he decided to try his luck elsewhere, fishing for whatever tips he could. Larken didn't mind though, she didn't really feel like talking. She was only here for this job, and if she did it right, then she might not have to come to places like this anymore. Larken just needed to know what Dominic had been up to, and hopefully, this dress and the few drinks he would no doubt consume would do the trick. The dress was nowhere near as small as the red one Dominic had picked for her to wear to the opera, but it felt just as tight. The hot pink fabric clung to her like a second skin, cutting off just above her knees. Her right shoulder felt open and vulnerable, and she had to keep herself from constantly grabbing at it.

The last time they went out like this together, she hadn't known where Dominic planned on taking her. He claimed he wanted to have dinner and go dancing, and they ended up at that bar. Luckily, Vallen had followed behind her and rescued her fairly quickly. When that drunk at the bar grabbed her, she lashed out, not caring about who saw. Larken stopped caring about a lot of things since coming home. No longer did she let her father's drunk friends ogle her at parties. She hadn't let the security guards around the Manor or any entitled men that hung around her mother degrade or proposition her either. Larken had been told that her actions were reflecting poorly on her family, but she stopped considering herself a member of the Hale family the night of the opera.

"Any idea where lover boy might be?" Delvon's voice sounded in her ear.

Larken impulsively reached up to touch her hair, making sure that it still covered her ear. "No idea," she murmured. "He isn't usually late."

"Well, I'm starting to get looked at."

"*I don't care*," she breathed, trying not to draw attention to herself.

"No, I mean in a bad way."

"Stop creeping around in the shadows and ask someone to dance then."

"And leave you unsupervised? I don't think so, Peach."

Larken bit back her first retort and said, "I told you to stop calling me that."

"And I told you that it was never gonna happen."

Rolling her eyes, she did a quick web search. Calling over the bartender, she asked, "Could I order a drink?"

He looked her up and down, giving her an unamused smirk. "That's what I'm here for."

Larken looked over her shoulder and quickly found Delvon leaning against a pipe that held the ceiling off the floor. She pointed and asked, "Do you see that guy?"

"The creepy one?"

"Yes," she turned back to the bartender, "could I buy him a drink?"

"What will it be?"

"Three fingers of 120-proof whiskey, please."

The bartender huffed a laugh. "Sure thing, sweetheart."

"Are you trying to get me drunk?" Delvon teased.

The bartender finished pouring and made his way over to him, and Larken said, "There, pretend to sip on that, it should help."

"Do you even know what you ordered me?"

"Something you aren't supposed to drink fast. Now, stop talking to me; people are starting to look at me like I'm crazy."

The minutes turned to an hour, and then an hour and a half. Larken had long since finished the juice, opting for water instead. Delvon complained every five minutes, and Larken was starting to get a headache. She wanted nothing more than to take out the earpiece, drop it in the water, and short-circuit it. Then she would leave Delvon here and find her own way home. She heeded a hot shower to wash away the stink of the bar. This whole night was turning out to be a colossal waste of time. She didn't know where Dominic was; she only knew that he had never been late before. Larken could only assume that she had been stood up.

The music changed, and the melody had her gripping her glass. The words to the song echoed through the dark room, and Larken swallowed back the tears that pricked her eyes. She was there again, in the gym getting ready to spar with a too-weak Soren. He had teased her about the song like he teased her about everything.

Her hand found its way to the pearl, and she squeezed it, closing her eyes. Why couldn't she have stayed? Why did she always have to do what her mother told her? Larken knew the answer, ashamed that she still somehow hoped that her mother would accept her.

Knocking back the rest of her water, Larken made up her mind to leave. Grabbing her communicator, she made to stand, but warm arms wrapped around her from behind. Soft lips pressed against her neck, just under her ear, and Dominic whispered, "You weren't planning on standing me up, were you?"

"You're the one who's almost two hours late."

"I know. I'm sorry."

"Why didn't you message me and tell me that you were going to be late?"

"Would you believe me if I told you my communicator died on the way here?"

"I wouldn't," Delvon muttered in her ear.

Larken ignored him. "Well, you did show up, not knowing if I would still be here." She felt his sigh of relief before he let her go. "So, where were you?"

"I got held up in a meeting."

"Anything exciting?" she asked.

"Just stuff for the base. Captain stuff. You know how it is."

"Seeing as I was never a captain, no, I don't."

Dominic barked a laugh, taking the seat next to her, and flagged down the bartender. Fishing out a small metallic case from his pocket, he pulled out a thin cigar and lit it. He took a drag of the black stick and exhaled a fog of blue smoke that smelled like blueberries. Larken coughed and tried to fan the smoke away as Dominic ordered his drink. Turning to her, he grinned. When she didn't return it, he asked, "What's wrong? Are you still upset that I'm late?"

"It's not that," she said, pushing the memories of another grumbly Captain from her mind. "It's this song. It always makes me a little sad."

"Nonsense. This song is great!" Dominic said over the music and then turned to accept his drink.

The lyrics pounded into Larken's soul, and no matter how hard she fought it, she couldn't get Soren's face out of her mind. He hadn't thought the lyrics were sad either, but instead of thinking it was great, he had thought it was stupid and made her laugh. She shook her head, trying to clear her mind.

Stop thinking about him. You have a job to do.

Larken leaned into Dominic just as he knocked back his drink. He signaled to the bartender for another and then gave Larken his full attention. Or, more accurately, he gave her chest his full attention.

"That dress looks good on you. Is it new?"

"*Is it new?*" Delvon mocked, and Larken had to fight to keep from snorting.

"No, Carl found it in my closet. I guess Cam left it behind or something."

It wasn't a lie. Carl really had found it in her closet, but he had been the one to order it. The stylist insisted that he did it in case she ever found herself in a situation where she would need to play the part of a femme fatal, but she hadn't quite believed him when she had seen the designer's name on the dress. She was one of Candy's favorites, and Larken knew that he ordered some things with her family's arii, hoping that she would pass on the clothes she didn't want to Candy.

Dominic grinned and met her eyes. "Well, I think it looks fantastic on you. I can't tell you how happy I am that you're here with me and not someone else."

"*Little does he know you're sneaking away with me later. After getting me drunk no less.*"

Unable to help herself, Larken shot Delvon a glare. He snorted and turned away, drink still in hand, just as full as when he got it.

Dominic followed her gaze and scoffed. Larken turned just in time to see him down another drink. He took another puff of his cigar and sighed. "How has it been with him?"

"Fine. I forget he's there sometimes. It's really no big deal."

Dominic leaned in, eyes serious. "If he's bothering you, you can tell me."

"I know, Dominic." She smiled, grabbing his balled-up fist and holding it until he relaxed. "Delvon has been completely professional."

"Forgot about our little hallway rendezvous already, love?"

She kept smiling, even though she wanted to pull out the earpiece and throw it at Delvon. He chuckled in her ear, and Larken let go of Dominic's hand. "So, tell me about your meeting."

"Nothing to tell really. We had an influx of volunteers, so it's mostly just been trying to find places for them."

"So, what are you doing about it?"

"Each squad has to fill their empty slots. Then we'll start looking into base transfers and all of that. It's mostly just annoying paperwork. Nothing that you need to worry about."

Fill empty slots…

Squad 19 was being forced to replace her. Larken reached up and rubbed at her shoulder, the muscle hurting suddenly. She felt sick; she wanted to go home and demand to know why no one told her that they…that he…

"You okay, Lark?"

Larken shook her head, forcing herself to focus. She could think about all of this later. Now, she needed to get as much information out of Dominic as she could. "Fine, why?"

"You look like you're in pain."

Smiling, she said, "Just thinking silly things, that's all."

"I doubt anything you could think would be silly."

"Gag," Delvon grunted.

Larken's smile turned a little more genuine. She realized she was holding onto her necklace again and dropped her hand. Dominic took another puff, and Larken asked, "What else is happening at base?"

Dominic laughed, signaling for another drink. "Don't tell me you actually miss it there."

Larken shrugged. "And if I do?"

He cupped her cheek, bringing her eyes up to his. They were the same shade of chocolate brown as they always were, but this time, they didn't melt her like they once had. She didn't know if she was too broken, or if what had happened the last time they had been this close was the reason, but there was nothing there.

"Everything you need is here, Lark. This is where you belong."

She wanted to say he was wrong, to tell him that she had belonged *there*, back at base with the rest of Squad 19. She wanted to scream and shout and *beg* to go back. Larken felt empty, like a piece of her was missing, and she knew exactly what it was, who they were. She felt homesick for the cold bedroom, Mr. Chin's food, and the kitchen where she could make everyone smile. Larken hadn't realized until that moment how lonely she really felt. Her throat went tight, and her eyes burned.

Grabbing the pearl again, she rasped, "I'm sorry, Dominic, but it's late. I need to go."

"But I just got here. Don't you want to dance before you leave?"

"No, I—" she grabbed his hand, squeezing it. "I have to get up early. I still have a lot I have to do before the party."

Dominic sighed and crushed his cigar in a nearby ashtray. Pushing up from his stool, he helped Larken to her feet. She stood, her legs shaky from sitting for so long. "Want me to walk you out?"

"No, stay and finish your drink," she insisted. "I'll be fine."

"Right." He glared at something over her shoulder, and Larken knew that it was Delvon. Looking back at her, he asked, "Let me know you got back safe, okay?"

She nodded, and then he leaned in and kissed her cheek. Not looking at him, Larken made for the exit. A few guys tried to get her to dance, but she ignored them. Blowing past the bouncer and the guests waiting to get in, Larken spilled out onto the lot. She stumbled and had to catch herself on a nearby hovercraft. Reaching down, she tore her shoes from her feet, suddenly unable to breathe.

She headed for where they were docked and managed to get three steps before a hand at her elbow stopped her. She rounded on

Delvon, who asked, "And where do you think you're going, Princess?"

Larken narrowed her eyes, brought her hand back, and slapped him. Delvon only glared at her as he held her in place. Larken's hand burned, and she shouted, "Why didn't you tell me?"

He said nothing, only stared at her with hard understanding in his grey eyes. It only made her more upset.

"Why didn't you tell me?" she asked again, voice cracking.

He pulled her a little closer, and she stumbled.

Not wanting his comfort or his help, she balled her fist and brought it down on his chest. "Why didn't—why—" Her breath caught, and Delvon crushed her roughly against him.

Larken broke, dropping her heels and clutching at his dark shirt. She sobbed against him despite her efforts to keep her tears locked away, hating herself for leaving the one place she had been happy, and hating that she never had the choice to stay, to begin with. What would happen to them when they found someone new? Would they move on and forget her? Would they realize that she really was more trouble than she was worth? Larken wanted nothing more than to run away, find a way back to base, and crawl into bed. She wanted to pretend that all of this had been a bad dream, and she would wake up and be back there again.

When her sobs turned to hiccups, Delvon let go of her. He bent down and grabbed her shoes, and then led Larken to the hover. After helping her inside, he crawled in and fired up the engine. He turned with a sigh and gave her a hard look. She didn't speak, only waited for him to say what he wanted to say.

He narrowed his eyes at her and said, "You tell anyone I was nice to you, I'll never stop calling you Peach."

CHAPTER 9

The party was only four days away, and Larken still hadn't told anyone what had happened that night at the club. Delvon didn't either, but she thought it was more from embarrassment over their tender moment than anything. Dominic had been messaging her constantly, convinced that his being late was what had made her upset. She let him think that, knowing that it was cruel, but couldn't help it. She had been honest with him once before, and it blew up in her face. He wouldn't understand that her missing the way things were wasn't about him. Dominic would only hear what he wanted, which would probably be along the lines of her missing Soren more than him. Which, of course, wasn't true.

"What do you think?" Carl asked, fixing the train. The grass-green gown she had been stuffed into wasn't ugly, it just wasn't her. It had a lace halter-style bodice that fit more like a turtleneck, leaving her entire upper back exposed. The skirts cut off above her knees and fell like a waterfall down her back. The dress just didn't feel right.

"It's...pretty," she admitted, fingering the lace at her chest. The pearl had been trapped between the fabric and her skin, and she couldn't help but wonder as she stared at herself in the mirror what Soren would make of this dress.

Carl sighed, dropping the train. The fabric pooled behind the heels of her emerald stilettos. "Go change."

"Carl, really," Larken insisted, "just tell me what to wear and I'll wear it."

"Tell me something," he said. "How was Cameron Brady associated with you in the media?"

"As the scumbag who had his face broken by his client?"

"No," Carl narrowed his eyes at her reflection, *"before that."*

"A renowned stylist who managed the world's most difficult client?" she asked, not sure what point he was trying to make.

"Yes, but his client was never photographed smiling."

"Yeah, but that wasn't his fault."

"So, your unhappiness had nothing to do with being forced to wear clothes that made you feel uncomfortable?"

Larken sighed. "Okay, fine. I get it."

She stumbled off the little dais and back to the changing room. Unzipping the dress, she let it fall to the floor in a green puddle. Leaving the shoes in the mess of fabric, Larken reached for the floor-length red dress that Candy would have loved. It hugged Larken's curves, and she had a hard time getting the zipper all the way up. Larken remembered the last time she had been struggling to zip up a red dress and had to remind herself that Loxly wouldn't be standing outside the changing room, ready to make a joke.

Pulling the curtain back, Larken emerged. Carl looked her up and down, and then twirled his finger. Larken turned, allowing him to finish zipping her up. He then helped her to the dais, where a pair of white pumps were waiting for her. Using the stylist for support, Larken wobbled as she stuffed her feet into the shoes.

"And you're sure heels are the best idea?" Delvon grumbled from his seat. Different sized pink tulle dresses hung behind him, making Larken smirk every time she looked his way. She wondered if Carl had put the chair there on purpose, wanting to get back at the bodyguard for all the snide comments about his profession.

Larken's ankle wobbled again, and she had to look down at her feet to keep her balance. Carl frowned. "As much as I hate to agree with you, I think flats might be best."

"I agree," Larken added quickly. She continued to hold onto Carl as she kicked the shoes from her feet. Heels were no problem when she knew she would be sitting a lot, but standing for the duration of a six-hour party? She didn't know how she would survive.

"I'll go see what they have," Carl said, and then disappeared.

Larken stood awkwardly in front of the mirror. The dress fit her nicely, but she still didn't like this one any better than the others. She wondered what would happen if she couldn't find anything. Larken didn't want to make her friend look bad, but these high-end dresses just weren't her. She knew she would have to pick something, though, because Loxly wasn't going to swoop in and save the day again.

Wrapping one arm around her stomach, Larken grabbed the pearl. Even dress shopping was an impossibility. Squad 19 had completely altered her life, and there was nothing that didn't remind her of them. Every time Vallen asked her to make dinner, she thought of Levi. Whenever Candy and Carl did something cute when no one was looking, she thought of Hinlee and Brecker. Whenever Vallen took Larken for a hoverbike ride, she couldn't help but think about how much Loxly would love it. And all she had to do was close her eyes, and she would see Soren, leaning in and telling her that he would never let her go. But, in the end, he had.

Eyes burning, Larken glared at her reflection and yanked her hand from the necklace. Trying to distract herself, Larken looked at Delvon. Even though the weather was still warm, he wore long, dark pants and a long-sleeved grey shirt the same color as his eyes. The growth on his jaw looked even thicker than usual, and his black hair hung in his face. He looked bored out of his mind, though his jaw ticked under her scrutiny.

He rose a dark brow at her. "You make up your mind yet?"

Larken smirked. "I'm thinking...*bear*."

Delvon grinned, and Larken had to admit that the smile looked good on him. She was glad that her heart had been locked away because she didn't think that it could survive anymore damage. And Delvon had heartbreaker written all over him…not that she was interested in getting close to any other grumps.

"If it took you that long to decide between bear and dog, then we're going to be here until your party starts," he groaned, annoyance coloring his words.

"Aren't boyfriends supposed to want to go shopping with their girlfriends?" Larken teased.

He scowled at her, obviously not liking that the media had taken him from simple bodyguard and promoted him to secret lover. Sucking on a tooth, he released it with a *pop*, and said, "That dress makes your butt look fat."

"That scowl makes your face look stupid."

"Always glad to see the happy couple getting along," Candy mused, walking up to Delvon. The smell of fried food accompanied her, and Larken's stomach rumbled. Candy dropped a bag onto Delvon's lap and said, "Here."

Without even a thank you, Delvon tore into the bag, pulling free an impossibly fat burger. He took a too-big bite and groaned. Candy turned to Larken, who moaned, "Candy, *please* tell me that you brought me something more than a salad."

Delvon laughed around the food in his mouth and continued to attack his burger. Candy looked suspiciously over her shoulder, no doubt searching for Carl, and then leaned in. Larken moved closer, not wanting to miss what she had to say. But instead of speaking, Candy pulled another bag from her giant purse and then ushered her into the changing room. Pulling off the dress, Larken left it in a heap on the floor by the green one. She threw on her clothes and sank to the floor, sitting as far away from the expensive fabric as she could. She tore into the packaging, feeling drunk on the smell of the greasy meat, and took a bite.

Larken swallowed, just as she heard Carl ask, "What's that smell?"

"I brought lunch for Delvon," Candy answered.

"Candy, I better not find Larken in that changing room eating a greasy burger in that 40,000 arii dress."

When Candy said nothing, Larken heard Carl stomp over to the changing room. Pulling back the curtain, he frowned down at the wadded-up dresses on the floor, and then at Larken. She stopped chewing and mumbled, *"I'm not."*

Carl sighed, rubbing at his temples. Larken swallowed, then took another bite as she watched him hang the dresses up. He muttered about the creases in the fabric, glaring at her every few seconds. When he finished, he looked at her and crossed his arms again.

Rubbing the back of her hand across her mouth, Larken asked, "What?"

He followed the movement with his dark eyes, then stared at her hand as he said, "I think I found the dress. Hurry up and try not to stain anything."

Delvon barked a laugh and Larken mocked it, quickly polishing off the rest of the burger. Pushing herself to her feet, Larken wadded up her trash. She threw it in the bin outside the changing room that had probably only ever seen loose bits of cloth and tissues. She was about to wipe her hands on her pants when Carl pointed at her and growled, *"Don't you dare!"*

Larken raised her hands as if the stylist was holding her at gunpoint. Carl pulled a packaged moist towelette from Candy's purse and tossed it to her. Larken caught it, scowling.

"Don't forget to clean your face."

Larken rolled her eyes but did as she was told. After she had tossed that into the bin as well, she turned to Carl. "You found a dress?"

He beamed. "Yes! Hidden away on the clearance rack by the shoes."

"Why didn't they bring it with the others, then?"

"Believe it or not, kid, the *Hale* name doesn't scream *clearance.*"

"Whatever, just give it to me so we can get this over with."

"What? Need a nap after clogging your arteries?"

"Carl, I'll punch you in the face."

"Yeah right, you love me too much." Carl walked to the clothing rack behind Delvon, who had perked up some, and grabbed the dress he had stashed there. The color caught her eye immediately, and she couldn't help the smile that tugged at her lips.

Larken took the dress from him, disappearing into the changing room. She quickly took off her clothes and pulled on the dress. Once she zipped it up, Larken looked down at herself. She grinned, running her fingers over the fabric. The off-the-shoulder sleeves didn't pinch her arms, and the neckline didn't go too deep. The pearl rested against the lace of the bodice, looking elegant against the simple design. The hem cut off just above her knees, and the matte satin was the same shade of pale blue as the lace. Larken thought of Jodi and how she would say the dress reminded her of the sky.

"How's it coming?" Carl called.

Brushing her hands down the front of the dress, Larken took a deep breath. She pulled back the curtain and stepped out into the boutique. Candy, Carl, and Delvon all stared at her, and Larken shrugged her shoulder, rubbing her jaw against it. She toyed with the hem and asked, "So?"

Carl motioned for her to stand in front of the mirror. She stepped up onto the dais, curling her toes as she bit her lip. She didn't know if their silence was a good thing or a bad one. Carl opened a shoebox and pulled out two peach-colored flats. He set them in front of her, and Larken stepped into them. Lip still between her teeth, she looked up at Carl. He grabbed her waist and forced her to face the mirror.

Larken's breath caught—the dress fit her beautifully, and she felt comfortable in the shoes. Carl looked at her like she was a supermodel instead of the Daughter of the Military, and Candy beamed at her. But none of that mattered because the only thing she could think of was how much she wanted Soren to see her like this.

CHAPTER 10

"The Military Heiress has been spotted again with her new stylist, Carl Habathorn. The man who once interned under Dave Carlisle, stylist for the renowned net-star, Ophelia Braves."

Soren refused to look up from his communicator, telling himself that he could care less about what was happening in Larken's life.

The reporter continued, his voice whiny and grating, *"The young stylist made his big debut the opening night of* Libri E Beaus *almost two months ago."* Soren couldn't keep his eyes from the television, knowing what photograph they would show. *"Where Miss Hale found this dress is as much a mystery as the man who accompanied her."*

There they were, the old Soren and Larken, looking so happy together. He couldn't tear his eyes away, as entranced by her beauty now as he had been then. He still dreamt about that night, sometimes bolting upright in a cold sweat, grabbing his side and hearing her shrieks of terror. Other times, he held her on that bench, kissing away her tears and telling her all the things he had been too scared to say when he was awake.

Loxly whistled and asked, "How surprised do ya reckon they'd be to find out that the four of us picked that dress out?"

"They'd probably laugh you out of the studio and claim that you were nothing more than a crazed fan," Hinlee answered.

"But *I am* a crazed fan," Loxly shot back.

"Don't we know it," Levi grumbled. He had been more himself lately, having something other than Larken's absence to focus on. He had been messaging back and forth with General Maxwell the most, hearing things as a field medic that the rest of them couldn't.

Brecker walked into the dorm, making his way over to the couch with Hinlee, and fell back on it. Resting his head in her lap, he groaned. "Those new guys are freaks."

Hinlee started brushing his hair out of his face, and he shut his eyes. Loxly chuckled and asked, "What do ya mean?"

"They wanted me to train a group of them, showing them what to expect out in the field. So, I led them through a workout."

"That doesn't sound so unusual," Levi said, crossing his arms.

"No." He opened his eyes and looked to the Second. "But when we were finished, they asked if we could run more laps."

"What's wrong with them?" Loxly asked. "Did you go easy on them or somethin'?"

"No," he answered, sitting up and grabbing a container of food from the coffee table. Stabbing a forkful of beef and broccoli, he stuffed it into his mouth. Brecker groaned and took another bite before saying, "I put them through the same one I have all the new recruits do to see where they should be placed."

"That is weird," Levi agreed, brow knitted.

"And there's something else," Brecker added, leaning back into the couch. Hinlee shifted, putting her feet up on his lap. "I heard one of them whispering about flowers."

"Well, that's not that weird. I brag about when you get me flowers," Hinlee said.

"You're not a guy." Brecker stuffed another forkful into his mouth.

"Maybe they were gettin' some for a girl they liked," Loxly offered.

"I don't think so. The whole thing was weird. They started out talking about the fires and then the flowers came up. Then they stopped talking about it when they realized that I could hear them."

"What kind of flowers?" Levi asked.

"Yellow ones, I don't remember what kind."

"Roses?"

Everyone looked to the field medic as Brecker stopped chewing. "I think that sounds familiar."

Soren raised his eyebrow at Levi in a silent question.

"I heard some of the trainees talking about yellow roses the other day. They were girls, so I didn't think it was that weird."

"But now?" Soren asked.

"Now, I think it might be more than just a coincidence."

"Well," Soren said as he stood, checking his communicator. "There's only one way to find out."

"What are you going to do, Decks?" Hinlee asked, voice tinged with worry.

"I'm going to ask Kelly about it."

"What would Kelly know about it?" the mechanic sneered, her distaste for the Captain evident in her tone.

"Kelly has had her new recruits for a few days now. If they've talked about it in the dorm, then she would know."

"I don't think you should be getting her involved."

"I'm not inviting her over for an in-depth conversation, Hinlee. I'm just going to ask her if she's heard anything."

"Just be careful," she warned. "You wouldn't want to say too much." Soren made for the door, and he heard her mutter, "*Or too little.*"

"*Hin!*" Brecker hissed.

Soren didn't stop or turn around. He deserved her harsh words. Hinlee wasn't stupid, and she knew that Larken would still be gone even if he had said something. They all knew it, but that didn't make him hate himself any less. He should have said something, anything, to let her know that he cared. He had promised her right before they crashed that he would never let her go, and he had. Soren had let her walk away from him, and now he was the only one who hadn't reached out to her since Loxly's video call. He couldn't face her, couldn't talk to her when he had told her that he meant every word he said, and then broke his promise only seconds later. She had been right to leave, and he had been right to let her try and forget him.

The heat of the afternoon had died down quite a bit, and a cool breeze hit Soren full in the face as he walked out to the courtyard. He could see Kelly stretching by the fountain and walked over to her. He had been running with her every night since his initial conversation with General Maxwell. Soren had no intention of filling Larken's spot, but he thought it would be beneficial to be on good terms with someone who was as chatty as Kelly. He had been right; most of the things he reported to the General had been things he had heard from her. Most of his peers were still upset with Squad 19, but Kelly had no problems talking to him or sharing base gossip.

When she saw him, she grinned and righted herself. Brushing invisible dust from her pants, a nervous habit that Soren noticed she had, she said, "You're late."

"Dinner went longer than planned."

"Oh." Kelly smiled at him and teased, "I thought you were going to stand me up."

The right thing to do would be to say he wouldn't dream of it, but Soren kept his mouth closed. He never said more than he needed to, and he hoped that his coldness would be enough for her not to take what he needed to ask the wrong way.

Kelly's smile faltered a little, and the two of them took off at a steady jog. It was still a good hour before sunset, but the new recruits forced Kelly to change her schedule a little. The two jogged in silence for a while, the place nearly empty as everyone was most likely still in the cafeteria. They jogged past the little flowerbeds, the cool air offering a steady comfort.

After they were far enough from the other people that were in the courtyard, Soren broke the silence. "Can I ask you something?"

"Of course!" she beamed.

"I was thinking about buying some flowers."

Her smile grew. "That's not a question."

"No, it's not," he agreed.

"So, are these flowers for a girl?"

"Might be."

"Do I know her?"

"I'm not sure if you've met, actually."

Her smile dimmed a little, and she said, "Oh."

Soren felt bad for hurting her, but he still asked, "Do you know what flowers are in season?"

"Some of the girls in my squad were talking about their boyfriends getting them roses. Yellow ones, I think. I thought it was really sweet that they would do that. Too bad Molly is allergic, and I had to put a ban on all flowers in the dorm."

Soren slowed to a stop, and Kelly did too. He looked her in the eye and asked, "So you think I should go with the yellow ones?"

"Honestly, Soren," her eyes dropped and she hugged her middle, "I think she would be happy just to know that you were thinking about her at all. I know I would be." Kelly looked back up at him with a sad smile. "Larken is a really lucky girl."

Soren's stomach fell as he was blindsided. "What do you mean?"

"I'm not stupid, Soren. I thought if there was ever a chance, it was now. But no matter what I do, I can't seem to get you to forget about her."

"I don't know what you're talking about."

"Don't you?" Her eyes crinkled at the corners, sadness twisting her features. "I've liked you from the moment I first saw you. And when I finally felt brave enough to tell you, she showed up." Kelly smiled despite her hurt. "I saw how you looked at her and how you smiled more whenever she was around."

"I still don't—"

Oh.

Kelly thought the flowers were for Larken. He suddenly felt like a jerk. "Kelly, I'm sorry. I didn't know, I shouldn't have—"

"No, don't blame yourself. I was the one who thought there was something more going on between us."

"Still, I—"

"Really, Soren, I'm fine. It's okay. I knew I didn't have a chance the moment she walked out of that hanger. I just thought that, with how upset you've been lately, you had moved on. I'm glad you're trying to work things out."

Work things out.

Soren wanted to laugh; it was too late to try and work things out. He had already burned that bridge with his own stupidity. There was no fixing what he had broken, no matter how much Loxly insisted that he could.

Sighing, he said, "Listen, Kelly—"

"It's fine. Anyway, I have to get back to my dorm. Let me know how it works out, though. Okay?" She looked up at him with that same broken hope that Larken had.

"Sure."

Kelly nodded once and then jogged back the way they had come. Soren waited a few minutes before he started walking back, unable to forget what Kelly had said. There was no way that Larken would forgive him. She had trusted him, let herself be open with him, and he abandoned her when she needed him the most. He knew now that she wouldn't have been able to stay. His conversations with General Maxwell made that very clear. She had only wanted to know that he wanted her to stay, and he did. But for some reason, the thought of admitting that out loud terrified him.

Soren walked back inside and made his way through the familiar halls to the dorm. The hallways were fairly empty; he hadn't realized how late it had gotten. Soren only passed a few people who wanted to squeeze in one last workout before lights out. Still, Kelly's words followed him.

I saw how you looked at her and how you smiled more whenever she was around.

Soren thought of the picture taken of the two of them the night of the opera, of the way he had smiled as he looked at her. He never smiled like that—he almost didn't even recognize the man in the photo with Larken. That man had been selfless, caring only about Larken's comfort, and doing whatever it took to make her happy. That smile didn't belong to someone like him, and he had stopped smiling the moment she had left. The last time he could remember feeling happy was that morning in the gym when he had teased her about that stupid song she went on and on about.

I knew I didn't have a chance the moment she walked out of that hanger.

He could remember how terrible Larken had looked that day, standing there, barefoot in that field and somehow managing to keep General Maxwell on his feet. Soren had known then that she was trouble, and that after that moment, his life wouldn't be the same. He had wanted to yell at her as soon as they were swarmed by the reporters and could still remember not knowing who to glare at—her or Braves.

I think she would be happy just to know that you were thinking about her at all.

Even if he did decide to reach out to her, what would he say? *Sorry that I broke the promise I made to you, just like everyone else in your life has?* No, he couldn't apologize for something like that if he wasn't going to do it in person. Then, he could at least give her the satisfaction of looking him in the eye as she told him exactly how much he had hurt her and that she couldn't forgive him this time.

Or, could Kelly be right? Was Larken just simply waiting for him to make that first move? He knew that she kept the necklace; maybe she really was just waiting for him. But he had messed things up too badly. He couldn't just call her and pretend like nothing happened. If things were still the same, he wouldn't call her anyway. He would just wait around for her to call him and complain about how late it was or ask why she needed to tell him about her shopping trips. Soren smiled, thinking of the things that could have been if he had just been brave and trusted her the way she trusted him.

Finally reaching the dorm, Soren pushed his way in and walked straight to his room. He would fill the rest of his squad in later, not wanting to interrupt the movie they were watching. Soren paused outside his door and looked at Larken's. He still hadn't gone in it, too afraid to see what was left behind. Shaking his head, he went into his room, pulling out his communicator as he shut the door.

General Maxwell answered on the second ring, asking, "Heard anything new, Deckard?"

Soren's lips twisted in a small smirk, finally feeling like he had something that could help Larken. "I've heard that yellow roses are in season."

"Have you now?"

CHAPTER 11

Larken suppressed a groan as Liam walked into the ballroom. She had hoped that her elder brother would skip her party and spend the night in some bar— somewhere away from her. Everything about him annoyed her. The way he walked like he owned the place, how he talked to everyone as if he were superior, and the way he made sure everyone knew he was the future Luminary of the Military District. He grinned and called to some rich Gadget Larken had seen him at the races with before.

She rolled her eyes and turned just in time to see Carl scowl at Delvon and murmur, "Alright, you listen here. You keep Liam *away* from Larken tonight. Is that understood?"

Larken couldn't help her grin at the sight of Carl trying to intimidate Delvon. He frowned, but nodded, causing her heart to swell. Delvon was a jerk, but he did care. He could deny it all he wanted, but she couldn't ignore the way he stood closer to her whenever Dominic was around or the way he glared at the reporters, chasing them away before they could get their pictures. She and Delvon weren't close like she had been with Loxly, but she knew that he would never let anything happen to her.

"There you are," Vallen said behind her. Larken grinned and

turned to him. He opened his arms, and she fell into his embrace. "Happy early birthday, runt."

Larken stood back. "Thanks." She looked him up and down, taking in his black suit before adding, "I forgot how good you look when you clean up."

"Don't get used to it," he growled.

Medic Ezra Lattic stepped in next, opening his arms as well. Larken hugged him, the scent of cinnamon and something spicy flooding her senses as he held her and murmured, "Happy birthday, Larken."

She pulled back, eyes catching on his coral-colored suit that complimented his skin, and said, "Thanks, Ezra."

She beamed, looking at her friends. They all looked great. Carl wore the same peppermint pink suit that he had worn when they first met. Larken thought that it looked great on him, and apparently, so did he. He always wore it when he wanted to look his best. Larken smiled when she realized that even though they started off on the wrong foot, he wanted to make a good impression on her.

Carl's hair had also been freshly trimmed and styled, and he wore a tie that matched Candy's floor-length lilac-colored gown. Her bodice was the same halter style as the green dress Larken had tried on only days ago, and her hair was done up in a fancy braid that hung over her left shoulder.

Even Delvon looked good, not that he didn't normally, but the slate grey suit Carl forced him into had been cut to his frame and fit him perfectly. Everyone who looked at him knew that he spent all of his free time in the gym, and Larken caught more than one woman having a hard time pulling their eyes away from him. And because Carl couldn't help but antagonize him every chance he got, Delvon wore a tie the same shade of blue as Larken's dress, claiming that every couple should match at parties.

Larken couldn't help but laugh as Delvon glared at her, clearly blaming her for his current discomfort. He looked like he would rather be anywhere but there, and she couldn't blame him. Larken knew she didn't belong among the white columns, the giant windows that were opened to allow an early autumn breeze to cool off the masses of people, or the expanse of bleached hardwood floors that had borne witness to too many of her embarrassing dance lessons.

Someone cleared their throat behind her, and Larken turned to find Wardell dressed in an adorable emerald suit and purple tie. He held a white box in his hands with a red bow on top. His nanny, Bailey, stood not too far away in a simple yellow dress, smiling down at him.

Grinning, Larken crouched down so she could look him in the eyes. He had the same dark brown eyes as their father, but everything else about him resembled their mother. "Hey, Wardell. What do you have there?"

His grin could chase away the clouds on a stormy day. He held out the box with his little hands. "I got you a gift, Sissy."

"That's very sweet. Thank you." Larken took the box and leaned in before asking conspiratorially, "What is it?"

He laughed, and then chastised, "You're not supposed to ask, silly."

"*Oh*," she said, feigning ignorance. Then she smiled and asked, "Should I open it then?"

He nodded eagerly, and Larken pulled the top off of the box. She found a glass dagger with a pewter handle inside, and her smile deepened into a grin. "It's beautiful. Thank you, Wardell."

He leaned in and whispered, "Bailey thought I should get you a bracelet, but I thought this would match your sword better."

"I love it," Larken said honestly. "This is much better than a bracelet could ever be."

"*I seriously doubt that,*" Carl muttered, which was followed by a grunt of pain.

Larken wondered if it had been Vallen or Candy that had gotten after him, but Wardell only laughed. "He's funny."

"He is," Larken agreed. "I like him much better than Cam."

"Me too. Cam was mean to you."

"Wardell," Bailey murmured, stepping closer to the boy. "Your sister has a lot of guests she needs to talk to. Would you like to go get some dinner while we wait for the dancing to start?"

He nodded, eyes glowing at the promise of food, and turned to leave. He looked back over his shoulder and asked, "Save me a dance, okay, Sissy?"

"I'll save you as many as you want," Larken promised.

He bounded off and Larken stood. Turning to Vallen, she found him smirking at her.

"What?"

"You'll see," was all he said as he took the box from her.

Soon people were swarming her, wishing her a happy birthday and expressing their joy at her safe return. Delvon and Vallen stayed close, and Carl kept his eye on Liam, letting the two men know when he got too close. Larken smiled and accepted everyone's well wishes with a nod. She recognized most of the people, having seen them at her parents' parties as she grew up. The ones she didn't know forced her to suffer through awkward introductions of how they knew her parents, watched her grow up, and were impressed with the beautiful woman she had become. But all conversation stopped when her mother walked in. Larken's hand found its way to the pearl, seeking Soren's protection even though he wasn't there. Instead of talking to her, though, Cornella decided to mingle. Larken blew out a breath of relief but stiffened again when Dominic walked in with her father. The two made their way toward her and Larken groaned.

"Need me to sneak you away for an evening tryst?" Delvon murmured in her ear, voice teasing.

She turned to look at him and felt a curl fall from her updo. "No, but thanks for the offer, sweetie."

"Just trying to help, love."

Larken's lips twitched, and Delvon grunted. He nodded, having done his job of cheering her up, and took a step back as the smell of scotch surrounded her. Larken turned to her father to find him beaming. He still looked as handsome as ever, dressed in a brick red suit that had his skin looking less sallow. His hair had been swept out of his face, and his beard had been freshly trimmed. He wasted no time wrapping Larken up in his arms.

"Larken," he murmured. "My sweet girl. Look at how big you are."

She tried not to let the words hurt her, but her voice sounded tight as she rasped, "Hi, Daddy."

He pulled back and cupped her cheeks with both hands. "You are *so* beautiful." Leaning in conspiratorially, he whispered, "I'm glad you don't look like your mother."

"Dad?"

He tapped her nose with his finger and said, "She doesn't deserve you."

Her eyes burned as she realized he knew that she knew. Larken swallowed thickly, and croaked, "Daddy, I—"

"Look at my pride and joy, Captain Braves," Trogar interrupted. "Isn't she the most beautiful thing you've ever seen?"

"Indeed she is, Luminary Hale." Dominic's eyes roamed over her body greedily, so different from the way Soren looked at her. His suit looked to be the same shade of navy blue that his uniform was, and it fit him well.

Her father waved away the title with his hand. "Call me Trogar, I insist."

Dominic grinned, chest puffing slightly with pride. He didn't know that Trogar asked everyone to refer to him without his title when he was drunk. "Of course, sir."

"Well, I'll leave you to it." He started making his way to the bar, but turned and called, "Save a dance for your old man, okay, Sunshine?"

Larken smiled and nodded, her heart breaking as he stumbled to the bar. She didn't have long to compose herself before Dominic pulled her into a hug. Blueberries chased away the smell of scotch, and Larken was grateful for it. "Happy birthday, Lark."

"Thanks, Dominic."

"You're going to have to wait a little bit for your gift though, okay?"

"Whenever's fine, but you didn't have to get me anything."

"Of course I did!" he said, pulling back with a grin. "What kind of a birthday would it be without gifts?"

Larken didn't say anything, not wanting to be honest and tell him that it would be like all of the others. She suppressed her shudder as he slipped his hand into hers, and then waved two people over. Larken knew the woman at once; Dominic was the spitting image of her. Ophelia Braves commanded the attention around her as if she were on a stage instead of at a birthday party. The navy dress she wore matched her son's suit, but the diamonds that clung to the fabric had the floor-length gown looking more elegant than anything Larken could ever dream of wearing. A gloved hand clutched a wrap around her, while the other held the elbow of a man Larken could only assume was Dominic's father.

As if in answer, Dominic stiffened at her side when the man's eyes landed on them, and he squeezed her hand a little tighter. Pulling her close, he whispered, "I know how you feel about parents, but they wanted to see you again."

"It's fine, Dominic," she assured, not sure why his parents would want to see her.

"Mom," Dominic said, letting go of Larken's hand and hugging the woman. "It's good to see you." She frowned and looked Dominic over when he released her. Then she turned her eyes on Larken as he said, "You remember Miss Hale, right?"

Ophelia's eyes narrowed as she took in Larken's dress. "The last time I saw you, Liam was chasing you with a handful of worms." Her frown deepened. "Then you punched him."

"Yes, well," Larken said, feeling Delvon step closer to her. "Liam has always had a way of bringing out the worst in me."

"Trust me, dear, you don't need Liam for that."

"Mom," Dominic warned.

"I'm just being honest, sweetheart. I'm sure Miss Hale is grown up enough to handle the truth."

Dominic leaned into his mother, hissing, *"You weren't invited here to insult her."*

Larken didn't catch Ophelia's response as Dominic's father took a step forward with a frown that could rival Vallen's. She took a nervous step back, landing on Delvon's foot. Not seeming to notice, Dominic's father looked her up and down, finally asking, "So you're the young lady that has my son finally acting like a grown man?"

"Um, yes?" she agreed, unsure, as Dominic barked, "Dad!"

Dominic's father stuck out a hand. "Colonel Marcus Braves."

Larken grinned and took it. "Cadet Larken Hale."

The man smiled, pleased with her introduction. Turning, he grabbed his wife's elbow and mumbled something as he led her away. Dominic stuffed his fingers into his hair and groaned, "Sorry about that. I didn't think—"

"It's fine," Larken said as she watched the couple track down her brother. Ophelia pulled Liam in for a hug, and Larken rolled her eyes. The woman obviously thought that Dominic was the bad influence, but Larken was willing to bet that half the things he was blamed for were Liam's idea.

Vallen cleared his throat behind her, and she peered back at him. He stared down at his communicator, grunting, "My gift just arrived."

"*Vallen?*" Larken asked skeptically, not liking the look on his face one bit. He met her eyes, and she narrowed hers. "What did you do?" He grinned as a guitar chord sounded through the ballroom. His grin turned devious, and she asked again, "*What did you do?*"

He stepped out of the way, and Larken looked behind him to the stage. The opening chords to *Sunset Dreams* surrounded her, and Larken watched in horror as Shadric Barlow leaned into the microphone and started to sing.

She forced herself to grin, and when she saw the way Vallen watched her, her smile turned genuine. "Are you surprised?"

"I have never been more surprised in my life." It was only half true; the only time she had been more surprised was when she had almost slit the singer's throat. "So, is this why you kept disappearing?"

"Mostly."

Dominic placed his hand on her waist, and she could feel the heat of it through her dress. He opened his mouth, about to ask her to dance, but Wardell's voice cut through his question.

"Sissy! You promised you would dance with me!"

Larken laughed as he blew past guests to get to her first. "I haven't forgotten."

She let him lead her out to the floor where other couples had already started dancing. Wardell led her around, the size difference making it a little awkward, but his smile made her discomfort worthwhile. Larken let herself have fun and laughed as she danced with her brother. This was what her last party should have been like. Instead, Liam had ruined it, and she refused to have another one. Her mother hadn't cared but insisted that they have one this year to celebrate her return as well. When the song ended, everyone clapped and Shadric hopped off the stage. He made his way over to Vallen, and the two men shook hands. His blond hair and light brown suit were a beacon in the sea of dark hair and rich fabrics.

Larken knew what was about to happen, but it didn't make her feel any better. She let Wardell lead her back to the group as the rest of the band started playing again. Larken reached them just as Vallen said, "—introduce Miss Hale."

Slowly, Shadric turned and looked at her. His eyes found her shoes, and she ignored the tingle that ran down her spine as they slowly made their way up. When their gazes finally locked, his bright blue eyes widened, and his mouth parted in disbelief. He looked just as handsome as that day in the woods, and Larken couldn't help but wonder what he thought of her.

Not knowing what else to say, Larken said, "It's a pleasure to meet you, Mr. Barlow."

His shock receded, and his eyes danced. He laughed a little, a musical sound that threatened her knees, and grinned. "I assure you, Miss Hale, the pleasure is all mine."

CHAPTER 12

Larken noticed the way Carl and Candy looked between her and Shadric and heard Candy mutter, *"Well, you're right. She does have blue-green eyes."*

Shadric either didn't hear the comment or chose to ignore it as he offered a hand and asked, "Care to dance, Miss Hale?"

"Sure," she breathed, hoping her voice came off as star-struck instead of terrified.

Shadric grabbed her hand and led her back out onto the floor. The flashes started the moment their hands touched, and Larken tried her best to ignore the cameras. Not that ignoring them was hard when the man she had imagined marrying up until recently pulled her into a dance. He smelled like a forest, rich and comforting, and Larken could get lost in just his scent alone.

Shadric smiled at her warmly as he said, *"Larken Hale.* Looks like I finally found you."

"Looks like," she agreed, voice shaky.

"First, I would like to apologize about the…" His eyes dropped to her shoulder and then met hers again.

Larken nodded, not able to speak.

"Second," he squeezed her hand a little. "I would like to say you look even more stunning than the last time I saw you."

She swallowed thickly, not sure what to say. Should she continue on as if nothing had ever happened between the two of them? Or should she ask him about it? Now would certainly be the right time to do it, with everyone around them inebriated and lost in their own little world. Then his words hit her.

"Oh, um, thank you," she said lamely.

He laughed, taking the tiniest step closer and causing her stomach to erupt into butterflies. "You're quite welcome."

"Do you perform at parties a lot?" She felt stupid as soon as the question was out of her mouth, but she didn't know what else to say. He had a way of making her mind go blank.

"Not normally, but I decided to make an exception when I heard who the party was for."

"Because you wanted to talk."

His eyes twinkled mischievously. "I would be lying if I said that the chance her pretty squad member might be here wasn't also a contributing factor."

"So what was the plan?"

"Talk to Larken, then look for you."

"And now that you know we're the same person?"

"I couldn't be happier about it." He looked sincere, so she decided to believe him. "I do feel like I need to apologize for not recognizing you that day, though. I might be in the media, but circumstances being what they are," he winked, "I don't pay much attention to it. The last time I saw you was when you were a kid."

Something inside her melted a little bit knowing that he wasn't keeping up with her family drama, endearing him to her all the more. Larken nodded, accepting his apology.

He smiled. "So, listen. About your initiation day—"

"I know it wasn't you. Or, your...*friends*."

"Right. I told you that part already."

"And I received confirmation from another source." Larken stared at his chest, unable to keep looking into his blue eyes. "What else did you want to tell me?"

"Not much you haven't already figured out, probably." His hand moved from her waist to her lower back as the music slowed into a new song, and he pulled her towards him as the new dance demanded. "I needed to warn you that there is a group parading around as Faithfuls that want you out of the way, and—" His cheeks turned a slight shade of pink. "I wanted to offer you a safe place to hide."

Larken felt her own face go hot.

"My offer still stands, by the way."

"Are you—" she needed to make sure she heard him right. Lowering her voice, she asked, "Are you asking me to run away with you?"

"It's not quite as romantic as you're making it sound, but, yes." Larken blushed hotly as Shadric continued to grin. "I actually like how you phrased it a lot better."

She choked. Larken wanted to look away, but his bright eyes sucked her in as he grinned at her. She felt lost, like the tiniest breeze would blow her away in a million little pieces, but as solid as stone at the same time. Shadric pulled her a little closer still, and Larken could now rest her cheek on his chest if she were brave enough.

Then, as if she wasn't frazzled enough, he asked, "By the way, I was wondering if you've heard my latest song?"

"Your latest song?" she asked, equal parts dreading and holding her breath at what he might say next.

His ears went an adorable shade of pink. "Yes. Have you heard it?"

So much like the sea, your blue-green eyes stop the heart in me.

There was no way, *no way* that this was happening. Her heart swelled both in mortification and joy. "I've heard it."

"What did you think?"

"Honestly?"

He nodded, eyes focused only on her. She took a second to bite her lip, buying herself more time before saying, "Honestly, I thought it was your best one yet."

"But?"

"*But*," she looked around, definitely not wanting to be heard, "I think it was incredibly stupid of you. It's not like we had many opportunities to meet while I was at base. What if someone figured it out?"

Shadric grinned, pleased with himself. "I thought you were worth the risk."

Larken sucked in a breath. She had finally heard the words she had been dying to hear her whole life, and it was *Shadric Barlow* that had said them. Larken was no longer convinced she was awake, and a part of her feared that Delvon would pound on her door any second, waking her up and demanding that she get her big butt out of bed.

"I know it was stupid, but I couldn't get you out of my head. You were everywhere, and I had hoped that, somewhere, you were listening to it and thinking of me too."

Larken thought she might faint, or swoon at the very least. She tried to get defensive, tried to tell herself that this was probably a line that he used on all the girls, but the way he looked at her pushed away all those doubts. He wasn't looking at her like a famous Star who only saw a conquest; she would know because that's how Dominic looked at her. He was looking at her like she was the only person in the room, like she was the only thing that mattered. He looked at her the way Soren did.

A lump rose in her chest, and Larken felt suddenly guilty. She was dancing with the most eligible bachelor in the country, and Soren was sitting locked in his room, angry that she had left him.

Something on her face must have reflected her thoughts because Shadric asked, "What's wrong?"

Before she could answer, someone tapped her shoulder. Larken looked to find Liam waiting expectantly. Shadric bowed out gracefully, handing her over to her brother who reeked of cognac. The singer made his way back to the stage, and Larken was left alone with her lifelong tormentor.

Shadric's tenor voice filled the ballroom, and Liam took Larken in his arms. He sneered at her and she demanded, "What do you want?"

"Mother thought it would be good publicity. Trust me, I'm just as unhappy about it as you are."

Larken only scowled. "Looks like you forgot your wine."

"Oh please. You would have found a way to make that about you, just like last time."

"You dumped wine all over *my* dress at *my* party. It was about me."

"Everything always is, dear sister."

"Are you stupid?" Liam looked like she had slapped him, eyes glossy and a little unfocused. Disgusted, Larken continued, "I can't tell if you're being difficult on purpose, or if you really are that stupid."

"I have no idea what you're—"

"All my life I have tried to stay out of the spotlight, hating the idea that everyone could look into my personal life whenever they wanted, and you always shoved me front and center. *I don't want Larken to have more media hits than me,*" she mocked, "*so let's pour wine on her dress at her birthday party so everyone can take pictures and talk about her.*"

Liam scowled at her, the expression so like their mother's. "You're the one who's sleeping with Dominic."

"I thought you didn't care," she scoffed. "That you—what was it you said? Dominic is the type of guy that would try to get with your sister *because* she's your sister?"

Liam's face went red, his anger making him grip her hand so hard that it hurt.

"I'm not sleeping with him. Not that it matters. The only thing that you're upset about is that someone might actually prefer me over you."

"You've always been Dad's favorite and you're not even his," he gritted out, the smell of the cognac reminding Larken of the reason for his sudden honesty.

Larken stopped moving, going as rigid as stone. There it was, the reason Liam had always hated her. He was jealous, was *still* jealous. The hatred in his eyes threatened to melt her, and all she could do was feel sorry for him. He had spent his whole life trying to prove that he was better than her. Not to hurt her, but to make their father see it too.

Tears burned her eyes as he let go of her and stormed away. She had always held out hope that whatever it was that had come between them could be resolved and they could someday be a real family. But she now understood that that was never going to happen. Her shoulder throbbed, reminding her of why that hope was stupid…of what happened the last time she had clung to it.

Feeling a set of eyes on her, Larken turned slightly to find her mother watching her. A cruel smile twisted her red lips, and the black dress she wore reminded Larken of the dream she had. The one where her own mother had pushed her to her death.

Cornella Hale stood taller and raised a hand, drawing every-one's attention. She looked like she had just taken a bite out of something sweet and couldn't wait for the second one. Everything around Larken quieted, and Dominic was suddenly at her side. He grinned at her, and Larken looked between him, her mother, and a very confused-looking Vallen. If he had been kept out of the loop, then whatever the Military District Lumina was about to say wouldn't be good.

"Thank you all for coming to help celebrate my daughter's twenty-first birthday." There was a spattering of pleasant applause, and Cornella waited for it to die down before continuing, her hands now clasped together in front of her. "As all of you know, it is my wish that Larken finds happiness in this life."

Larken narrowed her eyes at her mother, wondering how many people believed her lie.

"I believe that she may, at last, have found that happiness after the rough year she has had. Larken volunteered to fight alongside our brothers and sisters, sons and daughters, only coming home when she was honorably discharged after a horrific accident."

Larken heard several people sniffling around her. She wanted to roll her eyes, tell them that their fake tears helped no one, but she didn't.

"Even after all of her hardships, she still takes up the fight every day, continuing to support her fellow soldiers from home, encouraging them to do their best, and reminding them what it is we are fighting for." Cornella's smile turned devious. "And all the while, she has been chasing after happiness in the most *unexpected* of places."

Dominic grabbed her hand, but she barely noticed. Larken hadn't the faintest idea what her mother was talking about, and she suddenly felt very uneasy.

"So, it is with great pleasure that I give my blessing and announce the engagement of my daughter, Larken Hale, and Captain Dominic Braves."

Larken was back in her world of sunset glass, falling after her mother had pushed her. She couldn't feel the wind blowing past her, didn't fear the crash, and couldn't ignore the look of triumph on her mother's face. Cornella had won, had gotten what she always wanted. Larken would be sent away and be miserable for the rest of her life. Larken didn't feel the impact of the crash; she only knew that the man who had promised to never let her go wasn't there to kiss away her pain this time.

CHAPTER 13

Larken stiffened next to him, and Dominic hoped that it was only because everyone turned to look at the two of them. He couldn't help the smug smile that twisted his lips. He had done it— *Larken was his.* Cornella had put up quite the fight, trying to get every ounce of usefulness out of him that she could, but he made her see reason in the end.

If Dominic was honest, this wasn't how he wanted this to happen. Larken hated being made a spectacle of, but that was what had appealed to her mother the most. She approved the union and announced it in a way that no one could misunderstand what was happening. Larken Hale would marry him, and the two of them would leave the Military District forever. Dominic knew that he would have to apologize for how it was sprung on her, but he would have the rest of their lives to make it up to Larken. She didn't know that he was the one that she needed, the one who could give her everything she could ever want, but he would prove himself.

People started cheering, and Dominic dropped her hand. Grabbing her waist instead, he pulled her close to him. She felt stiffer than a board, so he started rubbing his thumb over the fabric of her dress, trying to comfort her. She wouldn't make a scene—that wasn't how she was brought up—nor would she want the extra attention on her. Larken would gracefully accept the well wishes, and then turn on him the moment they were alone. Dominic had until then to prove to her that this had been the only way. He would explain how her mother couldn't pass up the chance to try and humiliate her, and he would tell her of his plan to take her away from the family that never wanted her.

She took a small step back, trying to get away, and no doubt hide behind that new bodyguard of hers. He would be the first to go, General Maxwell the second. Larken wouldn't need either of them with him there. Dominic was fully capable of keeping her safe; she just needed to give him a chance to show her. She took another step, and he turned to her. Larken looked ready to bolt, so he pulled her close, taking her in his arms.

"I'm sorry," he whispered in her ear. "I know this wasn't how you wanted to find out, but your mother insisted."

Larken's breath hitched; she was starting to panic.

"Just ignore them and focus on me." He pulled back just enough to look into the teal eyes that had haunted him since that day she showed up to base beaten and battered.

Dominic hadn't lied when he told her that the way he thought about her had changed. The night of her eighteenth birthday party had him thinking thoughts of his best friend's sister that he shouldn't have been, but he couldn't stop. And the only thing that kept him from acting on those thoughts was that they never ran in the same circles. She was the beautiful impossibility that would always be out of reach. Then, by some miracle, she had ended up at the same base as him. But she quickly went from what he thought would be an easy lay to a soul-crushing obsession.

"Dominic?" she rasped, pulling him back to himself.

"I'm here."

"Wha—why didn't you ask me?" Hurt clouded her eyes, and he hated her mother for causing her this pain.

"Don't you see?" he asked. "It had to be this way."

"But I don't understand. You never seemed interested in marriage before."

"I keep telling you that I've changed, Lark. I'm done spending time at the races, partying, all of it." Her brow crinkled, and he wanted to reach up and smooth it away. "There's only one thing that I want now, and it's you."

Larken looked pale, and she wobbled slightly on her feet. The music had started back up again, and couples surrounded them, dancing and going back to what they were doing before the announcement.

"Would you like to get some air?"

She nodded, biting her bottom lip in a way that almost had him groaning. Larken pulled free from his grasp and blew past everyone. Guests stared after her as she made her way to the gardens. Dominic looked to find General Maxwell and Tanner making their way towards the door Larken had just disappeared through. Shadric Barlow hopped off the stage and followed them. Dominic frowned, not liking the way the singer had been looking at Larken while they danced.

Liam started laughing nearby, telling anyone who would listen that Dominic would make a terrible husband and that Larken would only keep him entertained for so long. Ignoring his childhood friend, Dominic slowly made his way over to where Larken had vanished. He nodded to people on the way, accepting their congratulations, and eventually strolled to the open door.

The early autumn breeze felt good—his suit was suffocating—and he silently made his way to the maze of giant rose bushes. Dominic entered, having spent more than one night exploring the maze as he chased old conquests, and started making his way to the middle. A distant howl sounded, the muffled note signaling the other beasts that Dominic usually tried to avoid. He stopped when he heard shuffling, listening intently.

"This is bad," he heard someone murmur. Dominic guessed it was Barlow since he knew the other voices. "What are we going to do?"

"Just keep to the plan," Tanner grunted.

Dominic smirked smugly; he knew there was something he

didn't like about the guy. Now he knew that Tanner was a treasonous traitor, as well as someone who tried to get between him and Larken.

"You two need to shut up. Anyone could be listening," General Maxwell warned.

"Right, sorry. I just...I can't believe it was her this *whole time*," Barlow muttered.

What? He can't be talking about Larken...can he?

"Well, if you had bothered to turn on a television, you would have figured it out a lot sooner. Not the sharpest blade in the set, are you?" Tanner asked, his tone mocking.

"I'm serious, Del. Do you know how much time I've wasted?"

"Well, I hate to break it to you, mate, but I'm not your only competition."

"You're not seriously interested in her, are you?" Barlow's voice sounded worried like the singer didn't think he could compete with the bodyguard.

"Do you two think it's wise to be discussing this in front of me?" General Maxwell asked.

"You can't get me worse than last time," Tanner mused, not sounding at all worried.

"Speak for yourself. I like my face the way it is," the singer said.

They were nearing the middle, and Dominic took the right turn in the fork instead of the left one the others had used. Creeping around the bushes, Dominic made his way to where he knew the branches were thinner. Peering through the yellow blooms and dark leaves, he saw Larken sitting on the edge of the fountain that her grandfather had commissioned for her grandmother. The thing hadn't been active in years, the stone nothing more than a statue of a woman standing over a drain. Larken was the picture of perfection, hugging her middle and staring up at the stars. There were no tear streaks staining her cheeks, and Dominic knew that she wouldn't cry. She wasn't the same girl he had stumbled upon in the bathroom all those years ago; she was strong.

Dominic watched, surprised when he saw Tanner walking up to

the fountain instead of General Maxwell. Tanner dropped down next to her and gazed up at the sky as well. Dominic's eyes narrowed in on the hand that covered Larken's.

With her other hand, Larken pointed to the sky and rasped, "That one is my favorite."

"Draca the dragon, huh?" Larken dropped her hand and put her head on Tanner's shoulder. He wrapped his arm around her, making Dominic see red. "I had you pegged as a Cabal girl."

Larken smiled, not taking her eyes off the sky. "I like the dog too."

Tanner reached up and pointed. "Do you know what that one is?"

"Kyrenia the mermaid."

"So you were a normal little girl after all."

"And you were an unusual little boy. How do you know what it is?"

"My mother liked it."

"What happened to her?" Larken asked.

"She died in the war."

"I'm sorry."

Tanner grunted before saying, "It was a long time ago, but whenever I look at the sky, I think of her."

"Well, I happen to know that only truly great people stop to look at the stars."

"Thanks, Peach."

"So," Larken mused. "How long do you think Vallen is going to hide in the roses?"

"He wanted to give us plenty of alone time, if you catch my drift."

Larken snorted. "Oh, I'm sure that's the case."

Tanner retracted his arm, and Larken straightened. He placed his finger under her chin and forced her to look at him. "You're tough. You'll be okay."

"Thanks for the reminder."

"Come on. Let's head back in. You still have a party to finish."

"Unfortunately."

"That's the spirit, love." Tanner helped her up, and Dominic made his way back to the ballroom, trying to relax his balled-up fists.

He would need to find a way to access all of the Manor security footage; he needed to know how deep Tanner and Larken's relationship went. It could simply be that her new employee had tried to cheer her up, or as Dominic suspected, it was something more. All he knew was that he had some decisions he needed to make. Should he tell Cornella what he had overheard? Or should he keep it to himself? He didn't relish the idea of getting caught with secrets, but he also didn't want Cornella to be able to use what he had learned against him. Not to mention, if he was the one who suggested that General Maxwell could be capable of treason, Larken would never speak to him again. No, he would keep what he learned to himself, and he would wait for the right time to act.

It wasn't long after he walked into the ballroom that Barlow snuck in and jumped back up onto the stage. Dominic would need to keep a close eye on him as well, and he thought he knew how. General Maxwell, Tanner, and Larken all walked in together, and Larken rose to her tiptoes so she could look over the crowd. She met his gaze and dropped back to her heels before making her way to him, her eyes determined. It would seem that he had failed to convince her, but that didn't matter. The Luminary had approved the match; she was bound to him and would only be free if both parties agreed. And Dominic had no intentions of ever letting her go.

Reaching him, Dominic saw a few more curls had fallen from their pins. Larken's hair no longer held that overpowering scent of grapefruit, and he was glad. The cheap shampoo wasn't her, and he would see that she had the finest things arii could buy. Larken looked up at him, brow furrowed, and said, "Dominic Braves, I accept your proposal."

Taken aback, Dominic grinned. He didn't care what had happened to make her change her mind, but he would forever be grateful. She would learn to love him, and he would do whatever it took to make her happy.

"I'm glad." He took her hand and led her to the stage. "I have another gift for you as well."

"Dominic, I don't need—"

"I know, but that's not the point. The point is that I *want* to do this for you. I want to make you happy, Lark."

She nodded, looking unsure, but continued to follow him. They reached the stage, and the three traitors looked at the two of them. Tanner sneered and General Maxwell eyed him suspiciously. Barlow only looked confused and asked, "Does Miss Hale have a request?"

"No, I do." Tanner snorted, and Dominic felt his ears warm. "What I mean is, I have a favor to ask of you."

"Sure," Barlow said, looking between him and Larken.

"You're my fiancée's favorite singer, and I would love to have you perform at the wedding."

Larken stiffened, and Dominic fought to hide his smirk as something cracked in the singer's eyes. Suppressing a frown, Barlow nodded. "It would be my pleasure."

"Perfect," Dominic said cheerily. "Then there's only one thing left."

Turning to Larken, he reached into his jacket pocket. Dominic pulled out the little silver box and opened it. Gently, he took out the ring he had spent hours picking out and grabbed Larken's left hand. He didn't miss the way her breath hitched as he slid it on. Holding her hand up, she looked wide-eyed at the ring.

When she didn't say anything, he asked, "Do you like it?"

Closing her parted lips, she let her hand fall to her side. She looked at him for a moment before saying, "It's pretty."

CHAPTER 14

Levi had offered to make breakfast, and no one had turned him down. They all smiled and chatted as they set the table while the field medic fried up some bacon. The whole dorm smelled of meat, and Soren couldn't remember the last time he had been this excited to eat a home-cooked meal. That was a lie of course, but he didn't want to think about the last thing Larken had made. Breakfast went smoothly, and Soren did a good job not thinking of her while he ate until Hinlee passed a bowl of strawberries to him. Levi hadn't said anything as he took the fruit and moved it down to the opposite end of the table, and Soren was grateful. Memories of Larken dishing strawberries onto his plate, and of him almost choking to death, flooded his mind. After that, Soren found he didn't have much of an appetite.

They had all agreed to spend the day lazing around the dorm. Since it was Saturday, they had nowhere they had to be, and Jing was due any moment. They had all just settled themselves on the couches when Jodi threw open the dorm door and marched in. With hair dyed in shades of black, grey, and blue, she looked like a living thunderstorm. Dark makeup made her look malevolent, and the onyx stud in her nose glinted whenever it caught the light.

"*Where is he?*" she seethed, not at all sounding like her usual bored self.

Hinlee snuggled into Brecker, relaxing as she muttered, "Looks like Decks is upsetting all the women in his life."

Soren glared and seriously considered saying something, but kept his mouth shut when he realized everything he wanted to shout at the mechanic sounded whiney and stupid. Instead, he watched as Jodi stomped up to him, frowning all the while. He gave her a second to try and melt him with her fiery gaze, before he demanded, "What?"

"Don't play dumb with me, Deckard. What are you going to do?"

Getting defensive, he asked, "What are you talking about?"

Jodi glared at him, and he glared back. After a moment, her eyes softened a little, and she looked at the rest of his squad. Her shoulders fell and she said, "You don't know."

"Don't know what?" Soren fought to keep his frustration in check but didn't like the look on the medic's face.

Scanning the room, her eyes fell on the remote that rested on the coffee table. Snatching it up, she took Larken's usual seat next to Loxly and turned the television on.

Two news reporters were laughing, the man smirking as his coworker giggled. The woman wore a tight-fitting orange dress that had her blonde locks looking like honey. She dropped her hand from her mouth, still grinning, and said, "*Honestly, Greg, you're too much.*"

"*Tell me where the lie is though. She took everyone by surprise. I didn't even know she was interested.*"

"*I'm sensing a little bitterness. Are you upset that you didn't get a chance?*"

"*Jan, every red-blooded male in the* country *is upset that they didn't get a chance.*"

Rolling her eyes, Jan looked all business as she explained, "*For those of you just tuning in for the day, we are happy to announce the engagement of Captain Dominic Braves and Miss Larken Hale.*"

Soren's stomach lurched so badly that he thought he might be ill. Hinlee gasped and covered her mouth with both of her hands. Levi looked like he wanted to break something, and Loxly and Brecker shook their heads in disbelief.

Footage of Larken standing in the middle of a ballroom, looking terrified, filled the screen. Braves grinned like he had finally won. Jan continued, *"The announcement was made last night at Miss Hale's twenty-first birthday celebration."* Braves pulled Larken in for a hug, and Soren could see how stiff she was. *"The happy couple are set to be married sometime next month and expect to make their first debut as a couple at the Night of Masks Celebration."*

"A month-long honeymoon seems a bit excessive to me," Greg complained as the screen switched back to him. *"It's like he's rubbing our faces in it."*

"Well, it would seem that you aren't the only one who thinks so," Jan said. *"I, for one, was shocked to learn that Shadric Barlow's latest hit,* Wanting You, *was really a confession to the Military Sweetheart."* The screen cut to a picture of the two dancing. Shadric held Larken close, grinning at her and making her blush. Soren needed to stop watching, but he couldn't. *"With no other clue as to who the mystery woman had been, there's no denying that the Daughter of the Military does indeed have* blue-green eyes."

"Son of a gun..." Loxly murmured.

"Did you ever hear if that guy showed up to the party?" Greg asked.

The picture of Soren and Larken filled the screen. She looked so happy and carefree, nothing at all like the woman who had been forced into her engagement. *"The mystery man did not show up, and we can only assume that the two had a falling out."* Jan leaned into Greg conspiratorially. *"Not that I blame her; that new bodyguard of hers is much more my taste. If that Delvon Tanner is in need of a new job once the couple is married, I would be more than happy to hire him."*

A picture of Larken dressed in olive-colored shorts and a faded denim top replaced the one of the two of them. Soren's eyes should have been drawn to her, but instead, they fell on a giant in a grey long sleeve shirt. Dark hair hung in his face, but it couldn't hide his grey eyes. Soren jolted, causing Levi to look at him. Balling his fists so tightly that his knuckles popped, Soren scowled.

He didn't look at Jodi as she lowered the volume of the television and asked, "Now that you know, what are you going to do?"

"Why do we have to do anything? She made her choice," Soren growled, trying to keep his voice level. He knew the words weren't true, that Larken would never pick Braves in a million years, but he still said them.

"She didn't make a choice at all, you moron!" His eyes snapped to her as Jodi continued, "She was *forcibly* removed and then *forced* into an engagement. Larken has been unhappy this whole time!"

"And how could you possibly know that?" Levi asked, narrowing his eyes.

"I have a new pen-pal."

"Have you been talkin' to General Maxwell too?" Loxly looked mildly surprised.

"Medic Lattic," Jodi admitted, her cheeks flushing so slightly that it was almost unnoticeable. Then, she glared at Soren again. *"What are you going to do?"*

Soren frowned at her for a moment, then looked back at the television. Jan was still fawning over the man that had held Larken at gunpoint. Ignoring Jodi, he stood and went to his room, communicator already out and requesting a video call with General Maxwell.

His door shut softly behind him, muffling the sounds of Jodi's snarls, and Soren wished he could have slammed the thing. His fists were shaking, and he prayed that General Maxwell had a good explanation, because Soren thought he might just fly to the Manor and kill him.

General Maxwell accepted the call, and his equally fierce frown filled Soren's screen. "This had better be important, Deckard. I don't have time to—"

"Are you aware that the man who has been employed as Larken's bodyguard is the same one that held her a gunpoint the night of the opera?" Soren interrupted.

General Maxwell's frown lost some of its malice, and the man sighed, looking tired. Then he asked, "Which answer would be easier for you to hear?"

Soren let out a slow breath, trying to gain control over his emotions.

"I knew this conversation was coming. I just thought I would have more time when you didn't notice him right away."

Soren sat on his bed, not wanting to admit that he had been avoiding anything that had to do with Larken. He didn't want to think about what it meant. And he didn't want to think about what it meant that General Maxwell noticed how complicated his feelings for Larken had gotten.

"I guess I'll start at the beginning. It was, let's see," he paused a moment, "seventeen years ago that I and the rest of Squad 12 were shipped out on a secret mission."

The one where his whole squad died…

General Maxwell's face went dark, and even through the video, Soren could see the hurt in his eyes. "We were sent into enemy territory, and then were immediately captured."

Soren's stomach soured, but he said nothing, only listened.

"Two months we sat in a jail cell. They fed us, let us out once a day for exercise and showers, and a preacher visited us each Sunday. Not only that," General Maxwell's voice went soft as he continued, "but each day, they requested a meeting with the Squad Captain."

"What did they want?" Soren asked, finally speaking.

"They wanted me to have a face-to-face conversation with their leader."

"And after those two months, you accepted?"

"I did." General Maxwell leaned back, and Soren could now see that he was sitting at a desk. "And I will never forget what they told me."

Soren waited, knowing that he wouldn't like what the older man was about to say.

"They started by asking me why I fought in the war. Being young and stupid, I told them that it brought honor to the country that raised me. Then they asked who I thought the war benefited."

"I'm guessing you gave the wrong answer?"

General Maxwell gave a hard smile. "I did. I told them that it would benefit every family that the Faithfuls were trying to attack." He smirked, eyes distant and remembering. "I had grown up in this District. I lived and breathed the military. I joined not knowing that Trogar and Cornella would agree to go to war over the idea of a group of Maxim following fanatics. After I gave my answer, the leader told me that the only ones who benefited in a time of war were the warriors."

"What does that mean?" Soren asked.

"It means that the only one who has control over this war is Cornella." Soren almost dropped his communicator as General Maxwell continued, "When the war started, Larken was already four years old. Trogar knew that his wife had been unfaithful and had started to drink. He loved Larken more than anything, and the pain of that drove him mad. Trogar couldn't understand how such a special, kindhearted girl had come from his wife's betrayal."

Soren's throat felt tight. So, her father knew. Soren wondered if Larken had figured out that he knew; if she blamed herself for his drinking.

"Cornella could see her life slipping away. She had married well above her station, and her fool of a husband threatened to tarnish the Hale name. There was even talk of the Magnate appointing a new Luminary, and Cornella refused to let that happen."

"So she used the Faithfuls as an excuse to go to war, ensuring she would keep her title," Soren said, stunned.

General Maxwell nodded.

A hole opened up under Soren and threatened to suck him in. All of this, the people he and his squad had killed, the people he watched die over the years, the families that sacrificed their own children for arii, it was all because of one woman. And she was the same one that had raised Larken.

Why does she hate me so much?

Soren's throat felt tight as he remembered Larken's words. She had sobbed against him, asking why the one person she had always wanted to prove herself to couldn't love her. Soren didn't have the answer then, and now that he did, he knew that Cornella Hale would never love her daughter. Larken represented everything she had almost lost. Fisher had wanted nothing to do with Cornella, and Trogar had clearly felt the same way. Then came baby Larken. With her wheat-colored hair and teal eyes, she was Cornella's greatest failure. Soren almost ended the call right there and ran to the hangar. There was no more doubt in his mind; he needed to see Larken. He needed to tell her all of the things he had been afraid to and tell her how much she meant to him. She needed to hear it from someone, and he hoped that he wasn't too late.

"What happened after you talked with the leader?" Soren asked.

"I was given two options. Either we would be allowed to stay on the edge of Camp and live out the rest of our lives in exile, or we could take up the cause."

"Are your squad members really dead?"

"No, but it felt like they were. When I was raising Larken, I couldn't go back and forth. She needed me, and I needed her too."

I blame myself.

Soren felt his eyes go wide. "It was you. You were the one that leaked the information about us training on Field E."

"I was, and I would never have forgiven myself if something had happened to any of you. We sent the men that we thought were most likely to recognize her, but they didn't and I put all of you at risk. I am deeply sorry for that."

"Did you really have the flu the night of the opera?" Soren asked. Four days in quarantine would have been the perfect cover for visiting the Faithful Camp.

General Maxwell smirked. "I knew I liked you. No, I wasn't sick. I was meeting up with some of my brothers. I had eyes on the inside, but I didn't know of the attack until you went down. I had no signal where we met, and Larken called as soon as I was back above ground."

"I'm assuming that it was your *eyes* that manhandled her and pointed the gun at her head?"

"He has been dealt with, I assure you."

Soren highly doubted that since the man was still alive, but there was nothing he could do about it now. "So, he's a member of the other group that attacked us?"

"Yes."

"And I'm assuming that they have something to do with the yellow roses?"

"The Vigilants. They're a group that Cornella's been gathering over the past few years. It is our belief that she's slowly been putting her soldiers into the bases and is planning something big."

"Are they the ones starting the fires?"

"That's what we've been assuming."

Soren's mind spun. "And she doesn't suspect that this guy is working with you?"

"It isn't her problem anymore. Delvon used to be the one who led the Vigilants, but I suggested that he be the one to look over Larken."

"So who leads them now?"

"You've already figured that one out, Deckard."

"Braves," Soren muttered, seeing red.

General Maxwell sighed. "I guess that it's my turn to give the ultimatum now. You have three options."

"Which are?"

"Option one, you and your squad can desert. I won't come looking for you, and no one will be able to track you. I will completely wipe you from the system, and it will be like Squad 19 never existed. Option two, you can forget we had this conversation, continue fighting, pick a new squad member, and move on with your lives."

Not liking either of those, Soren asked, "And the third one?"

"I will disband Squad 19, remove all record of you, and the five of you can come work for me as Larken's personal security team."

He didn't say it, but he didn't have to. Go protect Larken as traitors and become Faithfuls as well. Now that Soren knew everything, he felt dirty in his uniform. He wanted to rip it off and burn it, ashamed of all the damage he had caused in it. Soren believed that he had been doing good, that he was following the will of Maxim, and it had all been a lie. But maybe that wasn't completely true. Maybe he had been brought here—they had all been brought here—to meet Larken and help her. Perhaps they were all there to make a difference in this time of darkness.

Soren gave General Maxwell a look, his tongue feeling stuck in his throat again. He knew what he needed to do, what the others would want to do. General Maxwell's lips twitched, and then he said, "I'll be in touch."

The video call ended, and Soren felt lighter despite all the information that now held him down. Things were indeed a lot more desperate than he had originally thought, but they wouldn't be that way for long. Not if he had anything to do with it. Soren took a moment to say a quick prayer for the safety of his squad and Larken, then pushed off his bed. He left his room and a scowl turned his face the moment he heard the music.

Loxly complained loudly, talking over the song and saying that he still didn't believe that it was about Larken. Everyone gave him a hard time, claiming that it had only been a matter of time before the singer caught sight of the Military Heiress and fell head over heels. Jing's giggles told Soren that she had arrived, and he typed out a quick message to General Maxwell, asking that he saw to the safety of Jodi and the Chin family.

Soren reclaimed his seat next to Levi, Jodi watching him like a hawk. Hinlee insulted Loxly, and he asked, "Cap, what do you think?"

"About what?"

"Do you think the song is about Larken?"

"I think the song is annoying and that you should turn it off."

"Is he always like this, or is today just getting to him?" Jodi asked, her lips curling in annoyance.

Jing, who had been braiding a section of the medic's hair, paused and said, "I think he's just sad because Larken is getting married."

"We're all sad, darlin'," Loxly admitted, not looking at Soren.

"Yeah…" the little girl said, looking up at the sharpshooter. "…but Soren loves her."

No one said anything as Soren's heart stopped beating. Jing's face scrunched up like she thought she might have said something wrong.

Jodi, not caring about the heaviness that covered the common room, asked, "What makes you say that?" Her tone implied that Jing was brilliant for noticing something Soren hadn't.

Jing looked back to the medic and answered softly, "When Larken lived here, he looked at her the way Papa looks at pictures of my momma."

Soren swallowed thickly, wondering if what the small girl said was true. He remembered the photo of him and Larken, how he couldn't recognize himself in it. Not able to help himself, he looked over at Hinlee, who was already staring at him. Her eyes were still hard like they had been since Larken left, but there was something else in them as well. His heart squeezed, and he realized why Hinlee had been so upset with him lately. It wasn't because she blamed him for Larken's leaving; it was because she thought he had given up his only chance at happiness. He had, but now Soren was determined to make it right.

CHAPTER 15

Larken woke up to find the midmorning sun bathing her in light. Her room had a soft glow to it, and she felt like she was still in a hazy dream. Reaching up, she rubbed her face. Something sparkly caught her eye, and Larken held up her hand. Spreading her fingers, she took in the giant oval diamond that was almost as thick as her finger. The stone reached from knuckle to knuckle, and Larken frowned at it, letting her hand fall to the bed. She wanted to tell Dominic that she wouldn't marry him, but Vallen insisted that she proceed with the engagement, promising that everything would work out. She trusted him like she always had but still wanted to pull the ring from her finger and chuck it at Dominic.

Never before had she felt so lost. What was happening to her? Why did she feel so broken? Larken didn't know what to do. Every time she tried to pray lately, she only ended up feeling more alone than before. Was Maxim listening to her? Could He hear her, or was her voice muffled as she slowly drowned in the mess her life had become? Things had been so much easier at base. Larken felt alive, *free;* here she only felt weighed down by chains she feared she wouldn't be able to break when the time came.

She stared at the ceiling as her door opened. Estelle hopped off the bed and left to, undoubtedly, go find Vallen. Larken could tell without looking at the door that it was Delvon. He walked in quietly and then climbed onto the bed next to her. Rolling to face him, Larken found him smirking.

"Need a kiss to wake you up, Princess?"

"You always know just what I need," she murmured as she snuggled close to him and let him wrap her up in his arms.

He moved slightly, then breathed, "All clear."

Larken sighed, not moving. She wrapped her arm around her middle and grabbed the pearl. Feeling heavy, she let her eyes close again. Delvon rubbed a warm hand up and down her back, and she imagined that they looked like a sad couple being torn apart.

"General Maxwell wants to know what you want for tonight."

Larken snorted. "You needed privacy for that?"

"Unless you want to risk your new fiancé coming."

"No, I'm good." Larken thought a moment and sighed again. "I don't care, what do you want?"

"Come on, don't be like that."

Larken met his grey eyes. "What, you want me to tell you that I want Mr. Chin's food? You planning on going all the way to base to get it for me?"

"No, I'm not that nice. General Maxwell or Carl, maybe, but not me."

She shook her head, lips twitching. "No, eating that would only make me feel worse. I don't care what we have."

"Fish it is, then."

"Sounds great."

"It is. I make the best fried fish you'll ever eat."

"I look forward to it."

Delvon looked at the camera again before asking, "How are you now that you've had time to think about it?"

"Well, I can honestly say that I would much rather marry you."

"That would be quite the scandal. When do you want to announce that we eloped?"

"Last night at the party." Larken frowned. "Can you believe he asked Shadric Barlow to perform? He's *horrible*."

"I thought you liked him? Something about *dreamy eyes* or whatever."

She rolled her eyes. "I meant Dominic."

"Ah, that makes more sense." Delvon's lips twitched.

"He's just like Liam. Always thinking he deserves whatever he wants solely because he wants it, and then when he gets it, he rubs it in everyone's face."

"You wanna tell me what you're really upset about?"

Larken gripped the pearl tighter. Pressing her forehead against Delvon's warm chest, she murmured, *"I don't want him to hate me."*

Larken didn't explain who the *him* was, and Delvon didn't ask her to. A hot tear seeped from her eye before she could stop it. Delvon held her tighter, and she let out a long breath. She couldn't imagine what Soren must think of her. Larken had once told him that she understood Dominic and what it felt like to be confused. It hadn't been her feelings for the Star that had confused her though. And laying there, being held by Delvon, she couldn't help but remember that night in the medic-building when another grumbly man held her.

Soren had held her for hours, letting her cry her fill. Delvon was offering her the same thing, but it felt worlds different. The gruff bodyguard offered friendship, whereas she thought Soren might offer her something more. It wasn't fair that she'd had to leave, and now she would never know if Soren had wanted anything other than friendship.

Looking up, she met Delvon's eyes. She knew that she looked more vulnerable than he had ever seen her, but she didn't care. "Promise me that if Vallen can't fix this, you will. I don't care how you do it—kidnap me for all I care—just *promise me.*"

"I'll marry you myself before I let Braves touch you," Delvon assured.

Larken smiled, relieved, and couldn't help but tease him. "Even though I'm not your type?"

"You're growing on me."

Delvon loosened his grip around her, his signal that the audio of her camera had turned back on. Larken stretched, feeling cold now that she wasn't sharing his heat. Her communicator started buzzing on her nightstand, and Delvon reached back and handed it to her. Looking, she didn't see the message from Loxly she had expected. Instead, it was from that same unknown number that had messaged her when she first got back.

Happy birthday, my little songbird. I have something for you. Please meet me at the abandoned theater at the edge of the District. General Maxwell knows where.

A second message told her the day and time, and Delvon leaned in close after she went still. "Who's that?"

"An acquaintance," she answered.

Either he figured out that it was Fisher Fillmar by reading the message or he didn't care. Delvon didn't push the matter, nor did he stop her when she got out of bed and made her way to her bathroom. She quickly showered and found Delvon still sprawled out on her bed when she came out.

Crossing her arms, Larken asked, "Did you only come and check on me so you could slack off?"

"I think you already know the answer to that," he said, propping his head up with his hand. His eyes danced as he asked, "Need a hand getting dressed?"

Larken blew him a kiss before locking herself in her closet. She could hear his laugh through the closed door. She could also hear Candy walk into her room and call in a singsong voice, "Where's the birthday girl?"

"Be out in a sec!" Larken said loudly. She grabbed a pair of pink pants and paired them with a white lace top. She only knew the two matched because she had been with Carl when he bought them. Forgoing her leather sandals, she opened the door and was immediately attacked by Candy.

Laughing and pushing her away, Larken dropped to the chair in front of her vanity. Candy followed her and snatched up a comb. Working it through Larken's tangles, she asked, "Did you make a decision about tonight?"

"Delvon's making fish."

"Is your plan to get a parasite and die?"

"*Hey!*" Delvon barked over Larken's laughter.

"I have it on good authority that he makes the best fried fish."

"Well, we'll invite Ezra to eat with us, just in case."

Delvon growled and Larken smiled. She let Candy put her hair in curlers and listened to her hum one of her favorite songs. A violent buzzing sounded and Larken looked in the mirror just in time to see Delvon accept a call on her communicator. He frowned and Jing's voice demanded, "Where's Larken?"

Delvon scowled and Loxly asked, "Jing, what are you doin'?"

"Some guy has Larken's communicator."

"Why don't you ever ask me before you call her? What if she's busy?"

There was a second of silence. Then, "Is Larken busy?"

Delvon gave an exaggerated grunt before pushing off the bed and dropping the device into Larken's hands. Jing's little face grinned up at her, and Larken smiled back. "Happy birthday!"

"Thanks, sweetie."

Jing scrunched her face up and asked, "Was that man in your bed?"

Three different octaves of confused protests sounded over a feminine laugh. Loxly could be heard complaining, "There better *not* be a man in her bed!"

Candy peeked at the screen and crooned, "Oh, she is *precious*."

Smiling, Larken answered, "He's my bodyguard. He was sleeping on the job."

Jing opened her mouth to speak, but the communicator was taken from her. Loxly's and Brecker's faces filled the screen, both wearing almost comical frowns. "What's he doin' in your bed?" Loxly demanded.

"Yeah, why isn't he guarding you?" Brecker added.

"How has Braves's head not exploded yet with how close the two of you are?" Levi called from somewhere.

Larken looked at the two men and fought to keep her lip from trembling. Then let loose the laugh that bubbled up over her tears. "You guys are something else."

"Answer the questions, Little Bird!" Loxly demanded, not finding the situation at all funny.

"Candy! What are you doing?" Carl asked, barging into the room.

"Curling Larken's hair."

"Then use a curling iron! Her small face will look even smaller with those!" Carl stopped and looked at Larken. "No offense, happy birthday."

"Is that Carl?" Jing asked faintly. Larken imagined she was either getting a snack in the kitchen or playing with the stereo.

Total chaos broke out around Larken. The guys were still demanding to know about Delvon, who was still stretched out on her bed like an oversized cat; Carl and Candy bickered about her hair; and Hinlee and Jing laughed over it all. Larken smiled, never imagining that she could ever feel this happy on a birthday, especially after her engagement. Her eyes fell to the ring, and it felt suddenly tight. Setting the communicator down, Larken pulled the ring off. She would wear it in public, but there was no need to pretend she was happy about it alone in her room.

The ring clattered onto the vanity, silencing Candy and Carl. Making up her mind, she picked up the communicator again and asked, "When is the next visitor's day? I'm going to sneak over there and visit you guys."

Brecker's and Loxly's faces fell, but it was Levi who said, "They canceled visitor's day."

"What?"

"Rec time too," Hinlee added.

"Why?" Larken asked.

"Efficiency," they answered as one.

Larken deflated a little, and Loxly moved the communicator a bit so he was the only one in the screen. "Hey, we'll see each other again. Don't worry."

Larken nodded. Then her hand went to the pearl, suddenly realizing that she wanted only one thing for her birthday. Loxly watched her, and his eyes softened. "Soren had to run to the hangar, but he said if we talked to wish you a happy birthday."

Larken knew Loxly was lying, but she still said, "Tell him thanks."

Delvon hadn't been pulling her leg. The fish practically melted in her mouth. There was lots of laughing and good music, and Larken definitely ate the lion's share of the meal. Delvon teased her mercilessly, making her laugh and giving him a hard time right back. She liked that it was more than just her and Vallen, and she was glad that Ezra had been invited. Larken had always liked the medic and was grateful to have the opportunity to hang out with him without getting stabbed with needles.

She rolled her shoulder at the thought, thankful that being home at least meant she was back to her regular schedule for adjustments. It was a little funny that her shoulder was the only thing coming back had managed to fix. There were mornings that she still woke up uncomfortable, but it was nothing like it had been at base. The same could be said for her family life too.

Larken wore giant Candy-style curls, and Carl dolled her up. They pitched in with Ezra and got her a new weapon belt that strapped around her waist and covered the entirety of her left thigh. It had already been fitted to her sword and could fit six daggers and a gun. Vallen, despite renting Shadric Barlow for an entire evening, got her another present as well. A new silver handgun to match her sword, and it had the latest upgrades. She had learned that they had been testing magazines the day she had called to invite him to the opera. Her gun housed two of six different types of bullets and could fire without exploding. Vallen and his team had trouble with the Igniters and the Smokers reacting poorly together, and her new gun was technically still a prototype, but she loved it. Larken just needed to remember which order she loaded the bullets in before firing blindly.

Even Delvon had gotten her something, but she had to open it before dinner where the others couldn't see. The silver cuff rested against her left wrist and housed a pretty aquamarine-colored stone. Running her finger over it clockwise would jumble any minor wave frequencies, rendering communicators or any other small devices completely useless. It was perfect for having a secret conversation out in the open, and something that she desperately needed. That hadn't stopped her from teasing him about buying her jewelry, though, claiming that it was something only a boyfriend would do.

Vallen cleared his throat and leaned back in his chair. Everyone stopped talking to look at him as he grunted, "I have a job for you, runt."

"No work on birthdays," she said, popping a bright green grape into her mouth.

"It's not that kind of job, and you don't have to start until tomorrow."

"Alright," she caved, "what is it?"

"The last three rooms in this wing need to be furnished. I found you a new security team; they'll be arriving next week."

"What do I need to get? How many are there?" she asked, not liking the idea of more people following her around.

"Six." Estelle got up from her spot by Vallen's feet and draped herself over Larken's. "The beds should be big enough to fit Delvon."

"Did you by any chance make six clones of Delvon? Because that would be awful, we would always be out of food."

"You're one to talk. You just ate six pieces of fish. How do you expect to fit that big butt of yours into a wedding dress?"

"Because it's *fish*." Larken glowered at him. "And you're one to talk, you're *always* eating."

Delvon brushed her words away, unable to argue with her.

Looking back at Vallen, he said, "You'll probably want another few couches for this room too."

Larken took in the space around her. She had just finished redecorating her sitting room. It looked more like the Squad 19 common room than she cared to admit. The two couches were blue instead of crimson, and the armchair that Vallen sat in was the same color. Candy, Carl, and Ezra all sat on the couch opposite her and Delvon. Two more couches and another armchair should do it, but she didn't want the room to be too crowded either. Larken didn't relish the idea of sitting and hanging out with six other guys the size of Delvon, especially if they all acted like him.

Nodding, she asked, "Anything else?"

"Just one more thing." He pushed up out of the chair and disappeared to the communal kitchen. He walked back with a cake that was practically on fire with how many candles were lit, and everyone except Delvon and Vallen started singing.

Larken sat awkwardly, having always hated being sung to, and waited for it to be over. Finally, she was told to make a wish, and Larken took a moment to think. She stared at the flames, her vision going spotty from the light, and knew what she wanted to wish for. Closing her eyes, she focused on the one thing she wanted more than anything else in the world.

I want Soren to take me back home.

She blew out the candles, managing to get them all in one go. Candy cheered and Carl started pulling the half-melted candles from the yellow frosting. Every year Vallen made her a lemon cake, just like she did for his birthday. She would never tell him, but his tasted a lot better than the ones she made for him. Soon the cake was cut and eaten, and Larken was ready for bed. Sluggishly, she stood and bid everyone a good night. Delvon carried her gifts back to her room for her, and Larken let him. The exhausting day she had before, and the belly full of food, had her stumbling more than once.

When they reached her room, Delvon set all of her stuff down on her vanity. He glanced at the camera before pulling her in for a rough hug. He kissed the top of her head and said, "Goodnight, love."

"Night, night, sweetie," she said through a yawn.

He rolled his eyes before turning to leave, but she caught his smile. Estelle trotted into the room just before Delvon closed it. The android hopped up onto the bed and got comfortable. Larken made her way to the vanity and started putting her things away. Something small and yellowish caught her eye. Looking, Larken found a conch shell about the size of her palm sitting next to her engagement ring. Picking it up, she gaped at the shell openmouthed. It was beautiful and perfect. Grinning, she held it up to her ear and laughed. She could hear it, *the sea*. All the stories were true; she couldn't believe it. Noticing a piece of paper on the vanity, Larken picked it up as well. Shell still to her ear, she smiled as she read what the note said:

Happy birthday

CHAPTER 16

"Why do I have to be the one to do it?" Larken huffed, slouching against her vanity as she ran her finger over the shell. She had already been engaged for two days, but she still wanted to push the planning off for as long as possible. Especially if it meant not working closely with a certain blond singer.

"It's *your* wedding," Delvon scoffed, stretched out on her bed.

"I know it's my wedding, I just—" Larken blushed and turned away.

Delvon chuckled, and it made her face heat more. "Don't tell me that I actually have competition."

"You don't!" she insisted, only making him laugh more.

"So, if you don't have a problem with dreamy-eyed Barlow, then you can go over your setlist with him."

"Tell you what," Larken rounded on the bodyguard, "I'll go do some wedding planning, and you can get *off of my bed.*"

Delvon grinned at her. "Aww, don't be like that, love. I thought you liked your sheets smelling like me." His eyes glinted. "I like my sheets smelling like you."

Larken stood and walked away from the shell so she wouldn't accidentally throw it at Delvon's head. She snarled at him, and he laughed some more as he pushed to his feet. He followed her out into the hall and then wrapped his arms around her from behind. She elbowed him in the gut, trying to get free, but only ended up laughing when a member of the Manor staff rounded the corner. She stopped in her tracks and stared at the two of them wide-eyed before turning and practically running the other way while Delvon refused to loosen his hold. Larken managed to free herself, and Delvon fell into step silently beside her.

Looking up at his stern face, Larken realized she was glad that he was there. Delvon was nothing like Loxly, but he could still bully her into leaving her room and make her laugh like the sharpshooter had been able to. Delvon met her gaze, raising an eyebrow. Shaking her head, Larken looked forward and made her way to the ball-room. The sun made the white halls glow, and she wondered how Shadric would feel about sitting outside. She didn't think that a man who lived in the woods would have a problem with it, but the day was too nice to waste.

The security guard that stood outside the ballroom doors eyed Larken up and down as she walked past and Delvon growled at him. Larken hid her face, trying not to let the poor guy see her smile. A warm hand found its way to her lower back, and she knew that Delvon glowered at everyone that glanced her way.

She looked up at him and whispered, "Such a good boyfriend, keeping all the other men away."

"The best you'll ever have."

Larken grinned at Delvon and winked, "Well, I better go find your *competition*."

"I won't be far."

Delvon faded into the background like he usually did, and Larken looked around the room. The stage stood empty, and the doors that led to the gardens were open. Smiling, she made her way to them, the crisp afternoon autumn air wrapping its arms around her as she did. Stepping out onto the dirt, a guitar could be heard on the wind and Larken followed the sound. She disappeared into the maze, knowing that Delvon would wait for her in the shade. The man never wore shorts, even though he often complained about the heat.

As far as she knew, the fountain in the middle didn't have any cameras. Larken had a hard time believing that Delvon would bring up his mother and be so vulnerable with her if he knew that they had an audience. If the two of them had been able to talk freely, then that meant that Larken and the singer would be able to too.

The chords of a song that she had often sung at the tabernacle on base led her way, and Larken started to hum absent-mindedly as she walked. It wasn't long before she found Shadric, sitting on the edge of the old fountain. The thing had been empty for years, but Larken could still remember playing in it as a child. Vallen had sat on the edge, letting her splash him, then threatened to go in after her whenever she did. Her grandfather had built it, having married into the Hale name, and wanted to do something special for her grandmother. She had loved gardens, so he built the maze and surprised her with the fountain in the middle. Larken's mother had torn out the hedges before Larken had been born and replaced them with her yellow rose bushes, but the fountain still stood.

The stone woman in the middle was supposed to resemble her grandmother, but the years had chiseled away the features. Dressed in a simple dress that showed off her entire right leg, the statue held two items. One arm cradled a clay pot, tilting it to the side, and was supposed to be pouring out water, representing her grandmother's love for the District and her people. The other hand gripped a sword that she held straight up, pointing to the sky, representing her promise to always protect the people of the Military District. Larken used to pretend when she was little that the fountain could protect her too. After she had been yelled at or had a fight with Liam, she would run out here like she did after her surprise engagement. She would sit on the edge and cry as she waited for Vallen to come and find her. Then she grew up, and it became a place where she could sit alone in silence. Only, now it wasn't so quiet, and Shadric grinned at her when he realized he wasn't alone.

"Hey, I was wondering if you would find me."

"Hi, Shadric."

"Call me Shad." He smiled, and then stopped playing. Shadric made to stand, saying, "Sorry, we can go in if you want. The day just seemed too nice to spend it inside."

"No," she insisted, making her way over to him. "I was going to suggest coming out here anyway."

"You were?"

His smile caught her off guard, and she landed on the stone a little harder than she intended as she said, "Well, not this exact spot, but yes, outside."

Shadric's smile only deepened, making her look away. Thankfully he didn't mention her blush as he asked, "So, the setlist?"

"Right," she said, jumping on the chance to change the subject. "So, what songs were you thinking?"

"What songs do I think? For your wedding?"

"*Right...*" Larken dropped her gaze again. "Sorry."

"No worries."

Sighing, she asked, "Do you think we could get away with playing the same songs that were at the party?"

"We could." He looked at her and teased, "But I don't think your fiancé would like it very much."

"Well, I don't like that he didn't tell me that we were getting engaged, so it would make us even."

Shadric stared at her, open-mouthed.

She blushed again. "Sorry."

"No, don't be." A hand hesitantly covered hers. "I just wasn't expecting you to be so honest with me after..."

She smiled at her feet. "What happened when we met?"

"Yeah."

"Well, I've been told that I'm honest to a fault, so you won't have to worry about that around me."

"I wish I was more like that."

Larken laughed and looked at him. "Trust me, you are. I might be honest, but I'm not *write-a-song-about-how-I-feel* honest. You're brave in a way that I never could be."

Shadric's blue eyes reflected the sun as he smiled at her. "Want to know a secret?"

"Absolutely."

"All of those songs were fake. *Belong to You* was the only one that I wrote that had any real meaning."

Shadric's hand felt suddenly heavy on top of hers. "You're kidding."

"I'm not."

Larken laughed awkwardly and glanced away again. "Sorry, but I don't believe you."

He squeezed her hand, his voice serious as he said, "I promise I'm being completely honest."

Larken felt her heart skip a beat, and her stomach knotted with nervous excitement. She never thought that she would ever actually meet Shadric Barlow, and she definitely never thought that the singer might have feelings for her. Up until now, he had always been the impossible idea, an excuse for her not to date. But the way he looked at her, the way he didn't bother hiding his own feelings. It made her silly lie feel not so silly anymore.

Larken risked a glance at him, and her blush burned hotter. He looked at her the way he had when they first met, like she was nothing more than a dream. She dropped her eyes again, and Shadric let go of her hand to start playing once more. "So what songs do you like?" he asked. "They don't all have to be mine. I can play whatever."

"Can you?" she challenged, glad her voice sounded strong and clear.

Shadric made a face at her. "Of course I can."

Larken scanned her memory for the oldest hymn she could think of. It wasn't long before she raised an eyebrow and said, "*My Maxim, My Peace.*"

Without even stopping to think, Shadric started playing the melody, adding his own embellishments, and sang all four stanzas word for word. When he finished, he grinned.

"*Okay,*" she grumbled, realizing her mistake in challenging a

Faithful to play an old hymn. "What about *Crash Tonight* by Paisley—"

Larken didn't even finish speaking before Shadric started playing. The song sounded different on an acoustic guitar, rather than a steel one, but there was no denying that the Star knew it. They went on like that for a while, Larken thinking up songs and Shadric somehow knowing them. It didn't matter what genre they were, if they were new hits or old ones that Larken had stumbled upon in her youth, he knew them all.

When he had finished his own rendition of Emma Addison's *Whispered Dreams*, he looked at her and grinned as he asked, "What else ya got?"

Frowning, she said, "*Nuovo Amore.*"

Shadric's grin deepened as he strummed out the melody. Taking the part of Jon the stable boy, Shadric sang Larken's favorite song in *Libri E Beaus* perfectly. Without thinking, Larken jumped in with Estelle's part. Even though Shadric looked at her with surprised eyes, he didn't falter. Together they moved through the words, complementing each other's voices and speaking in a language only two people singing a duet would understand. Goosebumps broke out across Larken's skin, but she didn't stop to think that she was actually singing with Shadric Barlow. If she did, she probably would have swallowed her tongue. Instead, she let the music and the words flow through her, just like she did every time she sang it. The only difference now was that she had someone to sing it with.

When they finished, Shadric looked at Larken in a way that had her hugging her middle and asking, "What?"

"I didn't know you could sing like that."

She shrugged. "A lot of people don't."

"Why not? You would be great."

"I don't like the idea of singing in front of other people."

"So, I should feel special then?" he teased.

When she didn't answer him, Shadric turned serious. He didn't say anything for a long time, and Larken only met his gaze when she felt brave enough. He was looking at her like he had when they danced. She felt her cheeks heat but didn't look away. They were sitting so close, and Larken felt a sudden tug to move closer still. Shadric must have felt it too because he leaned in ever so slightly. His blue eyes heated before they dropped to her lips, and Larken was helpless as her eyes fell to his…wondering what they felt like, wondering what it would feel like to finally be kissed. Nothing else mattered in this moment; it was only her and Shadric. Larken held her breath as her eyes closed.

She could feel his lips close to hers, and her stomach flipped in anticipation. Her communicator buzzed in her pocket, making her jump and nearly stopping her heart. Larken let go of the breath she didn't know she had been holding and laughed slightly. "Sorry."

Shadric only smiled at her, his own cheeks a soft shade of pink, and turned his attention back to his guitar.

Pulling her communicator from her pocket, Larken accepted Carl's call. "Yeah?"

"Where are you?"

"What do you mean? I'm with Shadric."

"Well, that explains it."

"Explains what?" she asked, cheeks heating again for the hundredth time that day.

"You were supposed to meet with me and a possible designer ten minutes ago."

Larken pulled her communicator from her ear and checked the time. "Shoot. I'm sorry. I'm on my way."

Hanging up, she looked to Shadric, ready to apologize. His lips twitched. "Have to go?"

"Yeah, something about a designer. I don't really want one, but I promised I would meet them."

"Don't worry about it. We can pick the setlist another time."

Larken smiled, aware that her blush still colored her cheeks. She couldn't understand how Shadric seemed so calm and collected when she felt like she might lose it at any second. Nodding her agreement, Larken stood and made her way out of the maze, the chords to *Nuovo Amore* following her as she did.

Delvon stood waiting for her outside the entrance, leaning against a pillar with his arms crossed. He looked her up and down before raising a dark eyebrow and asking, "So how's my competition?"

Soren sat alone in his room, the dark nowhere near as heavy as his thoughts. There was so much that needed to be done, but not enough time. Soren felt pathetic, like he was trying to hold onto smoke knowing that his fingers were incapable of doing so. Everyone had been in agreement; Soren had barely gotten the question out of his mouth before Hinlee threw her arms around him and sobbed into his shirt. Loxly and Brecker couldn't stop smiling, and even Levi seemed livelier. Jodi had made a comment about him taking long enough, and he was still waiting on a response from Mr. Chin. Everything was looking up, but the impossible task in front of them seemed to be the only thing Soren could focus on.

Nineteen years. He had been a soldier of the Military District for the last *nineteen years.* What would he do when this was all over? What would any of them do? Hinlee and Brecker both joined when they were nine, and Levi when he was fourteen. This life was all any of them knew. Even Loxly had given six years of his life to the cause, and it would all be over soon. Too soon.

Maxim, what am I doing?

Soren pushed to his feet; sitting in the dark obviously wasn't helping. Leaving his room, he quietly closed the door. Soren stood there, leaning against the wood and letting his head fall back. It seemed like so much more than forty-eight hours, like the announcement of Larken's engagement and General Maxwell's confession happened years ago instead of just days before. Soren wondered how she was doing. He wanted to call her, to ask how her birthday had been, to ask if she had gotten his gift, but he was too much of a coward. Soren had a lot to make up for, and he was off to a poor start.

Without lifting his head from the door, Soren looked down the hall. He still hadn't gone into her room; none of them had. Fear of what had been left behind kept him away, but now his curiosity was getting the better of him. Pushing off his door, Soren made his way down the hall, remembering all the times Larken had wished him goodnight, and how he had nearly broken the door down her first morning there.

Slowly, Soren reached up and twisted the knob. Grapefruit washed over him, choking Soren as his throat went tight. Everything was just as she had left it, and Soren didn't know why he expected it to be any different. Maybe because her leaving had changed his life so drastically that he expected everything else to change too.

A thin layer of dust covered her weapons case. Soren walked over and opened the top drawer, remembering how he teased her about it being full of shoes when she first got it. He had been so wrong about her, had treated her so poorly those first few days. If it were him, Soren would have snapped and started a fight or transferred at the very least, not willing to put up with a Captain like the one he had been. But Larken hadn't. He didn't know who convinced her to stay, Loxly, Hinlee, or if it was her own stubbornness, but she had stayed and put up with him. Soren closed the empty drawer, stomach twisting. She had stuck by him then, but would she stick by him now?

Sighing, he walked over to her bed and sat down. The silence of the room felt wrong, and Soren tried to remember when the quiet had changed from relaxing to annoying. Was it after that day in the gym when he had made fun of that song, or when Hinlee had been playing the one he had always thought was a duet because of Larken? Maybe it was after his video call with General Maxwell when he knew for certain that he would be seeing her again.

Soren fell back on the bed, resting his hand on his stomach. Part of him worried that Hinlee would walk into the dorm any moment for her dorm shift and see him like this, but the other part didn't care. What had being proud and pretending he didn't care gotten him? Nothing. It had only caused a rift between him and the rest of the squad, and it could have ruined his relationship with Larken forever.

How was he going to make this right? Soren needed to do more than a lame birthday present he wasn't even sure she had gotten. He'd hurt her so badly, had treated her the same way her family always did. Instead of just being honest and saying she mattered to him, he let her go without a word. Soren might not have been downright cruel like Cornella or Liam were, but there was no way his silence hadn't cut just as deep.

Somehow, Larken found the strength to climb out of bed every day, smile for the cameras, and play the role of the Daughter of the Military. But Soren knew what really went on behind closed doors. His hand balled into a fist as he remembered hearing her cry through the door the day she had been activated. Soren turned his head, looking at the speaker closest to him. His mind shifted from Larken's secret tears to the day he caught her dancing. His lips twitched without his permission and he sighed.

Yes, the way he felt about Larken had definitely changed over the few months they had been together. If someone had told him the day he had rescued her that he would be going insane and nearly kissing her whenever they were alone, he would have laughed in their face. He would have been wrong, just like had been wrong about almost everything since she walked into his life. But now that Soren knew he was finally doing the right thing, how would Larken react? Would she be happy? Or would she treat him the way he deserved and turn him away?

CHAPTER 17

She had only been planning the wedding for a few days, and Larken already felt stressed enough to pull out all of her hair. No one listened to her, and she had to accept whatever was planned for her. So far the color scheme had been decided as hot pink and pale orange, and yellow roses were going to make up her bouquet. Larken didn't mind the pale orange so much, and she had found a new appreciation for pink thanks to Carl, but she hated her wedding colors. If it had been up to her, the colors would be tan and blue like the ocean, her bouquet would be made up of blue forget-me-nots, baby's breath, and peach roses. And the groom would be different as well.

Larken sighed, trying her best to pay attention to the coordinators and not scratch at her ring finger. The two Star women were arguing about the napkins. One wanted pink napkins with orange trim, the other wanted orange napkins with pink trim. Larken wanted to punch them both in the throat just to make them shut up.

"What do you think, Miss Hale?" Tina asked. She had a skeletal-thin frame and wore a yellow pantsuit. Her hair was jet black, and Larken thought the combo made her look like a half-starved bumblebee.

"I'm sorry, what?" she asked.

"The place settings," Stacy answered. She had what she had called *Military-brown* hair and asked Larken if it made her look like she was actually from the Military District. Stacy also wore a form-fitting lime green dress that complemented her olive skin.

"I thought we were talking about napkins?"

"We decided on the orange ones with the pink trim," Stacy answered, glad she had gotten her way.

"Oh, well, then I guess we pick the ones that match the napkins."

The sound of a guitar tuning in the background stopped, and there was a soft chuckle. Larken stiffened, feeling a blush start at her chest. She had been actively trying to forget the fact that Shadric sat only a few feet behind her in the ballroom, getting ready to try and run the setlist with her again. Larken hadn't been able to forget the way she had felt in his arms, how surprisingly easy it had been to talk to him, or what had happened the last time they tried to talk about music. Being with him distracted her. She didn't think about Squad 19 when they were together, and that confused her more than anything.

Tina gave Larken a puzzled smile and then said, "Maybe we should decide on the dishes and utensils first. That would narrow down things quite a bit."

"Sure, what were you thinking?"

Stacy grinned, cutting Tina off. "I think we should have pink crystal plates."

Tina gasped and exclaimed, "And orange crystal silverware and glasses!"

The two fell into ridiculousness, and Larken groaned as she rubbed at her shoulder. It throbbed dully, and she seriously considered exaggerating her pain just so she could leave. She let go of the muscle and stiffened as she felt warmth at her back.

Shadric leaned over her, reaching for the plans. He pulled the tablet towards him and sighed. Larken tried not to think about what had almost happened the last time they were this close, but she didn't succeed. Memories of him smiling, leaning in close, and the way she had closed her eyes as her belly flipped assaulted her. She tried her best not to blush.

"This looks awful," he whispered.

"You don't have to tell me," Larken grumbled, glad she didn't sound as nervous as she felt.

"Are they going to dress you in cotton candy to complete the look?"

Larken glared at him. "You want to say that a little louder so the peacocks can hear you?"

Shadric's bright blue eyes danced as he snorted. Helping her to her feet, he said, "Come on."

"Where are you going?" Tina demanded. "We still have work to do!"

"Miss Hale trusts your judgment. We still have to work out the setlist."

Both women's faces fell when they realized the responsibility that Larken and Shadric had just dumped on them. Larken had to turn away to hide her grin. Shadric grabbed her hand and led her to the stage. Letting go, he started packing up his guitar.

"What are you doing?" Larken asked, following his movements with her eyes.

Shutting his guitar case, he looked at her and answered, "We're getting out of here."

"What?"

He grinned, grabbed her hand, and then pulled her out of the ballroom. Past Delvon and Shadric's security team, the two ran out to the drive. Larken barely had time to think of anything other than the way his hand felt before she was stopped in front of a silver hoverbike she didn't recognize and given a helmet. She stared at it as Shadric strapped his instrument to the bike and jammed on a helmet of his own.

"Hurry and get that on before they realize we're leaving the grounds," he said quietly.

Larken grinned, feeling reckless and wild as she put the helmet on. It pushed her bun into her scalp, but she didn't care. Shadric threw his leg over the bike and started it up. Larken jumped on behind him and barely finished wrapping her arms around his middle before they shot off.

She couldn't help her excited squeal. Shadric was going much faster than Vallen had ever driven with her. Shadric laughed and it danced in the wind, making Larken feel lightheaded and giddy. They sped down the roads, passing buildings that slowly grew further and further apart. Soon, they were the only ones on the road, and Larken hoped the singer knew where he was going.

The giddy feeling eventually passed, and Larken let herself enjoy the freedom. She knew that Delvon would be furious with her for giving him the slip, but every second an aircraft didn't drop out of the sky to chase them down, the less she thought he would blow up when they saw each other again. Maybe he was glad that she could get away for the afternoon and wouldn't even mention it when she got back. Resting her chin on Shadric's shoulder, she tried to suppress a shiver. Her maroon capris and peach tank top weren't really keeping her warm in the onslaught of wind, but Shadric didn't seem to mind how close she was.

Eventually, they slowed down, and Larken looked around, seeing only trees. When the bike had fully stopped, Shadric reached up and pulled his helmet free. Hopping off the bike, he helped Larken to her feet. He took her helmet and set it next to his before grabbing his guitar case. Taking her hand, Shadric led her to the little wooded area that they were parked by. They passed through the trees, and Larken gasped when they reached the clearing. Before her sat a field of lavender, and Shadric grinned at her.

"What is this place?"

"It's where I come to write music." He pulled her into the flowers, and she quickly noticed the large quilt and picnic basket. Larken gaped at him. He shrugged, ears going slightly pink. "I thought you could use a break from all that wedding stuff."

Her own face going warm, she turned away from him, smiling as she did. Shadric wasn't at all like she expected him to be. Every time they were together, she expected him to start acting like Dominic, but he always proved her wrong. He had been nothing but kind to her after their initial meeting. A fresh wave of heat washed over her, chasing away her chill as she remembered just how kind he had been.

Reaching the quilt, Shadric helped her to the ground, making sure that she was comfortable. He set his instrument down, and then took a seat next to her. Larken looked up at him when he grabbed her hand again. He blushed slightly and said, "Sorry, we always held hands while we prayed. I can—"

He tried to pull his hand away, but Larken squeezed it, cutting him off. "This is fine."

"You sure?"

Smiling, she nodded. Shadric grinned and said a quick prayer. He prayed not only for the food, but also for her health and safety during her time of stress. Larken felt her eyes burn. No one had ever prayed out loud for her like that before. She was touched by the beauty and selflessness of it all.

"Are you okay?" Shadric asked when he finished and saw that she hadn't opened her eyes yet.

"Fine," she rasped as she looked at him.

"You don't look fine."

"It's just been a while since I felt like someone other than Vallen cared about me."

"I thought your bodyguard—"

"Delvon's great, but he isn't the type to openly say he cares about you."

Shadric smiled like he understood what she meant. "I have a few friends like that."

"That must be nice," Larken said, dropping her gaze.

"It is." His voice was warm as he thought about the ones close to him. Shaking his head, he asked, "Aren't you close with your squad? They seemed very protective of you in the woods."

"I was, but I'm starting to think that they realize what it means to care about me."

"And what does it mean to care about Larken Hale?" Shadric's blue eyes danced, making her stomach feel tight.

"It means that, eventually, you're going to get hurt."

"Well, I guess that means I'm good."

"What do you mean?"

He grinned. "You already shot me."

Larken's face went hot as he opened the basket and started pulling out the food. "I try not to think about that."

He laughed. "Why? It was one of the best days of my life."

She couldn't help but laugh as well. "Getting shot was one of the best days of your life?"

He met her gaze, eyes serious. "Meeting you."

Larken's breath hitched, and she couldn't look away. Her stomach flipped, remembering that he almost kissed her not even a week ago. That he meant what he said, that he *wanted* to kiss her. Not only that, but she was going to let him. Larken had wanted to have her first kiss be with Shadric, but did she still? She was drowning, and she wondered for a moment what would happen if she just let herself sink. What would happen if she let herself care about someone else? Would Shadric leave her too?

Looking away, she asked, "So, what made you join the Faithfuls?"

Smiling, but letting her change the subject, Shadric answered, "I was taken in by them. My parents died when I was young, and they practically raised me."

"So how did your career fit in with it? You might not have recognized me that day in the woods, but I definitely recognized you."

"Well to be fair, you are also *my biggest fan ever.*"

She blushed hotly. "Please tell me Vallen didn't—"

"He used the word *obsessed* actually. I was just trying to lessen the blow."

Larken reached up and covered her face as she groaned. She was going to *kill* Vallen. No wonder Shadric felt so confident; he already knew what she thought about him. Larken couldn't ever remember feeling so mortified in her entire life.

Laughing, Shadric pulled her hands free. "I'm sorry," he said. "Look, let's just eat, okay?"

Nodding, Larken let herself be handed a sandwich. Her embarrassment still threatened to make her run away, but she forced her legs to stay put. The food helped some, but not enough to where she wasn't constantly sneaking glances at Shadric. He didn't seem phased at all and smiled happily as he ate.

Unable to take it anymore, Larken decided to direct the focus away from her. "Can I ask you something?"

"Anything."

"How does Maxim fit in with the Faithfuls' ideals?"

His chewing slowed, and then he swallowed, considering her question. Instead of answering her, he asked, "Can I ask you something?"

She nodded.

"Who do you think Maxim is?"

Larken thought for a long time, trying to figure out the right words. Eventually, she answered, "I guess Maxim is my God and the only One who I'm truly afraid doesn't want me."

Something dimmed in Shadric's eyes. "Why do you think He wouldn't want you?"

"You're joking, right?"

Shadric looked completely serious, waiting for her to answer.

Sighing, she asked, "Why would he want me? I'm not special."

He grabbed her hand. "You are. You are *so* special, Larken."

"I know plenty of people who would disagree with you."

"And I know plenty of people who would disagree with *you*. Maxim doesn't care about who we are, where we came from, or if our parents are alive or dead." The way he said it made it sound like someone had once told him this very thing. "Maxim only wants to love you, and for you to let Him love you in return. He covers our weaknesses and is our greatest strength. He doesn't ask for anything, doesn't demand sacrifices or proof that you're good enough. Only you the way you are."

Larken's throat felt tight. Vallen had once told her something similar when she was young. She hadn't believed him; her own mother didn't even want her, the one person who had carried her and felt her life begin. How could someone as amazing and wonderful as Maxim possibly feel any differently? Larken was a nobody, a child that had been given up to the war to be slaughtered, just like all the other unwanted children. How could Maxim ever love her?

"If He only wants me the way I am, then why did He abandon me?" she asked, not bothering to hide the hurt in her voice. Larken hadn't planned on sharing her fears with anyone, but now that she had, she couldn't keep the rest in. "Why would He give me a home, a family, just to take it away? If He wants me, then why can't I feel Him here?"

"He didn't abandon you," Shadric insisted.

"He did!" Tears burned her eyes. "I was finally happy, and I finally thought that I might matter, and then *He took it all away.*"

"He didn't take anything away, Larken. You still have your family, even though they might not be with you now."

"You don't get it. You've always belonged somewhere. I don't have that; I'll never have that. I thought I did. I thought that I had finally found a home and friends. That I finally had a real relationship with Maxim. But I was wrong. He doesn't want me, and He can't use me. I was stupid for ever thinking that He would."

"That's not true. He loves you, and this is all just part of His plan. I promise."

She shook her head. "You're wrong."

Shadric cupped her cheeks, forcing her to look at him. "I'm not wrong. I knew it the moment I saw you. *You* are special, you are loved, and you will be the one to determine what kind of world we wake up to tomorrow."

"How can you be so sure? I don't even know if I'll be alive tomorrow. *How can you?*" she accused, pulling away from him. "What do you want from me, Shadric?"

"I want you to do what you were born to do."

"Which is?" she asked, voice feeling weak.

"To become Luminary and stop this war."

Larken couldn't breathe as the world around her stopped turning. "What?"

"We need you, Larken. Your mother, she's talking *genocide*. Cornella Hale wants all Maxim worship stomped out and to be the only one standing when the smoke clears."

"She's not perfect, but really? Genocide?" Larken couldn't believe it, *wouldn't* believe it.

"All those families, all those fires...Larken, did you really think that was us?"

"No, but—"

"Think, Larken. Really think about it."

The Faithfuls followed Maxim. There was no doubting that. They were all labeled fanatics that took His teachings too far. But if Maxim was a just God, one that loved all of His people, then why would a group following His teachings try to wipe out entire families that had always boasted about following Him? Now that Larken thought about it, she couldn't understand how she ever thought that what she had been told had made any sense. And the fires Vallen was trying so hard to keep from her...

She felt her eyes widen in horror, and Shadric only smiled sadly at her.

"My—my mother," she rasped, so quietly that she almost couldn't hear herself.

"Yes. Larken, we need you. Please, you have to come to Camp with me. We can keep you safe and—"

"And what, Shad? You can't just expect me to leave."

"But you can. There's nothing for you back there."

"I know!" she shouted, making him jump. Larken grabbed the pearl and whispered, "*I know*."

"Then what's stopping you? Let's go, right now."

"No."

"Why?"

"I have to see this through first. I don't know if you're right about why I'm here, but I do know that Vallen has a plan. If I just leave with you, we can be tracked. Or worse."

Shadric's face fell, but he nodded. It would seem that she wasn't the only one that let her emotions get the better of her. "You're right," he agreed. "We need a plan."

"I can try and talk to Vallen tonight, if you're okay with me sharing your secret, and see what he thinks. Okay?"

Shadric sighed and nodded. Larken knew that he wanted to say more, but she was glad when he didn't and instead grabbed the guitar case and pulled it towards him. Larken watched as he opened it and took out the instrument. Shadric strummed it a few times, tuning the guitar until it was to his liking. He looked at her and started playing the chorus of *Nuovo Amore.* Larken went from upset and hurt, to embarrassed and flustered in a single heartbeat. Shadric smiled at her, his thoughts reflecting in his eyes.

Looking away, she said, "You don't have to play at the wedding if you don't want to."

He didn't bother trying to hide the hurt in his voice. "It does seem a little unfair, doesn't it?"

Larken shrugged awkwardly.

"I mean, I've only just found you," he admitted.

She thought her face had felt hot before, but it was nothing compared to how it burned now. He laughed softly, and she turned to find him blushing as well.

"Sorry, I didn't—well, what I mean is—" he stopped playing and sighed. "I'm messing this up."

Larken burst out laughing, not knowing what else to do. He looked at her, raising a blond eyebrow. "I'm sorry," she gasped. "I'm not laughing at you. It's just, in all my life, I never thought that I would be the girl that *Shadric Barlow* would get flustered around."

He couldn't help but laugh as well. When they sobered, he smiled again and said, "I meant it when I said that, Larken. You are the most beautiful woman I have ever seen." When she didn't say anything, he asked, "Was it okay that I said that? You're not going to shoot me again, are you?"

Her lips twitched. "I don't have my gun."

"I have that going for me at least."

"That guitar isn't hurting either."

He grinned. Dropping his gaze, he asked, "So what other songs were you thinking for the wedding?"

Larken's cheeks heated again, remembering what had happened the last time they had tried talking about this. Pushing the thoughts away, she asked, "Got anything new about arranged marriages that the bride wants no part of?"

"I can write some."

"Sounds perfect."

"I have been working on something new, actually," he admitted. "But I don't think I can release it now."

"Why not?"

"I don't think it will be well received."

"You can play it at the wedding, I don't care."

"You might." He laughed bitterly.

"Try me."

Smiling sadly, Shadric started to play. The guitar filled the clearing, and Larken let herself get lost in the pretty melody. It was only after he started singing that she felt her blush return. Shadric's voice rose and fell, singing the most beautiful love song she had ever heard. It was somehow better than *Wanting You*, and just as heartbreaking. With lyrics like *wanting you is like slowly dying* and *the only thing I want to do is to belong to you*, Larken knew it was for her. Her eyes stung as she listened to it, and she realized just how much the singer cared for her.

Larken didn't think it was possible; no one wanted her. Dominic only treated her like she was some sort of conquest, and Soren… well he hadn't wanted her in the end, had he? But Shadric…he had no fear. He told her exactly how he felt about her, just because he wanted her to know. Larken knew her feelings weren't as strong for him, but the fact that she no longer had the option to choose, to see if they would be one day, wasn't fair.

When he finished, Larken blew out a long breath. She sniffed back her emotions and choked out, "Yes. I think you should play that."

"What? Really?" he laughed. "You're joking, you know that song's about—"

"Shad, I want you to play it." She pleaded silently with her eyes. "This is the only thing I get any say in, and that song was the most beautiful thing I have ever heard. Please play it."

"They're going to talk, you know."

"They always talk."

"I don't know what headline sounds more appealing. *Daughter of the Military Marries Captain Dominic Braves* or *Heartbroken Singer Confesses True Feelings During New Couple's First Dance.*"

Larken frowned. "How about *Military Sweetheart Runs Away with Wedding Singer and Bodyguard?*"

"Why, Miss Hale," Shadric mused. "I thought you'd never ask."

They fell into a comfortable silence, picking out songs for the wedding. Shadric teased her a few times, insisting that he play her favorites. She didn't ask how he knew but assumed that Vallen had told him. It wasn't long before the sun started setting and they were forced to return.

They pulled into the drive, where reporters and security guards were waiting for them. Delvon blew past them, pulling Larken against his side and leaving Shadric to fend for himself. The three of them managed to make it into the Manor, and Larken almost wanted to drag Shadric back out there just to upset Dominic. She knew that he would hate that she spent the day alone with him, and she couldn't be happier about it. Slipping off her ring, she stuffed it into her pocket and grabbed the pearl subconsciously.

"Well, that was exciting," Shadric said. He looked to Delvon and offered a hand. "Hey, I'm Shadric."

Delvon only grunted. Shadric awkwardly dropped his hand, and Larken looked between the two of them. Something about them together seemed familiar, and she couldn't quite put her finger on it. Shadric offered her a sheepish smile, and Delvon glared at her. Then, Larken remembered. Delvon looked like that man in the woods, the one that Brecker had hurt. They had the same face and were about the same height from what she could remember.

Delvon snarled at her, his eyes shooting up to a nearby camera. "Get up to your room, Peach. You've already given me enough trouble today."

Larken realized she was gaping at him. She closed her mouth and looked at Shadric. He shot Delvon a nervous glance, and she wasn't sure if he was intimidated, or if he was worried that they had been found out. Whatever it was, Larken would have to talk to Delvon about it. She needed to know if he was a Faithful too and, if he was, what that meant for her.

CHAPTER 18

It had been almost a week since Larken disappeared with that *Barlow*. In retrospect, having him sing for the wedding probably wasn't his best idea, and now Dominic looked the fool. The media had painted her as the fun beauty that had finally found joy in relationships but was now being forced to settle down, and he was the jerk who was forcing her to do it. All of this was a mess, and it frustrated him that Larken couldn't see that he held her best interests at heart.

But the media wasn't all wrong. Even now as he watched her try and talk to the wedding coordinators, he could see how stressed she looked. Not that she was the only one who was stressed. Dominic had tried to be patient, but against his better judgment he had snooped around a bit, trying to find any information about Tanner and Larken. No one told him anything, but after her escapade with Barlow, Dominic wasn't sure it was Tanner he needed to be worried about.

Her hair fanned out around her, looking softer each time she ran her fingers through it. He liked her with her hair down; it made her look elegant and not like she was about to go for a run. Dominic tilted his head, watching as she tried not to yell at Tina or Stacy; he couldn't remember which one was which. She tried to explain to them that yellow roses would be a bad idea to use as decorations because they were already in the bouquet. The Star wasn't understanding, and soon the other one was backing her up.

"I just don't understand what the problem is, Miss Hale. It's a good thing that they're in the bouquet; they'll match."

"The flowers aren't supposed to match, Tina. If they did, the bouquet wouldn't be special," Larken said, voice sounding short.

"All of the flowers will be special," the other girl interjected.

"Yes, but the bouquet—" Larken shut her mouth before she could start breathing fire and stuck her hand into her hair again.

Figuring she'd had enough for one day, Dominic left the bar area of the ballroom and walked over to save the coordinators. The two were talking over each other, trying to get Larken to understand that her way was wrong, and Dominic placed his hands on her biceps just as she clenched her fists. Worried that she might actually punch one of them, he forced her to take a step back.

"It's okay," he murmured. "We'll just get you a different bouquet that you can hide until it's time to walk down the aisle."

The fight went out of her, and she relaxed her shoulders so much that Dominic worried she might collapse. Larken nodded and made her way to a nearby chair. Sinking onto it, she propped her elbows on her knees and cradled her head. Her hair fell around her like a wheat-colored curtain, hiding her away, and Dominic kneeled before her. Rubbing his hands up and down her arms, he tried to soothe her.

Larken groaned and said, "I don't know how much more I can take of this. The wedding is almost two weeks away, and they keep —" she sighed and looked up. "We spent *three hours* talking about hairpins, Dominic. Hairpins! They aren't even doing my hair!"

Dominic tried not to laugh but failed. She groaned again and dropped her head back into her hands. Pulling her close, he kissed her temple. "Sounds like you could use a break."

"What I *need* is to stab something."

Dominic chuckled, letting go, and lifted her face so she would look at him. The pale blue halter top clasped around her neck made her eyes pop. She wore that pearl necklace that he assumed General Maxwell had gotten her since she never took it off, and Dominic couldn't help but hate the simplicity of it all. Larken deserved the finest things life had to offer, not plain clothes and jewelry. He wasn't sure where she had gotten the bracelet from, but it matched her ring, so he didn't complain. He would be hard-pressed to make her get rid of the jeans she wore though. They hugged her like a second skin and had him thinking dangerous thoughts.

Cupping her cheek, he asked, "Why don't we get out of here?"

She tried to turn her head to look at Tanner, who lurked in the corner like always, but he forced her to keep her eyes on him. "Where would we go?" she asked before nibbling on her bottom lip.

"I know a place."

"I don't think—"

"Let me help you, Lark," he said. *Trust me.*

She looked like she wanted to argue, but she asked, "Would Delvon come with us?"

"No, just you and me."

"Dominic, is that a good idea?"

He tightened his grip on her unintentionally. "So you'll run away with that Barlow, but not me? I'm your fiancé, Larken."

"I know." She pulled his hand away, and he saw pink skin where he had held her. "That's why I'm not sure it's a good idea. I don't want to..." She dropped her eyes, face turning red. "I don't want you to expect something that isn't going to happen."

Dominic smirked and put his finger under her chin. When she was looking at him again, he said, "I've waited this long, Lark. I can wait a few more weeks."

Out of excuses, Larken nodded. He pulled her to her feet and sent a warning glare to Tanner. The man stayed where he was, but he pulled out his communicator and started typing on it. They didn't have long if they were going to leave. Grabbing Larken's hand, Dominic led her to the drive where he'd left his hovercraft. A new sporty model in the Vixon line, with black chrome and a bright red undercarriage. It was the most expensive thing he owned, and he only had it because Larken couldn't get over her silly fear of flying.

Helping her into the hover, Dominic rushed around and hopped in as well. He wasted no time firing it up and jetting it out of the drive. The bright lights of nightlife were just starting to turn on, illuminating the darkening world around them. Dominic had a heady rush, and he almost forwent his plan for the night and took them to the house in the country he had commissioned for the two of them. He needed to be patient though; if he didn't do everything perfectly, Cornella would be able to find them, and it would all be for nothing.

Larken didn't say anything as she stared out the window, one hand holding her stomach, the other the pearl. Unable to help himself, Dominic placed his hand on her thigh. Her eyes fell to it, and instead of the heated glance he had expected, she looked back out the window. He blamed the stress and squeezed her thigh gently. "Want to tell me about it?"

"It's just…a lot."

"Is the wedding all that's on your mind?"

She was quiet for a moment, and then said, "Yes."

He knew she was lying; she was annoyed with him. Since her spontaneous date with the singer, he had ensured that the only time she had been alone was when she slept. When she wasn't working out, she spent her time working on the wedding or with him. Dominic didn't want to risk her running away again.

He leaned forward in his seat and let go of her. "Looks like we're here."

Larken looked as well and then sighed deeply. "Dominic, I'm too tired to dance."

"You won't be for long, trust me."

He hopped out of the hover and ran to help Larken out. Her outfit would have her standing out a little, but it didn't matter. Everyone would soon learn that looking at her would end badly for them.

Together they made their way into the club. Dominic quickly found them seats at the bar and ordered them both something strong. Once he finished, Larken asked for some type of juice before the bartender could disappear. It didn't matter what she ordered; the vial of chamomile extract he had would help her relax in no time. When the drinks arrived, she lifted hers, about to take a sip, but he stopped her.

"Wait, I have something for you."

With the straw still millimeters from her mouth, she asked, "What?"

Pulling the vial from his pocket, he uncorked it and grabbed her drink. "This is chamomile extract, it will help you relax."

"Really?"

"Yeah, just a little. It's basically like having a cup of tea."

She watched as he dumped the contents of the vial into her glass. He used the straw to stir it and then handed it back. She gave him a warm smile and then sucked down her drink. Dominic threw back his drink as well, and then the one he had ordered for her, glad that he had finally been able to make her smile since their engagement had been announced.

One glare had people moving out of his way, which was good because Soren felt ready to commit murder. Cameras flashed all around him, but he ignored them; the only thing that mattered was her. It was the first time in over a month that he had seen Larken, and this was not how he had expected to find her. He expected shouting, hitting, and her using his shirt like a tissue as she cried in his arms. Not her making a spectacle of herself, dancing on top of a table in a club that Dominic had dragged her to.

It wasn't like the last time Soren had caught her dancing. Then, Larken had been mortified, wearing a pair of shorts that Soren couldn't forget. Now, she wore skin-tight jeans and moved to the music like she didn't care who saw her. Larken had on a dreamy smile and didn't let her wobbling or stumbling deter her. Something in Soren snapped, and he felt like a bull ready to charge.

When he caught sight of Braves, he growled low in his throat. This was all his fault; Larken wouldn't even be here if it wasn't for him. Soren was also willing to bet he had something to do with the way she was acting. There was no other possible explanation. Larken Hale wasn't the type of girl to draw attention of any kind; there was no way she got up on that table without any encouragement from him.

Soren made his way to Braves as he pleaded with Larken to get off the table. She closed her eyes, moving like the only thing that mattered to her was the music that pounded through the speakers in the smoky room. Braves grabbed her hips, trying to pull her down, but Soren was on him before he even had time to turn around.

"Get your hands off of her," he growled. The people around them stopped dancing and drinking to watch.

Dominic stiffened and turned on him. "*Deckard*," he spat. "What are you doing here?"

"I'm here to take Larken back to the Manor after you kidnapped her."

"I didn't kidnap her! She was stressed and needed to have some fun."

"Larken doesn't think dancing on tabletops and drawing attention to herself is *fun*." Soren towered over the Star, and for the first time since they met, Braves looked a little afraid of him. "What did you do to her?"

His face went red and he roared, "I didn't do anything!"

"*What did you do?*"

"It's not my fault if a little bit of chamomile extract has her acting like a slu—" Soren punched Dominic in the jaw before he should finish the word and the Star crumpled. Soren didn't know if the man was unconscious or just trying to save face, but he didn't get back up. The cameras flashed with renewed vigor, and Larken's feet chose that moment to get tangled up.

She fell back and screamed, thinking she was going to hit the floor. Her arms were up in front of her face, bracing for an impact that never came. Soren caught her, pulling her close to him. Her skin was just as soft and warm as he remembered. The wild animal that had been rioting through Soren's chest since she left finally settled down now that she was back in his arms.

Slowly, she lowered her hands and blinked bleary-eyed at him. "Vallen?"

"No."

Her eyes focused some at the sound of his voice. Her lips parted and the loud music covered her small gasp. She reached up tentatively and touched his jaw, almost like she couldn't believe that he was there. Tears welled in her eyes and she whispered, "*It's you.*"

Soren stared down at her, his own throat feeling uncomfortably tight.

"I've missed you." She sniffed loudly and snuggled into his chest. "Take me back to the dorm. I wanna go back."

Soren's heart broke, and he got her out of that club as quickly as he could. He couldn't focus on the cameras or the fact that he was all anyone would be talking about for the next few days; he needed to get her home. Once they were out in the lot, he carried her to the hovercraft General Maxwell had lent him for the evening. Awkwardly, he managed to settle her into the passenger seat, and she didn't want to let go when he pulled away.

"Don't leave me again," she pleaded, hands gripping his shirt tightly. "I don't want you to leave me."

"I'm just getting into my seat," he assured. "I'll be right back."

Reluctantly she let go, and Soren almost tripped in his haste to get into the hover. Once in, he strapped her harness around her. She had a hard time keeping her eyes open, and Soren couldn't help but notice the pearl that hung from her neck.

Looking up, he found her watching him. "I kept it," she rasped. "I tried to throw it away, but I couldn't. That would have hurt more."

Soren grabbed her hand, and she tangled her fingers with his willingly. Raising it to his mouth, he kissed her knuckles. Then he promised, "I'm not leaving this time."

"You said that before. You said you wouldn't let go, and then you did." A tear slipped from her eye, and Soren wondered how much of this conversation she would remember in the morning.

"I was scared before," he admitted.

"Soren Deckard doesn't get scared. He's too pigheaded."

He snorted. "I am."

"And he's cranky."

"Yes, that too."

She yawned, reaching for him and resting her head on his shoulder. "And handsome."

Soren tried to smother his smile and hoped that she wouldn't remember any of this. If she did, she wouldn't ever be able to look at him again. Silently, he fired up the hover and made his way back to the Manor. He got past the gates with no problem and found everyone waiting for them in the drive.

Pulling to a stop, Soren got out and walked around to the side Larken was on as General Maxwell asked, "Any trouble?"

A giant grey and white beast ran up to the hovercraft and started to sniff at it, growling low in its chest as it noticed Larken. Soren's stomach twisted, hoping that the thing just smelled the chamomile and that Cornella hadn't turned one of the few things Larken actually liked about the Manor against her. It snorted and trotted off, telling Soren that his gut was probably right.

"She won't want to go out in public for a while. Or see Braves once she finds out he drugged her."

"He *what?*" Levi, Loxly, and Brecker demanded at the same time.

"Gave her too much chamomile extract," he said, pulling the door open. Soren unbuckled Larken, and she wrapped her arms around him. She murmured something into his neck that sounded like her asking for a pillow, and his lips twitched despite the seriousness of the situation. He pulled her out and turned to General Maxwell. "Where's her room?"

The older man just glared and turned. He led Soren and the others into the Manor, Delvon following behind. Soren wasn't quite sure what to make of the man, but he didn't like Braves, so Soren figured he was alright. Once they were in front of Larken's door,

Delvon opened it and Estelle raised her head. The android's tail beat against the bed, and Soren smiled at the sight.

He walked in and set Larken on the mattress. Taking her sandals off, he put them under her bed. Then he pulled the covers up over her, making sure she was comfortable. Once Soren was satisfied, he turned to leave, but Larken grabbed his wrist and stopped him. She pulled him to her, giving him no choice but to get on the bed. Larken fussed until he relaxed next to her, and she snuggled against him. Pressing her face to his chest, she took a deep breath and sighed. Soren waited a while for her breathing to even out. When he thought she was finally asleep, he made to get up. The hand on his bicep tightened, and she mumbled something into her pillow.

He bent in close to her and asked, "What was that?"

"Don't leave me again."

Soren kissed her forehead. "I'm never leaving you again. I'll see you in the morning."

"Promise?"

"Promise."

CHAPTER 19

Larken's head felt heavy when she opened her eyes. Her tongue tasted metallic, like she had fallen asleep with a coin in her mouth. Her head pounded, and she needed water. Larken felt like she had spent the night crying, but she couldn't really remember anything after getting into the hover with Dominic. Her skin didn't feel sore anywhere like a dermis gun had been used, so she didn't think she had been attacked, although her shoulder hurt and she knew she would need to seek out Ezra. Trying to remember what happened only made her head hurt more, so she gave up. Larken stretched slowly, relieving some of the built-up pressure in her muscles, and realized that Estelle wasn't in bed. She started to wonder what time it was when the door opened.

Not caring if they saw her, Larken rolled over and pulled a pillow over her head, pretending lamely to still be asleep. After two heartbeats, the bed dipped and a warm body pulled her close. She groaned, protesting as the pillow was taken from her, and Delvon's deep chuckles reverberated in her chest.

"If I would have known how fun you were, I would have spiked your drink a long time ago."

"What are you talking about?" she rasped groggily. His words had a hard time sinking into her brain, and she rolled over to snuggle him, trying to steal his warmth. The comforting scent of pine and salt soothed her and she mumbled, "Be a good pillow and be quiet."

"You still feeling it? That idiot gave you too much."

"Gave me what? Some water?"

"You thirsty?"

"My mouth tastes weird."

Delvon sighed and let go of her, getting off of the bed. He grabbed the water bottle on her dresser that she took to workouts and disappeared into the bathroom. Water started running, and Larken closed her eyes. Burying herself deep into her blankets to make up for the heat that Delvon had taken with him, she sighed contentedly. She saw only darkness at first, but soon she found herself standing on the edge of a cliff, watching a waterfall spit out foamy water, and readied herself to jump into the clear depths below. Then, Delvon startled her awake by touching her shoulder.

"You have to sit up."

"My head's too heavy."

He sighed and made her sit up. She held her head to try and stop the throbbing, and Delvon helped her drink. "Not only was it too much, but it was a shoddy product. Who knows what it could have been laced with?"

The water helped clear her mind a little, and she rolled her shoulder as she asked, "What on earth are you talking about?"

"I'm talking about Braves drugging you at a club last night."

Larken's head shot up and she met Delvon's grey eyes. "He did *what?*"

"*Drugged you,*" he said slowly, annoyed that he had to keep repeating himself.

Delvon reached out and pressed a hand to her forehead, and she batted him away. "Knock it off."

"Just making sure you aren't running a temperature. You've been asleep a long time; that's why they sent me in. Ezra was worried that you might not be reacting well to whatever it was Braves gave you."

"How long was I asleep?"

"Almost seventeen hours."

Larken gaped, waiting for the bodyguard to say he was joking. When he didn't, Larken leaned back against her pillows and grabbed the pearl. Someone had thankfully taken off her engagement ring, but her finger still itched. She wanted to throw the thing away, toss it out a window and never think about it again. She looked at Delvon, his frown not as severe as it normally was.

"Are you okay?"

She looked to the camera in her room, but he gripped her jaw gently and forced her to keep eye contact.

"Are you okay?" he asked again.

"Is the engagement off?"

He grunted. "They won't call it off just because your fiancé's an idiot." She frowned, and he said, "But that doesn't matter now. What matters is how you're feeling."

Larken realized that this was the longest they had talked since she ran off with Shadric. She had missed the grumbly bodyguard and nodded to assure him that she felt fine. He relaxed a little bit, still not taking his eyes off of her.

"Could I have some more water?" she asked, head still pounding.

He got up again and went to the bathroom. He called over the running water, "Do you remember anything?"

"Not sure yet," she answered. "It makes my head hurt."

"That's probably because you haven't had water in almost a day," he said, once again crawling onto her bed and handing her the water.

"I remember not wanting to leave without you and feeling stressed."

"Anything else?"

Larken looked at the man that stretched out beside her. She took a sip, knowing that she needed to ask him something, but couldn't remember what. Her head felt full of cotton and she was having a hard time remembering what happened yesterday morning, let alone last week. "Not really."

"Just drink your water, you'll remember something eventually." He reached for her communicator and handed it to her. "You better message Wardell. He's been worried about you."

Larken froze, remembering. She eyed him and took the device. Setting it in her lap, she said, "There was something I wanted to ask you."

"Were you wanting to run off into the sunset? Because that's not my style."

Larken huffed a laugh. "And what is *your style?*"

"Punch out the groom, steal the girl, and then—"

"Ride off into the sunset on a hoverbike?"

Delvon cracked a smile. "Well, I guess it's sort of my style."

Larken laughed but stopped when it hurt her head. She gulped down some more water, and then said, "No. I was wondering if you had a brother, actually."

Delvon went still. He closed his eyes and sighed before saying, "I knew that idiot would get me into trouble."

"So, you do?"

"Aye."

"And I met him."

"Yes, love. You've met him."

"So does that mean—"

"Drink your water," he interrupted, purposely not looking in the direction of the camera.

She complied and then asked, "Do the two of you get along?"

"What do you mean *get along?*"

Larken chose her next words very carefully, knowing that if she activated the cuff Delvon gave her, the Manor security team would know. "Do the two of you share any interests?"

He smirked, giving her that look that said he forgot how clever she could be. "For the most part. He prefers fishing over hunting though."

Larken understood. Delvon wanted to be on the frontlines, going after the prey; his brother liked sitting back and waiting for the fight to come to him. She took another drink and asked, "So if you like hunting, why didn't you go at the beginning of the Summer?"

"How do you know I didn't?"

Even though there had been many men that hadn't taken off their helmets, Larken felt like she would have known if he had been there. He smirked at her again, turning their conversation into a game, waiting for her to take her turn. Polishing off the rest of the water, she said, "You brag about the smallest things. I'm sure I would have heard if you got a big kill."

He grinned. "You're right. I didn't go." Sighing, he put his hands behind his head and relaxed. "I had other job-related responsibilities."

"Such as?" she asked, hitting the ball back into his court.

"I was a high-up security guard before I became your babysitter, you know."

She only laughed, and this time it didn't hurt her head, but her shoulder was making up for it. "Yes, we all know I ruined your life."

Delvon grabbed her hand, and she looked into his grey eyes. They were the softest she had ever seen them. He took a deep breath and forced out, "That's not true, love. You've given me hope for tomorrow."

Larken's eyes burned, and she knew that he would never be this open or honest with her ever again. His words twisted her heart, and she remembered what Shadric had said. She thought she might be sick, feeling like the world was waiting on her to be something she wasn't ready for. Larken wanted to protest, tell Delvon that they had all made a huge mistake, that they had chosen the wrong girl. But he didn't look at her the way Shadric had. Delvon didn't have bright hope in his features, only steely determination, and that was a look Larken could understand. She didn't know if she could make things better like Shadric seemed to believe, but she knew that she had what it took to stop her mother. It was all she could offer; she could convince them to pick a different Luminary later.

Larken sighed, and then sent her brother a quick message, telling him that she had woken up and that she felt fine. While she did that, Delvon messaged Ezra. The medic wasted no time coming into her room and setting up the portable bench he used when she couldn't leave her room. He quickly adjusted her, gave her an injection, and checked her vitals. When Ezra was satisfied, he packed up his things and left, but only after telling her to message him again if she needed something.

Stumbling, Larken made it to the bathroom just before it registered that she was still wearing the same clothes as the day before. Stripping, she readied herself for the day and pulled on her robe once she was out of the shower. The warm water had her body moving more fluidly, and she felt less muddled.

Opening the bathroom door, she found Delvon pretending to doze on the bed. She knew he would be at her side in an instant and wondered if the man was ever able to relax. With still no sign of her android, Larken asked, "Where's Estelle?"

"Getting familiar with your new team."

"They're already here?"

"Yup."

Larken groaned; meeting a bunch of new people was the last thing she wanted to do today. Well, that wasn't quite true, wedding planning and spending time with Dominic were lower on the list, but still...

Walking into the closet, she pulled on whatever was in reach. Kaki capris and an elbow-length shirt that boasted fat cream and coral stripes that Larken hoped matched. She looked everywhere for her sandals, but couldn't find them. Peeking her head out of the closet, she asked, "Delvon, do you know where my shoes are?"

"Which ones?" His voice had a bored tone, and she couldn't help a small laugh. She had had more excitement on base than she did here, and instead of protecting her from murderers, Delvon was helping her track down her shoes.

"The leather sandals."

"The ones under your bed?"

"Under the bed?"

"That's what I said."

Larken left the closet and stopped next to Delvon. Crouching down, she looked under the bed and found her sandals waiting for her. "How did they get under here?"

"Maybe you left them there last night?"

"No, I would have left them in the closet when I changed." But she hadn't changed, and she didn't know why. Standing with the sandals in hand, she asked, "What happened last night?"

"*I told you,*" Delvon huffed like she was being thick on purpose. "Braves drugged you."

"No, I mean, how did I get home?"

"Oh, one of your new team members went and got you."

Larken still felt like she was missing something, something important. Pulling on her sandals, she asked, "Why would Vallen send one of them to get me and not you?"

"Good question, why don't you go ask him?"

"Why don't you stop keeping secrets and tell me what's really going on?"

"Just go to the sitting room," he grumbled and then rolled over onto his side. "I'm on break."

"Why are you taking your break in my bed?" she scoffed.

"What kind of boyfriend would I be if I didn't sleep in your bed?"

"The *normal* kind."

Sighing, Delvon pushed up off of her bed. "Do you want me to go with you, is that it?"

Larken took a comb to her hair and then braided it. "I don't care what you do."

Delvon was behind her in moments, wrapping his arms around her. "I'll go with you."

"And if I don't like them?"

"I doubt you won't, but if you don't, I'll kick them all out."

"Good." Larken nodded at herself in the mirror, ignoring the ring that sat on her vanity. "I'm ready."

The two left her room, and she could immediately hear the loud music and laughter spilling from her sitting room. Estelle's barks punctuated the air every now and then, and Larken's nerves ebbed a little. If Estelle liked them, then they couldn't be that bad.

Delvon pulled the door open for her, and she screamed as a rogue dart flew towards her eye. Crouching, Larken covered the back of her neck as the dart flew over her head and clattered against the bright tiles in the hall behind her. People laughed, and a familiar woman's voice called, "You dumb hick, how can you be so bad at darts when you're a sharpshooter?"

Larken's head shot up at the words *dumb hick*, not believing what she had heard. Standing so fast she almost fell, Larken took in the room before her. Loxly, Hinlee, and Levi all grinned at her from the dartboard; Jodi sat on one of the couches across from Candy and Carl with Estelle resting in her lap; and Brecker reclined in an armchair with his communicator, no doubt reading a mystery. Tears welled in her eyes as she took everyone in, and she looked over the room again.

Turning, Larken ran for the training field, knowing that that's where she would find him. Her sandals clapped against the tiles, threatening to slip and slide as she ran. Delvon didn't follow her, and a single tear escaped her left eye. She couldn't believe it, *wouldn't* believe it, until she saw him.

Pushing open the door harder than she needed to, Larken stumbled out into the open. The warm autumn sun shone down on her, and Larken stilled, chest tight with disbelief. She waited, trying to calm her rapidly beating heart. Larken looked over the field, but couldn't see anything. Her heart fell, thinking that she had made a mistake, that he had stayed behind. She hugged her middle, feeling sick, and made up her mind to go back inside.

Just then, something big caught her eye and Larken turned. Running out from behind an excessively large rose bush, *he* saw her and slowed to a stop. Larken stared, openmouthed and not believing her eyes. He heaved, sucking in air as sweat dripped from his face. She took a step toward him, and then another. Then, she broke into a run as a sob escaped her. Not caring that he was drenched in sweat, Larken leaped into his arms, tears spilling from her eyes. He spun when he caught her, holding her close.

"*You came,*" she rasped, throat almost too tight to speak.

Soren didn't say anything, only tightened his arms around her.

CHAPTER 20

L arken was back where she belonged, and Soren wondered how he could have ever let her go. The night before, she hadn't been herself. Larken had said things that she never would have if she had been in her right mind. But this…this was so much better. She was herself again, and she still ran to him like he hadn't abandoned her all those weeks ago. Larken should be mad at him; it's what he deserved. He had been a fool, scared that she would realize that she didn't need him, just like it scared him to realize how much he might need her.

She smelled different, and he immediately missed the grapefruit. The scent fit her perfectly, and it felt like part of her was now missing. Something ran down his neck, and he couldn't tell if it was his sweat or her tears; he only knew that when her feet touched the ground and she pulled away, it was too soon.

Larken looked up at him, his hands still on her waist, not ready to let go just yet. She brought her hands up to her face, wiping at her tears. Laughing, she said, "Look at me, crying like an idiot. I must still be messed up from last night."

Soren's hands tightened. "So they told you?"

"Delvon did when he came to check on me, yeah."

"Are you—" Soren clamped his mouth shut, feeling more

exposed out in the training field than he ever had at base. Larken raised an eyebrow, waiting for him to finish. Thinking for a moment, he asked, "Are you okay with him here?"

"Who? Delvon?" Her lips twitched a little. "Yeah. He reminds me of you, actually."

"How?" Soren frowned, not believing that he could have anything in common with the man that had held her a gunpoint so casually.

"He's grumpy too."

Soren looked at her for a good minute before scoffing.

Larken laughed, making her teal eyes dance. They looked bluer than he remembered, clearer. "Let's go inside," she murmured. "There's a lot we need to talk about."

Soren nodded, and he followed her back into the Manor. The cool air felt good on his skin, and he wondered how Larken could stand working out in this heat every single day. He hadn't even finished a full workout, and he already wanted to take a cold shower and sleep for the rest of the afternoon. They paused before the sitting room door, and Larken peeked her head around the doorframe. Soren wondered why she didn't just walk in, but then he noticed a dart on the floor, and he assumed that that had something to do with it.

Still leery, she entered and he followed. Everyone grinned at the two of them, and Larken gasped as she looked at the dartboard. Following her gaze, Soren chuckled a little as she asked, "Who did that?"

"Loxly," Hinlee, Brecker, and Levi answered at the same time.

Larken walked over, demanding, "What, almost blinding the real thing wasn't good enough?"

Everyone laughed as the sharpshooter sheepishly rubbed at the back of his neck. "Sorry, Little Bird. I didn't do it on purpose."

Someone had stuck a paper photograph of Larken and Braves to the dartboard, and even though Braves's half of the picture held most of the darts, one had found its way to the middle of Larken's face.

"If it makes you feel better, we made him add an extra 300 points for it," Brecker offered, grinning.

"I suggested a million, but Brecker thought that was *excessive*," Hinlee said, her smile just as bright.

Larken pulled the dart free and dropped it onto the billiards table. It thudded against the felt, and she made her way to one of the couches. Larken took the open spot next to Delvon, leaving Soren to drop to her other side. Hinlee watched him, her eyes shining with unspoken words that Soren pretended not to understand. The stylist, Carl, looked between the three of them. He opened his mouth, then a woman with red hair elbowed him in the side, face impassive.

Soren looked at Larken and found her facing Delvon. He smirked at her and pulled her to his side. Kissing her temple, he murmured, "No need to be shy, love. They'll find out about us eventually."

Her eye roll was practically audible as she snuggled into his side. Something snapped in Soren and he almost pulled Larken to him instead, but General Maxwell chose that moment to walk into the sitting room. They all looked to him, his eyes on Delvon and Larken. He sighed deeply and then ordered, "Everyone to the hangar."

They stood as one and filed out the door. General Maxwell grabbed Larken's elbow and muttered that she didn't have to go if she didn't want to, but she only shook her head and joined the rest of the group. Estelle barked happily, stopping in front of General Maxwell. He frowned at the android. "You stay and make sure no one goes through Larken's things."

The pup whined, and then trotted to Larken's door. Sitting, the android snarled, warning whoever might come too close to stay away.

"Great guard dog," General Maxwell muttered. "Has a built-in camera."

"Perfect for identifying assailants," Soren agreed, suddenly fonder of the small, white monstrosity.

Larken had fallen into step with Hinlee and Loxly, and the sight of the three of them walking together again made Soren smile. Soren didn't care that General Maxwell saw his emotions, and he didn't mind that Loxly draped an arm around her shoulders; Soren was just happy to be near her again. She turned her face, laughing at something Hinlee said, and it squeezed his heart. He hadn't realized how empty he had felt after she left. His anger hadn't come anywhere near to filling the hole that grew each day they were apart, and now he thanked Maxim that he could finally breathe again.

General Maxwell talked with him the whole way, and Soren forced himself to pay attention. He wanted to do his best, prove that the General hadn't made a mistake by choosing him. It was so different from when he had first taken up the mantle of Larken's protector. Then he had only cared about her ability to do what she was told and how she might jeopardize Squad 19. Now, Soren only cared about her safety. He didn't know the exact moment everything had changed, but he knew that if Fletcher's Second in Command were to harass Larken now, she wouldn't even have the chance to break his nose because Soren would beat the guy half to death himself.

They reached the hangar, and it had the same bright tiles and white walls that made up the halls of the Manor. Each aircraft looked luxurious, even the military-level ones. General Maxwell moved to the front of the large group, leading them all to a sleek silver and cream-colored aircraft that looked like it could comfortably sit twenty-five people. It stood out against all the other black aircraft and clearly didn't belong. Soren looked over at Loxly, who gaped at the thing openmouthed.

Larken snorted, nudging him with her hip. "You gonna cry?"

"I might," he muttered, unable to take his eyes off the thing. "What is it?"

"The Harpy," General Maxwell answered. "I had it commissioned myself."

They all understood the words he didn't say. *This aircraft has no affiliation with Cornella whatsoever.*

General Maxwell typed in a passcode and then hit a black button on the side. The door opened, extending a set of black steps to the ground. Soren immediately remembered the day that he had watched Larken try to get herself out of the *Arsene*, the way she had hung herself off the side of the aircraft.

"What?" Larken demanded to his right.

Soren looked down at her, finding her teal eyes narrowed in a suspicious glare. He tried to frown to hide his small smirk, but he failed. "Nothing."

"Liar," she huffed, crossing her arms and looking ahead.

Unable to help himself, he asked, "Need help getting up there?"

Larken scoffed and stomped off, but not before he could see her blush. Chuckling, Soren followed her up the steps. Everyone had already found a seat, and Larken paused in the doorway. She stopped breathing and then took a step back onto Soren's feet. Jumping, she turned, and he could see the apology already forming on her lips. He reached for her cheek but gently grabbed her shoulder instead.

"You alright?"

Her breaths came in little gasps. "I thought I could—"

Soren grabbed her other shoulder, trying to get her to calm down. "We can go back."

"No, I—"

"We can go back, Larken."

"Delvon," General Maxwell barked behind him. "Take Larken back to her room."

"Yes, sir," Delvon said, standing.

"We'll go too," offered the girl with the red hair. She pulled Carl to his feet, saying, "We need to start shopping anyway."

Larken gripped Soren's forearms, clearly not hearing a single word over her panic. He slipped one hand to her neck and she looked up at him. Tears lined her eyes, reflecting the memory of the night of the opera. Delvon pried one of her hands from his forearm, and Soren jerked his face in the bodyguard's direction. He almost punched him; Larken wouldn't be having this panic attack if his buddies hadn't kept shooting her out of the sky. This was all *his* fault, and Soren would cut off his own hand before he let the man responsible for this take her anywhere.

"Larken, love," Delvon murmured. "We're going back. Come on."

Larken looked away from Soren and met the bodyguard's eyes. He reached for her again, and this time she let go of Soren willingly. All Soren could do was glare as Delvon led her off the *Harpy*. Carl and the girl followed, sharing dark looks. Soren glared at General Maxwell. He wanted to be the one that Larken could rely on. He owed it to her, he promised.

General Maxwell shook his head, slapping a matching black button that had the stairs retracting. "He already knows what's going on, you don't. You need to be here, Deckard."

Knowing that the man was right, Soren dropped to an open seat. The cream-colored leather and luxurious cab were lost on him as he fumed. No one said anything, their hearts all with their hurting squad member. None of them wanted to leave Larken. They wanted to go back, but no one moved. Loxly looked the worst but perked up some when General Maxwell asked if he wanted to learn how to fly the *Harpy*. He disappeared into the cockpit, and soon the beast fired up.

Trusting that General Maxwell would tell the sharpshooter where to go, Hinlee leaned into Brecker and murmured, "I knew she wouldn't like flying anymore, but I didn't think it would be that bad. We have to do something."

"And what would we do?" Levi demanded. "Have Loxly fly her around in a field again?"

Hinlee got defensive and snarled, "At least I'm trying! I can't just sit back and watch her suffer!"

"You think that's what I want?" Levi sneered. "You think I enjoy seeing her like this?"

"Guys," Brecker said, trying to stop the brewing argument. "We can work something out. It'll be okay."

"And what if we have to whisk her away, Brecker?" Hinlee

asked. "How will we get her into the air? We need to help her get over this."

"This isn't something we'll be able to fix." Everyone stopped and stared at Soren. "You weren't there; you didn't see her."

No one said anything, just stared at the floor silently. Soren looked at the houses that flew by underneath them. He was there again, holding her as she shrieked in his ear. He could remember wishing that he would go deaf if it meant that she would survive the crash. She shook worse than a scared animal, and even after all these weeks, he still had nightmares about it. Sometimes he would wake up before they crashed; other times he didn't and he had to pull her dead body from the wreckage.

"Well, maybe we don't get her back in the air," Hinlee said. "Maybe we give her something good to think about when she feels that way."

"Like what?" Brecker asked, looking at her skeptically.

"We never got to throw her a party, and I still have her gift."

"You want to have a party?" Levi rose an eyebrow.

"Sure! You can cook, Brecker and Loxly can help me decorate, and Soren can sit in the corner and brood about it."

Soren glared at her.

"What? You want to make the cake? Sorry, but I like Larken *alive*."

Levi and Brecker snorted, and even Soren couldn't help his smirk. It was true, he was the worst out of all of them and they all knew it. Larken didn't. She had never sampled any of his cooking, and he would prefer it to stay that way.

"Does anyone have a problem with the party?"

When no one said anything, Hinlee started bouncing ideas off of them. She talked about how they should decorate the sitting room, how they could keep Larken busy while they did it, and what they should have to eat. She pulled out her communicator and started taking notes. They agreed on lasagna for dinner, blue and white decorations, and a bitter lemon tart instead of cake for dessert.

Brecker asked about ice cream, but Soren reminded them that she preferred sorbet.

Hinlee smiled wickedly and then said, "Decks, you'll be in charge of stealing her communicator so we can play her favorite music."

"And how exactly am I supposed to do that?" he demanded, forcing his cheeks not to heat as he thought of the device that she always kept in her back pocket.

"I'm sure you'll think of something," she mused as they started their descent.

The *Harpy* hit the ground gently, and the engine died. Loxly jumped into the cab, grinning and saying, "You guys gotta try this thing!"

General Maxwell appeared and ushered them off the aircraft. They spilled out onto a vast field, much like the one that Soren and Larken had crashed into. Soren looked around them and then noticed a fair-sized metal door in the ground. Assuming that that was where they were meant to go, he made his way over to it. General Maxwell beat him there, reaching the bunker first and crouching down. Soren watched him punch in the code, and then the General looked at him. "You are to tell no one these numbers. Understood?"

"Yes, sir."

"Good." He stood, lifting the door as he did. "Everyone in."

One by one they climbed into the stale darkness. Little blue emergency lights were lit, so they had a general idea of where to stand. General Maxwell climbed down the ladder with familiarity and then smacked the wall. Lights turned on and the door fell shut, a loud clicking telling them that they were locked in.

Pushing his way to the front, General Maxwell led them down a few different halls. Doors with little windows showed cabins, each filled with two bunk beds. This place was old, much older than the outdated lights suggested. Soren could tell what had been updated and what had belonged to a time long forgotten just by looking at it.

They filed into a room that held a long table, fifteen chairs, and a large screen on one wall. Everything in the room looked to be brand new, and Soren took a seat without a word. General Maxwell sat at the head of the table and looked at each and every one of them.

"What is discussed in here is not to be repeated in the outside world."

They nodded.

"Welcome to the Faithfuls," he said. "From now on, you are to refer to me as Vallen. When we get back, you will tell people that we were doing team-building exercises."

"And what are we really doing?" Levi asked, his eyes more alive than Soren had ever seen them.

"What we will really be doing today, Mr. Jameson, is discussing the plan to get Larken out of her engagement and back to Camp."

"And then?" Brecker asked.

"And then, Mr. Wilton, we start a revolution."

CHAPTER 21

I will wear whatever you tell me to.

Larken had never regretted saying anything more than she did in that moment. After having that mortifying panic attack in front of everyone, Larken had decided to lock herself away in her room for the rest of the day. She had cuddled with Estelle, finished the book she had started on her communicator, and spent a few hours catching up on a net drama. The next morning, feeling rejuvenated and ready to take on the world, she had the brilliant idea to leave the Manor and get away from it all for a little bit. Now, she stood in a bridal boutique as Carl slowly descended into insanity.

She had assured him that it didn't matter what she wore, that there was no way she would be happy on her wedding day, and he could pick out whatever he wanted. Carl had gladly taken up the challenge, but he had slowly started to realize the weight she had placed on his shoulders. He looked to be cracking slightly under the pressure and had yelled at the store clerks more than once. Candy did what she could to help, but it seemed Carl was determined to suffer alone.

The bridal boutique seemed impossibly big, crammed with dresses of all colors and sizes. Mannequins stood, modeling the latest designs and looking just as lifeless as Larken felt. They didn't want to be there, and neither did she.

He had narrowed the whole boutique down to five dresses and seriously considered designing one himself. They had met with a few designers before, but Carl hadn't liked any of them. Larken didn't even have time to protest before he chased them off, not that she would; she hadn't liked any of them either. But if anyone could design the perfect dress for her, it would be Carl. The only problem was that she didn't want the perfect dress because she wasn't going to marry someone she loved. Not that she was in love with anyone, but there were certain men that she would have preferred to Dominic.

Larken chased away thoughts of grumbly Captains and blue-eyed singers and turned her attention back to the stylist. Carl's hair was mussed and the sight of it tugged at Larken's heart. The man who had always been so put together was fraying at the ends, and Larken couldn't help but feel responsible.

"Okay," he huffed, and Larken perked up. "I think we're ready for you to start trying them on." Carl turned on the four clerks that had hovered around their small group like a flock of vultures. "Go double-check that all of the windows are covered and that the cameras are turned off. If any pictures of her are leaked, we'll have to find another dress somewhere else."

The clerks jumped into action, afraid of what losing the Hale association would do to their business. With them out of the way, Carl grabbed the first garment bag from the rack. He led Larken to the changing room, then pulled the curtain closed, and Larken stripped off her clothes. Carl unzipped the bag and gently took out what looked like a fluffy white mess. He held the gown open for her, and Larken almost fell trying to get into it without stepping on the skirts. Once the bodice covered her torso, Carl disappeared behind her and started lacing it up.

Larken felt constricted and choked. She had never really pictured herself dating, hadn't even had her first kiss, and now she was trying on her first wedding dress. She would always remember this moment, and she would always remember how unhappy she was. Being Cornella's second child, Larken had thought that she would someday marry for love, if she married at all. What was supposed to be one of the happiest days of her life—picking out the dress she would wear as she tied herself to her perfect match—was now tainted by annoyance and a breaking heart.

Larken didn't realize her eyes were burning until Carl asked, "How does the front look?"

"Fine," she croaked.

She felt his hands stop, and then he came back around. Grabbing her hands, he waited until she met his eyes before saying, "You are a *warrior*."

"What does that even mean?" she scoffed, sniffing back her tears. Larken could feel everything inside her falling apart. Vallen said he had a plan, but the wedding was exactly twelve days away, and instead of running away, she was dress shopping.

"It means that you're brave. You stay and fight, even when others want to give up. I knew it the moment I saw your snarled hair, and you called me a *'prissy Star.'*"

Larken laughed bitterly at her first impression of Carl. If someone would have told her then how close they would become, she would have laughed in their face.

"You are *not* the first person to marry someone they didn't love." Larken nodded, dropping her head again. "But," Carl put his finger under her chin and had her meet his eyes once more. "You very well could be the first that has people standing by you, wanting to help however they can."

Don't give up hope. We're working on it.

Carl didn't say the words, but she heard them just the same. She nodded, squared her shoulders, and let out a slow breath.

"There's my girl." Carl went back to lacing her up and finished with one last tug. "There, all ready. What do you say we go show the others?"

"Go show Delvon my wedding dress?" she muttered. "I can't think of anything else I would rather do."

"That's the spirit!"

Carl yanked back the curtain and pulled her out despite her efforts to stay where she was.

Carl ushered her up onto a little dais, and Larken was forced to look at herself in three different floor-length mirrors as all of the clerks gasped. They talked over each other, telling her how pretty she looked and how the dress was made for her, but one glare had them shutting up. Candy suggested that they go look for some flats the exact shade of ivory as the dress. They quickly disappeared, not wanting to risk the sale by upsetting Larken.

Larken helped Carl fan out the skirts around her, and even bending that little bit restricted her breathing enough that she had to stop. Standing straight, Larken looked at the gown. The sweetheart neckline squashed her breasts together uncomfortably, and she pulled at it. Carl smacked her hand away, and she glared at him. Hundreds of little beads covered the bodice, making it sparkle and scratch against the inside of her arms. Larken didn't know what to do with her hands. The rough tulle of the skirts fluffed out every-where, and she didn't want to touch it and risk losing her hands in the fabric. She crossed her arms, not knowing what else to do, and narrowed her eyes at Delvon as he chuckled.

"Nice bra straps," Delvon teased. "The black adds just the right amount of elegance."

Larken turned, ready to jump on him and wipe that stupid grin off his face, but Carl grabbed her waist. "Not in this dress you don't! And you," he rounded on the bodyguard, "try not to make her want to murder you. You'll be the one paying if she gets blood on the dress."

Larken snarled, and Delvon blew her a kiss. She rolled her eyes. "I hate this dress," she grumbled.

"I thought you didn't have an opinion," Carl mused.

"Well, this one is too tight and I hate it. I'll need something more breathable if Delvon is forced to make good on his promise."

It was Delvon's turn to glare, but he said nothing, only running his tongue over his teeth. Larken tried to take a step, but then tripped on the skirt. Carl caught her, eyes wild. "Did you rip it?"

"No, I *didn't rip it*," she seethed as she grabbed an armload of the tulle.

She marched back to the changing room, trying to cool her anger. It wasn't Carl's or Delvon's fault that she had to spend her day this way. But that didn't stop her from wanting to pick a fight. Part of her wished that Carl hadn't held her back and that she could have had a full-out brawl with Delvon. She would have destroyed the dress, but at least she would feel better.

Carl followed her in, another garment bag in hand. He hung it up and got to work on her laces. Air flooded her lungs and she said, "No more laces."

"Anything else?" Carl asked, perking up some.

"No tulle."

"Right. What else?" Carl looked relieved, finally getting some direction.

"You know what I like, Carl. Just look for a dress like that. I don't care if it's designer, expensive, or *whatever*. I just need something that I can—"

"Run away in?" he offered quietly.

Larken sighed, but she couldn't deny his words. "Yeah."

"I'll have Candy help me if this next dress doesn't work out. Hold on." Carl grabbed the garment bag he had just brought in and disappeared.

Larken was left standing there, clutching the dress to herself to keep covered. She couldn't help but wonder if Carl had played her a little, picking a dress he knew she would hate in order to get some feedback. It seemed like something he would do. Not only that, but it would be that much more amazing when he showed her the dress she would undoubtedly pick.

Carl reappeared seconds later, smiling. "I think this one might work. *And* no laces."

Larken offered him a smile. "Sorry, Carl, I—"

He shook his head. "You can be as prickly as you want. I promise I've heard, and been called, worse. This is my job."

"Still..."

Carl wouldn't hear any more of it. He motioned for her to give him the dress, and Larken waited for him to hang up the gown. Carl pulled the new one from the second bag, and just looking at it, Larken knew she already liked it better. Maybe they wouldn't be spending the whole day there as she had feared. Carl helped her into it, and she smiled slightly.

"Like it?"

"It's *nice*," she admitted.

"I'll take it!" Carl beamed.

The skirts felt much lighter than the last dress, and Larken risked taking a few steps after Carl finished buttoning it up. Her upper back was completely exposed, the buttons fastening below her waist and at the collar around her neck. The bodice looked like its back had been completely cut out, and a sheer fabric rose from the sweetheart neckline to form the collar. Sparse lace patterns decorated the see-through fabric on her chest, and it continued from the collar in thick straps down over her shoulder blades, leaving her exposed skin in the shape of a diamond.

Nodding, she looked up at Carl, and he asked, "Ready to show the others?"

"Yup. Let's get this over with."

Carl pulled back the curtain, and Larken walked out of the changing room on her own this time. Stepping up onto the dais, she looked at her reflection. She smiled when she saw that her pearl necklace looked invisible under the lace. Larken could keep that little bit of Soren with her and no one would ever know. She brushed her hands on her skirts and then turned to Delvon and Candy.

"What do you think?"

Delvon smirked, and it make him look like he had figured out more than he should have. He confirmed Larken's suspicions by saying, "Looks easy to move around in."

She shot him a warning glare and he chuckled. Candy looked between the three of them, trying to piece together the unspoken words. "Well, I like it," Candy said, cutting into the silence. "Are there shoes?"

"I want flats," Larken said, lifting up the front of the dress and exposing her bare feet.

"Easy now, love," Delvon teased. "I already got an eyeful of your bra. Try to leave something to the imagination."

Instead of snarling, Larken dropped the skirts and laughed. She stepped off the dais and took the empty chair next to him. She reclined slightly, putting her feet up on his lap. Carl wandered away muttering, *"Where did those clerks go?"*

Candy turned on Larken and Delvon. "Please tell me that you're not planning what I think you are."

"Who are you to stand in the way of true love?" Delvon mocked.

Candy only sighed and pushed herself to her feet, off to go help Carl. Larken looked at Delvon to find his grey eyes already on her. She raised an eyebrow and asked, "You plan on keeping your promise then?"

Delvon grabbed her left hand and kissed her ring before saying, "I do."

CHAPTER 22

A rmed with only a bandanna and strict orders not to mess everything up, Soren made his way to the training field. Larken and her entourage had gotten back a little over an hour ago, and General—*Vallen* had put her straight to work. He thought that the party was an excellent idea and had a hard time not smiling whenever he looked at any of them. Vallen told them that he knew he made the right decision when he selected Squad 19 for Larken, and it seemed to be almost too much for the General. Soren could understand; the man had watched Larken grow up not being wanted by her family. Now, she had them. It reminded Soren of the promise he had made to himself. The one where he would tell her everything he had kept from her…and still hadn't.

The late afternoon sun warmed the small training field as Soren walked out onto it. It was nothing special compared to the other fields around the Manor, but it provided enough space to get work done. An open area of flat grey rock inside a box of yellow rose bushes provided a perfect place to spar, run drills, or do whatever else Vallen had thought up for Larken. Outside the bushes ran a fair-sized track. The hard dirt had been packed down over the years, and Soren wondered how many times Larken had run around the yellow flowers in her life. Off to the side, close to the Manor, sat a few sunbathing chairs that he was sure Carl and Candy made more use of than Vallen and Larken.

The music that blared from unseen speakers reminded Soren of his impossible task. He didn't know if it was better that she didn't have her communicator on her or not. On her, he would risk getting caught trying to pickpocket it. Finding it lying somewhere would make it easier for him to simply take it, but the music would be what gave him away. She would notice if the speakers just stopped spitting out their current melody.

Shadric Barlow wasn't playing; instead, it was loving, slow tune. A steel guitar twanged a song that had probably been lost to the ages until Larken had found it. Soren stepped onto the packed dirt and made his way to the middle of the field, curious as to what manner of cardio she could be doing to such a slow song. The man sang, begging his lady love not to leave him alone for the night, and Soren couldn't help a small smile. Her taste in music was certainly diverse, he would give her that.

Passing the bushes, Soren found himself transfixed. It was like that day he had caught her dancing all over again. Only this time, instead of dancing, Larken moved from one fierce-looking pose to another. She wasn't stretching, like a lot of women had done at base; that would have been worse to stumble upon. No, Larken looked to be fighting in slow motion. One second, she crouched slightly, fists pulled into her sides palm up. The next, she turned and slowly kicked out at the air. The music pushed her movements as she reached out, and then pulled back again.

Soren thought of water, of the ocean. Her movements were sure and strong, and she breathed in through her nose, exhaling through parted lips. He'd never seen anything like it before. He stood, watching her for a moment. Without even looking at him, she mused, "It's said that these movements are the secret to everlasting life."

"It is now?"

"The story goes that a man went on a quest for the elixir of life, but instead had a vision. He concluded that the elixir wasn't so much an elixir, but movements that would open the body's path-ways, granting them good health and a balanced spirit."

"Very interesting."

She finished just as the song did, and then turned to him. "Did you need something?"

"No," he lied.

She didn't look like she believed him. Larken brought her right arm over her head and bent it like she was trying to scratch her back. Then she grabbed her elbow and pulled. A small *pop* sounded, and she sighed as she rolled her shoulder.

"How has your shoulder been?"

"Good. It helps when I don't have to break in new mattresses all the time." She walked past him and then reached for a water bottle he hadn't noticed before. Grabbing her communicator as well, she tossed it to him as she took a drink.

Momentarily panicking, thinking that he had been found out, he asked, "What's this for?"

"I have a message on there that I wanted to talk to you about."

Soren's stomach fell. He'd barely said twelve words, and she already knew. Hinlee was going to kill him. Looking through the messages, he found the one with a number that wasn't saved in her communicator and opened it.

Happy birthday, my little songbird. I have something for you. Please meet me at the abandoned theater at the edge of the District. General Maxwell knows where.

Soren breathed deeply through his nose, trying to hide his quickly beating heart. The message wasn't party-related. If he managed not to mess up the next few minutes, it would stay a surprise.

"He messaged again, saying he wants to meet tomorrow," Larken said softly, now standing much closer than Soren had realized.

"Are you going to meet him?" he asked.

"I—" She looked away. "I was hoping that you would go with me." Larken took a deep breath and then rushed, "Vallen is busy and I don't really want Delvon to see that part of my life, and, well, now that you're here, I thought—"

"I'll go."

Larken looked up and met his eyes, her teal depths threatening to drown him. "Really?"

Soren nodded, suddenly unable to speak. Now would be the perfect time to tell her. Now, when they were alone, when she had reached out to him again after everything he had done. But his jaw locked, his self-preservation not letting him speak. She had proven herself to him over and over again. Why couldn't he just reach out to her?

Her smile melted him and she nodded. "Thank you."

Soren put the communicator in his pocket, and if she noticed, she didn't care. He followed her back to her room and then waited patiently for her to shower and get ready. She had started talking to him about shopping with Carl, shouting through the door of her closet about how annoying it had been. He listened, trying hard to stay put. The urge to track Braves down and murder him was almost too strong. He hadn't seen Braves since he punched him that night in the club, and Soren wondered if the Star might be avoiding him.

Larken walked out of her closet, hair snarled and still dripping onto her shoulders. She wore a nice pumpkin-colored T-shirt and brown pants that cut off halfway down her calves. The colors looked good on her, and he smiled when the pearl glinted in the light. She sat down at her vanity and took up a comb. Soren noticed the shell immediately and his breath caught. He wondered if she knew or if she thought it was a gift from Vallen.

"So, what are you thinking for dinner tonight? I was thinking something with pasta."

Perfect.

"Yeah, that sounds good."

"I'll have to ask Levi to help me though. I haven't cooked for this many people before."

"He'll do whatever you ask."

"Yeah. He makes a good big brother, doesn't he?"

"Anyone is big compared to you."

Larken threw the comb at him, and it bounced lamely off his chest. "I meant *older*, you jerk."

Soren grinned at her, causing her to laugh. Skies above, how he had missed that sound. He wished it was her laugh he dreamt about instead of her screams. "Right, sorry. Misunderstanding."

She quickly braided her hair and then pushed to her feet. "Well, then. Shall we?"

"One thing first."

She raised an eyebrow. "Oh?"

Soren pulled the bandanna from his pocket. "I have a surprise for you before we meet up with the others."

She looked at the navy cloth skeptically. "Sorry, I don't do blindfolds. Not since Liam locked me in a room with centipedes crawling everywhere."

Soren gaped and she shrugged. Then he asked, "Do you really think I would do that to you?"

"No, but you know how it is."

"If I promise that I'm only taking you down the hall, will you trust me?"

She sighed. "Fine, just get it over with."

Soren walked behind her and brought the bandanna up over her eyes. He didn't miss the way she stiffened when his thumb accidentally brushed against her neck or the way she stopped breathing. The scent of warm apples danced around him, and even though he liked her other shampoo better, he was suddenly starving for the red fruit.

Once he finished tying the blindfold, Soren leaned into her. Lips millimeters from her ear he asked, "Ready?"

She sucked in her bottom lip, biting it as she nodded.

"Good, let's go."

Soren walked around her and grabbed both of her hands. She gripped his tightly, letting him know that even though she trusted him, she was still a little nervous. He thought back to the moment when she had opened up Estelle and how wary of the gift she had been. Soren had wondered then if Liam had once given her a snake, but if he was willing to lock her in a room with creepy crawlies, maybe Soren had been too kind in his assumption.

Larken stumbled and Soren dropped her hands, grabbing her waist instead. She grinned and he returned her smile, even though she couldn't see it. "You okay?" he asked.

"Yeah." She laughed lightly. "You probably didn't miss having to protect me from breaking my ankles."

I missed everything about you...

Soren almost said it, he *wanted* to say it. Instead, he opened his mouth and, "Only you could break your ankle barefoot," spilled out.

She laughed again and placed her hands on his forearms. Releasing her waist, Soren found her hands again, her fingers brushing down the length of his forearms as he did. Soren was almost glad for the blindfold; he wasn't sure about how she would react to the look of confused desperation on his face. This was the most they had touched since that night she sought him out in the medic building.

Trying his best to make sure that she didn't trip or stumble again, Soren led her the rest of the way to her sitting room. Everyone watched them as they entered, and Hinlee gave him an approving smile. Delvon lay sprawled on one of the couches, and his grey eyes glinted with something that threatened to make Soren squirm. The bodyguard understood more than he let on, and that annoyed Soren more than it should have.

Soren tried to let go of Larken, but she gripped his hands tightly, silently asking him not to let go. Instead, Soren pulled one hand free and fished her communicator from his pocket. He tossed the device to Brecker, who caught it easily and passed it off to Hinlee. She messed with it for a few seconds, and Soren was grateful when the voice that spilled out of the invisible speakers around the room wasn't Shadric Barlow's.

Larken stiffened and Soren moved in closer. He pulled his other hand free, and she let him. Reaching up, he took the bandanna off, revealing her closed eyes. Her lashes fluttered and he whispered, "Keep them closed until I tell you."

Larken nodded and started nibbling on her bottom lip. Soren walked around behind her and put his hands on her waist. He told himself that the surprise might make her jump and she might trip, but even he didn't really believe that.

Leaning in close, he murmured, "Now."

Larken opened her eyes and gasped as she took in the room around her. Turquoise and white streamers hung everywhere, stretching from the ceiling to the walls, and midnight-colored balloons floated among them. Gifts had been piled onto the little coffee table, and the scent of baking lasagna wafted in from the communal kitchen on the other side of the wall.

Hinlee beamed and shouted over the music, "Surprise!"

Larken choked and then laughed. Rushing to the mechanic, she left Soren standing alone. He made his way to one of the couches, already exhausted. How he managed to not give anything away, he had no idea. He felt like Larken could tell what he was thinking just by looking at him, and Soren wondered if that had anything to do with his inability to speak around her. But if she already knew, then why couldn't he just tell her what he felt? Why couldn't he tell her that she was important, that she was everything that her mother refused to tell her?

Loxly pulled Larken to one of the couches and dumped a large gift bag onto her lap. Leaning back, the sharpshooter draped his arm over the back of the couch behind her. She leaned into him slightly, and Levi took the seat on her other side. Aside from Soren, those two had suffered the worst in her absence. Even he wanted to find a way to squeeze onto the couch with her, but Soren restrained himself. Vallen looked unnaturally comfortable in one of the armchairs, and Hinlee and Brecker crowded in next to Soren. Delvon got up, taking the free armchair so Carl, Candy, Jodi, and Medic Ezra could sit together. Soren caught the subtle glances between the two medics and smirked. *Pen-pals* might have been putting it lightly.

With urging from Loxly, Larken pulled the white tissue paper from the navy gift bag. Estelle barked playfully before hopping up onto Levi's lap and nipping at the paper. The white material got stuck on one of the android's canines, and her face scrunched up comically as she tried to free it. Larken pulled three clear tablets from the bag and tapped the top one. Three small pictures appeared that appeared inverted to Soren, and Larken beamed. She tapped the other two screens, one with four small pictures, the other with seven, and her smile only widened.

Leaning over to Loxly, she kissed his cheek. "Thank you, I've wanted to read these for a while.

"How do ya know they're from me?" he asked, grinning down at her.

"You used the same bag you brought your suit home in."

Loxly laughed and tapped her nose with a knuckle. "You're welcome, Little Bird."

The door flew open, and a small child Soren didn't recognize ran into the room. He held a pink box and almost tripped as he practically yelled, "Don't start without me, Sissy!"

Larken barely had time to hand Loxly the tablets before the child jumped up on her lap. Grinning, she wrapped her arms around him and asked, "Wardell, aren't you supposed to be in your evening lessons?"

The boy groaned before complaining, "Foreign language is so boring. Besides, everyone speaks the common tongue."

"It's not about communication," Larken chastised through her smile. "It's about learning culture."

"Culture is boring too."

She sighed and looked at Vallen. He pulled out his communicator and started tapping at it. Shaking her head, Larken asked, "Does Bailey at least know where you are?"

Wardell frowned. "No, I didn't want her to tell me I couldn't come." Then he offered up the box. "I even got you another present."

Larken took the box from him and opened it, revealing an assortment of salt covered chocolates. She smiled warmly at her brother. "Thank you, Wardell."

"You like them?"

"I love them."

"Good! I didn't know what your favorite was, so I asked your boyfriend."

Larken's brow crinkled in confusion and she looked to Soren. His heartrate picked up and he couldn't swallow, but he forced the panic away and shook his head. Her cheeks went pink and she turned her face back to Wardell. "You mean Delvon."

It was Wardell's turn to look confused. "Yeah. Isn't he your boyfriend?"

Larken, still pink, ruffled his hair. "You shouldn't go around saying that."

"Why not? The security guards outside my room said that you—"

"Which gift do you think I should open next?" she asked loudly, interrupting her brother.

Wardell slid off her lap, distracted by the presents, and Larken shot a withering glare at a chuckling Delvon. Her face had gone from an adorable pink to a deep red, and her glare only had the bodyguard's eyes dancing. Soren balled his fists. Wardell pushed the pink gift bag from Hinlee into his sister's hands, while Loxly rescued the box of chocolates from a curious Estelle.

Larken pulled a mint-blue dress from the bag, and Carl asked Hinlee about the dress as another gift was given to Larken. Hinlee explained that she found it on the Vendor and thought that Larken might need something to wear to service if she managed to find a tabernacle that she liked. Larken's lips twitched as Hinlee spoke. She pulled the lid off another box and fished out a ring shaped like a raindrop. Putting the ring on her right hand, she flexed her fingers, the silver catching the light, and she grinned at Brecker.

"Figured if you were going to keep punching guys, you might as well make it a little more memorable for them."

Larken barked a laugh as Soren's eyes narrowed at the dull point of the ring. Yes, one well-placed punch with that ring could definitely blind someone. Larken pulled another clear tablet from the box as well and tapped the screen. Grinning, she added it to the bag in Loxly's lap with the others. The dress had been passed down to Carl so he could get a better look at it, and Wardell grabbed Larken's hand. After a close inspection of the ring, he deemed it was suitable enough for his sister and handed her another gift.

Music played quietly in the background and Larken opened a thigh strap with seven tiny syringes resting side by side like bullets. Soren's stomach squirmed. Each one held a different concoction to counteract different poisons. Levi insisted that if she was going to keep getting shot at with infused bullets, these should help her. He said he trusted that she could memorize the different side effects of the possible infusions and which syringe would keep her alive.

Larken then opened a certificate that promised a massage at a nearby wellness spa from Ezra, special bullets from Vallen, the grapefruit and orange blossom shampoo and conditioner she had used at base from Carl and Candy, and a pair of black pumps from Jodi that Soren was surprised to see since Larken was so clumsy. Wardell crinkled his face at the shoes, but Larken narrowed her eyes at them. She looked up to the medic, who was smirking, and then pulled the heel off one of the pumps. Larken threw her head back and laughed at the hidden knife, pulling the shoe away from Wardell's suddenly more interested hands.

"Where did you find these?" Larken asked, putting the heel back in place.

"I had some help," Jodi answered, winking at Candy.

Candy grinned before saying, "The ones I bought are pink."

Wardell handed Larken another gift, pouting after Larken told him that her new shoes weren't toys. Soren watched her hands as she carefully tore off the black wrapping paper, exposing a dark canvas. Larken grinned at Delvon, her eyes sparkling.

Loxly peered over her shoulder at it, looking confused. She beamed at him. "Isn't it beautiful?" she asked.

"Sure," he offered. "Who doesn't love white dots?"

Levi snorted and Larken rolled her eyes. "They're *stars*, Loxly, not dots."

"Sure they are, Little Bird." The sharpshooter still didn't look convinced.

Larken turned the canvas around, showing everyone the smears of black, blue, and pink that were decorated with fifteen or so white dots. "It's the constellation Draca." She pointed at a small cluster. "This is his head." Larken then followed the long trail of stars with her finger. "And this is his body and tail."

"Where are his wings?" Wardell asked, looking at the canvas with wide eyes.

"You have to use your imagination," she said warmly. Soren was reminded of how good Larken had been with Jing and wondered again if she wanted children someday.

Wardell squinted at the painting, tilting his head. Larken looked to Delvon and mouthed a *thank you*. He nodded once and then grumbled, "I'm supposed to give you those flowers too."

Larken reached for the dried bouquet of lavender that had been bound with twine. Her face went pink again as she pulled free the note and read it. Loxly leaned into her, trying to see what it said, but she folded it again before he could. That didn't stop him from asking, "Did that say *secret admirer?*"

"*No,*" she insisted, going pinker and not sounding at all convincing.

"Come on, Little Bird. You obviously know who those weeds are from. Why won't you tell us?"

"Because it's none of your business," she shot back.

Larken glared at Delvon, and Soren could feel the unspoken conversation passing between the two of them. His hackles rose, not liking how close she was with the bodyguard. First, he held her at gunpoint; then, he *rescued* her from the *Harpy*. Soren was really starting to not like this guy, and the only thing that kept him from throwing punches was that Delvon was better than Braves.

Finally surrendering, Delvon rolled his eyes. "Look, love. I told him it was a bad idea, but he insisted."

"Well, then *you* can be the one to thank your hunting buddy."

He smirked. "I think he was hoping for more than a *thank you.*"

"Fine, pass along a kiss from me too then."

Delvon glared and Larken smirked. She added the bouquet to the growing pile on Loxly's lap as she stuffed the note into her pocket, and Loxly took the canvas and rested it against the side of the couch. Wardell held one last gift for his sister and Soren felt suddenly nervous. He wondered if she would like it or if she would think that it was stupid. Soren tried to think of what he could get her, and this was all his last-minute scrambling could come up with.

Larken took the black box from her brother, running her fingers over the smooth top. Estelle whimpered tiredly as she sniffed at it, making sure that it wasn't dangerous, like she had with all the other gifts. Larken scratched Estelle's head. "Good girl," she said. "Go take a nap."

Estelle wagged her tail once, then hopped off of Levi's lap. The android trotted over to a blue mat in the corner and curled up on it. A small *ding* sounded as Estelle connected to a power source, and Larken turned back to the gift as she explained, "I didn't like the idea of plugging her into the wall, so I got her a wireless charger. Now she just looks like she's on a bed."

"Nifty," Loxly said. "How long does the charge last?"

"A couple of days."

Larken took the lid off the box and pulled free another clear tablet. Grabbing it, she smiled at Soren before tapping the device. But instead of the book covers that she had no doubt expected, a picture of her and Loxly sleeping together on one of the dorm couches filled the screen. Her lips parted as the picture changed, cycling through all of the pictures Squad 19 had taken with her. Some were of her sparring in the gym with them, others were of her laughing with cards in her hands. Soren had asked his friends to send him all of the pictures they had, whether they were staged or not. He was surprised at the number of pictures Hinlee had secretly taken and kept one of him covering Larken's sleeping form with that black jacket of hers for himself.

Larken met his eyes, silver lining hers. She opened her mouth but closed it again when nothing came out. Soren nodded and she sniffed as she dropped her gaze back to the screen. Larken laughed when she saw the picture of Brecker laughing next to her as she guzzled water, red-faced after trying hot sauce for the first time. Wardell crawled up into her lap, not liking that the pictures looked backward to him. He asked about some of the pictures and Larken explained what was happening in them. Soren felt someone looking at him, and he looked over at Vallen. The man nodded gruffly, unspoken words dancing in his eyes.

You did good.

Soren nodded back, pride filling his chest. He'd finally done something right. Then he looked at Larken once more. He knew he would have to come clean and admit that this hadn't been the only gift he had gotten her, but that could wait for a little longer. Soren could tell her later, sometime when they were alone and not at risk of being interrupted. Maybe then he could work up the nerve to tell her all of the other things too.

CHAPTER 23

The good feelings from the night before were slowly disappearing, and Larken thought she might be sick. Even the masseuse that had worked on her back for a few hours that morning had commented on her obvious stress. Larken went back and forth between twisting the ring Brecker had gotten her and holding the pearl, even though Soren sat right next to her.

The previous day had started out rough but had ended more perfectly than she could have ever imagined. Wardell had surprised her most of all, asking if he could stay and eat dinner with her instead of running off to be with their mother. He apparently adored all of her new friends and told her that he wanted them to throw a party for him sometime as well. Her favorite part of the day had been when she got to tell him about her life at base.

After the delicious dinner that Levi had made, they broke out a lemon tart that had everyone but her and Vallen puckering. Afterward, she cornered Delvon and gave him a message to pass along to Shadric. Larken knew that he thought she was worth the risk, but she didn't. Every time he did something that drew attention to the relationship between herself, Shadric, and Delvon, she grew more and more afraid that someone would make the connection between them and the Faithfuls. And if they were discovered, then there was a good chance that Vallen would be too.

She still wasn't quite sure how her instructor fit into all of this, but if Delvon and Shadric were both Faithfuls, and Delvon reported to Vallen, then he was mixed up in it somehow. Larken knew that everyone else was in on it as well, but with everything being monitored, she couldn't risk asking about it. The security team would notice if she used her cuff to have a private conversation, and it would look suspicious if she kept meeting people at the fountain. The only way she would be able to ask her questions would be to go wherever they all went after she had her panic attack. But she would rather stay in the dark and trust that they all knew what they were doing than get back on the *Harpy*.

Soren grabbed her hand, forcing her to stop running her nail between the stone and the setting of the cuff Delvon gave her. He stared ahead as he muttered, "I don't think your boyfriend would be very happy if you broke that."

Larken sucked her lip between her teeth, locking in her retort of, *He's not my boyfriend.* Instead, she said, "Thanks again for coming with me."

He sighed, relaxing his grip a little. "Sure."

Soren looked over at her, an apology in his eyes. This was Vallen's hover; he had taken an aircraft to wherever it was he was going today instead of going with her. He hadn't shared what his plans were, leaving Larken to assume that it had to do with whatever he did with the rest of her friends. And since the hover had been issued to Vallen by her mother, the two of them knew better than to talk freely about things that might get back to her. Soren knew that she and Delvon weren't really dating, he had to, but that didn't stop her from feeling any less guilty about it. Or feeling guilty over her confusing feelings for Shadric.

Taking a moment to find the right words, Larken admitted, "The thing about Delvon..." Soren looked back to the road, and it made speaking a little easier. Sticking to the cover story the two of them had worked out, Larken said, "I didn't think I would see him again after I left for base. We had to pretend that we didn't know each other."

Soren squeezed her hand, the only sign that he understood what she meant. Larken and Delvon really didn't know each other; otherwise, she would have recognized him the night of the crash.

She continued, "We thought it best to go our separate ways after that. But when I came home, and he became my bodyguard, one thing sort of turned into another."

"And your engagement?" he asked, keeping up the pretense.

"It's hard, but we're managing."

Soren squeezed her hand again.

They sat like that the rest of the way to the theater, silently holding hands, and Larken remembered the last time they had done that as the building came into view. Everything had been so simple then. She had a home, a family, and her only worry had been if Dominic was planning on trying something during the show. Her free hand worked its way up to the pearl. They stopped just outside the crumbling theater, and Larken felt Soren's eyes on her. She met them and they glowed a warm green, telling her he was thinking about when he gave her the necklace as well.

Unable to meet his intense gaze any longer, Larken looked out at the building. Her stomach flipped nervously, and she sucked in a quick breath. Soren reached over and cupped her cheek, forcing her to meet his gaze once more. His eyes were hard as he said, "We can go back if you aren't ready."

Larken covered his hand with hers, tears burning her eyes. Memories of the two of them flooded her mind. The night Larken told him about her shoulder, when Soren had given her the necklace, the two of them in the garden after the opera, the words he had said before the crash, and that night in the medic-building. The memories that had caused her so much pain only a few days ago were now, once more, a comfort.

Soren's silent apology filled the cab, and Larken smiled at him as she whispered, "I forgive you."

Soren let out a long breath and pulled her close. She wrapped her arms around him as he buried his face in her hair. She almost missed his murmured, "I didn't understand what you were asking. I'm so sorry, Larken."

She tightened her arms in response, a few tears breaking free. When she pulled back, he looked more vulnerable than she had ever seen him, and she didn't stop herself from touching him. Larken cupped his cheek and he leaned into it for a moment before pulling away. They had spent enough time stalling, and they needed to move on to the next big obstacle of the day. Soren got out of the hover and walked around to open the door for her. He stuck out a hand, helping her out, and then the two of them made their way to the theater.

The building had definitely seen better days, but the gold and sand-colored bricks absorbed the sun, making the place look magical. Tall grass and wildflowers grew everywhere, and bees jumped from bloom to bloom. The wooden door looked like sun-bleached driftwood, and the hinges screeched when Soren pulled it open. The scent of dust hit them immediately, and even though the place hadn't seen a performance in over twenty years, it still held that awed silence that could be found in every theater.

Dust covered everything, sticking to the green carpet, wall hangings, and the brass accents that had been tarnished beyond repair. Larken reached out for Soren's hand and he silently moved closer. Her heart broke for the forgotten magic of this place, for the stories that it must know and would never share again. Larken looked at everything and swallowed thickly as they hurried through the foyer and towards the stage.

The double doors were already open for them, waiting expectantly for the first guests in years. A lone figure stood on the stage, the holes in the rafters creating natural spotlights. The wood had severe water damage in some places and burn marks in others. Larken didn't realize she was squeezing Soren's fingers until his free hand brushed her wrist. She relaxed her grip and looked up at him.

"He hasn't seen us yet," he whispered. "We can still turn back."

"No, I—" Larken looked back at her biological father. "I want to hear what he has to say. I want to know the truth."

"I'll be right here then," Soren assured, releasing her hand.

Larken watched him disappear into the shadows and faced the stage. Squaring her shoulders, she walked down the center aisle. The felt-covered seats matched the green carpet in the foyer, but most had been torn open in spots. Stuffing spilled out onto the ground, and Larken tried not to think about the animals that may or may not be living under the remaining upholstery.

When she reached the orchestra pit, Lark cleared her throat. Fisher stiffened and then turned. He relaxed when he saw her, an easy smile breaking across his face. Fisher looked the same as he had the night they met, only dressed more casually in a maroon long sleeve shirt and a pair of jeans that looked brand new.

"You came." He leaned over the pit, extending his hand. "Here, let me help you."

Larken grabbed his hand, instantly comparing it to Vallen's. Whereas her instructor's hands were scarred, calloused, and rough, Fisher's were the smooth hands of a performer. He helped pull Larken to the stage, looking her over when she straightened.

"Did you have any trouble finding the place?" he asked as she brushed some dust off of her olive capris.

"No, we found it okay."

"Is General Maxwell—"

"He couldn't make it. My friend came with me."

"The bodyguard or the young man from the opera?"

The knowing tone of Fisher's voice had Larken blushing slightly as she said, "Yes, Soren was the one you met that night."

"Good, I liked him." Larken looked at Fisher, raising an eyebrow. He looked away, mumbling, "Well, I—what I mean is, he didn't seem like he trusted Ophelia's boy, which I—"

Larken, taking pity on him, cut Fisher off by saying, "Yes, Soren is a good man."

Fished sighed and then ran his fingers through his hair. He laughed dejectedly and turned his gaze away. "I told myself that I wouldn't muck this up like I did last time, but it would seem that I'm already making a mess of it."

"If it's any consolation, I don't really know what I'm doing either," Larken offered.

He gave her a warm smile, then reached into his pocket. "I suppose this is as good a time as any." Fisher handed her a little mint-colored box, saying, "Happy birthday."

"You didn't have to..." Larken trailed off as she opened it. A beautiful hair comb rested on a small white satin cushion. The twisting silver design held six pearls, and Larken stared at it, open-mouthed.

"That belonged to your grandmother. She wore it during every one of her performances. It's time you had it."

Larken looked up at the man before her, his uncertainty palpable. She wanted to be upset like she was that night in the dressing room. But instead, she asked in a cracked voice, "I have a grandmother?"

"You did," Fisher answered quickly. "She passed away when you were six."

Larken looked back at the comb. "Did she know about me?"

"I never admitted my relationship with Cornella to her, but yes, she knew. You look just like her."

And you.

Larken closed the box so none of the dust floating in the air could land on the comb. "How did you meet my mother?"

Fisher sighed and stuck his hands in his pockets. He looked to the back of the room, and she wondered if he was looking for Soren. It was only when his eyes glossed over that she realized that he was falling into a memory. "I met your mother in this very theater, when I starred in *Libri E Beaus.*"

Larken felt like she had been hit. "You were in *Libri E Beaus?*"

Fisher smiled and looked at her. "Yes, many years ago. It was my second greatest achievement...after you." Larken blushed, and he moved on. "It was the only thing I wanted to do. And after I played Jon, the stable boy, I was ready to move on with my life."

"But how did you meet my mother? She hates music."

"She didn't use to."

Larken gripped the box tighter. It made sense. She had always assumed that her mother hated music because she hated her; Larken never thought that there might be another reason for it. But if she'd fallen in love with a man that loved music, she would probably hate music if he left too.

Fisher continued, "Back then, she could be found at every show that had received a good review, needing to see and hear it all. Wanting to get on the Luminary's good side, the director of my show gave Trogar three tickets."

"One for him, my mother, and Liam."

"Yes." Fisher ran his fingers through his hair again. "And in another attempt to get into Trogar's good graces, the director invited them to meet the performers after the show." He shook his head, teal eyes far away. "I fell in love with your mother the moment I saw her."

Larken closed her eyes, trying to imagine her mother as a different person, but she couldn't.

"Our affair burned like kindling, intense and quick. I grew to like Trogar, and I found my way back to Maxim. I ended things with your mother; she didn't take it well."

Larken laughed dryly. "I can imagine."

Fished sighed deeply. "I cut all communication with her. She retaliated by recanting her statement on the *Libri E Beaus* showing she had seen, saying that any director stupid enough to cast me deserved to have their shows tank. Those three months that we were together, and that I showed in *Libri E Beaus*, were the last time I ever set foot on stage. I ended our relationship, and she ended my career."

Larken's eyes burned. "And me?"

"Nine months later I saw you in a news story, and I've been watching you through a screen ever since."

Her voice broke as she asked, "She never told you?"

Fisher shook his head, his teal eyes haunted. "I can't tell you how many times I almost broke down and just showed up at the Manor. But I thought that might make your life harder or that you might not want…"

Larken's heart skipped a beat, and it felt painful when it started up again. "Want what?"

"Want *me*."

Despite her best efforts, a tear ran down her face, and then another. Her whole life, she had always felt like she wasn't wanted, and this man—*Fisher Fillmar*—had been on the other side of her mother's lie feeling the same way.

"I don't expect anything, Larken," he said, voice cracked. "I don't expect you to love me, or even call me Dad, but I want to be a part of your life. If you'll let me."

A sob escaped her, and she clapped a hand over her mouth in an attempt to keep it in. Somebody wanted *her*. Larken almost didn't dare believe it, but when Fisher crossed the stage and wrapped her up in his arms, she did. She knew that he had meant every word as he held her and wept. Somehow, they had found each other, and Larken didn't feel so alone anymore. Fisher would never replace her father or Vallen, but they could make this work.

They stood like that for a while, Fisher telling her over and over again how sorry he was, and Larken feeling overjoyed that someone wanted her for her. When they finally did say goodbye, the sun that poured through the rafters had turned a deep gold. Soren didn't say anything as he was introduced to Fisher, only shaking his hand, and then helped Larken back to Vallen's hovercraft.

Larken fell into the seat, wiping at her still watery eyes. She couldn't stop smiling and looked forward to the next time she would see Fisher. Soren hopped into the hover and Larken waved at Fisher's shrinking figure. When he was no longer in sight, Larken faced forward and let out a long breath.

"I take it it went well," Soren ventured.

"He told me about my mom, about how they met, and why he was never around." Soren didn't say anything, and she knew he wouldn't ask out of respect for her feelings. She answered him anyway, "My mother never told him about me. He only knew I existed because he saw my birth announcement in a news story."

Soren reached over and grabbed her hand. "But you're happy?"

Larken grinned at him. "Yes, I'm happy."

The rest of the way back to the Manor, Soren let her play music, even though most of the songs had his jaw ticking. Larken didn't care; she smiled and sang, feeling lighter than she had in days. She was with her family again, they were working to get her out of her engagement, and one of her parents wanted her. There was nothing that could upset her.

When they pulled into the drive, Larken almost didn't notice the stillness of the grounds. Soren gave her a look that had her staying put as he got out of the hover. He looked around for a few moments before walking over and opening her door. Soren grabbed her hand and helped her out, keeping her close as they made their way into the Manor.

Their breaths could be heard in the heavy silence as they walked. Larken looked around but couldn't find any security guards or other members of the Manor staff. Soren dropped her hand, wrapping his arm around her. She could feel how tense he was, and she didn't like it. The happiness she had felt in the hover slowly evaporated, and a paranoid worry took its place.

What in the world is going on?

Together, the two of them made their way to her sitting room. Soren pulled the door open, and a blackness pushed out to greet them. Larken peered inside and saw that Hinlee and Candy were crying into tissues that looked to be nearing their limits. Delvon pushed off the wall he was leaning against and made his way to Larken. He pulled her from Soren and back out into the hall.

Looking down at her, he frowned in a way that told her she wouldn't like what he had to say. Her heart squeezed as she thought about everything that could have gone wrong while she was away, but nothing she imagined could have prepared her for the words that came out of his mouth.

"General Maxwell was in an accident. Something went wrong with the aircraft." Delvon swallowed hard. "He didn't make it."

Larken stopped breathing; her heart stopped beating. The world tilted, and then pain shot through her knees. Delvon dropped in front of her, reaching for her as she shook her head. Blood pounded in her ears even though her heart no longer moved it through her body. This wasn't happening. It couldn't be.

"Breathe, love. You need to breathe."

Larken couldn't. Delvon brushed at her face, and she realized she was crying. She gasped in a breath before hissing, *"No."*

Delvon tried to help her to her feet, but she pushed him away. *"No!"*

Larken scrambled to her feet on her own and ran. She hurtled down the hall and took a right. Her lungs caught as she burst into his rooms. Larken looked everywhere, but he wasn't there. Figuring he must be in the training field, she turned to leave.

Soren was there, and he caught her.

"Let go of me!"

"Larken."

"I SAID LET GO OF ME!"

She was shaking, and Soren pulled her into his arms. Larken screamed and pushed at him, trying to get him to let go. She needed to go check the training fields, and the hangar, and…

Her knees gave out, and she sobbed. Larken beat weakly at Soren's chest as he held her. She kept screaming, refusing to believe that it was true. Larken would go out into the training field, and Vallen would be there, sweating and barking at her to hurry up and join him. He couldn't be…there was no way he was…

Larken started screaming again, scratching and kicking at Soren, pleading with him to let her go. She couldn't see past the tears that blinded her; she couldn't breathe. The world around her was going fuzzy, but she refused to give in. Vallen was alive and she would find him once Soren let go of her.

Delvon appeared, a hard look on his face, and Larken snarled at him. This was his fault; he was lying to her. She tried harder to get away from Soren just so she could claw out the pity filling Delvon's grey eyes. He walked closer, something in his hand that she couldn't make out.

"Let go of me!" she screamed. "I have to find Vallen!"

There was a sharp pain where her shoulder met her neck and Delvon murmured, "I'm sorry, love, but this is for your own good."

Tears spilled freely from her eyes, and she tried again. "Please, *I have to find him.*"

Then her world went dark.

CHAPTER 24

The black sky thundered, threatening to soak them all, but Larken didn't cry. This whole funeral was a sham. If Delvon hadn't guilted her into coming, she wouldn't have. People stood as the priest spoke, telling everyone what a good man Vallen had been, but he didn't know him. None of them did, only Larken. Only she knew the man he really was, the man who had unofficially adopted her as his own, the man who made the best lemon cake in the world, the man who hated the rain because it hurt his knee. These people, crying and mourning, they didn't know the real Vallen. If they had, they wouldn't be satisfied with an empty urn. They would know that no body meant that there was still a chance that he was alive somewhere. And Larken would do whatever it took to find him.

No one believed her. Not Candy or Carl, not her old squad members, not Delvon, and not Soren. Larken was all alone again. Only this time, Vallen wasn't around to tell her to trust her gut. No, she would have to do this alone, but none of it would matter when she found him. Everything would be the way it was before she went to go see Fisher. Larken would find Vallen, and he would save her from the wedding that was only five days away.

Five days. If I don't find Vallen in five days, then I'm running away on my own...

Cameras flashed and Dominic moved the black umbrella he held from one hand to the other. He wrapped his arm around her, appearing every bit the sympathetic fiancé. Larken hadn't seen him since the night he had accidentally drugged her. That was another thing she and Delvon didn't agree on. He thought Dominic did it on purpose to get her to spend the night with him, and Larken thought Dominic was too stupid to come up with a plan that well thought out. If he had planned it, then he would have tried long before that night. Dominic had plenty of opportunities to take advantage of her in the past, but she knew that he was too afraid of losing her to try anything that drastic.

The black teacup dress she wore felt suffocating in the humid air, and Larken wanted to rip it off. The dark clouds seemed reluctant to part with the rain, holding the water until a few drops couldn't help but spill out here or there. Thunder and lightning tried to convince the heavens to release their burdens, but still the clouds clung to what they could. It was only a matter of moments before the sky would open up, drenching them all. She wanted to lock herself away in her room, wash off her makeup, pull the pins from her hair, and get started on her search. But until the minister stopped speaking and she had listened to every condolence, she was stuck there.

A clap of thunder shook the world, and Larken knew that if Vallen was there, they would be curled up under that blue blanket he kept around for her and halfway through a film. She could almost feel the worn material of the blanket, see the hot water bottle resting on his extended knee. Another clap of thunder boomed in the air, and Wardell's hand shot up to hers. Looking at him, she saw tears rolling down his cheeks.

Larken pulled him to her, and he buried his face in her skirt. She ran her fingers over the back of his head, trying to comfort him despite Dominic's hold on her. The media would play it up about how heartbroken Wardell was to lose Vallen, but the truth was, he didn't really know him. Vallen had always been her caretaker, not his. He cried because he was afraid, and Larken's heart went out to him.

Focusing once more on the preacher, Larken pretended to listen. They had all gone over Vallen's will, and he had left everything to her. Her eyes drifted to the large hologram of him in his uniform. He smiled in the picture, and it looked wrong to her. He didn't smile. Part of her hated that this fake version of him was how most of these people would remember him.

Lightning sparked across the sky, making Wardell squeak. Larken wondered if her mother had chosen this day as one last attempt to spite Vallen. Everyone knew that his funeral would be held in General's Field; he had been a General after all. The decent thing to do would be to check the forecast and *not* hold an outdoor funeral when it was going to storm. But her mother wasn't decent, and Larken refused to look her way as her own form of protest. Cornella had sent her off to be killed in the war, brought her home when she had finally found a family, accepted a proposal from Dominic, and ruined Vallen's fake funeral. Larken was done letting her mother tell her what to do, and she was done caring what her mother thought. Larken tried to fight her smirk as she decided that she might end up running off with the wedding singer after all.

"Let us pray," the preacher droned, voice deep with age. "Oh great Maxim…"

Larken tuned him out, closing her eyes.

*Maxim, please, if You can hear me, please keep Vallen safe. I've been so alone, so confused. I'm begging You, show me which path to take. I've seen what life in the dark has done to the people I care about. I don't want to live that way. Tell me what to do; give me a sign. And please…*please *don't make me marry Dominic.*

The service concluded, and the hologram dissipated as if it had never been there. People got up and a few even made their way to where the Hale family stood. Larken felt the eyes of her security team behind her, but one set felt more prominent than the others. She knew that if she were to turn around, she would find Soren glowering, his eyes flashing gold as he tried to burn Dominic's arm with his gaze. More thunder sounded, and Wardell gripped her tighter, wrinkling her dress.

She loosened his grip just enough to crouch in front of him. Cupping both of his cheeks, she brushed away his tears the best she could. "Do you want Delvon to take you back?"

Wardell looked torn; he wanted to leave, but he also didn't want to leave her. Bailey hadn't been issued an invitation, and only the burly head of Wardell's security team, Casey, had accompanied him.

When he didn't answer her question, she asked instead, "Would you like *me* to take you back?"

"Are you allowed to?"

"I don't see why not. It doesn't look like people are wanting to hang around," she mused, looking over the crowd and then up at the sky. "It's going to start pouring any second."

Wardell looked behind him. Liam and their mother were already halfway back to the hover that had brought them there, and their father was nowhere to be seen. Facing her once more, he nodded vigorously.

Larken nodded as well before standing. Wardell clutched her hand and followed her out from under Dominic's umbrella, not that it had been big enough to cover her brother as well. Larken looked over her friends quickly; everyone except for Candy had expressions of stone. She cried into a bright pink handkerchief that didn't match the black everyone wore.

Silently, they made their way back to the hovercraft that had brought them to the General's Field. Wardell jumped in first, practically pulling Larken's arm off in his attempt to get her in as well. She wasted no time finding a seat, and Wardell took the seat next to hers, burying his face in her lap. To her annoyance, Dominic followed her and took the open seat to her right. He once more wrapped his arm around her, pulling her close in a lame attempt at comforting her. Both Delvon and Soren took up the seats opposite them, crossing their arms and scowling at the Star. The sight of them almost made Larken laugh, and she would have, if she wasn't still mad at them.

Delvon had knocked her out after he told her about Vallen, and she woke up in the medic wing of the Manor, cuffed to the bed. Ezra and Jodi had monitored her, only letting her go when they were sure that she was no longer a danger to herself. Delvon had yet to apologize and even though she knew he never would, Larken used it as an excuse to stay mad. Soren, on the other hand, had been distant and cold, like he had when she first moved to base all those weeks ago. She didn't know what had changed; he had seen her freak out multiple times before, but maybe that last one had been one too many. Maybe he had finally realized how messed up she was and didn't want to risk getting any closer to her. Either way, the anger fueled her. It pushed her, gave her something to think about other than her impending nuptials.

As if just thinking about it caught his attention, Dominic said for the hundredth time, "I really am sorry, Lark. I can't even imagine—"

"I'm fine," she interrupted. "You don't need to worry about it."

Dominic looked a little confused, and she wondered for the first time if he had been apologizing for her loss or what had happened at the club. Knowing him, it could very well be both. Looking at him, no one would suspect that Soren had knocked him out just over a week ago. He was his usual flirty, easy-going self and acted as if nothing had happened between him and Soren. The night had never reached the media and Larken honestly didn't know if it had been a threat from Vallen that kept the story secret or if Dominic paid everyone off to keep his embarrassment under wraps. Larken didn't care. She couldn't wait until she didn't have to put up with him any longer, and she shuddered to think that she had once considered what being with him might feel like.

The hover door started to close when a hand shot in, triggering the safety feature and opening the door once more. Shadric Barlow stumbled in, looking a frazzled, soaking mess. Larken hadn't noticed that the rain had started, and she gaped at him. His bright eyes heated when they landed on her before he looked over the rest of the cab. Shadric quickly found Delvon and took the open seat next to him. His unspoken *we need to talk* was almost audible, and

Larken wondered if Dominic picked up on it. The Star watched Shadric closely, making Larken panic. She did the only thing she could think of and grabbed Dominic's hand.

He looked at her, clearly surprised that she was the one who had initiated contact. She put on her best coy smile, trying not to look too obvious, and said, "It's good to see you again, Dominic. I missed you."

"You did?" he asked, looking hopeful enough to make her a little guilty. "I'm sorry. I thought it might be best to give you a little space."

She squeezed his hand. "I know it was an accident."

Relief flooded his features, and he pressed his forehead to hers. "It was, and it will never happen again, Lark. I *promise.*"

She smiled and allowed him to kiss her cheek. Her skin burned, but not like it once had. Before, he seemed to awaken her nerves; now he scorched her unpleasantly. Trying to keep his focus, but not wanting any more contact, she asked, "How has work been?"

"I won't lie, the disbanding of Squad 19 was difficult to work around, but one of my own was promoted and took over." Dominic didn't bother trying to hide his annoyance, but he didn't dare say anything about her old squad acting as her security team, knowing that if he did, it would upset her.

"And how are the recruits?"

"They all have squads or have been distributed to other bases accordingly."

Larken raised an eyebrow as Wardell murmured something incoherent into her dress. He had fallen asleep, and she would need help getting him inside the Manor when they got back. She refused to ask Soren or Delvon for help, but Brecker would be able to get the job done easily enough. Larken stroked her brother's light brown hair as she asked, "I take it that's a good thing?"

"Just one less thing that I have to worry about before the wedding."

"What else are you worrying about?"

Dominic squeezed her shoulder. "Nothing that I want you fretting over."

"But I'm going to be your wife. Shouldn't I know what's bothering you? Maybe I can help." Larken forced her eyes to stay on Dominic and not drift over to Shadric.

"Oh, my sweet Lark. I don't know what I did to deserve you."

Nothing. You went behind my back and asked my mother.

Larken smiled, hoping that her eyes didn't reflect what she really thought.

"I suppose there is *one* thing that you could do to ease my burdens a little."

"Anything," she said, almost afraid of what she was agreeing to.

"Don't leave the Manor until the wedding. I don't like the idea of you wandering around without General Maxwell looking out for you." In a voice quiet enough not to be heard over the muttered conversation between Shadric and Delvon, he added, "And I don't trust Tanner."

Larken leaned closer. "Why not?"

"It's silly." Dominic's eyes turned hard as he said, "But I don't like the way he looks at you."

"Dominic," she whispered, "it's just the media. There's nothing going on between us."

"I know, and I trust you," he insisted. "It's him that I worry about."

Larken looked away, unable to keep the charade any longer. She hadn't lied. There really was nothing going on between her and Delvon, but she still felt guilty. The two of them might not be romantically involved like Dominic seemed to think, but that didn't mean that they weren't trying to find a way out of the wedding. And for that, Larken knew that everything she had just told Dominic was a lie.

Shadric Barlow kept stealing glances at Larken, and Soren seriously considered gouging out his eyes. The singer had no business looking at her like that. Why he was even on the hovercraft with them Soren had no idea, but he intended to find out.

He tried his best to ignore Delvon and Shadric after they started talking about the wedding, not wanting to hear it. But when he heard Delvon grumble, *"I don't care if one of the musicians quit the band. You keep the setlist the same, just like we planned."* Soren thought they might be talking about more than music. If they were, then Larken's performance made more sense. Not only that, but it meant that she was in on whatever coded conversation they were having.

For the first time, Soren wondered how much she had been able to put together on her own under the watchful eye of the Military Manor's security team. He had assumed that she knew of the plan to get her out of the Manor and out of her engagement, but with the way she refused to look over in Delvon and Shadric's direction, Soren knew he had been wrong. And with only five days until the wedding, and her chronic fear of flying, he didn't think he would be able to pull her aside and ask how much she actually knew. Not that she would talk to him about it anyway; Soren had been ignoring her, and she knew it.

Larken was upset with him, and he didn't blame her. Seeing her screaming for Vallen made him realize how much it would hurt her if they continued the way they had been. Even now, as she soothed a stirring Wardell, Soren knew that she still didn't believe that Vallen was gone. Truthfully, what she had said after waking up made sense. A man as resourceful as Vallen wouldn't just simply vanish the way the media had claimed. He had walked into enemy territory, returned home as a spy, faked having the flu to go to a secret meeting for the Faithfuls, and now died without even so much as a tooth left behind at the crash site. If Soren was honest, he didn't really believe that Vallen had died either. But taking Larken's side in this would only bring them closer together, and that was unfair to her. Especially if Vallen really was gone. He couldn't give her that hope.

Wardell yawned broadly, stretching and rubbing at his eyes. He looked up first to his sister, then the burly man with the curly red hair on his other side. Blinking, Wardell took in the other people around him, and his eyes stopped on Jodi. His brow crinkled and he said, "Your hair looks like the sky."

Jodi offered the boy a smile. She hadn't changed her black, grey, and blue hair since arriving at the Manor, and Soren thought that the dark look suited her.

Wardell continued his perusal and then looked up to Larken. "Sissy, why is Shadric Barlow here? Is there going to be another party?"

"No, Wardell," she answered sweetly. "Mr. Barlow probably just had something for the wedding he needed to talk about."

Wardell's face scrunched a little more. "But why is he here? Was he friends with Vallen too?"

"He's friends with me. He came to give me his condolences and to try and make me feel better."

The boy looked to the singer, and then back to his sister. He whispered, but everyone heard him ask, "Didn't he write a love song about you?"

Soren's hand balled into a fist of its own accord.

Larken stiffened, and then cupped his cheek. "Who told you that?"

"I heard Liam talking about it, and then Bailey told Casey that she heard it on the news."

"No, sweetie," she said. "That's just speculation."

"What's that?"

"It means that people are just making guesses and that they don't really know."

The hover slowed and Wardell asked Larken if she thought their mother would be upset if he asked to learn the piano while his sister ushered him to his feet.

Delvon leaned forward and asked, "Carl, mind keeping an eye on Miss Hale for a few hours? I need to make a run with the team, look for likely places assailants could be hiding between here and the honeymoon destination."

"Of course," he agreed. "We have to do a run-through for her hair anyway. Perfect weather to stay locked up inside."

"Casey and I can help too!" Wardell insisted. "I don't have lessons today, and I can help watch her."

Larken glared at Delvon, silently blaming him for ruining her plans for the day. If Soren had to guess, he would say that she had planned to spend the afternoon combing through the news stories on Vallen's crash, looking for anything that might tell her what really happened.

"My team will be at the Manor as well," Shadric offered. "We still have to fine-tune the setlist and start rehearsal."

"Then we're all agreed," Delvon said as he stood, cutting off Braves who was no doubt going to offer up his help as well. Soren smirked.

One by one, they filed out of the hovercraft, each of them going their separate ways. Soren hung back only long enough to make sure Larken got into the Manor okay and that Braves didn't follow her. The man kissed her on the cheek, playing the part of an upstanding gentleman, and then glared at Soren the moment she turned away. Soren glared back, remembering the feeling of his fist connecting with the Star's jaw.

Turning, Soren joined the others who were quickly making their way to the hangar. Loxly punched in the access code to the *Harpy*, and they were loaded up and setting off before all of them had even found a seat. Jodi pulled out her communicator, most likely telling Ezra that they were going to be gone for another few hours.

What had been an hour-long trip before felt like only a few minutes. Loxly landed close to the bunker and cut the engines. They piled out of the *Harpy*, and Soren punched in the code when he reached the metal door. Silently, they climbed down into the darkness and made their way to the conference room. When Soren shut the door behind him, everyone started talking at once.

"Enough!" Delvon's voice cut through the chatter, silencing everyone. "We continue as planned."

"We can't!" Hinlee insisted.

"And why not?" the bodyguard demanded.

"Because we barely had a plan to begin with," Brecker answered, siding with Hinlee.

Delvon sighed. "Well, what do you have?"

"A general idea," Levi said as he scratched at his beard. "Vallen wanted to get a better feel for how the ceremony would play out, so we mostly focused on what would happen *after* we got Larken to Camp."

"Okay," Delvon grumbled, irritated. "Then what's your general idea?"

"Rescue Larken from the weddin', get her to a secret location, then," Loxly drawled, "we somehow get her in the *Harpy*, and we fly away."

Delvon glowered and sat in the chair that Vallen had used the last time they were there. He looked exhausted, not that Soren could blame him. Since losing Vallen, the man had taken over everything —on top of his job protecting Larken. Delvon rubbed at his temple and said, "If anyone has any ideas, now would be the time to speak up."

Silently, everyone looked to Soren, to their Captain. Swallowing, he took a seat as well. This was the moment Vallen had readied him for when he had placed Larken in Squad 19. Not to take care of her when she had been harassed, not to keep her when Braves tried to get her transferred, and not to be used as a shield when they crashed out of the sky. Soren had been tried and tested for this exact moment, and he suddenly felt the full weight of that responsibility.

"Well, *Captain Deckard?*" Delvon mocked.

"I have somewhat of an idea. All of us will have to work together to pull it off. It might sound a little crazy, but—"

Delvon's grey eyes glinted, cutting him off. Then the bodyguard opened his mouth and said, "The crazier, the better."

CHAPTER 25

Larken didn't know what she was doing. She was supposed to be in her room with Carl and Candy talking about the big day. Instead, Larken lied about wanting to find Estelle and now stood in Delvon's usual spot in the ballroom, lurking in the shadows, waiting for…something.

Shadric talked and laughed with his band, looking like he was having the time of his life instead of practicing. But Larken supposed that since he played the songs so often, he could afford to goof off a little. Not like her. She couldn't do anything fun anymore, and she didn't want to. Larken couldn't afford to waste any time… and she didn't know who else to turn to. Shadric had offered to take her away, and Larken seriously considered letting him.

Finally, Shadric noticed her. It was during the bridge of his newest song, *Belong to You,* and for a moment, Larken was back in that field. She could almost smell the lavender as her heart slowly worked its way up to her throat. Shadric didn't take his eyes off her, his voice taking a pained edge. Larken's eyes burned, and she thought about leaving.

What am I doing? I shouldn't be here.

And she shouldn't. Larken should be turning to Delvon or Soren, but she was still so angry with them. Not to mention that even if she asked Soren to talk about what had happened, he would probably ignore her. And she was so sick of being ignored.

Shadric finished up the song and told his band to take a break. Larken didn't wait around, only kept to the shadows and quickly made her way to the fountain. The cool evening air nipped at her bare arms and feet. She hadn't bothered grabbing a jacket, but she didn't really care either. At least if she felt the cold, she was feeling something other than hopelessness.

The rain stopped a few hours ago, but the world still clung to the grey clouds above. Humidity had each breath she took feeling sticky. Larken could already hear Carl yelling about the mud that had fused to the bottom of her feet. A leaf or two stuck to her wet skin, but she didn't bend down to brush them away.

Reaching the fountain, Larken waited, staring up at the weather-beaten face of her grandmother as one of the new hybrids howled somewhere. She had been silly to think that a hunk of stone could ever protect her, and she was stupid for wishing that it still could. Larken's eyes caught on the sword pointing to the dark sky.

Luminary.

How do they expect me to be Luminary when I can't even protect myself?

Larken shivered as a breeze kicked up loose pebbles and twigs around her, chaffing her arms. A jacket was wrapped around her, and Larken turned to find Shadric smiling at her. "Here."

"Thank you."

He had changed out of his suit and now wore ratty jeans and a white T-shirt. The black leather jacket he had given her felt warm, like he had just taken it off, but he hadn't worn it on stage while he practiced. It smelled like a campfire, and she stuffed her arms into the over-sized sleeves.

"I'm sorry about General Maxwell. I know the two of you were—"

"I need your help," she cut him off.

"My help?"

"Yes, no one else will listen to me."

Shadric scratched at the scruff on his jaw before he asked, "What kind of help?"

Larken took a step closer to him and looked him in the eye. Taking a deep breath, she whispered, "I don't think Vallen's dead. No one believes me, and I need help finding him."

Shadric's eyes softened, and he opened his mouth. Whatever he was about to say, he thought better of it and closed his mouth. He shook his head. "I'm sorry, Larken, but I can't help. I wouldn't know the first—"

Larken let out a long breath and hung her head. Taking a few steps away, she said, "Never mind then. Thanks anyway."

A hand grabbed her elbow, stopping her. Larken couldn't look at him. The last time they were together, he had assured her that she wasn't alone, that she hadn't been abandoned. But she had never felt more alone than she did right now. Her eyes burned with her hurt and anger. No, Maxim didn't care for her; there could be no other explanation. Either none of her friends believed her and had pushed her away, or things were worse than she chose to believe and Vallen was gone. If he were, then Larken really was all alone.

"Larken, wait. Please."

"Why?" she croaked. "So you can tell me that I'm not as alone as I feel? That this is all part of Maxim's plan?" Larken tried to pull her arm free. "You already said all of that last time, and things have gotten worse. So forgive me if I choose to not take you seriously this time."

"Larken."

"I'm tired, Shadric. I'm tired of fighting, I'm tired of hurting, and I'm tired of being alone. I may not love Dominic, but at least he will—"

"Will what?" Shadric demanded, voice harder than she had ever heard it. "Will help get you out of here? Will take you away from your cushy life as a Luminary's daughter? Will believe you when you tell him what you just told me?"

Larken closed her eyes, pretending that the tear that had just escaped past her lashes wasn't running down her cheek.

"I know you're in pain and that you feel like the sun won't rise tomorrow, but I promise it will."

"Yes, because tomorrow is when you need me to take up your cause and play your puppet. What about after tomorrow?" She turned on him after clearing away the tear, giving into her anger. "What about the day after that? And the day after that, Shadric? I don't care about tomorrow. So far every *tomorrow* I've had only built my hopes up and then took everything I've ever cared about away from me!"

Larken had started shouting, but she hadn't noticed until she stopped speaking and realized the crickets had gone silent. Shadric still looked at her, and she assumed his eyes found only a pathetic broken mess.

She turned her face away and rasped, "Don't look at me like that."

A warm hand brought her face back up, and Shadric brushed his thumb across her jaw. This wasn't how she had planned out this conversation. As a Faithful, Shadric was supposed to believe her. He was supposed to believe her and offer to help find Vallen. She wasn't supposed to be breaking in front of him, and she wasn't supposed to feel like maybe she had been wrong after all.

Her lip trembled and Shadric pulled her tight against him. His chest muffled the sound of her dry sob. The singer said nothing as they stood together, didn't offer any words of comfort, didn't try to tell her that things would get better, and she was glad. Saying those things would have only made it worse.

Even after Larken composed herself, she didn't move. Shadric didn't loosen his hold on her, hugging her like she would disappear if he let go. He had started humming at some point and Larken could have melted. She didn't know the song, but it somehow reminded her of the moon. Haunting but beautiful.

"What is that?" she whispered.

"I don't know. I just remember that my mom used to sing it to me when I was scared."

"It's lovely."

"I think so too."

Larken was silent for a moment, and then said, "Sorry I yelled at you."

"I understand. I was angry after I lost my parents too. But when the Faithfuls took me in, I started to understand things better. I knew that my parents wouldn't want me suffering, and I needed to make the most of my life. I know I'll see them again, though. And I didn't want to tell them about how I spent my life angry and bitter."

"That's a wonderful way of looking at it, but..." Larken trailed off, not wanting to finish.

Shadric sighed. "*But* General Maxwell's not dead."

"Right."

"Larken."

"No." She looked up at him. "Please don't. Just let me pretend for a little while longer. I'm already getting married, and all my friends are ignoring me. Vallen can't be dead too."

"Okay," he said, looking deep into her eyes. His ears turned pink and he looked away.

"What?"

"Nothing."

"Tell me."

"Now isn't the right—"

"Shad, just tell me."

"Did you get the flowers?" he blurted out.

Larken's own cheeks warmed. The beautiful words in his note burned into her memory.

I could bask in the beauty of your smile forever, drown in the oceans of your eyes.

"I got flowers, but I'm not sure who they were from. The note only said *secret admirer.*"

Shadric chuckled, looking at her warmly. "I knew I should have signed my name."

Larken gasped, pretending to be surprised. "You mean they were from *you?*"

He grinned, his beautiful face chasing away some of the darkness in her hurting heart. Larken couldn't help but smile back, wanting to forget herself in this moment of warmth. How could he care for her so openly? He should be broken like her, but there was something different about him. He had a brightness and Larken felt drawn to it. She didn't know if it was just who he was or if Maxim had anything to do with it, but she wanted whatever it was. She wanted to be bright too.

"How can you be so sure of everything?" she asked. "How can you know that Maxim is doing what's best for you, even when it hurts?"

Shadric looked up at the dark sky. "Look at the stars."

Larken did, confused. When he didn't say anything else, she said, "I can't see them."

"Exactly. The storm clouds are in the way. But the stars are still there, right?"

She sighed. "Right."

"The world is dark and ugly right now, but the stars are still burning on the other side. And when the sky clears," an opening appeared in the clouds as if to prove his point, "the stars look more beautiful than before."

Larken remembered a conversation she had with Hinlee, saying that she wished she could have more faith in the plan that Maxim had for her. But how could He use her? She was too lost, too broken; He didn't need her. Larken stared at a patch of three stars that poked through the heavens. Shadric was right. They were more beautiful than she could remember them being, and those three stars shone more brightly against the black sky.

Larken looked down at him and asked, "Is your offer—"

"Yes, of course." Shadric dropped his gaze from the sky as well. "We can leave tonight if you want."

She shook her head. "No, not tonight. I want to try and find Vallen first. But if nothing works out, I'll come find you before I walk down the aisle."

"Whatever you want."

He made it sound like he was talking about more than what she was asking for. Suddenly, Larken felt more aware of the arms around her. They tightened as if he could tell what she was thinking and her breath hitched. She couldn't tear her gaze away no matter how hard she tried. Shadric's eyes only seemed to suck her in more. Larken felt helpless as his head dipped closer and her eyes fell shut.

Her communicator started buzzing.

Shadric's helpless laugh puffed warm against her lips. Larken couldn't help a small smile of her own. "Sorry."

"I don't like that this is becoming a habit."

"It does seem like someone is out to get you, doesn't it?" She pulled the device free and accepted the call. Holding it to her ear, she mumbled, "Hey, Delvon. What's up?"

"Where are you?" he demanded.

"Relax, I'm safe. I just went for a walk."

"If you're not back in your room in the next three seconds, I'm ordering a Manor-wide man-hunt for you."

"Well, you better get the men ready because I'm not hiding in my bathroom."

"*Get back here now.*"

He hung up and Larken rolled her eyes. Stuffing her communicator in her back pocket, she made to take off the jacket, but Shadric put his hands on her shoulders. "No, you keep it."

"Won't you get cold on your way home?"

"I didn't bring my bike today, I'll be fine."

"Are you sure?"

"Positive." He smiled and then blushed slightly. "It looks better on you, anyways."

Larken's lips twitched. "Thanks."

"Do you want me to walk you back?"

"It might be better for you if you don't. Delvon's in a mood."

"I'll just walk you to the ballroom then."

"Such a gentlemen," Larken teased.

Shadric grinned at her before taking her hand. They were silent as they walked, and Larken wished it could have lasted a little longer. She had thought she was completely alone, but she didn't feel that way with Shadric. He understood her in a way that no one else did…and as much as her heart went out to him for his pain, she was glad for it.

They reached the ballroom, and Larken bid Shadric a goodnight. His promise moved between them silently, and she knew that he would do whatever it took to help her. Leaving him with the rest of his band, Larken made her way back to her room. The white halls reflected the dark world outside, and she didn't bother to turn any lights on. The Manor hardly ever had any shadows, and when it did, Larken could pretend that she was invisible.

Delvon waited for her outside her bedroom door and looked her up and down once before deepening his frown. "What?" she demanded, crossing her arms.

He pushed off her door and started walking down the hall. He didn't even look back at her as he said, "Bad idea, Peach."

CHAPTER 26

Dominic forced himself not to pull at his tie. He felt out of place in his suit, wishing again that he could wear his uniform. But judging by how late Cornella had kept him last time, he didn't want to take any risks. He would rather be dressed for the rehearsal dinner that evening than risk being late again. At least last time he had had enough sense to keep a spare outfit in his aircraft.

Dominic received many appreciative glances as he walked through the familiar halls of Base 14. Some he recognized from past encounters, others were simply trying to catch his eye, not knowing that he had changed. Which he had; he hadn't looked at another woman since his engagement, and he was going crazy. He couldn't wait until they were married and he could finally enjoy his new wife. Dominic would be lying if he said that he didn't think about sneaking away with her whenever they spent time together, but he knew Larken, and she would only ever engage in that sort of *activity* with her husband. Knowing that made her that much more desirable, and Dominic couldn't wait to be her first.

A familiar sounding gait fell into step with his, and the women who had been admiring him only seconds before suddenly found somewhere else to look. Cornella laughed, her voice dripping with venom as she mused, "I hope that you're not already looking for a mistress. You aren't even married yet."

"I have no plans on looking for a mistress anytime soon, Lumina."

Or ever.

"I see," she sighed. "And how is my prize bloom today? Ready for tonight?"

More than you can imagine.

"Yes, I will admit that I'm looking forward to it."

"Well then, we better make sure that we make this meeting fast. We wouldn't want to keep my daughter waiting."

Cornella sped up, beating him to the door at the end of the hall that led to Base 14's conference room. Dominic widened his own strides and opened the door for Cornella as soon as he reached it. She walked into the room as gracefully as if she had been floating and took the seat at the head of the table without a word. Dominic followed, taking the seat on her left.

Avery Sutton sat across from him, beady brown eyes narrowed, no doubt calculating how to get him out of the way and secure the title of *Cornella's Dog* for himself. The man had been in his father's squad and knew nothing of integrity. He did whatever he could to get ahead, making his father regret ever bringing him on board. Dominic knew he had been the man for the job the moment Cornella asked him to find a replacement. Loyal only to himself, Sutton would do whatever he was told to move up in the world.

The rest of Dominic's squad were in attendance as well. Squad 19 hadn't been the only one to be disbanded, but they were the only ones to desert. He had been furious to learn that General Maxwell had gone behind his back and hired those degenerates to be Larken's personal security team. But, in the end, it wouldn't matter. Little accidents happened on the job all the time, just like the server virus that had infected the military aircraft that General Maxwell had just happened to be using the day of the crash. After reaching a certain altitude, the engines seized, and General Maxwell fell to his death.

Dominic had second thoughts at the beginning, not wanting his fingers to be caught in the same pot as the men that tried to kill Larken more than once. He told himself that the job was a gift, that he should be thankful that he now controlled the men that had wanted Larken dead for so long. With him sitting at the top, he would control who they went after and what moves they made. The fires were a stroke of genius on Cornella's part, and he ran with it, wanting to keep the Vigilants as far away from Larken as possible. And now that he had used them to remove one obstacle, he knew the rest of Larken's security team could be taken out just as easily. He would save Deckard for last though, force him to watch as the woman he had tried to steal away turned on him. She would realize that it was all Deckard's fault, and then beg Dominic to finish the nuisance off.

Cornella looked over the room, her hard caramel eyes landing on the empty chair. Without looking at him, she asked, "Captain Braves, where is Mr. Tanner?"

Not skipping a beat, he answered, "I thought his services would best be used to protect Miss Hale today."

Cornella turned her eyes on him, the very job she had taunted Dominic with thrown back in her face. "Is there a threat against her life that the rest of her *security team* couldn't handle?"

Dominic bristled at her words; he still hadn't told her of his suspicions. He had concluded that, once he and Larken were set up in their new home, Cornella deserved to have the empire she had fought so hard to build be torn apart around her. Dominic wanted the Faithfuls, or whomever it was that Tanner worked for, to take her down. He wanted them to destroy her world the same way she had destroyed Larken's.

"With the last-minute preparations and all the people coming and going from the Manor, I thought that it might be suspicious if the bodyguard that she is always photographed with wasn't there. Especially since we move forward with our plan soon."

Cornella's lips curled into a silent snarl, but she knew that he was right. "Fine," she said. "You can inform him of our plans when you next meet."

"Of course, Lumina."

She had no idea that he didn't regularly meet with Tanner, that Dominic had assigned someone else to pass along the messages. There would be nothing to tie him to Tanner and whatever happened to the Military District after he left. The only thing that mattered anymore was getting Larken to safety.

Dominic hadn't believed Tanner when he had talked about securing the way to the honeymoon after General Maxwell's funeral, but it didn't matter. He wasn't taking Larken to that beach house anyway. He would load her up into his hover, slip her something to knock her out, switch to his aircraft, and then fly them to their new home. Whatever Cornella did after that was none of his business; he didn't care what happened to her. Only Larken mattered.

Cornella moved on with the meeting, asking about how the Vigilants were adjusting to their new lives on base. She had plenty to say about how she wanted things to move forward after the wedding. Cornella wanted to use the ceremony, and the media attention it would have, to make the first move. Base 14 would ship out during the nuptials, leaving the Vigilants behind to burn the base to the ground. The District would see it as a threat, not knowing that all the people who stayed behind actually lived. They would only see the flames and the falsified numbers. Every single Vigilant represented a fake soldier that would die, and the deaths would push the District into action.

"Are you sure this is wise, Lumina?" Sutton asked. "If we burn down the base, we're destroying a perfectly good hiding place for the rest of the Vigilants."

Cornella glared at him hard enough that Dominic thought she might have him murdered for speaking out of turn. "And what would happen, Chief Administrator Sutton, if we *don't* burn the base down after we present our cleverly crafted story, and someone stumbles upon a fully intact Base 14 full of my special operatives?"

Sutton went pale. "I-I'm sorry, Lumina, I didn't mean—I didn't think—"

"That's right, you *didn't think.* That's the problem here. The only ones who seem to be *thinking* are me and Captain Braves." She rounded on Dominic. "You couldn't find anyone more competent?"

"If you had wanted competence, Lumina, you should have told me when you gave me the order to look for someone malleable."

She frowned at him again, having no one to blame but herself. Leaning back in her chair, she brushed invisible dust from her black sweater and sighed.

Cornella listened as the rest of the newly appointed Captains in the room gave their report on the Vigilants they were responsible for. Each one puffed out their chest as they spoke, wearing their yellow rose pins proudly. Dominic only half listened and kept one eye on the time. Now that Cornella had what she wanted, she had no more need of him. After the ceremony, both he and Larken would be free of her, and they would never have to come back to the Military District again.

The thought threatened to have his lips twitching, but he kept his face expressionless. He was glad he did when Cornella glanced over at him. She looked him up and down, taking in his brown suit and the teal tie he got specifically to match Larken's eyes. She smirked at him before returning her attention back to the others. Dominic might have plans to leave and never look back, but a little voice told him that that might not happen. That he could try and run all he wanted, but Cornella had no intention of letting him go.

CHAPTER 27

Aflute of champagne had been shoved into her hand, and Larken almost threw it in the smirking waiter's face. He winked before disappearing into the crowd with his tray but didn't stay away for long. He bobbed in and out of her vision, looking her up and down every chance he got and clearly hoping that the stressed and aggravated bride-to-be would seek him out for a little distraction. She couldn't find Carl anywhere, which was unusual since he was *her* stylist.

Candy laughed, standing close to Hinlee. The two had grown close over the last few days, Larken's upcoming wedding sparking conversation about the ones they hoped to have. The two had whispered in the chapel nonstop as Larken practiced walking down the aisle. Soren and Loxly had disappeared as well, not that it mattered. They still weren't speaking—Loxly giving Larken her space, and Soren just ignored her as always. He wasn't the only one she actively tried to avoid though; Larken hadn't talked to Delvon since the night of the funeral. If he had been able to recognize Shadric's jacket that quickly, then the two were a lot closer than what he had let on. It didn't help that he had ignored her and belittled her theory about Vallen still being alive, but he had also given her advice she didn't ask for.

What was it to him how close she and the singer were becoming?

Larken tried to take a breath, but her lungs felt too tight. The pink dress she wore restricted her to the point that, if she were to drop something, it would be stuck on the ground until someone was kind enough to pick it up for her. The sweetheart neckline dipped dangerously low, but with the laces in the back being as tight as they were, the fabric wouldn't be shifting anytime soon. The gown had a small train that dragged slightly behind her, and the front of the dress cut off just above her ankles, showing off the white pumps that her poor feet had been stuffed into. Thankfully, a built-in slip protected her legs from the coarse tulle. The inside of her arms weren't so lucky though, and they brushed against the scratchy bodice every time she moved. If Larken had her way, she would have made a different statement, wearing the same dress she had worn to Vallen's funeral. But her mother had selected her attire for the evening, and Larken hadn't been allowed to refuse.

Standing in the same spot she had been in for the last thirty minutes, Larken watched as her fiancé walked around the ballroom, talking to everyone that caught his eye. She was glad that Dominic hadn't made her go with him. It was hard enough standing in her heels, and she couldn't imagine trying to maneuver around her skirts as well. Her communicator buzzed in her hand, and Larken couldn't help but smile as she read the message.

You look beautiful…and very uncomfortable.

She looked around, trying to find Shadric. When she couldn't spot him anywhere, she sent out a message of her own.

Where are you?

You can't see me?

Larken shook her head at the device.

If I could, I wouldn't be asking you.

She waited, but a reply never came. Looking around the ball-room once more, she decided that he wasn't there. If he had been, Dominic would never have left her alone. Once more she scanned the room, but this time she met the eyes of that hopeful waiter. He smirked, delivered his last flute of champagne, and made his way toward her.

Larken didn't wait for him to speak before she set her drink on his tray and grabbed her skirts. She caught the briefest look of irritation on his face before turning away, surprised that Dominic hadn't noticed the way the man had been keeping tabs on her. Taking a step, she tested her weight on the pump. The polished wood beneath her feet slipped and slid under her new shoes, and Larken tried to find whatever friction she could. She should have scuffed up the soles, but Carl would have killed her. The simple-looking white pumps had been more expensive than the dress. Her communicator buzzed again, and Larken dropped her skirts.

Colder.

Turning, she took another step. The device vibrated again.

Colder.

Facing the open doors, Larken made her way to the gardens. She should have guessed that he would be there; he was outside whenever he had the chance. Larken wondered if it had anything to do with growing up in a camp or if that was just who he was.

A new message shook her communicator, and she stopped to read it, not trusting her balance to keep her upright if she were to read and walk in heels.

Warmer.

Grinning, Larken took up her skirts once more and pushed into the gardens. The air had goosebumps breaking out across her skin, but she didn't stop. People smiled at her, offering their congratulations and well wishes for the following afternoon. Larken only nodded at them and didn't let them deter from her mission. Little baubles floated in the sky, fighting the stars for attention. The rose bushes, the night sky, and the lights had everything feeling magical. Larken felt like a princess in a fairy story as she walked into the maze. The foliage muffled the orchestra that Dominic had hired for the evening, and Larken didn't pass a single person on her way to the fountain.

Most people didn't know their way through the maze, so when

her parents threw extravagant parties like this, the intoxicated guests were warned to stay away from it. The security team had gotten tired of walking through it the next morning in their search of unconscious socialites. Apparently, the security guards either trusted that Larken could find her way back—or they just didn't care—because no one came after her.

When she reached the center, Shadric was nowhere to be found. She didn't waste any time looking for him though. Instead, she walked up to the edge of the fountain and dropped her skirts. Wrapping her arms around herself, Larken looked up at the statue she had stared at through most of her childhood. The only defining feature left on her grandmother's face was her lips, turned up in a small smile. Larken had always thought that the statue had a great secret, one that would forever remain hidden.

"She looks like you, you know," Shadric said softly, somewhere behind her.

Without turning around, she asked, "You think so?"

"I do. You're both strong. Facing whatever the world throws at you. Smiling when the wreckage clears and you're still standing."

"I never looked at it that way before."

"Sometimes, we can't always see our best qualities, and we need someone else to point them out to us."

Larken turned. "And what do you think my best qualities are, Mr. Barlow?"

He stepped closer until he stood right in front of her. He had shaved, and his blond hair had been styled. Shadric looked extremely put-together in his light grey suit and forest-green tie. "You, Miss Hale, are the sun. You are unrelenting, resilient, constant, and you force people to look at things in a way they never have before."

"What do you mean?"

He smiled. "You nearly killed me and somehow tricked me into developing feelings for you."

Larken laughed. "To be fair, you *were* trying to kidnap me."

"I would do it all over again too."

"Even if that meant I would shoot you again?"

"If it meant meeting you," Shadric reached out and grabbed her free hand, "then yes."

Larken sighed, dropping her gaze. She wasn't the only one who had the power to turn others' worlds upside down. Shadric had blown into her life as a knight in shining armor, confusing her as he threatened to steal her heart. But it wasn't just him. Someone else threatened to steal her heart away as well. Only, since that day in Vallen's sitting room, Larken didn't think that Soren wanted to anymore.

Shadric gently pulled her communicator free and set it on the edge of the fountain. He didn't say anything as he grabbed her waist and pulled her close. The two of them stepped seamlessly into a dance, the soft notes of the orchestra pushing and pulling them like water. Larken stumbled more than once, her heels catching on her train, but Shadric caught her each time. His hands felt warm against her cold ones, and she wondered what he was thinking.

As if he could sense her unspoken question, he murmured, "I don't think I've seen your hair down like this."

Her curls felt heavy against her shoulders when she said, "Dominic likes it like this."

"And what do you prefer?"

"I like it pulled back. I don't want to have to worry about it getting in my eyes if I have to fight."

Shadric grinned. "I don't know why I expected a different answer."

She laughed softly. "And what about you?" Larken moved her hand from his shoulder to his jaw. "I don't think I've ever seen you clean-shaven before."

"Your fiancé said that if I wanted to keep my job, I couldn't look like I just rolled out of bed."

Larken hummed, moving her hand back to his shoulder. "Well, I for one happen to like that style. When Cam worked for me, he used to say that's how I always looked."

Shadric smiled at her. "The guy you punched, right?"

"How do you know about *that*, but not what I looked like when we met?"

"I heard about it happening from a friend, and after I realized that you were *Larken Hale,* I looked it up."

Larken should have been mad that he had used her unwanted media attention to his advantage, but she had been following him in the media since she was thirteen. Instead of frowning at him, she only rolled her eyes. He smiled and pulled her closer. Larken didn't think twice about letting go of his hand and wrapping her arms around him. Resting her cheek against his chest, she absorbed as much warmth from him as she could, losing herself in the wooded scent of his grey suit.

"How has your search been going?" he asked, changing the subject.

Her heart sank as she was forced to admit, "Not well. I was hoping to find more, but there's nothing. It was like he was never here." Larken didn't say that that was the main reason she was convinced that he was still alive, but she didn't think she needed to either.

"Did you make a decision about the morning?" His voice was soft, as if her answer would set things into motion that he had been waiting a lifetime for.

"All I know so far is that I won't go quietly, if at all."

Shadric splayed his hands across her back, resting his jaw against her hair as he released a deep breath. Here in his arms, she wasn't the Daughter of the Military or the ex-cadet of Squad 19; she was only Larken Hale. She was all he wanted, and she couldn't tell herself anymore that she didn't want him. Her heart felt torn between two impossible choices, but she couldn't help but think that the choice had been made for her.

How could she choose between the two men that plagued her thoughts when one acted like he wanted nothing to do with her anymore? Did she still even have a choice? Soren didn't want her. She thought he did, but if the way he was acting lately was any indication, then he had decided that she wasn't worth the trouble. But

Shadric was here, and he made sure that she knew how he felt. Why shouldn't she let him sweep her off her feet? What was so wrong with letting him take care of her? She was tired of always being the strong one, and with him, she felt like she didn't have to be. Larken could live in his world of sunshine and music. Together they could write their own story; she could live in exile with him as a Faithful and never look back. Life with Shadric seemed so perfect—he offered her everything she had ever wanted. A home, family, acceptance, and understanding. So why couldn't she just reach out and take it? What was stopping her?

Larken's eyes snapped open, and she looked up at Shadric. His bright blue eyes chased away the image of the hazel ones she realized she had been thinking about. Her cheeks heated, guilt twisting her stomach in a way that made her feel sick. Shadric's brow crinkled, and a look of confused worry crossed his face. "Larken, are you okay?"

"Fine," she huffed. "Just a little lightheaded."

"It's that dress," he grumbled. "You haven't taken a full breath this whole time."

"I should get back to the party before they notice I'm gone."

"Are you sure?" he asked, that same worry coloring his voice.

"Yes, I'm sure." She didn't meet his eyes when she added, "I would hate for Dominic to come looking for me and find us here. I don't want to think about what he might do."

"If he touches you—"

"Not to me." Larken reluctantly met his gaze, heart still twisting with guilt. "I'm worried about what he might do to you."

Without waiting for him to reply, Larken grabbed her communicator, lifted her skirts, and made her way out of the maze. Levi stood waiting for her at the entrance, and she refused to look at him; she didn't know what he was thinking, and she didn't want to. He knew more about her complicated relationship with Soren than anyone, even though he never said anything about it. She still got embarrassed thinking about the rash incident and how Levi had been the one to make fun of her for it.

She walked past him, but he still said, "It would be the smarter decision, you know."

"I don't know what you're talking about."

"It would be easy. No baggage, no mixed signals, and definitely less fighting."

Larken sighed, eyes burning. She looked over her shoulder at the field medic. "But?"

"But nothing. If you would be happy, then it's the right choice for you."

Levi walked past her back into the ballroom. The orchestra started up a new melody that had her shoulder throbbing. Levi's words danced in her head, and she realized that Shadric would be the right choice, the *easier choice*. But she didn't know if he would be the choice that made her happy. Larken thought back to the last time she had been truly happy, and the pearl resting against her chest suddenly felt heavy enough to bring her to her knees.

CHAPTER 28

Larken barely made it two steps into the ballroom before Dominic appeared at her side. He looked her up and down, making her feel guilty even though nothing had happened. Well, nothing in the way he was obviously thinking. Larken felt her hand wander up to the pearl, and his chocolate brown eyes followed the movement. His features softened and he sighed.

Pulling her near, he murmured, "Please try and stay close, Lark. You never know what the men here might try after a few drinks."

Her defenses rose as she released the necklace and muttered, "I can take care of myself."

"I know you can. Believe me, I do. I just don't want anything to happen to you."

"You were the one who wanted an open bar."

Dominic ignored her like he always did when she disagreed with him. It made her ball her hands into fists, and she thought about punching him. Larken was getting so tired of the way he treated her, and if it wasn't for the promise she had made to Vallen, she would have called everything off right then and there. Larken had to trust that he was still out there and had a plan.

Deciding it would be better to leave than to stick around and do something that she might regret, Larken tried to step out of

Dominic's hold on her. He gripped her arms tighter, not ready to part with her. "Where are you going? I just asked you to stay here."

"I wanted to spend some time with my father," she lied. "He had a hard time during the rehearsal. I wanted to make sure he was okay."

Dominic raised a blond eyebrow. "You promise you weren't just trying to sneak back outside?"

Levi's words sounded in her mind as if they were from years ago, not just minutes. Larken dropped her gaze and said honestly, "I felt overwhelmed."

Dominic sighed again, pulling her close once more. "I know you hate this, Lark, but this time tomorrow it will all be over."

"I know," she mumbled into his chest, biting her tongue before she could tell him that that's what was bothering her.

Dominic finally released her and sent her off with, "Give Trogar my regards."

Larken made her way over to the bar, eyes narrowed in on the stool her father sat atop. The cute bartender looked to be flirting with him, and Larken could hear her father's jovial protests and laughter from where she stood.

Reaching the stool next to the Luminary, Larken dropped her communicator onto the bar before she pulled herself onto it. Her skirts hung around hers and the stool's legs like a tulle tablecloth. Her Father barked another laugh before saying, "That's sweet, honey, but you're younger than my daughter. You should find someone your own age."

The bartender beamed at him, not at all offended by his refusal. Then again, she probably propositioned him because he hadn't tried pawing at her like his drunken friends would have. Larken's respect for the bartender increased and the brunette looked at her and asked, "What'll it be, Miss?"

"Just some water, Brandi. My daughter doesn't drink," her father answered for her.

Larken wondered what other things he picked up on over the years. If he knew about Fisher and her hatred of alcohol, it had to be more than what she thought. Maybe he had noticed that she was at base and only pretended to make her absence easier. Or maybe he only remembered what he heard while he was drunk *when* he was drunk.

Trogar turned to her and cupped her cheek. His smile faltered a little and he asked, "Why is my Sunshine so dim tonight?"

"Just have a lot on my mind."

"Does it have anything to do with why you're sitting at the bar with your old man instead of dancing with your fiancé?"

The bartender dropped off the water and Larken huffed out a slow breath. Wrapping her hands around the cold glass, she remembered all the times when she was little that her father had seen through her mask. Even now, he looked at her with those same dark eyes that seemed to understand more than what he let on. She looked up at the first man she had loved and admitted, "I feel a little lost, Daddy."

"Course you do. You're getting married after all."

"No, I mean, more than that." Larken looked around to make sure no one was listening and then leaned in close to her father. "I don't love him."

The words were like a weight that fell from her shoulders as she said them. She wondered briefly if she had ever actually said them out loud before, but Trogar's sympathetic smile chased away the thoughts. "I understand that too well."

"Then why did you agree to it? Why not let me choose?"

"Because, Sunshine," her father pulled back and downed the rest of his drink, "he will treat you well."

"How do you know?" Larken felt her heart squeeze.

"He was willing to do whatever it took to be with you, and a man like that will stop at nothing to make sure that you're happy." Trogar looked back at her. "And your happiness is all I want."

And all I want is to get away from here...

Larken looked at her father as he ordered another drink. Surely if her father could see how unhappy she was he couldn't expect her to stay, could he? Her stomach soured. Did he know about her plan to run away before the wedding?

As if he could read her thoughts, Trogar said, "Just give him one more chance, Sunshine. He might prove you wrong." Then he bitterly added, "Just like your mother did to me."

Before Larken could respond, everyone started clamoring for the bride and groom to share a dance. Dominic grinned as he made his way over to her, and Trogar helped her from her stool before she could even take a sip of her water. Larken stood on her tiptoes and kissed her father's scratchy cheek. Tears lined his eyes, as if he knew that this was goodbye, and she whispered, "I love you, Daddy. Thank you, for everything."

He cleared his throat and rasped, "Make me proud."

"I will," she promised. Dominic grabbed her hand and led her out onto the floor, and Larken had no choice but to leave her communicator behind with her father. Out of the corner of her eye, she saw Delvon made his way over to the bar and stuff the communicator into his pocket.

Dominic pulled her in close before the music even started and asked, "You have a good talk?"

"I think so," Larken answered, throat tight.

"Good. I don't know when we'll be able to see him again."

"What about your parents?" she asked, wanting to direct the conversation away from her.

"What about them?"

"When have you last talked to them?"

"I spoke with them earlier. Mother was upset that I chose to marry a soldier, and Father insisted on telling me that I'm not good enough for you."

"I'm sorry, Dominic. That's awful."

He shrugged, fixing a suave smile on his face. "It's true. There's no use denying it." He pulled her closer, and Larken's stomach flipped uncomfortably. "I don't deserve you, but I'm happy you're letting me try."

She didn't know what to say, so she just stayed silent, pleading in her mind for him to back off a little. As they danced, it was impossible for Larken not to compare Dominic to Shadric. She and the singer had moved as if the music tugged at their souls, like they were of one mind. And then there was that night in the dorm, the one where Soren had taken her in his arms and made her feel lighter than air. That night had been so long ago, and those people who had danced together didn't seem to exist anymore. The thought tugged at her heart, and Larken wished again that none of this had happened. She forced herself to stop because she knew that she didn't want to go back to the way things were.

Back then, she didn't know what her mother had planned. Larken wouldn't know anything about the Faithfuls, and she never would have become friends with Delvon, as mad as she was at him. Things might be simpler if she had the power to turn back the clock, but only cowards focused on what they wished they could change. Vallen hadn't raised her to be a coward; he raised her to take life by the reins and charge in the direction of her destiny. And even though she would be charging blindly in the days to come, Larken would do whatever it took to keep moving forward.

Dominic brought her back to herself by pulling her in closer still. His whole arm wrapped around her, and she had the choice of resting her face against his chest or staring into his neck. Larken chose the latter, not wanting him to think that she was finally starting to let her guard down again. He took whatever he could get, and the Star stuck his face into her hair. He took a deep breath and then murmured, "Grapefruit?"

"I got some for my birthday."

"Larken, you don't need to be using that cheap shampoo. You're better than that."

"Actually," Larken interjected, annoyance touching her tone, "Carl said that it was really good for my hair type and that Cam should have had me on a similar formula to begin with. Besides," she added, "I *like* it."

"But you deserve so much more," Dominic tried again.

Larken wouldn't hear it. She pulled back just enough to look him in the eyes. "Stop acting like you know what's best for me. You don't."

"I do," he insisted, hands tightening on her. She wondered if he knew he was doing it but didn't get a chance to tell him his grip was starting to hurt because he continued, "I do know what's best for you because I've seen the kind of life you've had since you've been back." Dominic's cheeks flushed slightly in anger as he spoke. "Since your return, everything has been difficult for you, and I'm sick of it. That's why I asked for you. I was tired of watching the woman I love suffer. And if I had known it was going to be like this, I would have never asked—" Dominic's voice cut off, choked by anger.

Larken's gaze snapped to him, and she narrowed her eyes. "Asked *what?*"

Still not looking at her, Dominic sighed and answered, "Nothing."

Larken stopped dancing, almost making him trip. She didn't care who was watching, where she was, or about anything other than what he had meant to say. A sinking feeling in her stomach told her that she already knew the words he had left unspoken, but she needed to hear them. She needed to know who exactly was to blame.

Seeing the look in her eyes, Dominic visibly started to panic. "Look, Lark, I didn't know. I thought I was helping you."

"I told you to stop helping me right after I got to base," she snapped. "What did you ask, Dominic?"

"Larken, I—"

"*Tell me!*" she hissed, demanding an answer.

"I asked your mother to bring you back home so we could finally be together."

There it was. She had been right all along. Her mother had never cared about her safety; the only reason she had come home was because Dominic had made a deal with her mother. Larken thought she might be ill or pass out. "What did you trade?"

"Excuse me?"

"She never does anything for nothing. What did you trade? What did she make you do for bringing me home?"

"I have been helping her with things around the different bases, that's all."

All the conversations between her and Delvon rushed to the front of her mind so fast that she became light-headed. Dominic was the missing piece. All the questions that she couldn't answer; he was the thread that tied them all together. He wasn't just helping around the bases; he was a part of that group that tried to have her killed over and over again. Though that wasn't the worst of it in her mind. Larken knew she was wrong for thinking it, but she couldn't keep the thought from forming.

Dominic was the one that took me away from Soren.

Before she could scream, cry, or even knock him out, Dominic pulled her close. He held her tightly, filling her lungs with the scent of blueberries and betrayal. "Please don't hate me, Lark. I was only trying to do what was best for you, what was best for *us*."

"I could never hate you," she rasped, voice cracking through her honesty. If anyone deserved her hate, it would be him and her mother, but she just couldn't bring herself to hate him.

She was too soft, too *weak*. Larken had always been too quick to forgive, even though she could never forget. She could no more hate her mother than she could Dominic, even if her mother was the one causing her all this pain. Larken didn't care what Dominic's next promise would be, or even how he would phrase his next apology. The only thing that mattered was getting away from here. And she would not rest easy until she was free.

She fixed a fake smile on her face, assuring him that she understood, and let him lead her through the rest of the dance. Larken kept her broken heart hidden away and told herself that Dominic had been right about one thing. This time tomorrow, this would all be over, and she and whoever would help her would be very, very far away.

CHAPTER 29

L oxly gave a low whistle as Carl turned the lights on. Larken's closet stood before them, and it had been stuffed with more clothes than had been at that Star boutique Soren had purchased his suit at. Carl just sighed, saying, "I know. All my hard work." Then a little louder, he said, "Thanks again for coming. Packing for a honeymoon is one thing, carrying all of it to the aircraft is another."

"Course, Carl. Happy to help." Loxly's voice sounded smooth and not the least bit worried, whereas Soren could only grunt, too afraid that just opening his mouth would give them away.

Estelle whined in the doorway, dropping to the floor and exposing her belly. Carl ignored the android as he motioned Loxly forward and started stuffing outfits into the bag the sharpshooter held. Loxly asked about certain choices, but the stylist assured him that everything he picked was Larken's favorite. Soren let the two be, leaving the closet. He trusted Carl to know what Larken would want, seeing as he had been dressing her for the last month. Soren paused as Estelle whimpered up at him and he crouched down. Rubbing her belly, he murmured, "Don't worry. We won't forget you."

In answer, the android let her tongue loll out of her mouth.

"Security will be minimal over the next month; she'll need all the help she can get."

Estelle flopped onto her belly and jumped to her feet. She scampered away, and then out of the room. Soren stood, figuring that the android made her way to Vallen's couch. He would have to remember to grab her *bed,* as Larken called it, and added it to the mental list of things to pack. He walked over to Larken's dresser and pulled open the first drawer.

"Remember, only pack what Miss Hale won't be able to live without on her honeymoon," Carl called from the closet.

The reminder didn't help, and Soren started to panic for an entirely different reason as he stared openmouthed at the contents of the drawer.

When Soren didn't respond, Loxly poked his head out of the closet. "You okay, Cap?" Soren closed his mouth and looked over just in time to see Loxly chuckle. "Please tell me you didn't find what I think you found," the other man teased.

"I—what? No!"

Loxly only laughed again and Carl looked out of the closet as well. The stylist rolled his eyes, taking Soren's side. "Trust me, it's not what you think."

The sharpshooter passed the bag off to Carl and walked to Soren's side. He peered into the drawer and sighed. "Of course it's books. What else would our Little Bird use a place to keep clothes for?"

Soren, still panicked, looked to his friend for help. "Which ones do I take?"

"All of them?" he offered.

Carl groaned from the closet and then walked over to them as well. He reached into the drawer, barely able to pull free one of the clear tablets that had been packed in. If each tablet held a series or more, Larken could very well have more books than the base library. Carl looked over the tablet and then put it back. He grabbed another one as he said, "General Maxwell said that they had to start getting the hard copies because her communicators kept short-circuiting.

Apparently, Miss Hale would max out the memory on the device and then some."

"How's that possible?" Loxly asked. "Brecker has more books than anyone on the squad, and he hasn't come close to needing a new one."

Carl handed Soren a beaten-up tablet that had been chipped in a few spots. He gave Loxly a sad smile as he said, "Brecker also had all of you. When Miss Hale wasn't working out with General Maxwell..."

She was here, alone, reading...

Soren looked at the tablet again, running his finger over one of the deeper gouges. Carl started walking back to the closet, saying, "If they look like that, pack them."

Soren looked over to the sharpshooter, who was now glaring at the tablets. Soren knew that Loxly wasn't mad, even though he looked it. He was hurting for his friend. Loxly was no doubt remembering all the times he had helped pull Larken from her hurt at base when she had been ostracized for being a Hale. At least, that's what Soren was remembering. Growing up in the Manor, she didn't have that. She had her sound system and her books. No wonder she had latched onto Jodi and Brecker, talking with them about books as if they were her favorite food.

"What ones did you get her?" Soren asked, pulling Loxly from his thoughts.

The sharpshooter grabbed the newest looking one in the lower right-hand corner. He hit the screen and handed it to Soren. "This one." Loxly grabbed the two that were next to it, looking them over as well. "And these, but she might have finished them already. She likes readin' more than fightin'."

Soren thought back to all their spars and couldn't help but smirk. "Doubt it."

"You're a special case, Cap."

"Says the man who's afraid to talk to her too early in the morning."

"I'm smart, not afraid," Loxly shot back as he rejoined Carl in the closet.

Soren started looking over the tablets, grabbing all the excessively battered ones he could find. Once he had the tablets in her bag, he shut the drawer and opened the second one. The weapons had been less of a shock, and Soren called Loxly back out. He passed off the gun that Vallen had given Larken for her birthday, and the sharpshooter sat on her bed to examine it. He fawned over the handgun as if it were a newborn, and Carl emerged from the closet with a small leather bag. One look from him warned Soren not to go looking through it if he wanted to keep his eyes. Soren gave him a nod.

After packing all the weapons and belts, Soren moved down to the third drawer. He huffed a laugh as he saw all the shoes that had been crammed into it, and Carl only grumbled something that sounded like, *"Don't care if they were from Cam. Absolutely no respect."*

Pushing the drawer back in, Soren moved down to the bottom one. His heart wrenched when he found that black jacket Larken had always worn around the dorm folded with a sterling silver medal resting on top of it. Soren remembered when they had been called in for the reading of Vallen's will. Larken had stood there, refusing to look at any of them, angry that they hadn't believed her. The portly lawyer had wasted no time saying that everything went to her, but Soren would never forget the look in her eyes as she was handed Vallen's General's medal. Her teal eyes had wavered, and he knew that, for the first time, she was wondering if she had been wrong.

Soren packed the jacket and the medal with the General insignia on it, just to be safe. It wasn't too long ago that Soren had wanted this same medal for himself. And he would have worn it proudly too. Soren stared at the snake that wound its way up the simple sword for only a moment before dropping the thing into the bag. The sword, protection of the world, and the snake, ever-changing and ever-adapting, doing whatever it took to remain the protector.

They were the symbols that had guided his life, and now they were only a bitter taste in his mouth.

Soren reached into the drawer again, pulling out clear tablets that held photos of Vallen and Larken as she grew up. He also found the album he had given to her for her birthday. Soren felt a sting of pain, wondering why she had felt the need to hide his gift away, but then he remembered where he was. Larken seemed to keep everything that truly meant something in this drawer, and his gift had been in there as well. He couldn't help but look over at her vanity. The ring that should have been there was gone, Larken having to play pretend for one more night, but the shell was still there. The painting that Delvon had given her had been hung up on her wall close by, and as much as he hated it, he knew he would have to bring that as well.

That was another thing Soren had been forced to come to terms with. Delvon wasn't the enemy, as much as Soren had wanted him to be. Should Delvon have done what he did the night of the crash? No. But how much worse would it have been for the two of them if he hadn't? Soren and Larken would have had to choose a side right then and there, and thinking back to that night, Soren was afraid that if it had come down to that, he would have made the wrong choice.

Estelle chose that moment to reappear, huffing and snarling, dragging a blue blanket behind her. Soren couldn't help his small smile and walked over to help the android. Grabbing the blanket, Soren folded it and tucked it into the bag as well. He added the painting and the shell and turned to the mutt. She would need to be charged before he packed away her mat. As if she could tell what Soren was thinking, she yawned and wagged her tail halfheartedly. The retrieval must have taken a lot out of her. Soren crouched down and scratched at the same spot behind her ear that Larken always did.

"You did good. Go take a nap."

Estelle licked at his fingers with a dry tongue, and then made her way to the sitting room. Soren looked over Larken's room. Everything of worth appeared to be packed. Carl insisted on bringing a few more outfits than Soren thought Larken needed, but the stylist claimed that he had been right the last time Larken needed a specific outfit, and he was sticking with his gut. Soren couldn't blame him because trusting his gut was all he was doing anymore.

Loxly took the two bags that Carl had handed him and slung one over his shoulder. "Let's go get these on the *Harpy*. I don't think *Captain Braves* will want to wait for us to pack up before settin' out."

The way Loxly said Brave's name almost had Soren chuckling. The constant security had forced them to get creative, and the squad had taken it upon themselves to be as sarcastic as possible when discussing Larken's fiancé. No one knew that they were really making fun of the idiot except the people who also knew he was an idiot.

Soren grabbed what he could as well and replied, "We'll have to come back for Estelle."

"I'll pack her up with my things tomorrow. She can ride with me so she doesn't disturb the newlyweds." Carl gave Soren a wink that would look suggestive to the security team watching Larken's room but told Soren a completely different story.

Soren nodded and his eyes fell on the leather bag that Carl carried. Rolling his eyes, he looked away and followed the two men to the hanger. In less than twenty-four hours, if everything went according to plan, they would be far away from the Military District Manor and Larken would be with them. Safe and, Maxim willing, still single.

CHAPTER 30

Larken's alarm went off, startling her out of one nightmare and thrusting her into another. She rolled over, pulling a pillow over her head, and groaned. Larken was back at square one, hiding in bed, wondering what would happen if she didn't show up to her next attempt at public humiliation. It was starting to look like she would have no other option but to find Shadric. The covers were pulled from her and Larken whined. Gentle hands silently encouraged her to get up, but she didn't move out of spite.

Still mad at Delvon, she mumbled, "Go away."

"Love, Carl has been knocking at your door for the last five minutes."

"And yet you felt the need to barge right in." She pulled the pillow from her face and glared at him. *What if I had been naked?*

"Out here, in the open, in front of your camera?"

She frowned for a moment before rolling back over and reaching for another pillow. "Shut up."

The mattress dipped and Delvon cuddled her. She let him, trying not to let his sudden affection burn her eyes. His lips brushed against her ear and he asked, "Do you trust me?"

Larken wanted to say no, but it wasn't the truth. She nodded, turned to him, and buried her face in his black shirt. Carl and Candy could be heard walking into her room, and Larken tried not to cry.

Delvon chuckled, tightening his arm around her. "This mean you forgive me, Peach?"

Larken finally broke, and through her tears, she sobbed, *"Don't call me that."*

Delvon chuckled some more, still holding her. He kissed the top of her head and rubbed a hand up and down her back. Larken didn't want anyone to see her—not her friends, and especially not Soren. She was mad at all of them for ignoring her and keeping her in the dark. Larken had tried to figure out a plan on her own, but she couldn't come up with anything. All her plans revolved around finding Vallen, but she didn't, and now her five days were up. But at least she still had Shadric.

"Candy, dear, can you do something about that camera? We need all the space we can get, and that closet isn't going to cut it." Carl sounded strangely calm, not at all like he was about to either make or break his career.

There was an unfeminine grunt, and then Candy complained, "It's too high."

Delvon pulled away with a sigh, and Larken followed his movements with her now-dry eyes. He walked right up to the camera and ordered, "Turn this thing off." When the blue light continued to defy him, he said, "No one is allowed to see her until the ceremony." Still, the blue light shone. Delvon pulled off one of his boots. "Last chance, mates," he warned.

When nothing happened, Delvon raised his arm and broke the camera with his boot. Larken sat up, not believing he'd just done that. Then, he turned on her, silently ordering her to get out of bed. She jumped off the mattress and realized for the first time that morning that Estelle wasn't in her bed. Looking around, she noticed that quite a few of her things were missing. Her birthday gifts, the photos of her and Vallen, the shell that she kept on her vanity, even the painting of Draca that Delvon had given her.

"Where's—" Larken looked at the camera that now hung from a

few wires. Not taking any chances, Delvon pulled it from the wall. The wires snapped with finality, and she tried again. "Where's my stuff?"

Not answering her question, Delvon said, "You get ready like nothing is happening. I'm going to go smooth over this mess before we get unwanted guests sniffing around this wing."

"What about—" Larken almost slipped and asked about Shadric. Instead, she asked, "What about your promise?"

Delvon paused and then smirked like he knew what she really meant to say. "If you still want me to marry you after all of this is over, then I will. But I don't think your boyfriend would like it very much."

"He's not my boyfriend!" Larken shouted, knowing that he wasn't talking about the singer.

"Sure, Peach. Keep telling yourself that."

Larken grabbed a pillow and chucked it at him. It missed by a lot, and Delvon's laughs could be heard as he closed the door behind him.

"Why is everyone so obsessed with me having a boyfriend?!" she demanded.

Candy laughed, not looking away from what she was doing.

"Okay, nightgown off," Carl ordered, dressed in pale salmon-colored pants and a turquoise polo.

Ignoring him, Larken ran to her closet. Throwing the door open, she saw that all her absolute favorite outfits were gone, as well as a few of the dresses Carl had insisted she get. Her heart picked up, daring to hope that whatever Delvon had planned might work.

"Come on, kid. We have to get you to the first checkpoint so we can get ready too."

"Right," she said, turning to Carl. "Sorry."

Larken rushed to the bathroom and got herself ready for the day as quickly as she could. Before she had been sent out to base, Larken took her time brushing her teeth and hiding in the shower; now she figured that the shower she had taken after the rehearsal to wash off the feel of Dominic's presence was good enough. With a final spit into the sink, Larken dried her mouth on the back of her hand and left the bathroom.

She pulled her nightgown up over her head on her way to the vanity and let it drop to the floor. Candy held open her robe, and Larken stuck her arms into the selves. Now she knew why Carl had been so frantic the day before, trying to do whatever he could to get her ready before the rehearsal dinner. She had shouted at him, not wanting to get waxed or even leave Vallen's small sitting room. Sulking and snuggling with Estelle was where she ended up spending most of her time. She would have spent it riding, but her mother had gotten rid of Buttercup, and none of the new wolf hybrids knew her. That blue blanket was the only thing she had of her old life, and she had used it to hide from the world and catch her frustrated tears.

Carl motioned with his hands for her to hurry up, and Larken sat in the chair so fast that she almost slid off it. Carl's fingers lost themselves in her hair, pulling free tangles and working their magic. Candy started applying makeup to Larken's face, saying that they didn't want to waste any time, that they needed to get to their checkpoints as soon as they could in case something went wrong.

The curling iron that Carl had plugged in was now hot, and he got to work too. She never thought that she would ever find comfort in the smell of hairspray and mascara, but Larken found that she did. It wasn't so much that she enjoyed getting done up, shopping, or discussing possible outfits, but she did enjoy spending time with Candy and Carl.

Candy opened her mouth, and Larken mimicked her, letting her put on the muted mauve lipstick. Candy hummed and smiled as she said, "This could be your signature color." Then she stuck the lipstick in the pocket of her yellow pants with a wink.

The two of them worked in tandem getting Larken ready, and it wasn't long before she was shrugging out of her robe and stepping into her wedding dress. Candy disappeared into the closet and grabbed Larken's shoes as Carl got to work on the dress' buttons. Larken twisted the ring Brecker had given her since Soren's pearl was trapped under her dress. She eyed the engagement ring on the vanity and wondered who had packed up all her things without anyone noticing and how they snuck them out of the Manor.

Candy kneeled in front of her, and Larken pulled up her hem to make it easier on her. Larken wobbled slightly, balancing on her left foot, but managed to stay upright. "Honestly," Carl muttered behind her. "You're one of the best fighters I've ever seen. How can you be so clumsy?"

"It's a gift," Larken answered, telling him the same thing she had always said when Vallen had made fun of her unfortunate lack of elegance.

When Carl and Candy stood back to admire their work, Larken sighed. She walked to the vanity and reluctantly put her ring on. Turning, she let out a determined breath. "I'm ready."

"Good," Carl said, before striding over and knocking on her closed bedroom door twice.

He stepped back and Brecker came in wearing a black suit. He eyed her up and down before saying, "You look ridiculous."

Larken laughed. "Thanks, so do you."

"You should have stuck with the dress we got you."

"That would have been a sight. Show up to the wedding in a dress I wore on a date with another man." She smiled. "Can you imagine the headlines?"

Brecker opened his mouth to respond, but Carl cut him off. "Any trouble?"

A chime sounded, and Brecker pulled out his communicator. Nodding, he said, "We're good." Brecker looked up at Larken and motioned to the door with his head. "Let's go."

Candy and Carl each snagged a quick hug before disappearing down the hall. Larken walked over to Brecker, who held out his arm and Larken placed her hand in the crook of his elbow. "Thanks."

"No problem." He led them into the hall and towards the Manor chapel. Their pace was slow and steady, as if they had all the time in the world and Brecker smiled easily, asking, "How has your day been so far, Miss Hale?"

"Surreal," she answered honestly. Larken looked to the cameras they passed, and each of them boasted a yellow light. She raised an eyebrow at Brecker.

"The yellow means that the audio is turned on, but the video is off. Delvon went a little overboard earlier, but don't worry, Miss Hale. Your beautiful dress won't be seen until you walk down the aisle."

Larken understood the unspoken warning and kept up the pleasant small talk. Brecker winced occasionally when she talked about what she thought married life might be like. She knew that it wasn't the mention of marriage that he disliked; it was picturing her being married to Dominic that had him looking slightly ill. They walked and talked, ignoring the Manor staff they passed, all the way to the little room that connected the Manor to the chapel. It was where her mother had waited for her father, and where her grandmother had waited for her grandfather.

The room had no cameras and three doors. Pale olive paint covered the walls, the musty scent somehow complimenting the smell of roses and macaroons seeping in from the chapel. Two white wooden chairs sat next to a little table that held an arrangement of fake pink flowers. The door they had walked in through looked to be made of the same pale wood that the other two had been crafted with. The one that led to the chapel was unadorned like the door Brecker just closed behind them, but the one that led to the outdoor venue held a diamond window made of fragmented glass. A hundred little rainbows were caught in the edges of the glass, making the room glow with a warmth that didn't feel right for the situation.

Brecker positioned her by that door murmuring, "It's not ideal, but it's the best option we have. Don't leave until it's time, and whatever you do, *do not* go into the chapel."

Larken took the few steps to the chapel door and locked it. She moved back over to the spot that Brecker had originally put her in and looked up at him.

Nodding, he said, "You should lock this one after I leave."

"You're leaving me?"

"I have to make sure Carl and Candy get where they need to be. You'll be okay. Just stick to the plan and everything should work."

"*Should?*"

"*Will*. Now, don't make a sound; remember, the audio is still on out there."

Larken swallowed thickly but nodded. Brecker opened his arms, and she hugged him quickly, praying as she did that this wasn't goodbye. After she released him, Brecker snuck out of the room as quietly as he could, and Larken locked the door after he shut it. She stood there, all alone, with no weapons. The only thing she did have was the hope that all of this would work out somehow.

Never had she felt so unsure about her future. Larken looked to the door that separated her from the chapel. Raising her hand, she placed it on the wood. The thing was a far cry from an altar, but it was as close to one as she could get.

Maxim, please help me. Please let this work. I don't know what You have planned for me, or even what the next five minutes will bring, but I trust that You hold my future in Your hands.

Larken breathed deeply through her mouth, her nose already starting to plug up with her sudden onslaught of emotion. She still couldn't believe that Dominic was the reason she had come home, but she had to trust that Maxim knew what He was doing.

I know I've doubted that You might care for me, but if You do, please Maxim, let this work. I will go wherever you lead me; I will fight whichever cause You choose. Just please let this not be the end.

Larken finished her prayer and took up her spot by the window. Green grass and blue sky blurred together in the glass, and instead of the pearl, Larken's hand wandered up to her shoulder. It throbbed, reminding her of the last time she had taken a risk this big. Pushing the thoughts from her mind, she started fiddling with the ring Brecker gave her as she waited.

And waited.

And waited.

CHAPTER 31

She hadn't noticed him leaving the dining hall the night before, and if she had, she didn't say anything. Soren hated that she was back in his life, that he was helping her, and that he was still managing to mess everything up between them. He didn't know if it was better that she was upset with him, drawing attention away from any escape plan he might be trying, or worse. Had it only been the week before when she had jumped, crying, into his arms? She had been so hopeful then; he had *felt* it as he held her in his arms. Larken was happy that he had come for her, *knew* that he would save her. But now Soren feared that he was about to make things so much worse for the Military Sweetheart.

Loxly hummed some song that Soren knew Larken favored, and he wished that the sharpshooter wasn't so jovial. So many things could go wrong, and if they did, it would all be Soren's fault. He was the one that had given everyone their designated tasks, and he would be the one letting her down if any of them failed.

Loxly helped Hinlee and Levi look for any trackers or anything else a Vigilant could have attached to the *Harpy*. Soren had to wonder if Vallen had planned this all along; the aircraft was the fanciest one in the hangar, and everyone readily believed that it was the one that would be sweeping Larken and Braves off to their honeymoon.

There was no need to look inside the beast for any trackers; Soren and Loxly were the only two left who knew the access code. And even if someone managed to figure it out, they had that cuff Larken always wore. Delvon insisted that it would be enough to jam any signals coming or going from the *Harpy*—they would just have to remember to activate the cuff once they had her. All their communicators had been looked over by Delvon when they were last in the bunker, and he had personally removed anything that could be used to track them. Levi had been worried about Larken's, but the bodyguard had admitted to looking into hers when he had been promoted to her guard dog, and again after the funeral. Vallen had made sure her communicator had been cleaned, and Delvon confirmed it. The device currently weighed down Soren's pocket, and he was acutely aware of how still his was in the pocket opposite.

Soren pulled out his communicator, looking for the coded messages that his team was supposed to send out when they completed their designated tasks. Delvon and Brecker had already sent their first messages, telling him that the camera in Larken's room had been taken out and that Brecker was waiting for Larken outside her room. They needed Jodi's message, signaling that she and Ezra had obtained the information and supplies they needed. Ezra didn't want to set out without anything for Larken's shoulder, and Jodi wanted to get some chamomile extract for Larken. That way Larken would be able to get into the aircraft without having another panic attack if she actually agreed to taking the extract. Soren wasn't so sure after the incident with Braves, but he was willing to try anything that might help her anxiety.

Jodi had brought up all her concerns the last time they had been in the bunker, and she only got defensive when none of her questions could be answered. She worried that the Vigilants had something hidden up their sleeves and that sheer force didn't seem like Cornella's style. Soren wanted to disagree, knowing what she had put Larken through and how ruthless the woman could be, but Delvon had the same feeling. Since Braves had cut the bodyguard out of the inner workings of the Vigilants, they couldn't be sure that the information he had been given was completely trustworthy. The bodyguard claimed that putting a plan in place and then revealing something sneaky that she had been planning without anyone's knowledge was exactly what Cornella would do. Jodi agreed to get whatever information out of the Manor lab that she could, and, with it, maybe they would have a better understanding of what Cornella was up to.

Jodi hadn't been the only one suspicious of Larken's mother though. The day after Soren had gone to the theater, Soren had received a message from an unknown number. He knew who it was as soon as he read the words: *I don't trust her; we need to protect our songbird.* Soren assumed Vallen had given the man his number, though he had no way to ask now. He had put Fisher in touch with Delvon since Vallen was no longer around.

As far as Soren knew, Fisher would be waiting at Camp for his daughter, wanting to step up and be there for her now that Vallen was gone. But Soren couldn't get that one word out of his head— *our.* It danced in his mind as he tried to sleep at night and when he followed Larken during the day. He didn't know what Fisher made of Soren's relationship with his daughter, Larken never said, but he had to know something. Otherwise, her father wouldn't have implied that Larken belonged to him as well.

Soren still couldn't wrap his mind around what had happened to Vallen. The more he thought about what had happened, the less it made sense. But he also could just be in denial like Larken. If Vallen was alive, he wouldn't have left Larken's escape up to him. Vallen had been a General, a mastermind when it came to planning and strategizing. For him to leave his pride and joy in Soren's hands... the thought only made the fear of failure that much worse.

After what felt like an hour, Soren pulled out his communicator again. It had only been four minutes, and Loxly informed Soren that the three of them hadn't found anything. Soren told him to double-check, just in case, and looked at his communicator once more. Silent prayers had been running through his mind like a mantra, but not even that helped to calm his nerves anymore.

Finally, he received Jodi's message. She sent a little image of a brown feather, telling the group that they had completed their task without any problems. Delvon's followed two minutes later, his white feather saying he had gotten to the surveillance room but had a little trouble and they should proceed with caution.

This was it—they were about to find out if their too few days of planning would amount to anything. Soren gave Loxly, Hinlee, and Levi a nod, telling them to move out. The three got into the *Harpy*, and it quietly fired up as Soren made his way out of the hangar. Following the path Delvon had instructed him to take, Soren walked quietly under the cameras that sported a yellow light. Soren sent out a blue feather, signaling that he was on the move, and it was followed by blue feathers from Brecker, Loxly, and Jodi. Carl sent a yellow feather, telling the group that he was waiting for Brecker to come back and get him and Candy. Delvon sent another white feather.

Soren hurried his pace but forced himself to look natural. He was a fair distance away from the hangar now, and he wouldn't be able to explain to anyone he might pass why a member of Miss Hale's security team was so far away from her. So many things could go wrong. Someone could argue that the *Harpy* wasn't scheduled to take Larken on her honeymoon, or Delvon could be caught in the surveillance room with who knew how many unconscious bodies. Even worse, Soren could get caught before he made it to the garage where all the hovercrafts were parked. If he were to get caught trying to take one, then everyone would know that Larken was in danger, and their whole plan would be ruined.

Voices had Soren stopping in his tracks and doubling back. He pulled open the nearest door and hid behind it. By the sound of the steps, Soren guessed that they belonged to two women, and he pressed his ear to the door. Their voices grew clearer the closer they got, and soon Soren could make out what they were saying.

"It's really a shame that she hadn't listened to us more. I thought the yellow roses were a nice touch. But, no, the spoiled brat had to do everything *her* way."

"*Exactly*," the other one agreed. "I mean, why even hire us if she wasn't going to consider our suggestions? She landed a man that any of us would kill for, and she acts like she doesn't even want to marry him!"

"This whole thing is a little over the top if you ask me. She doesn't deserve him, any of them."

"First Captain Braves, then that handsome bodyguard, and Shadric Barlow on top of all that? It makes me sick that everything comes so easy to her. Maybe they should get to know the *real* her. I don't think they would like…"

The voices trailed off as they stepped out of earshot. Soren breathed as his heart started again, beating twice as fast to catch up. Creeping out of the room, he continued on his way. Thankfully, he didn't have any more run-ins and managed to get all the way to the garage. The open room looked like the hangar, all white tiles and big windows. Out of everyone, Soren was now the furthest away from Larken, making his job easier to mess up. If he didn't make it to her in time, if they didn't get to the next checkpoint, if they didn't— Soren jumped as his communicator went off.

Brecker sent a brown feather, and then a blue one followed three seconds later. He had Carl and Candy, and they were now making their way to the *Harpy*. Only, Loxly hadn't sent his yellow one yet. The *Harpy* was still airborne somewhere, or worse, they had been caught. Soren knew it was too risky not to have any of them waiting in the chapel. They were *Larken's* team after all, and none of them were there to protect her; someone was bound to notice.

A door opened somewhere, and Soren ducked behind a large hovercraft, hating the brightness of the garage. His communicator buzzed and Soren worried that whoever had just walked in would hear it. Heart in his throat, he counted to five. When no one seemed to be coming his way, Soren looked at the message. Loxly's yellow feather stared up at him. Delvon added a blue feather to the thread, and Jodi sent a yellow one as well. The medics were safe, waiting for the bodyguard to get them. Everyone was making their way to the *Harpy* now, and then they would meet at the next checkpoint.

Hands slick, Soren stuffed his communicator in his pocket. Deciding that it would be better to gauge his surroundings before sending a message, he tiptoed around the hovercraft. When he could see the black hover that had belonged to Vallen, Soren froze. A dark-skinned woman held a tablet, ducking as she looked into the windows. A muffled sound came from her, but Soren couldn't tell what it was. She turned, and he shrunk back, afraid that she might see him.

The door behind her opened again, and a loud man who looked a little older than Soren walked in. Letting the door slam behind him, he asked, "How much?"

The woman didn't answer, just kept looking over the hover and making occasional notes. Walking up to her, the man pulled something from her ear, and Soren realized she was listening to music. It would explain why she hadn't heard his communicator vibrate in the silent garage.

The man asked again, "How much?"

"Not as much as you were asking for, but it's in good shape. We can offer forty."

"*Forty?*" the man boomed. "We bought the thing for a hundred!"

"Yeah, twenty years ago maybe. They don't even make this model anymore." She bent and looked in the window again. "I'm surprised you would make someone as high up as the General use this actually."

"We didn't make him. He insisted he didn't need a new hover as long as this one worked."

The woman sighed, righting herself. "Forty, take it or leave it."

"Forty-five," the man countered.

There was a brief pause, and the woman agreed. "Fine. I'll move this out to the transporter, and we can start the paperwork."

Soren watched in horror as the woman got into the hovercraft and fired it up. It was the only hover in this place that he had the access code to, the only hover that he could have used to get Larken to the checkpoint, and he just watched it get sold.

Skies above, don't they realize there's a wedding today? Why are they selling hovers?

But Soren knew the answer. Larken was about to marry a man she didn't love, and the icing on the cake would be finding out her only chance of escape had been sold off. Cornella might not know that their plan had already been put into motion, but she had counted on Larken trying to get away at some point and that Vallen's hovercraft would be the only one she might know how to use.

Soren pulled out his communicator, about to send a red feather to tell the team that he hit a wall and couldn't get to Larken, but an opening door had Soren pausing. He looked up, expecting to find someone else walk in, probably a security guard coming to tell him that he had been found out. Instead, he saw the man leaving and the door swinging closed behind him. The woman pulled the hover forward, as the garage door opened for her. Soren followed her with his eyes, watching his only chance at getting to Larken leave. Then something sleek and black caught his attention.

Hope once more flooded his chest, and Soren nearly collapsed from the rush of it. Glancing at all the cameras he could find, he made sure that they all had red lights. Soren sent off a grey feather, letting the team know that he had to change the plan a little, but could still move forward. He leaped out of his hiding spot before the man could come back and prayed that the door would stay open. The sale might have worked in his favor after all.

Soren threw his leg up over the hoverbike after giving it a once over, making sure it hadn't been equipped with trackers, and punched in the same code that unlocked the hovercraft. It didn't work. Soren tried again, forcing himself to go slow so he didn't mess it up. The screen blinked red a second time. Panicking, Soren wracked his brain. Taking a chance, he typed in the code to unlock the bunker. That didn't work, and neither did the one for the *Harpy*. Soren stuffed his fingers in his hair, just as the garage door creaked.

Looking, he watched the door's slow descent, and he jammed in the code to unlock Estelle's security footage. The bike roared to life, its rumbles bouncing off the tiles around him. Soren grinned and his pocket buzzed. He looked long enough to see Loxly's blue feather and then stuffed the device back in his pocket. Revving the engine, Soren shot off. He ducked low over the bike, just managing to squeeze through the closing door, and then took a right.

Stealth was no longer an option, so he went for speed. The engine wasn't as loud out in the open, but he still attracted a few glances from various staff members who were working outside. He shot around the Manor, looking for the eight-point star that marked the chapel. Soren hoped that Larken was ready because the bike would attract the attention of everyone inside. Pushing the bike faster, he tore through the expanse of lawn and garden that made up the outdoor venue. Larken would be going down an aisle after all, just not the one that led to Braves.

Skidding to a halt, Soren looked over as a door with a diamond-shaped window flew open. Larken was a vision as she held up her skirts and ran to him. The grin on her face melted away any doubt he had that they wouldn't be able to pull this off. Without a second's hesitation, she jumped onto the back of the bike and wrapped her arms around him. A door in the little room she had just left fell to the ground as someone put their foot through it.

Larken screamed in excitement as Soren shot off once again. Men piled out of the room, shrinking behind them as they got further and further away. Larken laughed and let go of his middle. Thinking that she was falling, Soren turned and made to grab onto her. Instead, he found her waving to a figure with blond hair. When she turned back to him, she hugged him tightly and rested her cheek against his back. Soren pushed the bike faster, grinning as he did.

CHAPTER 32

The wind pulled at Larken's hair, and it was only Carl's excessive use of hairspray and pins that kept it in place. Her gown trailed behind them, making her feel more like the heroine in an action film than someone who had just been kidnapped. Each breath she took tasted of weightlessness and freedom, and Larken had to force herself not to hyperventilate as she tried to take in as many lungfuls as she could.

Somehow, they had done it; her friends had managed to work together and rescue her. She didn't know where Soren planned on taking her, but she knew that wherever it was, it couldn't be worse than married to Dominic Braves. The feeling alone made her wonder if she could fly, and she never wanted to get off this bike.

It felt different, riding with Soren. With Vallen, she had felt at peace, just like she had when Loxly took her out to that field all those weeks ago. Then, with Shadric, excitement had every single one of her nerves singing and she had felt alive for the first time since coming home. He had taken her on an adventure, pulling her from her seemingly endless stress, and brought her to a world of magic and lavender. But with Soren, it didn't matter if they were fighting, or even speaking with each other, it felt safe. It felt...*right*.

The endless blue sky stretched out above them, creating the

perfect backdrop against the red, orange, yellow, and brown trees that reached for it. Larken didn't know where they were going, but she trusted that Soren did. She didn't know how many times he had left base before; but even if he did just get them hopelessly lost, at least they would be together.

Tears pricked her eyes like the cold wind pricked her bare skin. Larken tightened her hold on Soren, listening to his heartbeat. His warmth was enough to keep the chill away, but it could be snowing and she wouldn't care. They hadn't spoken in days, still hadn't spoken even though he had just kidnapped her, but he was the one she held onto. Not Loxly or Delvon, *Soren*. It was always Soren. The two of them always managed to find their way back to the other, no matter what came between them. Distance, harsh words, or heartache—none of it mattered. Soren hadn't kept his promise when he let her go, but he kept it now as they sped away from the Manor. He had come for her, and even though she was the one currently holding on, Soren left no doubt in her mind that she was safe in this moment.

A tear leaked from her eye, and Larken laughed. Soren turned his head slightly and hollered, "You having a mental breakdown or something?"

"No!" she called back. "I'm just happy!"

She felt his grunt through his chest as they continued to tear down the open roads, the trees thinning the longer they sat on the bike. The sky seemed to pale, even though it was past noon, and the clouds were a soft white that reflected the bright sun. Larken closed her eyes, content to just sit with Soren and let the stress of the wedding fade away.

Eventually, she realized that she was smiling again and that only made her smile more. She couldn't get over the fact that she was finally leaving, that she had left. Part of her wished she could have seen the look on Dominic's face as she rode off, and the other part was glad that she hadn't. What would he do? Would he simply let her go?

No, Dominic isn't the type of guy who willingly gives anything away.

He would come after her; it was only a matter of time. Larken hoped that by the time he did, she would be long gone, somewhere untraceable. She had asked Maxim for a sign, to tell her which path to take, and if Soren rescuing her on Vallen's hoverbike wasn't a sign, she didn't know what was. All she knew was that wherever Soren planned to take her, that was where she would make her stand. It could be some forgotten old house that no one would think to look in, or it could be another military base that hadn't been infiltrated by her mother yet. Wherever it was, Larken would tell Delvon that she was ready for whatever came next, and they could start forming a plan.

A subtle shift in the air had Larken opening her eyes. They were zooming up a hill, and she noticed a whooshing sound that fought to be heard in her wind-numbed ears. Larken looked up to the sky, suddenly afraid that an aircraft would drop out of the clouds over them any second.

Soren, no doubt feeling her grip tighten, turned his face slightly and shouted, "What?"

"I think we're being followed!" she answered. "I think I can hear an engine!"

Soren tensed and gripped the bike tighter, causing them to speed up. Larken still kept her eyes on the sky, panic making her palms damp. The air took on a new smell, and Larken felt her heart stop, sure that someone was chasing them.

No, not yet. We haven't had enough time, it's too soon.

Larken shut her eyes, pressing her forehead into Soren's back; she gripped him tightly, refusing to let him go. They would have to pry her from him, and she would fight the entire way back to the Manor. Larken refused to go willingly; she had tasted freedom, and a taste wasn't enough.

They slowed to a stop, and a crash had her jumping. Larken's eyes shot to the sky once more but then fell when something gold caught them. Soren pried her fingers from the death-grip she had on his dark grey shirt and got off the bike. He grumbled about something, but she didn't catch what he said, focused instead on the expanse of sand and sea before her.

Tears welled in her eyes, and she wasn't sure if it was from the beauty of it all, or if sand had been blown into them. She suddenly felt so small in this world, hit with how great Maxim truly was. He had created all of this, and yet, had still answered her prayers. Larken's stomach flipped as a wave turned to white froth and crashed into the shore. Her hands trembled and she balled them into fists, digging her nails into her palms to remind herself that she wasn't dreaming.

Soren grabbed her waist, and she let him help her off the bike, not once looking away from the water. He gave her another moment to stare before cupping her cheek and forcing her to look at him. Larken met his soft eyes as he asked, "Are you okay?"

"I'm happy I'm not married, if that's what you're asking."

His lips twitched. "Well, I'm happy you're not married too. But I asked if you were okay."

"I'm…" Her eyes drifted back to the ocean. "I'm perfect."

"Take your shoes off."

Larken laughed. "Why?"

"Are you telling me that you're content just to stare? Take your shoes off."

Larken grinned at him. "We have time?"

He raised a dark eyebrow at her. "Do you see the *Harpy* anywhere?"

Not waiting to be told twice, Larken ignored the nervous flip of her stomach at the mention of the *Harpy* and kicked off her shoes. With an armful of skirts, she ran out onto the sand and almost rolled her ankle. She never imagined that sand would be so firm and supple at the same time.

Soren chuckled behind her, grabbing her waist to hold her steady. "Careful." Larken looked down and found he had taken off his boots as well. She stared and he asked, "What?"

"I didn't know you had feet," she said, meeting his gaze again. "You only ever wear those boots."

Soren scoffed and helped her get closer to the water.

Larken fell silent, sucked in by the crashing waves. She had no words to describe what she saw or how she felt. Larken had always felt small and insignificant at the Manor, but it was nothing compared to the feeling that now squeezed her heart. The water looked so blue that the sky seemed to dim in comparison. She felt like her whole life had led up to this one moment, and now that she was here, Larken started to feel a little lost.

She remembered the day she had been shot, the last time she had looked out of the *Arsene* at the sea. Larken had felt homesick, and now that she stood before the foaming waves, she wondered what was left for her. Seeing the ocean in person was something she dreamt about for so long that, now that it had happened, she had no idea what to do next or what there was left to hope for. What would keep her going? She had no more dreams, no other impossibilities that would keep her fighting.

Soren's hands on her waist suddenly felt heavy, and she tried to ignore them. He wasn't the safe choice, Shadric was; Larken knew it, and Soren probably knew it as well. So why did they keep finding themselves in these situations? Larken was a flame. She burned and hurt whoever decided to get involved with her, and Soren acted like the moth that couldn't help but come back time and time again. Who was the real Soren? The one that ignored her and pushed her away, not wanting her to get too close, or the one in the aircraft that promised to never let go? Who was the man standing next to her, and why did she care? Larken's heart beat in sync with the crashing waves, not wanting to think about anything other than the perfection before her. Shadric was the best choice; Soren was a risk she didn't know if she could take anymore. It was too dangerous. She couldn't let her heart go down that road, but part of her knew that it already had.

Soren watched her, holding his breath. She had dropped her skirts not too long ago and now hugged her middle. His hands were still at her waist, and he didn't want to let go, not yet. Surely, she knew he had done this for her; that everything he did—it was for her.

Larken looked out at the sea like nothing else mattered, and he desperately wanted to know what she was thinking, how she felt at this exact moment. Soren knew all he had to do was ask and she would tell him. Only, he wasn't sure he was ready for the conversation that would follow. Yes, he purposely planned this spot as the final checkpoint, but he still wasn't sure why. Even standing there with her, he felt more confused than he ever had in his life. Was he hoping that she would put everything together? The pearl, the sea, and realize that the shell was from him as well? Or was it more than that?

As if she could read his thoughts, she murmured, voice strangled in a rasp that he had never heard her use before, "It was from you, wasn't it?"

Soren didn't say anything, just waited for her to look at him. Her eyes held an emotion that he couldn't read, like she was trying to figure something out but didn't know if she wanted to.

Still, she asked, "Why didn't you say anything? Why didn't you tell me?"

"I couldn't…" he admitted.

The silent explanation danced between them. He didn't know how she would have reacted, and that not knowing had been torture for him. Larken silently assured that she would have been happy with just knowing he had tried to reach out to her, that he should know that about her by now. Her eyes drifted back to the sea, that same look in them as the water pulled her back in. The waves retreated, readying themselves to break against the shore again. Soren wondered if Larken knew she held that same sort of power, that anyone who stood before her couldn't help but be awed and transfixed. Inside her was the force to lead her fellow countrymen, the drive to move forward no matter how many times she was pushed back, and the unrelenting compassion and beauty to capture even the most hardened of hearts.

Soren's stomach twisted, realizing what was happening. Larken had blown into his life, and the reason he always felt so unsure around her was that she took everything he thought he knew and turned it upside down. If it hadn't been for her, he would still be a military soldier, blindly doing what he had been told. He would have gone on undefeated in the sparring ring, not knowing that there was someone other than the great General Maxwell that could possibly take him out. Soren would have been comfortable, and he only just now realized how awful that would have been.

Now his life was full of laughter, music, and color. Soren had smiled more in those few months that Larken had been at base than he had in his whole life. He had spent tokens on something as frivolous and as useless as a necklace just because he thought it would make Larken happy. Soren had bought a suit and sat through an *opera* just so Larken could go and not have to worry about her now ex-fiancé trying something. And, as if all of that hadn't been enough to prove something in him had changed, he had danced. Soren had danced in the common room with Larken, holding her close, smiling at her, and somehow had a good time. Suddenly, all of Hinlee's and Loxly's knowing glances made sense, and that scared him more than anything in his life ever had.

Unable to deal with his terrifying thoughts any longer, Soren decided that it would be better to risk asking Larken what she was thinking about. A wave crashed into the shore, spraying them with salty mist, and almost covered his murmured, "Larken."

As if pulled from a trance, Larken gazed up at him with eyes that seemed to have absorbed the ocean. Gone was the confliction, and in its place, a teal so deep that it stole Soren's breath away. A tear streaked down her cheek, and Soren lifted his hand, brushing it away with his thumb. Recoiling the slightest bit, Larken reached up to her face as well. Feeling the moisture, she brushed away the evidence of her reverence and apologized.

"What do you think?" he asked, ignoring the apology.

Larken looked at him again, open vulnerability on her face. "It's everything that I ever hoped it would be."

Soren was left with even more questions. He had always thought that the sea held a special memory for her; he hadn't known she'd never seen it in person.

Before he could ask her anything though, she turned back to the waves and said, "I never thought I would get to see it. I've always wanted to, but then I was sent to base, and I thought I was going to die. When I didn't, I started to hope again."

"Then you were sent home." Larken blinked slowly, unable to look away from the force of nature before them, just as he was unable to look away from her.

"There's just one thing I don't understand."

Soren didn't say anything as he waited for her to continue. She swallowed hard, like what she was going to say would change everything between them. Soren wondered if this had anything to do with that look she had given him, and he didn't know if he wanted her to speak, but he did know that he didn't want her to stay silent.

"Every time I think something is impossible, you're always there." Soren's heart stopped, but she kept going. "A home, the opera, the wedding, the sea, *a friend*." She looked at him, tearing her eyes from the water. "You are *always* there. Why? Why would you defy the impossible time and time again for *me*?"

The look on her face, it was the same one she had before she left; only this time she wasn't asking for an impossible answer. She was asking for something much, much worse. Honesty.

"I don't know what you're talking about," he tried.

Larken wouldn't have it. "Why did you bring me here, Soren?"

"It was convenient," he lied. "A place away from the Manor with plenty of space for the *Harpy* to—"

"Cut the crap, Soren." She glared at him, her annoyance starting to boil over. "You ignore me for a week, and then you bring me here. *Why?*"

"You know why!" Soren barked, his own frustrations getting the better of him.

Larken looked like she had been struck, and he could see in her eyes that she did know, but she was going to make him say it anyway. "I don't."

Soren let out a long breath as she turned fully towards him. Her dress was ruined, collecting ocean spray and sand that the breeze tossed around. The lace covering her chest bubbled in a spot, and he knew that even though she was prepared to walk down the aisle towards Braves, she still wore his pearl.

"I don't know," she said again. "Tell me, Soren."

His hand moved on its own accord from her waist to her neck and he didn't stop it. Larken grabbed his wrist with one hand, still looking into his eyes, and placed the other on his chest. He was drowning in her teal depths again, and Soren felt suddenly afraid. How could he be so honest with her when it had never worked before? A little voice in his head told him that that wasn't true, that he had never been honest with her, that the reason he kept finding himself in this situation was *because* he refused to be honest with her.

Pushing the thoughts away, Soren lied. "I wanted to apologize for how I've been treating you."

Larken's eyes fell, and she was unable to hide the look of disappointment on her face. "Is that all?"

Soren brushed his thumb over her jaw, and her eyes reluctantly met his again. He hadn't planned on saying it, but the word slipped quietly past his lips. "No."

Her breath caught and Soren was surprised she could still breathe; he had stopped after she first looked out at the water. Larken bit her lip, and he couldn't help but stare. As if her lips held a tether to his own, Soren leaned in. Larken's hand slid up his chest as he moved, and she released her lip as her eyes fluttered close. They were once again in that moment, lost, and the only safety net was each other. Grapefruit danced on the wind, and Soren knew that the real Larken was back.

Just as his lips were about to brush hers, an engine could be heard overhead. Soren sighed as he pulled away, ready to kill Loxly for ruining their moment…again.

Larken backed away from him, face pink. He let her, but then grabbed her hands when he realized her flush wasn't from embarrassment. She watched the *Harpy* land in the sand, and her breaths came as quick puffs of air. Soren pulled her close, saying, "It's okay. Loxly is flying."

She rounded on him. "I don't care who's flying, I'm not getting on that thing!"

"Larken," he grumbled. "You knew this was the plan. I told you."

"And I was hoping that you were lying!" She turned away, her breaths harsh gasps, and one of her hands clutched her stomach.

Larken looked ill as the door to the cream and silver aircraft opened. Jodi and Brecker jumped out onto the sand. Brecker ran for the hoverbike, and Jodi fished for something in her pocket.

Reaching them, Jodi pulled a vial free and offered it to Larken, saying, "Drink this."

"What is it?" she demanded, looking at Jodi's offered hand skeptically.

She shrugged. "Chamomile extract."

"I'm not taking—"

"It's the proper dosage for your bodyweight. Besides," Jodi looked Larken up and down, "do you really want to get on that thing while you're awake?"

Larken glared at the medic before snatching the vial.

She knocked it back and grimaced as Jodi said, "Don't worry, I won't let them draw on your face or anything."

Larken only scoffed, tossing the vial back to her. Jodi laughed as she caught it and made her way back to the *Harpy*. Soren watched as Brecker loaded the hoverbike into the cargo trunk, and then tossed their shoes in as well before smacking the button that closed the hatch. Brecker hopped up the steps behind Jodi and Larken swayed on her feet.

Soren reached out to her, keeping her steady, and she grumbled, "Why is sand so hard to walk on?"

"It just takes practice."

She beamed at him. "Does this mean you're going to bring me back?"

The chamomile was doing its job, and Soren grunted, leading her to the aircraft. Larken chatted nonsensically about the water and how next time they needed to go swimming. Then she laughed, wondering aloud if Soren even knew how.

"I can swim," he assured her.

"Good," she sighed. Then she added, "Do you have a swimsuit, or do you swim in your clothes?"

"What are you talking about? Of course I don't swim in my clothes."

"Well, I haven't seen your feet before now, so how am I supposed to know?"

Soren grumbled under his breath, helping her up the steps. They reached the top, and she turned and ran bodily into him.

"What?" he demanded.

"I forgot something."

"What did you forget? Sand?"

She laughed. "No, silly. I forgot something else."

Soren moved out of the way for her, but instead of walking down the steps, she pulled off her engagement ring. He watched as she tossed it out into the sand and leaned against him for balance.

Her eyes drooped heavily and she wobbled, so Soren picked her up and carried her the rest of the way into the cab. Everyone except for Delvon and Levi cheered, and Carl even went as far as to call, "There's the happy couple!"

Soren scowled, making them laugh, and then tried to set Larken down. She tightened her grip on him and murmured, "Let me sit by you. You're warm."

Everyone got ready for takeoff, and Ezra tossed that black jacket Larken used to wear to Soren. He caught it easily and settled Larken on the seat next to him. She readily took the jacket, smelling the lapel and sighing. She murmured something that sounded like *Vallen* and then snuggled up next to Soren.

"Do you need to sit so close?" he grumbled. "You have a jacket."

"Fine," she slurred. "I'll go sit with Delvon. He's warm too." Larken glared at him. "And he wants to marry me, *so there.*"

Soren sighed, pulling her back to his side. "Will you just shut up and go to sleep already?"

"Hinlee," she whined. "Soren's being mean."

"Be mean back," she suggested.

Larken thought for a moment and then said, "You're not nice."

"Not your best work," Hinlee mused. "But at least you tried."

"Have Soren wake her up in an hour!" Loxly called from the cockpit. "She'll be plenty mean then."

Everyone except Larken, who was having trouble keeping up with the conversation, laughed. Even Delvon smirked, and Soren's blood went hot thinking about how the bodyguard could possibly know that it was true.

"Ready or not!" Loxly hollered over the laughter. The *Harpy* shifted, and then they took to the air, leaving the beach and Larken's engagement ring behind them.

CHAPTER 33

The chapel around him was in shambles. Pews were broken in half, missing legs or smashed against the walls. The flower arrangements had been destroyed, the yellow roses mocking him with voices that sounded a lot like Cornella's. They asked him if he had really believed that his plan would work, if he had really believed he would be able to leave the District behind so easily. The pale orange rug that Larken should have walked down with Trogar hours ago had been shredded, and candlesticks lay broken on the floor. Dominic had put his foot through the marriage altar and tossed the pieces through one of the ornate windows. The sun had started to dip, slowly pulling him into the darkness, and he welcomed it.

He took a long drag of his cigar and held his breath, willing the opiate to calm him down after the many hours of destruction. Dominic's mind raced, jumping from one extreme to another. Why had she left? He thought he had made it clear that he would take care of her, that he had her best interests in mind. Dominic didn't think he could risk telling her his plan to take her away, but as he sat there on the little dais they should have stood on together, he wondered if he had made a mistake by keeping it from her. He wanted it to be a surprise, to make a grand gesture and show that he had been listening to her, that he understood her need to leave, even if it meant turning his back on everything he had ever known. But now it didn't matter; Deckard had stolen her away from him.

"Well, well," a too-familiar voice sang. "What do we have here?"

Dominic released his breath, emitting a fog of blue.

"Are you quite finished with your little temper tantrum?" she asked.

He dropped his gaze, too angry to try and mask his emotions. "What do you want, Cornella?"

"My, how informal. I'm not your mother-in-law quite yet, you know."

Dominic stuck the cigar between his lips, keeping himself from saying something that he would regret.

Cornella crossed her arms, looking him over as her face twisted with disgust. The sun shone in through the open door behind her, trying to illuminate the dark chapel. It gave Cornella an almost angelic look; too bad she was anything but. "Look at you. *You're pathetic.*"

"Flattery won't get me in your bed, Cornella," Dominic mused. "I'm only interested in your daughter. You know, the one that turned against you and disappeared."

She snarled. "I don't need to lure you into my bed when I can just join you in yours. You know the one I mean," her voice dripped with hatred, "the one in the Thresh District."

"What do you want?" Dominic demanded, furious with himself. "What more do you need from me?"

"I *need* my daughter back."

"Go find her yourself." Dominic crushed his cigar on the dais. "Besides, even if I still considered working with you, I would never bring her back here."

Cornella laughed, the melodic tinkling grating against his raw nerves. Never had he failed at something so completely. Dominic had managed to lose the only woman he had ever loved, and somehow, his plan had been discovered by the one person he wanted to keep it secret from. He wondered how long Cornella had known, and he wondered if she was somehow responsible for Larken's escape. Letting Larken go would ensure that he at least stuck around to find her.

The black floor-length gown Cornella wore clung to her, and the red sash at her back matched her lipstick perfectly. She looked ready to spew venom, but her eyes were hard, calculating. "It is still my intention to give Larken to you, Captain Braves. But if you refuse to help me, then there is no telling what accidents she might end up having."

Dominic jumped to his feet and rushed at the woman. He shoved her up against a wall, his forearm pressed to her throat. She grinned as he seethed, "You lay one hand on her, and you will regret ever enlisting me into your little cause. I will destroy everything you have built up around you." He put more pressure on her throat so she would know he was serious. "Starting with that drunk husband of yours and your two heirs."

"Well now, color me impressed," she mused, not at all concerned that Dominic could easily kill her. "Maybe inviting you to my bed wouldn't be such a bad idea after all."

Dominic pressed into her harder. "*Stop talking!*"

"Why?" she asked. "Am I confusing you?" Cornella laughed. "Tell me, Captain, how long has it been? Weeks, if anything you've said is to be believed."

Her hands brushed up his sides, and Dominic jumped away from her, heart pounding as he saw red. She only laughed, enjoying herself as she played with him.

"What do you want from me, Cornella?" he asked again.

"As I said, I need help finding my daughter. Her running off could be detrimental to the both of us."

"And what will happen if I help you? Will you use and manipulate me again? Toy with me and string me along like some mindless puppet?"

"Enough of the dramatics, Captain. I had enough of that from your fiancée. All her life, nothing was ever good enough; everyone was out to get her."

"Everyone *was* out to get her."

Cornella sighed. "Even if that were true, it doesn't make it any less annoying."

Dominic dropped to a partially intact pew, propping his elbows on his knees and sticking his fingers into his hair. "What would you need me to do?"

"Find her, marry her, and make sure she never steps foot in my District again."

"Tell me something." He didn't look at her as he continued, "Did you have anything to do with her escape?"

"That would seem like something I would do, wouldn't it? Let her go, keep you here, force you to stay and help me until you were once again reunited, and I was able to kill you both." Dominic looked up just in time to see her smile as if she had been lost to some pleasant memory. "But, no, I didn't let her go. I was under the impression that one of my own would dictate security for the day, but it would seem that Mr. Tanner had other plans." Cornella pushed off the wall and prowled towards him. "But you already knew that, didn't you, Captain Braves?"

He laughed. "Do you want me to lie and say that I didn't hope that you would choke on the oppression you caused?"

"I didn't think that you cared about those Maxim worshipping fools."

"I don't. I care about you getting what you deserve."

"Your hands are covered in just as much ash as mine are, Captain, so don't pretend you're just some tragic hero doing whatever it takes to save his true love. It doesn't suit you."

"So what does that make you?"

"All of the great men and women of the past were a villain to someone, just as I will always be the villain to my worthless daughter."

"You're something, alright, but *villain* isn't quite the word I would use," Dominic said, fishing out his cigar case. He lit another one and sucked in a lungful.

"I like this new you," Cornella mused. "It's almost like you actually have a spine."

"I've always been like this." Blue smoke floated around him, looking almost grey in the golden sunlight. "I just don't see the point in pretending to be your loyal dog anymore."

"And what part are you playing now?"

"The man who won't kill you as long as you keep up your end of the bargain."

"Well, in a gesture of good faith, I have something that I think you'll want to see." Cornella left the chapel, walking over the door he ordered to be kicked down to get to Larken.

Dominic followed, not bothering to put out his cigar. She led him all the way to the surveillance room, receiving many glares as he smoked in the Manor halls. He didn't care anymore; the only thing on his mind, the only thing he *needed*, was to get Larken back. His carefully built-up image could be torn apart for all he cared. He wouldn't need it on the farm anyway.

The three men that sat in their chairs in front of the many screens turned to look at them. Cornella crossed her arms and ordered, "Everyone out."

No one waited around to be told twice. Cornella marched forward and started messing with one of the screens. Dominic dropped to one of the now-abandoned chairs and crushed his cigar on the desk. If Cornella noticed, she didn't say anything, and he didn't care if she did. What was one desk compared to all the wealth of the Luminary?

"My security team are a bunch of inept morons. You will have to find new ones. You should see what Mr. Tanner did to the ones in the medic wing."

"Whatever you say, Cornella."

"Larken and Mr. Tanner were able to use our security regulations to their advantages."

"What do you mean?"

"See for yourself," she said, moving away from the screen.

Dominic gripped the arms of the chair so hard that his knuckles popped. Larken was in bed, swaddled up in an absurd number of sheets and resting against so many pillows that it was a surprise that they all fit on the bed. Only, she wasn't in bed alone. Tanner was with her, holding her, *kissing her forehead.*

"What are they saying?" he barked, rounding on Cornella.

"We don't know." She let out a long sigh and added, "We have a privacy protection buffer set in place. To prevent scandal, any form of intimate conversation is muted so our team can claim ignorance. Anything more and the video cuts completely."

Cornella changed the video feed, and the screen showed Tanner kneeling in front of Larken at her vanity. Tanner ran a dermis gun over her arm, and she looked at him intently, her focus on whatever he was saying.

"And you know that they were only speaking?"

"I'm honestly not sure. At first, the team thought it was only a secret romance, but after things started to progress, someone decided that this was something I should become aware of. Knowing Larken, I figured she was just trying to get back at me, so I thought nothing of it."

Dominic tried to listen, but his mind caught on one phrase and couldn't move past it. His voice trembled with anger as he asked, "What do you mean *secret romance?*"

Cornella changed the feed again, and Dominic watched in horror as Larken was pressed up against a wall and Tanner kissed her. His eyes zoned in on her hands that she stuck in his hair, and then as she clutched at his shirt as if it was the only thing keeping her from losing herself forever.

"I can imagine how you must feel, but you need to believe me when I say we want the same thing. You want to get her back and hide her away, and I want Larken out of my way." Dominic felt torn between snapping Cornella's neck for showing him this and vomiting. He didn't look towards her when she said, "We need to work together, Captain. It's the only way we'll find her."

"And what makes you think I know where she is?" he gritted out.

"Come now, Captain. I know you are nowhere near as stupid as I think you are, so try to give me the same courtesy."

Dominic stood, pulling out his communicator. He hadn't wanted to let Cornella in on his plan, wanted to wait until this blew over to begin his search, but he no longer had that option. Who knew what Larken and Tanner were up to this very second? This whole time Dominic had thought her innocent, not willing to move forward because she was afraid or just infatuated with Barlow. But he had been wrong. When she had stopped him all those weeks ago in the dorm, it wasn't because she wasn't ready; it was because she didn't want *him*.

We'll just see about that. I wonder who you'll choose when I'm the only option left.

After accessing his tracker, Dominic said, "She's at a beach about two hours away."

"I'll ready an aircraft for you since yours is a few hours away as well."

Dominic glared at her but said nothing. Instead, he made his way to the hangar and jumped into the waiting aircraft. Three burly men followed him, two with dark skin, one with more freckles than was necessary. Still, Dominic was silent, not wanting to give in to his rage until he was alone.

The ride seemed to take only minutes, but no matter how fast Dominic flew, he couldn't forget what he had seen. Her hands, the hands he could still remember pressing against his chest, pushing him away, they had touched someone else. And it wasn't only that, but the fact that she had *wanted* to touch someone else. Was that why Deckard was so protective of her? Because he had those same hands touching him at base? Well, if that were the case, he wouldn't need to worry much longer. Dominic would put him out of his misery once he was finished with Tanner and the other members of her old squad. Deckard had always gotten whatever he wanted— the titles, the squad, *the recognition*—but Larken was one thing he wouldn't get away with. She belonged to *him*, and Dominic wouldn't rest until she was in his arms once again.

They landed on the beach as the sun hit the horizon. It didn't look like anyone was there, and if they had been, the wind and shifting sand had covered any evidence. Dominic still gave the order to spread out and search. He had to force himself not to chuck his communicator into the ocean. Instead, he opened the tracker once more to see which direction they went.

The device said that Larken was still at the beach, so he smacked it against his palm. When nothing changed, his heart fell. Dominic ran out onto the sand, searching frantically. A glint in the sand caught his eye, and Dominic stared, disbelieving. Slowly, he made his way to the spot and crouched down. Brushing the sand away, Dominic uncovered Larken's ring, the one he had given her, the one he had told her multiple times to never take off.

No…

Dominic stood and threw the ring into the sea, roaring. His blood boiled, and he stormed back to the aircraft. Without waiting for the men to get back, Dominic shot into the sky with only one thought pounding in his mind.

I will find you, Larken, I don't care if I have to burn down the whole world. I will find you, and when I do, you won't have anywhere to run. You're mine!

CHAPTER 34

"Will you sit still?" Soren grumbled.

"This dress is uncomfortable. I want to take it off," Larken whined as she tried to lift her skirts for the third time. Sand still clung to her bare feet, and Soren couldn't help but stare at her pink toes.

"Larken!" Carl barked. "If you don't sit still, I will personally throw away all of your pants so you are forced to learn proper dress etiquette."

"Why don't *you* wear it if you like it so much?"

"I'd like to see you try to squeeze that big butt of yours into his pants," Delvon jabbed. He had moved to Larken's other side to try and help contain her, but he only made things worse, antagonizing her every chance he got.

Larken looked up at Soren, eyes watery. "Soren, is my butt big?"

"Why are you asking me?" he demanded, trying not to choke.

Everyone tried to smother their laughter, but Larken didn't notice. "Because friends tell the truth!"

"I'm not having this conversation with you, Larken."

"Seems to me like he isn't a very good friend, love." Delvon smirked at him over Larken's head.

"Well, you're not either! All you do is tell me that I have a big butt and that I'm annoying. A good fiancé would give me their pants!"

"If you wanted my pants, Peach, all you had to do was ask."

"Delvon," Candy warned.

"What?" he looked back at Larken, but she looked just as confused as he did. "What did I say?"

"Fiancé?" Jodi asked, her honey eyes dancing. She was no doubt committing everything to memory so she could harass Larken about it later.

Larken only grinned at her, then leaned over and gave Delvon a noisy kiss on the cheek that had Soren seeing red. "Delvon promised to steal me away and marry me so Dominic wouldn't be able to. Isn't he a good friend?"

"The best," the medic agreed.

"Yeah," she sighed, leaning her head on Delvon's shoulder. "He even helped me when we were at the club and—"

"They don't need to hear that story," he interrupted.

"Oh, I think we do," Jodi insisted.

"You keep calling me Peach anyway; it doesn't matter what I do," Larken whined.

"Just keep your big mouth shut."

Larken turned back to Soren. "Do I have a big mouth?"

"Stop asking me weird questions," he grunted, swallowing hard and trying not to stare at her lips.

"How is that weird? Don't you like my mouth?"

"No!" Soren lied, getting frustrated with his embarrassment.

Larken frowned, crossing her arms. "Well, what do you know? Plenty of people like my mouth, like Sh—"

"Larken, shut up!" Delvon barked.

"Why is everyone being so mean to me?" Larken stood shakily and stuck her arms out for balance.

"Where do you think you're going?" Soren asked, his tone exasperated.

She rounded on him. "I'm going to go sit with Loxly. He'll be nice to me."

Larken took a step and tripped. Soren stood and caught her before she could hit the floor, then sat back down. Larken squirmed in his lap, and he had to wrap his arms around her to keep her still. When she still tried to get away, he practically shouted, "Stop moving!"

She let out a pathetic whine and ordered, "Let me go."

"Not until you calm down. You're going to hurt yourself."

Larken tried to get away a few more times before giving up. She rested her face against his chest and murmured, "You smell good." Then, she finally passed out.

"Well, that was fun," Jodi said.

"At least she's not dancing on tables this time." Delvon kept his eyes on Soren's hands, and Soren scowled.

"Dancing on tables?" Hinlee and Brecker asked at the same time.

Levi looked skeptically at Jodi, and Soren did as well. She hadn't reacted to the bodyguard's words, which made Soren think that she already knew. How much did the medic know about Larken's life at the Manor exactly?

But it was Carl who answered, "Yes, our dear Captain Braves slipped her too much chamomile extract after taking her to a club."

"We already knew that part, but *dancing on tables?* Really?" Hinlee rounded on Soren. "Why didn't you tell us?"

"Do you think Larken would really want us to know?" Brecker asked instead. "Let it go, Hin."

She huffed and leaned back into her seat.

"Besides," Levi interjected, "we have other things that we need to discuss that are more important."

They all looked to Delvon, who was frowning. He sighed, and then reluctantly asked, "What do you want to know?"

"What's going to happen to Larken?" Hinlee asked, voicing the question they were all thinking.

"She'll be fine. We won't make her do anything she doesn't want to do."

"And what are you hoping she'll do?" Levi narrowed his eyes, even more protective of Larken now than he had been before she left.

"Obviously, we want to make her Luminary."

"You *what?*" Brecker and Levi asked.

"She'll hate that!" Hinlee insisted.

"I know she'll hate it, but do you really think Liam is a better option?"

"Well, no, but—"

"But what?" Delvon scowled. "You think that once we get Cornella out of the way everything will just magically work out? What's stopping Liam from finishing what his mother started?"

"And what did Cornella start exactly?" Levi asked, his face dark.

"Genocide." No one said anything, so Delvon continued, "When Fisher left Cornella after recommitting his life to Maxim, she decided that it was Maxim that needed to pay."

"The fires," Jodi said.

Delvon nodded. "Right now they're too random and spread out for us to do anything, and the only people targeted are wealthy families who worship Maxim. It just isn't enough for us to go on."

"But what can Larken do about that?" Hinlee demanded. "You can't tell me you expect her to kill her own mother!"

"No. The plan is to get her to the Magnate, tell him what's really happening, and have Cornella put away. We don't want to murder anyone." Delvon's eyes hardened. "Enough people have died in this war, and the Faithfuls don't want to add to those numbers. But, if she leaves us no choice, we will do what we must, and Larken will have no part of it."

"So what part will Larken play?" Levi asked.

"She'll be our representative. Most of us that are still able to fight grew up at Camp; we don't know anything about society or Luminary etiquette. It'll be Larken's job to find out where the Districts really stand and plead our case to the Magnate."

"And if she doesn't want any part of it?" Soren demanded.

Delvon looked at Soren, his grey eyes dancing. "If the Princess doesn't want to help, we'll hide her away and she can live the rest of her life in ignorant bliss. But you and I both know she won't just stand by and watch, mate."

Soren's arms tightened around her subconsciously. She shifted a little, getting more comfortable, and placed her hand against his chest. The black sleeve covered most of her palm, and she mumbled something unintelligible. Larken sniffed and parted her lips, breathing through her mouth. She was completely out of it, and Soren could have sat there and watched her forever if it meant never letting her go.

Delvon was right—she wouldn't be satisfied just letting others take care of the mess her mother had made. More likely than not, she would see it as her fault. If her mother and father had never met, if they never had their affair, if she had never been born. Somehow, she always saw it as her fault, and maybe if Soren had just been honest with her before now, she might not feel that way.

He had a choice he needed to make. No more taking one step forward, then two back; it wasn't fair to her. He needed to decide if he was going to run to her like she always ran to him or let her go altogether.

Every time I think something is impossible, you're always there.

Why would you defy the impossible time and time again, for me?

Her words, her *question.* Looking down at her sleeping form, he knew the answer, and he knew in this way they were too similar. She didn't think she was worthy of a home, of friendship, of love. Just as Soren knew that the reason for his silence was because he didn't think he was worthy of her.

CHAPTER 35

Larken groaned, her head feeling heavy. Someone shook her shoulder and poked at her. She groaned again, wanting to keep sleeping. She had been having the most wonderful dream, that she had managed to escape the wedding, was taken to a beach, and then Soren almost—

"Larken."

Her eyes flew open, and she saw an expanse of dark grey. Warmth cushioned her cheek, and a steady heartbeat sounded in her ear. Slowly, she looked up and found Soren's eyes glowing green as they watched her.

"We're here."

She sat up, never taking her eyes off him. "Why am I in your lap?"

"We didn't have any restraints."

"*Oh no,*" she moaned. "Please tell me I didn't start dancing again."

"No, but you did try to take your dress off more than once." He grinned. "And I owe you a congratulations."

"For what?" She ran her tongue over her teeth, trying to get rid of the metallic flavor in her mouth.

"On your engagement. Am I invited to the wedding?"

"What are you talking about?"

"You told everyone about your plans to marry Delvon."

Larken glared at him. "*HA HA*, very funny."

"Seriously, am I invited? I need to know if I should be looking for a gift." His grin deepened. "How about a juicer? You know, for all the peaches you and your new husband will eat together."

"You suck."

Soren laughed and the sound vibrated through her whole body. Larken realized she was still on his lap. She blushed, turning away and trying to stand. Soren held onto her and asked, "How are you feeling?"

"Better than I did the morning after I was drugged. Can you let go now?"

He cupped her cheek, rubbing at something under her eye with his thumb. "Not until I make sure you're okay."

"I'm fine, will you—"

"Can you just humor me this once?"

Larken fell silent, the serious look in his eyes holding her tongue. She let him look her over, realizing as he did that he hadn't thought the plan would work. Soren had thought that he was going to lose her, so she sat still, ignoring the burning of her cheeks.

Trying to lighten the mood, she asked, "Will I live?"

"Don't." He held her gaze, one hand still cupping her cheek, the other finding one of hers. "Don't do that. You don't know how worried I was."

Her hand went up to her chest, forgetting that the pearl was trapped under her dress. Dropping her gaze, she murmured, "Probably not nearly as worried as I was." Her hand clutched at the lapel of Vallen's jacket instead. She didn't know how she had gotten it, but that didn't matter. "I honestly thought I was going to have to marry Dominic and that I would—that I'd never get the chance to..."

Soren didn't say anything, just pulled her close. Larken hesitated for only a moment before wrapping her arms around him as well. She didn't want to leave this spot. Here, they were Soren and

Larken, the way they were always meant to be. Here, they could be themselves, silently assuring the other that they would never leave and that they would never hurt the other. Larken wanted to stay like that; outside she didn't know what would happen, or who would try to come between them.

"Dominic made a deal with my mother. That's why I had to leave," she whispered, breaking the silent rule to not talk about that day.

Soren didn't say anything, but she could picture his frown as his arms tightened around her.

"He said that to repay her, he was helping her with base stuff. I think he's working with that other group, but you probably already knew that."

"He is, and I did."

"Did someone tell Fisher what happened?" she asked into his chest, not wanting to cause anyone else any pain.

"I'll take care of it unless he's here."

"And where exactly is *here?*"

"Why don't we go look together?" Soren made to help her up, but she refused to move. As if he could sense her fears, he sat her up and looked into her eyes. "This won't be like last time. Okay?"

"How do you know?"

"Because," his eyes hazel eyes deepened to a fierce shade of green that glowed gold, "I made you a promise, and this time I'm keeping it."

Larken sighed and nodded. She let him help her up, and he grumbled about his legs being numb. Soren held onto her after she took a wobbly step and helped her through the cab. Her feet were still bare...she couldn't remember what had happened to her shoes. The smooth floor felt cool under her feet. Larken looked out through the large windows and over the spacious seats. She didn't really get a chance to appreciate it the last time she was in it, freaking out the way she had. The cream and silver were so different from the grey and black of her mother's aircraft. She couldn't help but smile, knowing that Vallen had designed it this way just for her.

Soren helped her down the black steps, and Brecker stood waiting with her shoes. He held Soren's boots as well, and the two paused a moment to get them on. Standing upright, Larken took in the space around her. There were giant trees everywhere, and little bungalows were scattered under the branches. The sound of children laughing danced in the air. All the people who watched her gave her an easy smile. The scent of cooked meat had her stomach rumbling, and a shriek had her jumping back onto Soren's foot.

A little ball of energy charged towards her and only stopped when her arms were around her. Sobs wracked Jing's small body, and she moaned into Larken's skirts how much she missed her. Larken crouched so she could hug her properly, and Mr. Chin walked out of the closest bungalow. He grinned and waved at Larken, too proper to run at her the way his daughter had.

"What about me?" Carl demanded somewhere close by, and Jing soon rushed to him as well. He introduced her to Candy, who was grinning at Carl, and Larken knew that he wouldn't be able to push off marriage or children for much longer.

Someone else rushed to them, and Larken momentarily panicked when she saw the blond hair, but it was Shadric, not Dominic, that pulled her into his arms. "Larken, I was so worried."

"Shad, what are you doing here?" she asked as her belly flipped. Larken felt Soren stiffen behind her, and her stomach twisted with guilt.

"Once Del told me that you guys were on the move, I snuck off. There's no need for a wedding singer if there isn't going to be a wedding." Shadric caught Soren's fierce scowl and let go of her, offering his hand to Soren instead. "You must be Soren, Larken's old Squad Captain."

Soren took the offered hand, and a tick in his jaw told Larken that he was trying not to crush Shadric's fingers. "And you must be Shadric Barlow."

Shadric grinned. "Call me Shad."

Shadric turned before he could see Soren's frown deepen, and Larken elbowed him in the gut, glaring at him. He only turned his frown on her. She narrowed her eyes further, silently telling him to be nice.

Soren rolled his eyes and helped her over to where Delvon and Shadric were standing. Everyone else was already being led off, and strangely Larken wasn't worried about it. She knew without being told where she was, so she offered Delvon and Shadric a grin. "Looks like I made it."

"Looks like," Delvon grunted. "And I managed to keep my pants, so I'd say our trip was successful."

Shadric's smile fell. "Wait, what?"

Delvon smirked down at Larken. "Peach here tried very, *very* hard to get me out of my pants on the aircraft."

"*What?!*" Shadric demanded.

"*Oh skies above,*" Larken groaned. She turned on Soren. "I thought you told me everything!"

"Why would I do that? Jodi would kill me in my sleep if I ruined her fun."

Larken made a face at him, but his smirk looked more like a smile than it normally did.

"How about we get you out of that dress?" Delvon asked. "I can show you somewhere private where you can take it off." His grey eyes danced. "Unless you'd rather strip right here out in the open."

Soren grunted and Larken glared at both of them. "Why do I even talk to you two?"

"Well, we're engaged for one," Delvon said.

"And I smell nice," Soren added.

Larken stared at them for a long moment before saying, "I liked it better when you two weren't friends."

"We're not friends," they said at the same time, and then glared at each other.

"Uh-huh, real convincing." Larken crossed her arms. "If I didn't know any better, I'd think you two were brothers."

"Del, Shad, what took you?" a thickly accented voice that Larken recognized demanded.

Speaking of brothers…

Larken turned, finding Delvon's doppelgänger approaching them. The two looked exactly the same, scowl and all, and Larken wondered if she would even be able to tell them apart if they didn't have separate accents.

The man stopped before her, glaring over Larken's head at Shadric and Delvon. "Did you idiots get lost or just distracted by a pretty face?"

Shadric made a choking sound behind her, and Larken knew Delvon's glare matched the one his brother wore. "Watch yourself, mate."

Delvon's brother's eyes fell from him to Larken, and his features softened. Then, he did something that shocked Larken so much that she almost took a step back. He smiled. "Sorry about them, lass, I hope they didn't give you any trouble."

"Nothing I couldn't handle."

"My name is Ewan Tanner. I'm Delvon's much nicer, more charming younger brother."

"Well, even a blind man could see that," she offered with a smile.

"We look the same, idiot," Delvon muttered.

"I don't know," Larken mused. "There's definitely something more appealing about him."

"Why don't you ask him to take his pants off too then?"

Larken spun so fast that she almost fell. "Delvon!" He smirked wickedly, and Larken turned back around to Ewan. "I'm so sorry, I don't know—"

"It's okay, lass," Ewan assured her, a deep blush on his cheeks. "My brother's antics are nothing new to me." Then he narrowed his eyes at Delvon. "I just wonder what Blade will say when he hears about what he said."

"Who's Blade?" Larken asked.

Ewan's eyes moved back to her. "The leader of the Faithfuls. He'd like to see you right away if you are okay with that."

"Yes, of course." Hope sparked in Larken's chest. Maybe this *Blade* person, whoever he was, could help her find Vallen. Maybe he could tell her what really happened.

"Are you sure? He won't mind waiting a little longer if you wanted to change. Your new home is already set up; we just need to bring your things over."

"I'm sure. I've survived this long in the dress, a bit longer won't hurt."

"You sure about that?" Delvon asked.

Ewan opened his mouth, but Larken looked over her shoulder at Delvon. She batted her eyelashes and asked, "Why? Are you saying *you* want to take it off for me?"

Delvon sucked on a tooth as Ewan barked a laugh. Soren smirked and Shadric smiled, still looking adorably confused. Larken turned back to Ewan and nodded.

"I've heard many good things about you, lass, but I think that little show just put you at the top of my favorite persons list."

"Well, someone needs to humble him every now and then. His head is already big enough."

Larken could hear the unspoken, *not as big as your butt, Peach,* behind her back, but thankfully Delvon kept the comment to himself.

Together, the four of them made their way through the Faithful Camp. Children ran around barefoot in the setting sun, and their parents called for them to come home for bed. The bungalows were nothing fancy, visibly missing the electronics that even the poorest homes in any of the Districts had, but the occupants looked happier than Larken thought possible. The Camp itself seemed to glow with an unspoken power, and Larken knew that Maxim was here. She could feel Him in the earth and air around her, and she almost stopped just so she could bask in the feel of Him a little longer. If she had any doubts about where she was meant to be before, they were gone now.

People of all Districts watched her as she walked past them, and she wondered what they thought as they stared. Dressed in a wedding gown and a too-big leather jacket, she certainly didn't look like the Daughter of the Military. She wondered if they expected the same thing from her that Shadric had; she wondered if they were disappointed. If she were them, she knew she would be.

A hand pressed against her back, and Larken looked up to Soren. He silently asked her if she was okay. She nodded, but he didn't move his hand away, and Larken was grateful. She needed to remember that she wasn't alone anymore, and maybe since Soren was willing to stand by her side with this, he would be willing to help her find Vallen too.

They reached a large building that sat in the center of Camp. The eight-point star made of twigs and branches marked it as a tabernacle, and Larken felt nervous to go inside, like she was dirty and didn't belong. She hadn't stepped foot in a tabernacle since leaving base, not knowing where she could go without drawing attention to herself. If she were brave, she would have risked her mother finding out, but instead, she had cowered in her room on Sunday mornings, watching net sermons on her communicator like she had before she was enlisted.

When Ewan realized that Larken had stopped walking, he turned to look at her. "You alright, lass?"

"Fine," she lied.

Shadric leaned into her, whispering, "Remember what I told you. Go ahead."

He doesn't ask for anything, doesn't demand sacrifices or proof that you're good enough. Only you the way you are.

Larken took a deep breath, forcing herself to step forward. She had made her own promise that if Maxim got her out of her wedding, she would go wherever she was called. But that didn't stop her from sending up a quick prayer for bravery and strength. She also prayed for wisdom; she wanted to make the right impression on this Blade person.

The tabernacle was stunning. Everything was made from wood, and giant windows let in so much sunlight that there was no need for the lights that hung from the rafters. The sight took Larken's breath away, and she felt like she stumbled into a forest sprite's home from a fairy story, rather than a place of worship. The only stone that could be found in the place was the altar that stood on the stage, and Larken felt a pull to it so strongly that she couldn't help but take a step in that direction.

"Blade is up here," Ewan said, indicating a staircase.

Larken looked at the altar one last time and followed. She could pray later, once she was settled and could give Maxim her full attention. Now, she needed to do what she was brought here for.

They made their way up the stairs single file, Soren right behind her, and she asked, "Do you hold all your meetings in the tabernacle?"

"We try to. We like to take time to pray before any decisions are made, and we find that easiest to do here."

"I can see why," Larken murmured, letting her fingers trail against the wooden walls as they climbed.

They reached the top, and Ewan announced, "Blade, we're here. Miss Hale is with us."

"Very good. Thank you, Ewan."

That voice.

Larken stiffened, not believing her ears, convinced that they were playing a cruel trick on her. It was only after Ewan moved out of her way and she saw him that she let herself believe. He stood there, just as large, strong, and constant as ever, looking naked without the jacket hanging from her shoulders. Larken's breath caught. Tears flood her eyes, but she refused to let them fall. Maxim had answered more than one of her prayers today, and she would never doubt Him again.

Soren's presence behind her was suddenly all she could feel. Not long ago Larken had blown out her birthday candles, wishing that he would bring her home. At the time she had pictured the Squad 19 dorm, but this was so much better.

Larken choked, and Blade grinned. "Hey, runt. How you doin'?"

She couldn't hold back a sob as she ran to Vallen and threw her arms around him. Larken was finally home.

**READ ON FOR A PROLOGUE OF
BOOK 3...**

VANQUISHER

Why marry for love when money can ensure your happiness?

It was the question Cornella Hale had always asked herself. Why have love when she could have a life of luxury, a life of ease, or a life filled with music? She had fallen in love the moment she heard the first note sounding from a pianoforte.

When she was a child, she would sit in front of the television and watch old operas and concerts boasting of forgotten music. As a teenager, while her friends were off galivanting with a new boy every week, she would sneak into the theater and listen in the rafters since she was too poor for anything else. Cornella made herself a promise that she would marry above her station and one day be able to afford a seat out in the open. She would wear fancy dresses, laugh, and cry in the audience. And...she would finally be happy. Then Trogar came along and offered her everything she had ever wanted.

It came as no surprise that Cornella eventually fell in love with a man who made the most beautiful music she had ever heard. Not only was Fisher a skilled musician, but he was extremely handsome, as well. He made her feel like she was the greatest, most precious thing in the world. It was a feeling that Cornella became addicted to. She put everything on the line for him and was rewarded with a heart torn in half. More than anything, she wanted to keep her wealthy life of music, but she was just as willing to give it all up so she could only hear Fisher's.Then, Fisher found his way back to Maxim and broke her heart.

Hating him, and Maxim, for everything that had been done to her, Cornella ruined him and promised to forget him. Music no longer held the same joy it once had, but now she could afford to find new interests. Cornella devoted herself to her son and raised him to demand what the world owed him.

Then *she* came. Cornella had convinced herself that the baby was her husband's, but that wheat-colored hair and those eyes didn't lie. She came and ruined everything. Trogar started drinking shortly after that, and the Magnate began talking about finding a new Luminary. Cornella had already lost music; she refused to lose her life, as well.

She pushed and pushed, forming the Vigilants, and started the war against Maxim. Wardell was an afterthought. What better way to pull at the heartstrings of others than with a baby? Cornella had successfully painted herself as the tragic mother who had to lead the war efforts.

So, with all of the pieces in place, and even more sway than the Magnate himself, why wasn't she happy? Cornella looked out of her window, hands gripping her arms. Captain Braves was sprawled in a chair, smoking those awful cigars that were constantly hanging out of his mouth since Larken's betrayal. The smell only added to her crippling migraine, but she kept her frown firmly in place. This Maxim-forsaken house was getting on her last nerve.

Stagnant air surrounded her, the heat and the blueberry fog making her back sweat. Her heels, though gorgeous, were completely impractical for the task at hand. Not that she had plans to join the men and women running drills outside. Larken was off playing in the woods somewhere, while Cornella had literally been left here to rot. One of the drill Sergeants blew a whistle that had her right eye twitching. All she needed to do was get through this, then she could drug herself on the aircraft and sleep the whole way home.

"Something bothering you, Lumina?" Braves mocked. "The view not to your taste?"

"Perhaps you should get off your lazy backside and join them. What woman will want you if you get fat off drinks and cigars?" she retorted.

He huffed an annoyed laugh, and she saw out of the corner of her eye as puffs of blue spilled past his lips with each exhale.

Cornella had to fight not to roll her eyes. The man was a disgusting failure. He had become lazy, *obsessed* with only finding her daughter. Braves was barely useful anymore. If it wasn't for the fact that he was so devoted to tracking Larken, Cornella would have taken care of him weeks ago.

Another breath almost choked her. She needed to get out of this room. Letting her eyes take in the padded wallpaper and old furniture once more, Cornella brushed her hands on her black pants and walked out into the sun. Another shot of pain stabbed behind her eye, but it didn't stop her from walking away from her childhood home. After her parents died, she had considered burning the place to the ground, since it was more land than home. But she ultimately thought up another use for the crumbling farm.

The Sergeant with the whistle still resting in his mouth gave her a nod of respect. Cornella ignored him. She had finished what she had come here for. She'd looked over the soldiers, checked the stats of the Vigilants that had infiltrated the bases of Koraythea, and taken the unpleasant, involuntary trip down memory lane that she always did whenever she saw her childhood home.

Walking as fast as she could while still coming across as elegant, Cornella made her way to her personal aircraft. The pilot was waiting inside for her, probably sweating more than she had been in the small house. She didn't care though. The only thing she wanted was the sweet release hydrocodone could give her.

The aircraft started up as soon as her foot hit the carpeted floor. Cool air blasted out of the black vents, hitting her in the face and giving her the first sense of comfort she'd had in the last five hours.

Cornella didn't bother to shut the door behind her; the pilot could do it automatically and knew by now to do so. It started to close just as she hit the button to black out the windows. Darkness began to slowly encase her until the only light left shone from the screen sitting above the drink dispenser where she finished imputing her commands. Instead of her usual shot of tequila, a clear liquid of another sort appeared before her. Without waiting for even a second, she knocked the hydrocodone cocktail back. She made a face at the flavor of licorice that coated her tongue but felt the effects almost immediately.

Soon her eyes grew heavy in the darkness, and the last thought she had was of finally extinguishing the yellow light that was Larken Hale.

ABOUT THE AUTHOR

C.C. Urie is a Multi-Genre Christian Author who lives in Michigan. Her whole world revolves around her family, and her favorite time of year is when the leaves start to change. She's always had a love for reading, and enjoys sharing her stories with others. Her true calling in life is using her books to help spread the Good Word and show others how God has changed her life for the better.

OTHER BOOKS BY THIS AUTHOR